Elizabeth Rundle Charles

Diary of Mrs. Kitty Trevylyan

A story of the times of Whitefield and the Wesleys

Elizabeth Rundle Charles

Diary of Mrs. Kitty Trevylyan
A story of the times of Whitefield and the Wesleys

ISBN/EAN: 9783337011727

Printed in Europe, USA, Canada, Australia, Japan

Cover: Foto ©Andreas Hilbeck / pixelio.de

More available books at **www.hansebooks.com**

DIARY OF MRS. KITTY TREVYLYAN.

A STORY OF

The Times of Whitefield and the Wesleys.

By the Author of

"CHRONICLES OF THE SCHÖNBERG-COTTA FAMILY,"

_&c. &c._

London:

T. NELSON AND SONS, PATERNOSTER ROW.

EDINBURGH; AND NEW YORK.

1883.

DIARY OF MRS. KITTY TREVYLYAN.

I.

Wednesday, May the First, 1745.

MOTHER always said that on the day I became six-teen she would give me a book of my own, in which to keep a Diary. I have wished for it ever since I was ten, because Mother herself al-ways keeps a Diary; and when anything went wrong in the house,—when Jack was provoking, or Father was passionate with him, or when our maid Betty was more than usually wilful, or our man Roger more than usually stupid,—she would retire to her own little light closet over the porch, and come out again with a serenity on her face which seemed to spread over the house like fine weather.

And in that little closet there is no furniture but the old rocking-chair, in which Mother used to rock us children to sleep, and a table covered with a white cloth, with five books on it—the Bible, Mr. Herbert's Poems, Bishop Taylor's " Holy Living and Dying," Thomas à Kempis on the " Imitation of Christ," and the Diary.

The four printed books I was allowed to read, but (except the Bible) they used in my childish days to seem to me very gloomy and grave, and not at all such as to account for that infectious peacefulness in Mother's face and voice.

I concluded, therefore, that the magic must lie in the Diary, which we were never permitted to open, although I had often felt sorely tempted to do so, especially since one morning when it lay open by accident, and I saw Jack's name and Father's on the page. For there were blots there such as used to deface my copy-book on those sorrowful days when the lessons appeared particularly hard, when all the world, singing birds, and bees, and breezes, and even my own fingers, seemed against me, and I could not help crying with vexation,—those blots which Mother used to call "Fairy Fainéante's footsteps," (for Mother's grandmother was a Huguenot French lady, driven from France by the cruel revocation of the Edict of Nantes,—and Mother taught us French).

It made me wonder if Mother too had her hard lessons to learn, and I longed to peep and see. Yes, there were certainly tears on Mother's Diary. I wonder if there will be any on mine.

So white and clean the pages are now, and the calf-skin binding so bright and new! like life before me, like the bright world which looks so new around me.

How difficult it is to believe the world is so old, and has lasted so long! This morning when I went up over the cliff behind our house to the little croft in the hollow where the cows are pastured, to milk Daisy for Mother's morning cup of new milk, and the little meadow lay blue in the early dew before me, and each delicate blade of grass was glittering around me, and, far beneath, the waves murmured on the sands like some happy mother-creature making soft contented cooings and purrings over its young; and far away in the offing, beyond the long shadow of the cliffs, the just risen sun was kissing the little waves awake one by one,—it seemed as if the sun, and the sea, and the green earth, and I were all young together, and God like a father was smiling on us all.

And is it not true in some sense? Is not every sunrise like

a fresh creation? and every morning like the birth of a new
life? and every night like a hidden fountain of youth, in which
all the creatures bathe in silence, and come forth again new
born?

It often seems so to me.

I am so glad Mother lets me help Betty about the milking.
At first she thought it was hardly fit work for Father's daughter
(he being of an ancient and honourable family), but I like it so
much better than any work in-doors, that since there are only
Betty and Roger, and we must help in some way, she was persuaded to let me do what I enjoy. Mother always says, since
Father chose poverty with her rather than riches and honours
with his great relations, we must all do all we can to make it
easy to him. Mother thinks it was such a great sacrifice for
him to marry her, a poor chaplain's daughter. But it is impossible for me to think it a sacrifice for any one to have
married Mother.

It was delicious to sit milking Daisy and thinking of these
things, and of how Mother would welcome me with my cup of
new milk on this my birthday morning, while every now and
then Daisy, the friendly creature, looked round and thanked
me with her great kind motherly eyes, or rubbed her rough
tongue on my dress. There is something that goes so to my
heart in the dumb gratitude of animals.

However, as I was walking home with my milk-pails, singing,
I met Toby Treffry riding his widowed mother's donkey, beating
the poor beast with a huge stick,—blows which resounded as if
from the trunk of a tree,—and shouting at it in those inhuman
kind of savage gutturals which seem to be received as the only
speech comprehensible to donkeys.

It stopped my singing at once, and I chid Toby severely for
his cruelty to the creature, and it so thin and starved.

"It has had a better breakfast than I am like to get, mistress,"
retorted Toby surlily; "and if I was as lazy as the brute,

surely master would whack me harder. And there's mother at home without a crust till I come back."

Toby is a lank, lean-looking lad, and I chid myself for not remembering how his temper might be tried by poverty, and thought I could do no less to make up for my hard words to him than offer him a drink of milk and a crust I had in my pocket, and gently commend the beast to his tender mercies.

Methought the lad was hardly as thankful as he might have been; indeed, I am not sure he did not regard the gift as a kind of weak attempt at bribery. And so he went on his way, and I on mine. But the current of my thoughts was quite changed, and everything around seemed changed with them.

Beneath me, on the white sands in the cove, lay the wreck of the fishing-smack that was lost there last winter. Those sunny waves now fawning so softly on the shore had not yet washed away the traces of their own fierce work of destruction.

The thought of Toby's donkey brought before me all the mute unavenged sufferings of the harmless beasts at the hand of man. The thought of Toby's widowed mother lying sick and lonely, waiting for a crust of bread, led me down a step deeper into the sorrows of earth,—to want, and pain, and death. And the thought of Toby himself avenging his sorrows on the poor helpless beast led me to the lowest depth of all; for if the end of all this want, and pain, and sorrow, was to harden instead of soften, to make worse instead of better, what a terrible chaos the world and life seemed to be!

Thus, instead of the creation seeming the ladder of light on which just before my spirit had been rising to heaven, from love to joy, and joy to love, it seemed to have become a winding staircase into the abyss, from sorrow to sin, and from sin to sorrow.

The matter was too hard for me, but I resolved to ask Mother, and at all events to carry some bread and milk at once to Widow Treffry.

I therefore set down my pails in the dairy, gave them in charge to Betty, cut a large slice off the great barley loaf, took it with a jug of milk to Widow Treffry, and was back at the door of Mother's closet with her cup of new milk scarcely after the appointed time.

Yet Mother had been looking for me, for when she answered, she had this beautiful Diary of mine all ready beside her own.

She smiled at my rapture of delight. But it is so very seldom that anything new appears in our house, on account of our not being rich, that I never can help enjoying a new dress or a new hood, or even a new ribbon, as if it made the day on which it came a high day and a holiday, just as I used when I was a child; although now, indeed, I am a child no longer, and ought to estimate things, as Parson Spencer says, with a gravity becoming my years.

My new treasure entirely put all the great mysteries of toil and sorrow out of my head, until Mother, laying her hand fondly on my head as I knelt beside her, said,—" Your cheek is like a fresh rose, Kitty ; the draught of morning air is as good for thee as the new milk for me ;" and then, pointing to her old worn Diary, she added,—" Thou and thy book are as suitable to each other as I and mine."

A passionate, fervent contradiction was on my lips. Our precious, beautiful Mother ! as young in heart as ever. But while I looked up in her dear thin face, I could not speak ; the words were choked in my throat, and I could only look down again and lay my cheek on her hand.

" Do not flatter thyself, Mrs. Kitty," she said, with her little quiet laugh, " as if the comparison were all in thy favour. May there not be something in the inside of this poor worn old book worth as much as the new gilding and white emptiness of thine? Mine is worth more to me than when it was clean and bright as thine."

I thought of the blotted page I had once seen by accident there, and I said,—

"But what if there should be pages there stained with tears?"

"The pages blotted with tears are not always the darkest to look back on," she said.

Then the thought flashed on me,—"Perhaps it may be the same with the world's history. The tear-stained pages, nay, the blood-stained pages, may not be the darkest to read by-and-by;" and I said so, and told Mother also about Toby and the donkey, and Widow Treffry.

She paused a moment, as if to read my thought to the end, and then she said, in a low calm voice,—

"*One* page of the world's history stained with the bitterest tears ever shed on earth, and steeped in guiltless blood, is not the darkest to read. Child, it is in the light of that sorrow and that sin thou must learn to understand all the rest. All these hard and bitter questions are answered there to the lowly heart, and nowhere else, and to none else, as far as I have seen. But each of us must learn it for himself, and learn it there. I cannot teach it thee, darling, nor, I think, can God Himself teach it thee, in one lesson. But He is never weary of teaching, child; only be thou never weary of learning: and hereafter, when all the lessons are learned, and we wake up in His likeness, thou and I will sing together the Hallelujahs and the Amens it took us so long to learn, and then we shall be satisfied."

Thursday, May the Second, 1745.

I meant to have written a great deal more last night, but as I recalled those words of Mother's, I fell into a long musing, and then I must have fallen into a long doze, for the next thing I was conscious of was the hooting of the white owl that has built in the ruined side of the house.

So I never got beyond breakfast-time. It is quite plain that a Diary cannot be meant to be a record of all that happens in any one day, because it would take all the day to write it, and then there would be nothing to write.

Who would think, until they began to write, how much is always happening; how many words are spoken and how many things are done on every one of those days which seem so like each other, and are over almost before they seem properly begun?

As it passes, a day seems just a moment; but while we try to recall what it brought, a day seems a life-time.

I have heard old people say all life to look back on is just like a summer-day. And yet, when we stand at the judgment bar of God, and all the days are unrolled before us, will not each day seem like a life-time in its early resolutions broken, its irrevocable opportunities lost, its sins unrepented, its blessings uncounted? It is a discovery I have just made in my precious Diary, which has set me on these grave reflections.

On the last page I find Mother has written with her own hand these passages from Bishop Taylor's "Golden Grove:"—

"AGENDA, OR THINGS TO BE DONE.
"THE DIARY, OR A RULE TO SPEND EACH DAY RELIGIOUSLY.

"1. Suppose every day to be a day of business; for your whole life is a race and a battle, a merchandise and a journey. Every day propound to yourself a rosary or a chaplet of good works, to present to God at night.

"2. Rise as soon as your health and other occasions shall permit; but it is good to be as regular as you can, and as early. Remember he that rises first to prayer hath a more early title to a blessing. But he that changes night into day, labour into idleness, watchfulness into sleep, changes his hope of blessing into a dream.

"3. Never let any one think it an excuse to lie in bed, because he hath nothing to do when he is up; for whoever hath a soul, and hopes to save that soul, hath enough to do to make his calling and election sure, to serve God and to pray, to read and to meditate, to repent and to amend, to do good to others, and to keep evil from themselves. And if thou hast little to do, thou oughtest to employ the more time in laying up for a greater crown of glory.

"4. At your opening your eyes enter on the day with some act of piety—

"(1.) Of thanksgiving for the preservation of the night past.

"(2.) Of the glorification of God for the works of the creation, or anything for the honour of God.

"5. When you first go off from your bed, solemnly and devoutly bow your head and worship the Holy Trinity—the Father, Son, and Holy Ghost.

"6. When you are making ready, be as silent as you can, and spend that time in holy thoughts; there being no way left to redeem that time from loss but by meditation and short mental prayers. If you choose to speak, speak something of God's praises, of His goodness, His mercies, or His greatness; ever resolving that the first-fruits of thy reason and of all thy faculties shall be presented to God, to sanctify the whole harvest of thy conversation.

"7. Be not curious nor careless in your habit, but always keep these measures :—

"(1.) Be not troublesome to thyself or to others by unhandsomeness or uncleanness.

"(2.) Let it be according to your state and quality.

"(3.) Make religion to be the difference of your habit, so as to be best attired upon holy or festival days.

"8. In your dressing, let there be ejaculations fitted to the several actions of dressing: as at washing your hands and face, pray God to cleanse your soul from sin; in putting on your clothes, pray Him to clothe your soul with the righteousness of your Saviour; and so in all the rest. For religion must not only be the garment of your soul, to invest it all over; but it must also be as the fringes to every one of your actions, that something of religion appear in every one of them, besides the innocence of all of them.

" 9. As soon as you are dressed with the first preparation of your clothes that you can decently do it, kneel and say the Lord's Prayer; then rise from your knees, and do what is necessary for you, in order to your further dressing or affairs of the house, which is speedily to be done; and then finish your dressing according to the following rules.

" 10. When you are dressed, retire yourself to your closet, and go to your usual devotions; which it is good that at the first prayers they were divided into seven actions of piety :—

" (1.) An act of adoration.

" (2.) Of thanksgiving.

" (3.) Of oblation.

" (4.) Of confession.

" (5.) Of petition.

" (6.) Of intercession.

" (7.) Of meditation, or serious, deliberate, useful reading of the Holy Scriptures.

" 11. I advise that your reading should be governed by these measures :—

" (1.) Let it not be of the whole Bible in order, but for your devotion use the New Testament, and such portions of the Old as contain the precepts of holy life.

" (2.) The historical and less useful part, let it be read at such other times which you have of leisure from your domestic employments.

" (3.) Those portions of Scripture which you use in your prayers, let them not be long; a chapter at once, and no more. But then what time you can afford, spend it in thinking and meditating upon the holy precepts which you read.

" (4.) Be sure to meditate so long, till you make some *act of piety* upon the occasion of what you meditate : either that you get some new arguments against a sin, or some new encouragements to virtue ; some spiritual strength and advantage, or else some act of prayer to God, or glorification of Him.

" (5.) I advise that you would read your chapter in the midst of your prayers in the morning, if they be divided according to the number of the former actions ; because little interruptions will be apt to make your prayers less tedious, and yourself more attent upon them.   But if you find any other way more agreeing to your spirit and disposition, use your liberty without scruple.

" 12. Before you go forth of your closet, after your prayers are done, set yourself down a little while, and consider what you are to do that day, what matter of business is like to employ you or to tempt you ; and take particular resolution against that, whether it be matter of wrangling, or anger, or covetousness, or vain courtship, or feasting ; and when you enter upon it, remember upon what you resolved in your closet.   If you are likely to have nothing extraordinary that day, a general recommendation of the affairs of that day to God in your prayers will be sufficient ; but if there be anything foreseen that is not usual, be sure to be armed for it by a hearty, though a short prayer, and an earnest, prudent resolution beforehand, and then watch when the thing comes.

*   *   *   *   *

" 22. Towards the declining of the day, be sure to retire to your private devotions.   Read, meditate, and pray.

" 23. Read not much at a time ; but meditate as much as your time and capacity and disposition will give you leave; ever remembering that little reading and much thinking, little speaking and much hearing, frequent and short prayers and great devotion, is the best way to be wise, to be holy, to be devout.

" 24. Before you go to bed, bethink yourself of the day past.

If nothing extraordinary hath happened, your conscience is the sooner examined; but if you have had a difference or disagreeing with any one, or a great feast, or a great company, or a great joy, or a great sorrow, then recollect yourself with the more diligence: ask pardon for what is amiss, give God thanks for what was good. If you have omitted any duty, make amends next day; and yet if nothing be found that was amiss, be humbled still and thankful, and pray God for pardon if anything be amiss that you know not of. Remember also to be sure to take notice of all the mercies and deliverances of yourself and your relatives that day.

"25. As you are going to bed, as often as you can conveniently, meditate of death, and the preparations to your grave. When you lie down, close your eyes with a short prayer; commit yourself into the hands of your faithful Creator; and when you have done, trust Him with yourself, as you must do when you are dying.

"26. If you awake in the night, fill up the intervals or spaces of your not sleeping by holy thoughts and aspirations, and remember the sins of your youth; and sometimes remember your dead, and that you shall die; and pray to God to send to you and all mankind a mercy in the day of judgment."

I have taken so long reading these holy rules, and thinking of them, and thinking of Mother's goodness in writing them out with her own dear hand, that I have no time to write any more.

To-morrow I hope to begin in good earnest to put them in practice.

Only those last I certainly cannot put in practice; for I never remember waking in the night for long enough than just to hear a gust of wind through the tall old elms, and perhaps a rook cawing a remonstrance at being blown out of his nest, and the rain pattering against the window-panes; and then to thank

God for my bed, and feel how comfortable it is, and fall asleep again.

Also, I have no beloved dead to remember. None. My beloved are all living—Father, and Mother, and brother Jack, and Hugh Spencer; and if I stayed awake till cock-crowing, how could I thank God enough for that?

Friday, May the Third.

Early as I woke this morning, the birds were awake before me. First came the cawing of the busy rooks, from their nests in the elms, far above the roof; then the twittering of the sparrows in the white-thorn under my window. And these seemed to me like the tuning of the instruments in the church before the psalm, which was soon poured out in a delicious flow of continuous song from the throats of the thrushes and the blackbirds.

Yes, the choir was all ready for me; and when I opened my casement, the hawthorn and the lilacs sent up their delicate fragrance, like another kind of music.

I felt so happy as I looked out on the humble creatures all sending up their incense of content to God, that my eyes filled with tears, and I knelt and said aloud the Lord's Prayer, and then I said in my heart,—

"Dear creatures of God, ye seem never able to utter what ye would of His praise; and yet you do not know half His goodness —not half of what we know. Ye bask in the light of His smile, but we know the secret love of His heart. Ye praise Him for the overflowing of His riches, which cost Him nothing; we praise Him for the sacrificing love which cost Him His Son. The earth is full of Thy riches; but we only know, O our Saviour, the love of Thy poverty and Thy cross."

For the words Mother said to me on my birthday morning have been much in my mind ever since.

So it seemed to me most natural this morning that every act

should be something like what the Catechism says the holy sacraments are—"An outward visible sign of an inward spiritual grace." And as I opened my window, I thought, "Jesus, my Sun, I open my heart to Thee! Let Thy light and Thy Spirit flow into my soul, as Thy light and air into my chamber." And was not the pure cold water one of His own consecrated images? and did not the very clothes I put on recall the white robes, made white as no fuller on earth can white them, in a fountain no hand on earth could open or close?

I had no temptation to "light discourse," for Betty had just left the room inside mine, and she is seldom very conversational; and not a creature else, except the birds, was awake.

When I was dressed, I thought how I might best fulfil the good bishop's directions as to "retiring to my closet." At first I thought I would ask Mother to let me clear a small chamber in the turret above the apple-room. But then I thought it would be rather like the Pharisees praying in the corners of the streets, to go up there in the sight of all to perform my devotions; and I should lose the sweet feeling that no one knows what I am doing but God.

So I came to the conclusion that no place could be a better closet than a young maid's chamber like mine, with such sights and scents and sounds to be had from my casement.

But this inward debate occupied some time, so that I had not much time for the "seven actions of piety." Indeed, the first two of adoration and thanksgiving seemed necessarily much the longest for me, because I have so endlessly much to give thanks for, and so little to wish for. I must ask Mother whether this is right, and also what the act of oblation means. Also I am not quite sure whether I made the right kind of "*act of piety*" in reading the Holy Scriptures. My chapter was the first of St. Matthew, but I did not get beyond the twenty-first verse, because it seemed to me such a wonderful promise that Jesus our Lord will really save us from our sins, from being impatient

2

and discontented, and all the things which make us unhappy.
Before I got any further it was high time for me to be going
a-milking. Therefore I resolved, that instead of sitting down to
think what temptations were likely to come on me, I would do
this on my way to the cliff, to the pasture where the cows are.
That was how it happened that my temptations came on me
before I had time to think of them and guard myself; although
indeed in general it seems to me the very essence of temptations
is that they come just when and where one does not expect them.

On my way to take the milk-pail from the dairy, I went to
see if some cough syrup I had made for Widow Treffry, and
had left to stand there all night, had settled. When I came to
the shelf on which I had laid it, it was gone. On my questioning Betty (very gently, I am sure, for it was washing-day, and
we know she has all her prickles out then), she replied she could
not let such rubbish stand by her cream to tempt all the flies in
the country. She had put it on the window-seat in the kitchen,
and the cat had upset it. It was a mercy the cup was not
broken, and that the poor cat was not poisoned. She would
not have such filthy stuff in her dairy. To which I retorted
warmly that I had certainly as much right to the dairy as she
had, and that she might have known the cat always sat in that
window-sill when there was sunshine.

Betty replied that she was not going to be ordered about by
those she had brought up from the cradle; and I retired from
the contest, worsted; as I might have known I should be.

On my return to my room, before breakfast, I found all my
drawers in disorder. On my complaining at the breakfast-table,
Jack laughed, and said he had only been looking for a piece of
string, and asked if I intended to put it in my Diary.

I coloured, and said he had no right to pry into my drawers,
nor indeed to enter my room without permission.

Mother interposed, and said I should not make such a storm
about trifles.

And Father smiled, and asked me if my Diary was to be like that of the citizen in the "Spectator." Monday—Rose and dressed, and washed hands and face. Tuesday—Washed only my hands.

I ought to have laughed, but I could not. A profane touch seemed to have brushed the bloom off my new treasure, and so, somewhat heavily, the day passed on.

How very much everything has changed with me since this morning. At all events I have no difficulty in finding enough to-night for "confession" and "petition."

But to confess truly, I must, I think, be just to myself as well as to others. I have noticed that sometimes one can fall into a passion of self-accusation, which seems to me no more true repentance than a passion of accusing other people. I think one has no right to rail at one's self, any more than at any one else. Besides, it seems to me so much easier to burst into a flood of tears, and sob, " I am a wretch, a miserable sinner, the chief of sinners," than to say with quiet shame, from one's inmost heart, " I was unjust to Betty to-day ; I was cross and selfish with Jack. I was impatient even with dearest Mother."

Disappointment and vexation are not repentance. Exaggerated self-reproach is not confession. In the midst of our tears we secretly congratulate ourselves on our sensibility ; or the heart rebounds against the excess of its self-accusation, and ends by estimating the sin as very little, and its penitence as very great.

No : before all things I want to be true to myself and to every one. I want really to overcome my sins—not merely to have the luxury of weeping over them ; and therefore I must try to know exactly what they are. It was my hasty temper that led me wrong in all these things. But what makes my temper hasty ? *What was it* that Betty touched to the quick in asserting her right over me ? I suppose it was my pride.

What made me so angry with Jack ? He certainly had no

right to appropriate my property; but I had no right to be angry. It must be then that I care too much about my things? What fault is that? Can it be avarice?

And then, what made me impatient with Mother? I thought she did not justly stand up for my rights.

My dignity! *My* things! *My* rights! How mean and selfish it looks!

What would have made me overcome? If I had thought of Betty's rough but most unselfish care over us all these years; if I had loved Jack more than my miserable *things;* if I had loved and honoured Mother as I ought, and thought how tenderly faithful her reproofs are, and how I need them.

What I want, then, is love—more love. Yes, there is enough to confess, and enough to ask to-night.

Saturday, May the Fourth.

This morning was very wet and windy, and as I came down into the dairy I found Betty there already with the pails full of new milk.

"Do you think I was going to let such a young thing as you go over the cliff in this storm?" said she, letting down the pails with her stout, stalwart arms. "The wind would have blown over a dozen of you."

Yet Betty has rheumatism, and certainly her clothes are more precious to her, and more difficult to replace, than mine.

"Betty," I said, in a flood of gratitude, "I never ought to have spoken to you so yesterday about the dairy."

"Young folks must have their tantrums," said Betty, no doubt thinking it her duty not to miss such an opportunity of carrying on my education.

The glow of my repentance was somewhat chilled, when Betty added,—

"There is not a creature that comes near her that Missis does not do her best to spoil. There'd be no order in the house but for me. From Master Jack to the cat, not a creature would know what it is to keep in their place."

The universality of the censure took off its edge, and I could not help laughing; which I found do my temper much good.

I do think in good books something should be said of the good it does one sometimes to laugh at one's self. I think it often would do people more good than to cry.

I think religious people now and then perplex themselves by giving their faults too grand religious names. It is necessary, indeed, to dig among the roots of our sins; but occasionally I think we may accomplish as much by lightly mowing the blossoms. For the blossoms also have seeds; and weeds spread by the seed as well as by the root.

Sunday, June the Ninth.

Sundays are always delightful days. The very taking of the Sunday clothes out of the chest where they have lain all the week among the lavender, the sight of the clean swept stone floor of the hall where we take our meals, give one such a fresh, clean, festive feeling.

We have not very many Sunday books. Mother sometimes brings down the "Holy Living and Dying" from her closet; and when I sit at her feet, and she reads it to me, I feel as if I were walking with one of the old Saints through some King's Garden, full of all manner of fruits and flowers, and adorned with strange antique statues of gods and heroes and saints all mixed together, with stately foreign robes and faces, and garlanded with exotics; while the air is heavy with fragrance and sunshine, and musical with the regular flow of artificial fontinels. I enjoy it so much.

And then to read a chapter of the Bible afterwards is like coming from that royal garden straight up to the cliff behind our house, feeling the crisp fresh grass under one's feet, and the fresh sea-air on one's face,—looking over the fields where the cows and sheep and God's other common creatures are enjoying

themselves,—looking over the great and wide sea, with its countless emerald and purple waves, to which we see no end,—looking up to the great sunny sky to which there is no end;—and
through it all listening to a Human Voice like our own, telling
us in simplest every-day words things that touch our inmost
hearts; and knowing that the Human Voice is also Divine,
and that the things it tells are all true, for ever and for ever.

Then there are the Homilies, and, of course, the Prayer-book.
I do not wish for any more religious books. Besides, Betty has
Foxe's Book of Martyrs, with terrible pictures, and stories of
agonies willingly borne for Truth's sake—of heroic patience and
joy in death which brace the heart, as a strong pure air braces
the limbs—especially now that I am old enough to know how
to avoid the tortures and the dreadful pictures.

Monday, June the Tenth.

I wish I could feel easy about Jack. It is not that he has
any great faults. He is honourable and truthful as our Father's
son could hardly fail to be; and he has little gracious kindly
ways which remind one of Mother, and often melt Betty's heart
when she has most reason to be indignant with him. I do not
know what it is that makes me uneasy about him, except that
he never seems to me to do anything he does not like. He will
work in the harvest time as hard as any of the men, and do as
much; but no efforts of mine or Betty's can get him up in the
mornings, although he knows how angry Father is about it, and
how hard we all have to work to make up for it. He will
wander away for a day's shooting or fishing, just when every one
is busiest, and then return with birds or fish, and a jest, which
pacifies Betty, but not Father, and makes Mother sad. He
loses or spoils his own things, and comes on all of us and claims
our things, as if their chief use was to make up for his waste,
and then calls us mean and stingy if we remonstrate, and often
succeeds in making us feel as if we were, when he says, "Is he

so ungenerous as not to share anything with us?" But is it generosity to share your things with others, if you regard their property as a kind of inexhaustible fund to draw on in return?

He is never in time for church, although he knows Mother loves nothing more than to have us all walk into church together, and the vicar looks quite angry as he saunters up the aisle, and once even stopped in the Psalms, so that everybody looked; and sometimes even he alludes to such habits in his sermons. "How can people make such a fuss," Jack says, "about a little thoughtlessness?" But what is at the bottom of thoughtlessness which pains those dearest to us?

It would give me more pleasure than almost anything to see Jack do anything he really disliked, or give up anything he really liked, just because it was right. I am sure Mother is often anxious about him, especially since Aunt Beauchamp's husband, who is rather a great man in London, promised to get him a commission in the army. There are so many terrible temptations in the army, Mother says, for those who go with the stream. I cannot think Jack would ever do anything mean or disgraceful; but the opposite of right is wrong, and one never knows where a wrong turn may lead.

When we were children I never saw this. Jack was the best playfellow in the world. If he got me into scrapes, he always knew how to get out of them; and if not, I was quite content to be in disgrace with him; and if he liked to lead, I liked quite as much to follow. So I think there never could have been happier children than we. What princes could have had a better play-room than the dear old court behind the house? with the felled trunks of trees, and the ruinous sheds, and the old pigeon turret with the winding stairs, and our dog Trusty, and the cat, and the fowls, and ducks, and pigeons living in the freedom Betty's love of animals ensures to them, going where they like, and doing what is right in their own eyes. It was as good as a fairy tale any day, and better than Æsop's Fables, to watch the stately ways of the cocks, and the system of education pursued by the mother ducks, and the hens, with their tender anxieties; and to see the grand patriarchal airs of Trusty, and the steady, stealthy pursuit of her own interests by the cat. The farmyard was a world to us. The children who lived long ago in this house, when the three sides of the quadrangle were perfect, and all was stately and complete, never could have loved the old house as we do in its ruins.

Then we had the cove by the sea at the end of our valley— the cove with the white and sparkling sand, which the sea fills at every tide, sometimes creeping on in quiet ripples, but oftener leaping up in great white waves, far taller than we, and thundering on the shore like kindly giants pretending to intend to swallow us up, only we knew them too well to be afraid. What an enchanted place it was to us! Every day the sea washed us up something new, some glittering pebble or shell; and then there was the cave with the white sand heaped up at the end and the pool at the entrance, where we made a causeway "like Alexander the Great at Tyre," Hugh Spencer said.

For our happiest days were when Hugh Spencer, the vicar's son, came to play with us. He is three years older than I am, and he knew so much history that he was always linking our plays with great men and women who lived, and great things that were done, long ago; so that playing with him always felt like something real and great. And then he had a wonderful history of a man called Robinson Crusoe, written by a Mr. Defoe of London; and although Jack did not like the trouble of reading, he was always ready to listen to the wonderful stories of the island, and the cave, and the savages.

And Hugh always made a kind of queen of me, being the only girl, and seemed to think he could never do enough to save me trouble or to give me pleasure. He cut those nice steps down to the cove for me, that I might climb up easily when the tide was in. And he never would let Jack order me

about as he did at other times, although I had no dislike
to it.

I suppose it makes a difference to boys, not having sisters of
their own. Hugh's only sister died when she was seven years
old. One Sunday evening Hugh took me into his father's
study, to see her miniature. Such a little, fair, grave face, with
large, thoughtful, open eyes—grave and beautiful as an angel's,
I thought. It only wanted the wings, to be much more like a
cherub than any of the cherubs in church, which the clerk is so
proud of having painted with red cheeks and blue wings.

I suppose the memory of the little sister in heaven gives
Hugh that kind of gentleness he has with little girls and
women—even with Betty.

The memory of that little sister, and of his mother, who died
soon after. He watches Mother, and is as reverent to her as if
she were a saint—which, indeed, I believe she is.

It must make everything seem very sacred to have any so
very near us in heaven.

It does seem as if this world were a more sacred place to
Hugh Spencer than to most people. He looks so differently
on many things. For instance, last Sunday, as we came back
from church, Hugh walked with us. As we came near a
miners' village which lies in a hollow below the church-path,
sounds of wild drunken revelry came up to us from it.

Jack said, "The miners seem merry to-night."

"That dreadful place!" Hugh said softly to me, for we were
walking behind the rest. "I cannot sleep sometimes for thinking of it."

"Why?" I said. "Betty says they are not poor."

"No, but they are immortal!" he said; "and I do not think
the name of God is known there except in oaths. I saw a
dying woman there a few weeks since, and she had never heard
of our Lord Jesus Christ."

"Do they never come to church?" I asked.

"Only at weddings or funerals," he said ; "and if they came, what would the beautiful words be to them, untaught and untrained as they are, but so much music? You might as well talk to an infant in Greek."

"The vicar does say a good deal that is like Greek to me," I said (for our vicar is a very learned man, and of course he would not be respected as he is if his thoughts were always level to the comprehension of the congregation). "He knows so much," I added, fearing I had said something disrespectful, "of course, one cannot always expect to understand. The sermons always make me feel how ignorant I am. It makes one understand, too, how many wise men there have been in the world—Socrates, and Aristotle, and St. John Chrysostom, and so many others whose names I cannot even pronounce—that, altogether, it raises one's mind, and humbles one very much at the same time, only to think how much there is to be known and how little one knows. And then it is such a comfort the lessons are always plain."

"But there are people who know as little about Christ as you do about Socrates," he replied ; "and I cannot help thinking that if St. John Chrysostom, or, far better, St. Paul himself, had been here, they would have found some way to make the people understand—even such people as those miners."

It was a new thought to me that the sermon could ever be as plain as the Bible; for Mother never allowed us to discuss anything said or done in church. I was afraid we were on dangerous ground.

But Hugh pursued his own thoughts, and said, "I am going to Oxford soon, and when I have taken my degree, and learned how the Greeks and Romans used to speak, before I take orders I should like to go to another kind of university, to learn how the poor struggling men and women around us speak and think —to live among the fishermen on our coasts—to go to sea with them—to share their perils and privations—that I might learn how to reach their hearts when I have to preach; and then to live among such as these poor miners—to go underground with them—to be with their families when the father is brought home hurt or crushed by some of the many accidents, and to speak to them of God and our Saviour—not on Sundays only, and on the smooth days of life, but when their hearts are torn by anxiety, or crushed by bereavement, or softened by sickness or deliverance from recent danger. Men who have hearts to brave death over and over again to maintain wife and children, ought not to be left to die around us as ignorant as the heathen."

"But," said I, "you do know all the fishermen and miners in the county, Hugh, as it is. I am sure they all greet you when we meet them, like an old friend; and I never heard of any clergyman finishing his studies in the mines or among the fishermen."

"Did you never hear of any sermons preached on the sea-shore to fishermen?" he said, in a low reverent voice; "or of any life much of which was passed among the homes of the poor? I sometimes think," he continued, "it would be a good rule if every clergyman were obliged to begin by being something else, that he might know what the trials and temptations of ordinary people are; and that sermons might be more like heart speaking to heart, and less like a dry metallic echo of human voices, once living, but silenced long ago in death."

I was silent for some time. Hugh's words made me think; but then I thought of Mother, and I said,—

"Mother never lived in fishermen's huts or among miners. For years she has not been strong enough to go much beyond the garden, except to church, and her youth was spent in my grandfather's quiet parsonage; yet she seems always to understand what every one feels. People of all kinds pour out their sorrows before her, and she has words of comfort for all."

"Yes," replied Hugh, thoughtfully. "Perhaps any kind of

trial which makes the heart tender and deep, like your mother's, opens to it the depths of all other hearts. Perhaps some may learn, like her, to know all men and women simply by knowing Him so well who knows what is in all. But every one can scarcely become like your mother."

In the evening, when I went out into the kitchen to toast the bread, Betty said,—

"What a wonderful fine discourse the parson gave us to-day! It rolled along like the sea."

"What was it you liked so much in it, Betty?" I asked.

"Bless your heart!" said Betty, "do you think I would make so bold as to understand our parson? Why, they do say there is not such another scholar in all the country. But it was a wonderful fine discourse. It rolled along like the waves of the sea."

Thursday, July the Eleventh.

To-night, as we were supping, and Hugh Spencer with us, Betty came, in great agitation, into the room, and exclaimed that a Church parson had been mobbed, and all but killed, at Falmouth.

He had been preaching to the people in the open air, and was staying quietly in Falmouth, when the mob were excited against him, and, led on by the crews of some privateers in the harbour, attacked the house in which he was, swearing they would murder the parson. The family fled in terror, leaving him alone with one courageous maid-servant. The mob forced the door, filled the passage, and began to batter down the partition of the room in which the parson was, roaring out, "Bring out the Canorum? Where is the Canorum?" Kitty, the maid (through whom Betty heard of it), exclaimed, "Oh, sir, what must we do?" He replied, "We must pray." Then she advised him to hide in a closet; but he refused, saying, "It was best for him to stay just where he was." But he was as calm as could be, and quietly took down a looking-glass which hung against the wall, that it might not be broken. Just then the privateers' men, impatient of the slow progress of the mob, rushed into the house, put their shoulders to the door, and shouting, "Avast, lads! avast!" tore it down, and dashed it into the room where the clergyman was. Immediately he stepped forward in their midst, bare-headed, that they might all see his face, and said, "Here I am. Which of you has anything to say to me? To which of you have I done any wrong? To you?—or you?—or you?" So he continued speaking until he had passed through the midst of the crowd into the street. There he took his stand, and, raising his voice, said, "Neighbours, countrymen! do you desire to hear me speak?" The mob stood hesitating and abashed, and several of them cried vehemently, "Yes, yes; he shall speak!—he shall! Nobody shall hinder him!" and two of their ring-leaders turned about and swore not a man should touch him. Then they conducted him safely to another house, and soon after he left the town in a boat.

"A brave heart the parson must have had, truly," said Father. "I had rather face an army than wait to be pulled in pieces by a mob. But what did the mob attack him for?"

"Because he will preach in the fields, master," said Betty, "and the people will go to hear him; and the parsons won't have it, and the magistrates read the Riot Act on him the day before."

"But parsons and privateers' men do not usually act in concert," said Father; "and the Riot Act seemed more wanted for the mob than for the parson."

"I have heard of them, sir!" said Jack. "Some say this parson has been sent here by the Pretender. The common people go to hear him by thousands, and he speaks to them from a hedge, or a door-step, or any place he can find; and the women cry, and fall into hysterics."

"Not the women only, Master Jack," interposed Betty.

"My brother-in-law, as wild a man as ever you saw, was struck down by them last summer, and he has been like a lamb ever since."

"What struck him down, Betty?" said Mother in a bewildered tone.

"It is the words they say," said Betty,—"they are so wonderful powerful! And they do say they be mostly Bible words; and the parson is a regular Church parson—none of your low-lived Dissenters—and if he comes in our parts, I shall go and hear him."

"But, Betty, you must take care what you are about," said Mother. "There are wolves in sheeps' clothing; and I do not understand women going into hysterics and men being struck down. There is nothing like it in the Acts of the Apostles. I hope, indeed, it is no design of the Jesuits."

But Betty stood her ground. "I am no scholar, Missis," said she; "but I should like to hear the parson that turned my brother-in-law into a lamb."

"And I," said Father, "should like to see the man who can quiet a mob in that fashion."

"And I," said Hugh Spencer quietly to me, "should like to hear the sermons which bring people together by thousands."

I do not know that I should have thought so much about it, if our vicar had not preached about it on the next Sunday.

The things our vicar preaches about seem generally to belong to times so very long ago, that it quite startled us to hear him say that in these days a new heresy had sprung up, headed by most dangerous and fanatical persons calling themselves clergymen of the Church of England. This new sect, he said, style themselves Methodists, but seditiously set all method and order at defiance. They had set all England and Wales in a flame, and now, he said, they threatened to invade our peaceful parish. He then concluded by a quotation from St. Jerome (I think), likening the heretics of his day to wolves, and jackals, and a great many foreign wild beasts. He gave us a catalogue of heresies from the fourth century onward, and told us he had now done his part as a faithful shepherd, and we must do ours as valiant soldiers of the Church.

Betty thought our vicar meant that we should be valiant like the privateers' men at Falmouth ; but I explained to her what I thought he really meant.

But in the evening, as I was reading in the Acts of the Apostles how the magistrates and the mob seemed to agree in attacking the apostles, and about the riot at Ephesus and the calmness of St. Paul, I wondered if the apostle looked and spoke at all like that brave clergyman at Falmouth.

And my dreams that night were a strange mixture of that old riot at Ephesus, and this new riot at Falmouth, and Foxe's Book of Martyrs.

Hugh says the clergyman's name is the Reverend John Wesley, and that he is a real clergyman, and fellow of a college at Oxford.

II

TO-DAY a letter came from Aunt Henderson to Father, inviting him and me to pay a visit to them and Aunt Beauchamp in London. She said 'twould be a pity to let slip this opportunity, it was time I should be learning something of the world; and Aunt Beauchamp, who was staying at Bath for the waters, would fetch me in her coach from Bristol, if we could get as far as that.

Father would not hear of going himself, saying he had seen enough of the world, and had done with it; but he was very earnest that I should go. He said I ought not to mope my life away in this corner.

Mother turned rather pale, and spoke of the perils of the world for such a child as me.

But Father would not heed her: he has found a ship about to sail from Falmouth to Bristol, and he himself will accompany me thus far. So all is settled, and Mother says no doubt it is best. 'Twere a pity my mind should grow narrow, and I should come to think our little world was all. But to the primrose in the wood her world is not narrow; she sees as far around her as the rose in the King's garden, and looks up all day through the fretted windows of her countless green leaves to the sun, and at night beyond the sun, into God's world of countless stars.

I do not see how our world can be wider than just so far along the path God makes for us as He clears the way for us to see. And I do not see that it need be wider than home and heaven.

Father and Jack say it shows how much I need a change, that I am so unnatural as not to wish to go. And Mother is busy all day ransacking her stores for remnants of old finery to deck me withal. So I suppose it is just *the path* for me, and I must go.

Sunday Evening.

My box is packed, all but the corner into which I must squeeze my Diary, if it were only for the precious words at the end in Mother's handwriting. =

I am glad, now it is settled, that it is so near. I cannot bear to meet Mother's eyes and see her try to smile as she turns them away, and feel how long they have been resting on me.

And I cannot bear to see Trusty watch me in that wistful way and hammer his tail on the floor whenever I look at him. The poor beast knows so well I am going away, and I cannot tell him why, or how soon I shall be back again. And I know to-morrow evening he will come snuffing about all my things, and up to the empty chair where I sit, and then go to Mother and sit down gravely before her and whine, and feel as if I had forsaken him and done his faithful heart a wrong. And no one will be able to explain it to him.

Oh, I wish I were back again, or that things need never change!

A terrible thought came to me to-night as we were all sitting quiet in the great hall window, after we had sung the evening hymn.

I thought how what made me dread this parting is only because it is a faint uncertain shadow of the dreadful certain changes that must, *must* come; and that every day of these happy unvarying days, we are going on, hand in hand, heart to heart, on and on, always, always, to the point where our hands must be unclasped.

3

Partings are terrible because they are the foreshadowing of death.

But life, life itself, joyous growing life itself, is leading us on to death !

These vague yearnings, and regrets, and presentiments of evils which perhaps do not come—they are not vague, they are not delusive: they are indeed but shadows, but echoes; but they are shadows from the valley of the shadows, which is the one only certainty life brings us: they are echoes of farewells which must be said at last—and not answered !

Mother came in as I had finished these words, and brought me some little bags of lavender she had just finished to lay in my linen. She saw I had been crying, and bade me go to bed at once, and finish my packing in the morning.

Then she knelt down with me by the bedside, as she used when I was a little child, and said the Lord's Prayer aloud with me, and saw me safely into bed, and tucked me in as when I was a little child, and kissed me, and wished me good-night in her own sweet quiet voice.

But when she went away I cried, and almost wished she had not come.

All the days and nights I am away from her shall I not feel like a child left alone in the dark ?

But then came on me the echo of her voice saying, "Our Father which art in heaven," and if I can keep that in my heart, I cannot feel like a child alone in the dark.

I suppose that is why our dear Saviour taught it to us, and not only taught it us, but said it with us, that we might feel, as it were, His hand in ours when we say it, and so be wrapped all round with love.

Hackney, May the Twentieth.

It has happened as Mother said. The first few days were dreadful. I felt like a ghost in another world,—I mean a kind of heathen ghost in a world of shadows it did not belong to.

But now the world begins to look real to me again, especially
as eight days of my absence are really over, and I am all that
truly and surely nearer home.

Mother stood like a white statue at the door when I rode
away on the pillion behind Father; Jack laughed and made
jests, partly to cheer me up and partly to show himself a man;
Betty hoped I should come back safe again, and find them all
alive, " but no one ever knew;" and then she cried, and her
very dismal forebodings and her honest tears were, somehow or
other, the most comforting thing that happened to me that
morning: for Betty's tears opened the flood-gates for mine, and
then her forebodings roused my spirit to find a refuge against
them; and the only refuge I could find was to fly from all the
uncertainty straight to Him with whom all is light and certainty;
to fly from circumstances to God himself, and say,—

" Thou knowest. Thou carest. Keep them and me."

And then I became calm, and could even talk to Father as
we rode along, and think of the last requests I wanted to make
for the animals and the flowers, which had to be cared for
while I was gone.

Hugh Spencer met us on the shore, and helped us on board
with my trunk. I do not remember that he said anything particular to cheer me, but I felt better for seeing him. And I
begged him to go and see Mother often. And it comforts me
to think he will, until next month, when he is going to
Oxford.

It was fortunate for me that there was a poor sick woman on
board who had a little child, which, as she was too ill to notice
it, fell to me to take care of; because it made me feel that God
had not left this piece of my life out of His care, but would
find something for me to do. And, besides, the pleasure of
little children always makes one happy in spite of one's self.

When we landed at Bristol it was in a small degree like
leaving home again. The little child clung round me so lov-

ingly, and the poor woman was so grateful.   She said she could
never thank me enough for being so condescending.

She took me for a great lady.   That must have been because
of Father's looks.   It did make me proud to see how noble he
looked in his plain old suit of clothes.   Every one knew he was
a "born gentleman;" and when cousins met us in their velvets,
and laced suits, and hats, I thought he looked like a prince in
disguise among them.

It is worth while coming into the world a little, if only to
learn what Father is.

And cousins felt it too.   One of the first things Cousin
Harry said to me, when we were all in the coach on our way
to London, was,—

"Your Father looks like an old general, Kitty.   One would
never think he had been rusticating for a quarter of a century
among the Cornish boors."

"Captain Trevylyan could not fail to look like a gentleman
and a soldier," said his father, Sir John Beauchamp.

I like Sir John's manners far better than Cousin Harry's.
He is so grave and courteous, and attends to all I say, as if I
were a princess, in the old cavalier manner Father speaks of;
and never swears, unless he is very angry with the groom or the
coachman.   But Harry spices his conversation with all kinds of
scarcely disguised oaths, and interrupts not me only, but his
mother or Cousin Evelyn, and is as free and easy as if he had
known me all my life.

Yet I think he is good-natured; for once when I coloured at
some words he used, he was quite careful for an hour or two.
Cousin Evelyn and he had most of the conversation to themselves, although Evelyn was not very talkative.   Frequently
when I looked at her I found her large dark eyes resting on me,
as if she were reading me like a book.   Aunt Beauchamp was
buried among her furs and perfumes, and seemed every now
and then on the point of going into hysterics when the horses

dashed round a corner into a village, or the carriage jolted on the rutty road.

In one place not far from Bristol she was very much frightened. We had to stop while way was made for us through the outskirts of a large mob, who were collected to hear a great preacher called Whitefield. Uncle Beauchamp says he is a wild fanatic, and that the magistrates were not worth their salt if they could not put such fellows down. Aunt Beauchamp said we might as well travel through some barbarous country as be stopped in the King's highroad by a quantity of dirty colliers, who made the air not fit to breathe.

But as we waited I could not help noticing how very orderly the people were. Thousands and thousands all hanging on the words of one man, and so quiet you could hear your own breathing! All quite quiet, except that as I listened I could hear repressed sobs from some, both men and women, and I saw tears making white channels down many of the sooty faces.

And the preacher had such a clear wonderful voice. He seemed to speak without effort. His whole body, indeed, not only his tongue, seemed moved by the passion in him; but the mighty musical voice itself flowed easily as in familiar conversation, and the fine deep tones were as distinct on the outskirts of the crowd where we stood as if he had been whispering in one's ear. He looked like a clergyman, and the words I heard were very good. He was speaking of the great love of God to us all, and of the great sufferings of our Lord for us all.

I should have liked to stay and listen with the colliers. I never heard music like that voice; yet the words were more than the voice; and oh, the reality is more than the words! It made me feel more at home than any words since Mother's last prayer with me; and I should like Hugh Spencer to have been there.

Uncle Beauchamp asked me soon after we had gone on what made me look so thoughtful.

I said I was wondering if these were like the people they called Methodists in Cornwall, who came together in thousands to hear a clergyman called Wesley preach.

"Are they there too?" said Uncle Beauchamp. "Confound the fellows, they are like locusts. The land is full of them; but if ever they set their feet near Beauchamp Manor, I shall know how to give them their deserts!"

"They have met their deserts in more places than one, sir," said Harry; and he proceeded to relate a number of anecdotes of Methodist preachers being mobbed, and beaten, and dragged through horse-ponds, which seemed to amuse him very much.

But they made me think again of Foxe's Book of Martyrs.

Suddenly Cousin Harry paused, and said,—

"Cousin Kitty looks as grave as if she were a Methodist herself; and as fierce as if she could imitate the Methodist woman who once knocked down three men in defence of a preacher they were beating."

"I cannot see any fun in hundreds of men setting on one and ill-using him," I said.

"Well said, little Englishwoman!" interposed Uncle Beauchamp. "I have no doubt if she did not knock the assailants down, she would have picked the preacher up and dressed his wounds, in face of any mob."

"I hope I should, Uncle," I said.

And since that Uncle Beauchamp generally calls me his little Samaritan.

But Aunt Beauchamp checked the further progress of the conversation by languidly observing that she thought we had been occupied long enough with colliers, and mobs, and Methodists, and all kinds of unwashed people.

"John Wesley is certainly not that," said Harry. "He looks as neat and prim as a court chaplain."

"Is the fellow a dandy too?" exclaimed Uncle Beauchamp; —"more contemptible even than I thought."

" Dandy or not," said Harry combatively, " I have heard he is a gentleman."

" At all events he is not a dandy of Harry's school," said my Cousin Evelyn, " whose highest style is that of a groom unwashed from the stable."

Thus the discourse glided off to the subject of dress, which proved to be inexhaustible; and my russet travelling suit did not fail to come in for much good-humoured ridicule, although Mother had Miss Pawsey the milliner express from Truro to make it, and she comes up to London at least once in three years to learn the fashions.

It was three days before we reached London, and then I was not so much surprised with it as my cousins wished.

The streets were certainly wider, and the houses higher, and the shops grander, and I saw more sedan-chairs, coaches, and magnificent footmen in an hour than I had seen in all my life before; but that seemed to me all the difference. The things man makes seem to me, after all, so very much alike—only a little larger or smaller, or a little richer or poorer.

The great wonder is the people, and that is quite bewilder-. ing, because the stream never ceases flowing any more than the river or the sea at home.

I wonder if it is like the river or like the sea;—I mean, if it is really the flowing on of the river—the stream always the same, and the drops always different; or if it is more like the waves beating on the shore—the waves always different, but the water always the same, heaving, tossing, struggling, beaten back, pressing on again, and again, and again.

I think it is more like the sea.

And so many of the faces look so white and wan and defeated, as if the people had been tossed and broken and beaten back so very often. Only God will not let his human creatures struggle and be tossed about and baffled for nothing; I am quite sure of that.

What a blessing it is that the things we are dim and doubtful about are only the things *half-way up*, and that at the very
top of all, all is perfectly clear and radiantly bright !

For. God our Father is there; and his Son, the Lord Jesus
Christ, who is also the Son of man, is there; and God is
love.

Yes; at the top of this mountain of the world are not cold
snows and empty space, but heaven and God. And when we
are there, too, everything will be clear to us, as it is to Him.

And meantime Thou thyself, O blessed Saviour, art with us
here; and Thou, who lovest each of us more than our dearest
friend, more than Mother loves me, and knowest all things, and
knowest God, art satisfied that *all is right.*

And I am satisfied too.

Only I wish the preacher I heard near Bristol—Mr. Whitefield—could speak to these poor London crowds. I think he
might comfort them. Perhaps he *has* spoken to them, and has
helped those who would listen.

Hackney, near London.

The place Aunt and Uncle Henderson live in is called Hackney. I had no idea a merchant's house could be as pretty as
this is. Father always spoke of his Sister Henderson as " Poor
Patience," implying that she had lowered herself irremediably
by marrying a " tradesman ;" but I find that Aunt Henderson
as commonly speaks of Father as " my poor brother," apparently
regarding Cornwall as a kind of vault above ground, in which
we lead a ghostly existence, not strictly to be called life.

And indeed, as to what are called riches—handsome furniture
and costly clothes—Aunt Henderson is certainly right.

God's riches, of which the Bible says the earth is full, overflowing from heaven as from a fountain over-full, are of course
hers as well as ours, if she would look, so that they do not
count in the comparison.

It is very strange to me the idea some of the people in London seem to have, as if the rest of the world were a kind of obscure outskirts of this great town.

Aunt Beauchamp and my cousins seemed in a polite way quite grateful that I did not eat with my fingers or talk like a ploughboy. They condescended to wonder that I had such a pretty manner, considering I had seen nothing of "the world."

And Aunt Henderson, I believe, is sincerely thankful that I have not a hump, or long ears, or any other appendage that might be expected in a human being born out of " town."

But since London is not the City of the Great King, nor even the centre of the earth, perhaps the wonder is not so very great after all.

There is a nice large garden behind the house, and my bed-room looks over it across a long reach of marshy ground to a range of blue hills which look wavy like our moors. I feel sure there must be furse and heather there, and a kind of longing has possessed me every morning to feel my feet on the turf again, and smell the flowers. One morning I rose early to walk to them. But as I was leaving the garden, Uncle Henderson came down in his night-cap and Indian dressing-gown, quite breathless with hurry, and said,—

" Child, where are you going at this time of day ?"

" I am going to those hills, Uncle," I said. " They look like the hills at home. I am used to long walks, and I think I can be back by breakfast-time."

He looked at me with a kind of compassionate kindness, as one would on a half-witted person, and taking my hand, led me back to the house.

At breakfast Aunt Henderson told me never to venture alone outside the garden walls. " And as for Hampstead," she said, " neither your Uncle, nor I, nor any respectable citizens like to be seen there, since they have set up that wicked place at

Belsize, where they meet to dance and gamble. Besides, the
roads are infested with highwaymen. Child, I tremble to think
what would have become of you."

To comfort me, Uncle Henderson took me in form round the
garden after breakfast, and showed me a great many young,
new, spiky little trees, which he said had come from all kinds
of places I never heard of, and one of which he said was the
only one in England.

After that I could not help looking with respect and even a
kind of tender interest on the puny banished trees, although it
was impossible for me quite to agree with my Aunt, who said
she did not see how any person with a well-regulated mind
could ever desire to wander beyond such a garden as Uncle
Henderson's.

Before now I have always said my morning prayers looking
towards those blue hills. Which way shall I look now? I can
look straight up to the sky; for my other window looks towards
London, with its smoke, and its dull world of houses, and its
sea of people.

Yet perhaps *that* is the best way to turn my prayers, after all.
For the Bible says, God looks on the earth, "to behold the
children of men." After all, the hills are only perishable dust,
and in the city are the imperishable souls.

It is those poor wan men and women who were made in the
image of God, not this beautiful earth.

And perhaps even the stars themselves are only perishable
dust compared with the men and women toiling and struggling
in that great city.

If there is one heart suffering there, surely our Saviour cares
more for it than for all the *things* in the world; and I am
afraid there must be so many.

And if there is one heart praying there—and surely there are
thousands—that heart is nearer God and more sacred than the
highest star.

I wonder if God meant me to come to London partly to learn that.

The sea and the hills and the skies are so glorious; but God cares more for any poor, fallen, suffering human creature than for all the skies and hills and seas together. Hugh Spencer has often said so.

But I never felt it as much as now, since I heard the preacher near Bristol, bringing tears down those rough black faces, just with speaking to them about God and our Saviour.

Uncle Henderson is a Dissenter.

Mother warned me a little against this. But I find they have their own good books, just as we have, although they are not the same.

Quite a different set of names there are on the book-shelves in the best parlour,—Baxter and Howe and Owen, and a number of tall old books, bound in calf, which do not look much read, and which seemed to me to go on very much the same from page to page, with very long paragraphs.

It must be out of one of these books, I think, Uncle Henderson reads the sermon on Sunday evenings, because it seems to go round and round just like that, without getting on, so that one never knows when the end is coming, which I think is a pity. It is so much easier to bear anything patiently if one can only see the end, although it may be ever so far off.

Some of the books, however, seem to me as good as Bishop Taylor, and easier to understand, especially "The Saint's Rest," by Mr. Baxter, and a small book called "The Redeemer's Tears over Lost Souls," by Mr. Howe.

There are also some new hymns, some of which are delightful, composed by Dr. Watts and by Dr. Doddridge.

I do not think Mother knows anything of all these good people. She will be pleased when I tell her. It is so pleasant to think how many more good books and men there are and have been in the world than we knew of.

Uncle Henderson, however, does not seem at all pleased with Mother's good books. When he asked me one day what we read at home on the Sabbath, and I told him (although Mother does not read her religious books only on Sunday), he shook his head very gravely at Bishop Taylor, and said he was very much in the dark, quite an Arminian, indeed, if not a Pelagian, besides his natural shortcomings in common with all Prelatists.

Then I said that Mother's principal good book was the Bible, and that I liked it much the best of all.

And Uncle and Aunt Henderson both said,—

"Of course, my dear, no one disputes that."

Uncle Henderson always calls Sunday "the Sabbath." I daresay it is just as right a name. But I do not like it so much. It sounds like the end instead of the beginning. The Lord's Day is the first day of the week now, not the last, as in the old Jewish times, and I cannot at all see that Sunday is a "heathen name," as Uncle Henderson says; because, certainly, the *sun* is not heathen, and I like to think of Sunday as a kind of sunrise and dawn among the days.

Neither do I like the service in Uncle Henderson's chapel very much.

At home the sermon was very often beyond my understanding, but then there were always the prayers, and the psalms and lessons. But here the prayer seems as difficult as the sermon, and is nearly as long, and all in one piece without any break. And when it is done I feel as if I had been only hearing about sacred things, instead of speaking to God (although, of course, that is my own fault). The minister does not preach about Socrates and St. Jerome, like our vicar; but somehow or other, when he speaks about God and the Lord Jesus Christ, it seems just the same—*as if they had lived in the past*, and made decrees and done great things a long time ago.

But I do not think the people generally like it much more than I do. They seem so very glad to go. They rise the moment the blessing is finished (there is a rustling of silks and a settling of dresses long before), put on their hats, and seem to try which can get out first.

Uncle Henderson says they put on their hats to show that we must not have any superstitious reverence for places.

The sermons are very long. Last Sunday there were five-and-twenty heads, and each head was nearly as long as our vicar's Christmas-Day sermon, which certainly is always rather short, on account of the puddings.

And the people do not look interested. They are all, however, very handsomely dressed. Aunt Henderson says she has counted five coaches at the door—almost as many, she says, as there are at the church Lady Beauchamp attends at the West End.

I suppose the poor go somewhere else. I should like to know where.

Uncle Henderson says this was quite a celebrated chapel in the days of the old Puritans. The minister used to preach in it, and the people to come to it, at the risk of their lives, or at the least of having their ears slit, and being beggared by fines.

I should like to have seen the congregation then. Probably none of them went to sleep. And I suppose the poor came there then, and the coaches went somewhere else.

On our way home from the chapel to-day I saw where the poor people go.

It was in a great open space called Moorfields. Thousands of dirty ragged men and women were standing listening to a preacher in a clergyman's gown. We were obliged to stop while the crowd made way for us. At first I thought it must be the same I heard near Bristol, but when we came nearer I saw it was quite a different looking man; a small man, rather thin, with the neatest wig, fine sharply cut features, a mouth firm enough for a general, and a bright steady eye which seemed to command the crowd. Uncle Henderson said —

"It is John Wesley."

His manner was very calm, not impassioned like Mr. White-field's; but the people seemed quite as much moved.

Mr. Whitefield looked as if he were pleading with the people to escape from a danger he saw but they could not, and would draw them to heaven in spite of themselves. Mr. Wesley did not appear so much to plead as to speak with authority. Mr. Whitefield seemed to throw his whole soul into the peril of his hearers. Mr. Wesley seemed to rest with his whole soul on the truth he spoke, and by the force of his own calm conviction to make every one feel that what he said was true.

If his hearers were moved, it was not with the passion of the preacher, it was with the bare reality of the things he said.

But they were moved indeed. No wandering eye was there. Many were weeping, some were sobbing as if their hearts would break, and many more were gazing as if they would not weep, nor stir, nor breathe, lest they should lose a word.

I wanted so much to stay and listen. But Uncle Henderson insisted on driving on.

"The good man means well, no doubt," he said, "but he is an Arminian. He has even published most dangerous, not to say blasphemous, things, against the immutable divine decrees."

And Aunt Henderson said,—

"It might be all very well for wretched outcasts such as those who were listening, but we, she trusted, who attended all the means of grace, had no need of such wild preaching."

But he was not speaking of the immutable decrees to-day, nor of anything else that happened long ago. He was speaking of the living God, and of the living and the dying soul, of the Saviour dying for lost sinners, of the Shepherd seeking the lost sheep.

And I am so glad, so very glad, the lost sheep were there to hear.

Because in Uncle Henderson's chapel it seems to me there

are only the *found* sheep, or those who think they are found; and they do not, of course, want the good news nearly so much, nor, perhaps on that account, do they seem to care so much about it.

I wonder if the Pharisees, when they said our Lord was beside himself, thought His parables might nevertheless be of some use to those who did not (as they did) " attend all the means of grace."

I have found a friend.

At the end of Uncle Henderson's garden he has fitted up a little house where an aged aunt of his lives with one servant to take care of her. Every one calls her Aunt Jeanie.

She is a widow, more than seventy years of age. Her husband was killed when she and he were quite young, which is perhaps one reason why her heart seems to have kept so fresh and young. He was killed by King James's soldiers who were sent to disperse a congregation of poor people to whom he was preaching in the open air on the Scotch hills, just, I suppose, as Mr. Whitefield and Mr. Wesley preach to the poor people now.

But Aunt Jeanie does not seem to have a bitter thought about it. " How should she," she says, " now that the sorrow is so nearly over?" At first, indeed, she did feel bitter; but what is the use of God sending us affliction unless it takes the bitterness out of us? And now the years of separation are so nearly over, and her Archie, who has all these years been growing like her Lord, will be waiting to welcome her home.

" But then," I said one day, " it would have been sweeter to be prepared on earth together. A year in heaven must make any one so far beyond us on earth, we could hardly under-stand each other."

" My poor bairn, what thought have you then of the holiness of the saints? It is the pride, lassie, that separates us from one another, not the goodness. I know well the greatest

saint in heaven would be easier to speak to than many a poor
sinner on earth. Have you forgotten the Lord himself, and
how He let the sinful woman kiss His feet?"

Aunt Jeanie always calls me either my bairn or lassie. I
cannot, of course, write down her Scotch, but it has an unspeakable charm to me. Her voice has a tender cadence in it
I never heard in any English voice. It touches me like an
echo of some voice dear and familiar long ago.

She has beautiful histories to tell me of good people. She
has known so many.

Best of all I like to hear her speak of the family of Mr.
Philip Henry of Broad Oak in Flintshire. The farm-house
plenty and homeliness about the life, blended with such learning and piety, seem to me so very beautiful. The family
prayers in the great farm-house kitchen; the brother and four
sisters all growing up in the double sunshine of the love of
God and of their parents; the father in his study, or preaching, or visiting the prisoners or the sick; the mother, like the
woman in the Proverbs, rising while it is yet night, "giving
meat to her household, and a portion to her maidens," stretching out her hands to the poor, yea, reaching out her hands to
the needy;—it all seemed as simple and sacred and happy as a
bit of the Bible.

Then old Mr. Henry had such good sayings. "Prayer is
the key of the morning and the bolt of the night," is one
which I have written at the end of Mother's words from "The
Golden Grove."

Yet this holy family were all Presbyterians.

Aunt Jeanie does not know much of Mother's good books
any more than Uncle Henderson, but she does not shake her
head when I speak of them. She says,—

"There is no saying the strange ways by which people may
get to heaven, if only they love the Lord Jesus Christ and try
according to their light to follow Him. Was there not actually

an English minister, calling himself Archbishop of Glasgow in the worst days of the Prelatists, who wrote a book on the Epistles of St. Peter than which John Knox himself could not have written a better?"

So whenever I am more than usually wearied or perplexed by anything in Uncle Henderson or his chapel, I creep out to Aunt Jeanie, and she puts me all right again.

Sometimes she smiles dryly, and says, "I am doubtless a wise bairn, as wise as the man in the *Spectator* who turned the Whole Duty of Man into a book of libels, by writing his neighbours' names opposite each particular sin." Sometimes she smiles tenderly, and says, I am a poor bewildered lamb, and fears the wilderness is rougher and drier than usual just now for the little ones, since it perplexes even those who have been toiling long; "but the Good Shepherd," she adds, "doubtless knows the way, and will guide His own all the more tenderly because it is difficult."

Yet Aunt Jeanie is a *Presbyterian*, and I think a *Puritan*, as much as Uncle Henderson (the things of all others Father hates); and indeed I think she is worse. Her husband at least was a *Covenanter*; and whatever that means, I know it is something exceedingly dangerous, because I remember our vicar, speaking of it when he was congratulating us on living in such a Christian country, spoke of the "seditious canting Covenanters" as the lowest depth of the degradation to which Presbyterianism had reduced Scotland.

Dead Puritanism seems to me a very terrible thing. There is just the death, without the balms or the spices, or the beautiful sepulchre. Yet perhaps it is as well dead religions should look dead, that people may know it all the sooner and turn and seek for life where it is to be found.

But how beautiful Christian *life* seems in any form, and how much alike, whether in Mother or in Aunt Jeanie! Alike in being *life*, and yet how delightfully unlike in each!

4

Cousin Tom Henderson has come home. He has not Cousin Harry Beauchamp's free and easy manners. He seemed at first very shy and awkward, but now he is getting used to me and I to him; we are quite friends, and his large questioning eyes which at first gleamed so suspiciously from under his shaggy eyebrows now meet mine quite confidingly.

To-day, as we walked in the garden after the service in the chapel, he said to me,—

"Cousin Kitty, could you ever remember the *heads?*"

"Our sermons never had any heads," I said, "they were all in one piece."

"Then I suppose you did not mind going to chapel?" he said.

"I always liked going to church," I said.

"Why did you like it?" he asked.

"Mother liked it so much," I said; "and then it was Sunday, and something different, something better and more than any other day, and the corn-fields never seemed to look so golden, or the sea so bright, as when I walked to church with Mother's hand in mine. And coming home she let me gather a nosegay of wild flowers, and they and all the world always seemed fresh and clean as if they had a kind of Sunday clothes on like the rest of us. That was when I was a child, and now I like Sunday and going to church for a thousand reasons."

"Were you allowed to gather flowers on Sunday?" said Tom. "Did Sunday seem something *better* and MORE to you? It was always something *less* to me. I was not allowed to read the books I liked, or do the things I liked. Certainly such a walk to church, and a sermon without heads, would have made a difference. But then Nurse always said it was no wonder I did not like the Sabbath, because I was not converted. Cousin Kitty," he added abruptly, looking earnestly in my face, "are *you* converted?"

The question startled me very much, and I did not know what answer to give.

" Because," said Tom, " you know God does not love any one who is not converted."

" I am sure God loves me, Tom," I said, " if that is what you mean. How could I be so wicked as to doubt it for an instant, when He has done me nothing but good all my life long, and has forgiven me so many wrong things that I have said and done, and has borne with me so gently, and shown me my sins, and helped me against them whenever I have really asked Him ?"

" But all that is nothing, they say," said Tom, " unless you are converted, and you know you cannot always have been converted. No one is."

" But then there is the Cross, Tom," I said. " There is the Cross ! How can I doubt that God loves me when I think of the Cross ?"

" But they say the Cross will sink us lower in hell than anything else unless we are converted," said Tom. Then seeing me begin to cry, for I could not help it, he added in a gentle tone,—

" Do not cry, Cousin Kitty. Perhaps you *are* converted ; you attend the Lord's Supper, do you not ? so perhaps you are. It does seem as if God had been very good to *you.*"

There was something so sad and bitter in the emphasis which he gave to that " you," that I forgot my own perplexities altogether in pity for him, and I said,—

" Cousin Tom, God is good to every one. The Bible says so. He is good to every one because He is good, not because we are good. I cannot tell about being converted, but I am sure of that."

But at night when I was alone in my room, and opened my Bible, and knelt down by it, and made it all into a prayer, it all seemed to become clear to me.

Our Lord does certainly say, " Except ye be converted, and

become as little children, ye shall not enter into the kingdom
of heaven."

He said it to the disciples when they were debating who
should be the greatest in the kingdom of heaven.

To the poor wandering multitudes he said not, " Be converted," but " Come unto *Me.*"

Then it came into my heart.

" Lord, I do come unto Thee. I have come before. But I
come again now—to Thee, to Thee. I turn to Thee, I would
not turn from Thee for the world. Is that to be converted ?
See I am at Thy feet ; and if *not*, see *I am at Thy feet*, and
Thou wilt surely do the rest, since Thou knowest what I want,
if I do not. Lord, I *am* a little child—thou knowest I am
helpless, weak, unable to lead myself. Heavenly Father, I am
a helpless little child, and Thou art our heavenly Father. I
am not a little child half as much as I should like in truthfulness and simplicity, but I am a little child in wanting Thee, in
being able to do nothing without Thee. Not because I am
child-like, heavenly Father, but because I am helpless, help me.
Not because I am converted, O gracious Saviour, but because
I want Thee, help me ; not because I love Thee (and yet I do
love Thee), but because Thou lovest me, because Thou diedst
for my sins, help and save me. And help that other poor
wandering sheep who does not seem to have come back to
Thee at all, and save him, not because he is returning, but
because he is wandering, and it is so wretched to wander in
the world without Thee !"

I never lay down to sleep with a happier feeling than that
night.

The next time Tom and I were alone (it was by the window
in the best parlour ; Uncle was smoking a quiet pipe in the
garden-house, and Aunt was taking a dish of tea with a friend),
I said, " Cousin Tom, I have been thinking of what you said,
and you must not say God does not love you because you are

not converted. I am sure that is not true. Because our Saviour goes after the sheep when they are actually wandering and lost, which cannot be the same as being converted. And, of course, He goes after them because He is loving them. But you must *be* converted, Cousin Tom," I said.

His tone was altered from the time he had spoken last; it was not so much sad as bitter and sarcastic, and he said,—

"Cousin Kitty, you are a poor theologian. How am I to be converted unless God converts me?"

I did not know what to say, until at last I said, and I am afraid it could not have been the right thing,—

"God *is* converting you—taking you by the hand as it were to turn you round—I mean He is doing all He can, He is calling you, watching you, pitying you, seeking you in a thousand ways, He only knows how many and how often."

"Then I suppose it will be all right one day," said Tom, "for who hath resisted His will?"

I was very much grieved, his tone was so bitter, and I could not help saying, it came so forcibly into my heart,—

"Cousin Tom, you *are* resisting His will, with all your might —you *will* not come back to our Saviour."

"And you are contradicting St. Paul, Cousin Kitty," he said.

"How I wish you could hear Mr. Whitefield or Mr. Wesley," I said, for I felt my logic failing.

"Father says Mr. Wesley is an Arminian," said Tom, with a satirical smile; "but, perhaps, you are little better. Mother always said poor Sister Trevylyan was 'little better than a Papist.'"

At first I felt angry at his levity, but then all at once I thought it was only the laughter of a heart ill at ease, and I said gently,—

"Cousin Tom, you know you do not care in the least whether Mr. Wesley is a Calvinist or an Arminian. I am sure you are unhappy about something this evening. Can I help you? Jack says it often helps him just to tell me anything, and you have no sister."

"Nor any one that cares for me," said Tom.

"Oh, Tom," I said, "you must not say Uncle and Aunt do not care for you."

He had been sitting with his elbows on his knees and his hands on his face; now he rose, and said in a low voice, like the grinding of an iron heel on stone,—

"No doubt they care that *I should grow rich!* But, Kitty, this life is more than I can bear. While you are here it is a little more cheerful, but in a few weeks you will be gone, and it will be duller than ever. It is one incessant 'Thou shalt not,' from one end of the year to the other; or only one 'Thou shalt' to counterbalance it, '*Thou shalt make money* and be rich;' 'Thou shalt not go to the play; thou shalt not dance.' And I do go to the theatre and to the opera when I can. It does me less harm, I am sure, than sitting at home and hearing Aunt Beauchamp and Cousin Harry and nine-tenths of our acquaintances pulled to pieces as reprobates. But I dare not tell Father, because he would never believe I do these things without doing a thousand worse things which I do not. So I am living a lie, and I hate myself for it, yet I see no way out of it."

"There is a way out of it," I said. "You must give it up. It is better to lead the dullest life in the world than to do wrong, and I am sure you would find it happier."

"There is one thing I will not do, Cousin Kitty, I will not be a hypocrite. I will not put on a smooth face and pretend to like all the whining Pharisaical cant I hear. If I am to go to the bad end, it shall be by the honest broad road, and not by the narrow prim path of the Pharisees which leads the same way."

"But, Cousin Tom," I said after a little while, "there is no need for you to be either bad or a hypocrite. You can be *good*, and you must try."

"Do you mean I must be converted?" he said almost fiercely.

"I think," I said, "you should give up thinking about being converted, and should just *turn* to God, just look away from your sins and other people's sins, and from *everything*, to our Saviour, and ask Him to help you to be really good. Of course, it is all real with Him. And I am sure He would."

He did not answer, and I went on,—

"It seems to me you put conversion between you and Christ, as if it were a kind of shut door to get through, instead of just going up to the *open* door. For the door of the kingdom of heaven is open, I am quite sure. Our Lord says, 'I am the door;' which must mean that there is no door, no closed door, but that He himself stands at the entrance instead, to welcome us and lead us in. Think of the difference between a door and a friend's face, and a friend's hand stretched out to grasp ours. And then such a Friend! we have done Him so much wrong, and He is so ready to forgive all; and such a Hand! pierced to the cross for us. St. Thomas saw the prints of the nails."

My heart was very full, and when I looked up, Tom brushed his hand over his face and moved away.

But I went up to him and ventured to say,—

"Cousin Tom, tell Aunt Henderson what you have told me; I am sure it would be right, and perhaps it might help you both."

"You don't know in the least how hard it would be, Kitty," he said; "Mother thinks all sins are on the same level. If I told her I had gone to the opera, she would think me as bad as a thief. And yet," he exclaimed, "I do not know but I *am* just as bad. Have I not been living a lie?"

Just then Uncle Henderson came in, and I went to join Aunt Henderson in the best parlour.

She was just then comparing poor Aunt Beauchamp's system of education with her own, and complacently dwelling on the necessary difference in the results between her Tom and "poor Harry," who had just, she understood, lost a small fortune in betting on the race-course. From this she glided into an instructive dissertation on her household management. Other people, she said, were always complaining of their servants dressing like their betters, and even taking tea and snuff. But she never had such difficulties. She would like to see the hussy who would sport a silk gown or a snuff-box in her house. The visitor, a gentle, little woman, seemed quite depressed by my Aunt's superiority, and soon after took her leave in a meek and subdued manner.

A large portion of Aunt Henderson's conversation consists in these compassionate meditations on the mistakes and infirmities of her neighbours. She does this "quite conscientiously." "It is so important," she says, "that we should observe the failures and errors of our neighbours, in order to learn wisdom."

It seems as if Aunt Henderson thought the rest of the world were a set of defective specimens expressly designed to teach her wisdom, just as we used to have ill-written and mis-spelt sentences set before us to teach us grammar.

But I always thought we learned more by looking at the *well*-written sentences. In that way one's writing and spelling grow like the copy without thinking about it. And it is so much pleasanter to have the beautiful right thing before one constantly instead of the failure.

Besides, Aunt Henderson's grammar may not be exactly the standard after all.

And it must matter just as much how the *other* copies are written; at all events, to the people who write them. I suppose no one is sent into the world exactly to be a kind of example of failure, even to make Aunt Henderson quite perfect by the contrast. But only to think of Aunt Henderson calling Mother a Papist!

To-day I had a great pleasure. Last Sunday we went to another chapel, in Bury Street, and heard the venerable old minister called Dr. Watts preach. It was a sermon on safety in death, to comfort parents who had lost little children. And I am sure it must have comforted any one; it went so far into the sorrow with the balm. He spoke of this world as like a garden in a cold place, from which God, like a careful gardener, took the tender plants into His own house before the winter came to spoil them. Yet sweet and touching as it all was for those whose hearts were already awake to listen, there was nothing of the rousing penetrating tones which awake those whose hearts are slumbering.

The good old man spoke so tenderly I thought he must have felt it all for himself. But Aunt Henderson says he is a student and an old bachelor.

And to-day she took me to see the place where he lives. It is a beautiful park belonging to Sir William and Lady Abney at Stoke Newington. And there, five-and-thirty years ago, they brought Dr. Watts to be their guest for a week when he was lonely, and poor, and in delicate health. And they have kept him there ever since, caring for him like a son, and reverencing him like a father. He has nice rooms of his own; and they always are grateful when he joins their circle, so that he can have as much solitude and as much company as he likes, and have the good of riches without the responsibilities, and many of the pleasures of a family circle without the cares.

It seems to me such a beautiful use to make of riches. The holy man's presence must make their house like a temple; and when the dear aged form has passed away, I think they will find that the garden-walks, where he used to converse with them, and the trees under which he used to sit, and the flowers

he enjoyed, will have something like the fragrance of Eden left
on them.

So they *have* their reward ; yet not all of it. There will be
more to come, when they see our Lord, and He will thank them
for taking care of His servant.

Dr. Watts writes such beautiful hymns. They have not the
long winding music of John Milton's hymn on the "Nativity,"
or Bishop Taylor's in "The Golden Grove ;" but they have a
point and sweetness about them which I like as much, especially
when one thinks that the very best thing in what they sing of
is that it is *true*, for ever true.

They sang one at the chapel on Sunday, which I shall never
forget :—

> " When I survey the wondrous cross
>   On which the Prince of Glory died,
> My richest gain I count but loss,
>   And pour contempt on all my pride.

> " Forbid it, Lord, that I should boast,
>   Save in the death of Christ my God ;
> All the vain things that charm me most
>   I sacrifice them to His blood.

> " See, from His head, His hands, His feet,
>   Sorrow and care flow mingled down ;
> Did e'er such love and sorrow meet,
>   Or thorns compose so rich a crown ?

> " Were the whole realm of nature mine,
>   That were a present far too small ;
> Love so amazing, so divine,
>   Demands my soul, my life, my all."

It made the chapel seem as beautiful to me as any cathedral
while they sang it, because one seemed to look through it
straight into heaven, where our Lord is. And anything which
helps us to do that makes it matter so little whether what we
look through is a white-washed ceiling or a dome like St. Paul's.

And then the comfort is, the poor can understand it as well as the most learned.

While we were at Abney Park, a consumptive-looking minister from Northampton was there, a great friend of Dr. Watts. Lady Abney had just brought him from London in her coach—a gentle, thoughtful-looking man, called Dr. Doddridge. He also writes beautiful hymns, they say. Lady Abney told me he has a dear little girl who was once asked why every one loved her. She looked very thoughtful for a moment, and then said, " I suppose because I love every one."

To-morrow I am to leave Aunt Henderson to stay with Aunt Beauchamp at the West End of the town, in Great Ormond Street. I am afraid Tom has not made any confession to his mother yet. But he has promised to try to hear Mr. Wesley, and to go often to Aunt Jeanie.

Aunt Henderson has been talking to me very seriously about the dangers to which I shall be exposed. She says poor Aunt Beauchamp's is a thoroughly careless family, and they live quite in "the world."

Does "the world" then begin somewhere between Hackney and Great Ormond Street?

Mother seemed to think I should meet it as soon as I left home.

And the Catechism speaks of our having to renounce it from infancy, like the flesh and the devil.

If we have always to be renouncing it, it must be *there,* everywhere, always; one thing to Mother, another to Aunt Henderson, another to Cousin Tom, or Aunt Beauchamp; one thing to me when I was a child, another to me now—yet always there, always to be renounced.

What is it then? St. John says, " It is not of the Father."

Does it mean *whatever* gift of God we make a pedestal for our pride, instead of making of it a step of God's throne on which to kneel and look up, and adore?

III

Great Ormond Street.

HEY were all so kind to me when I left Hackney, I felt very sorry to go, and should have grieved more, had not the leave-taking been like a half-way house on the journey to my dear home.

Uncle Henderson gave me a purse with five new guineas in it, saying some people had found a fortune grow from no bigger beginning, and who knew but my guineas might expand into a "plum!" (a hundred thousand pounds.) I do not very well see how, because I have spent the whole over ten times in my mind already; but I know it will bring me in pleasures as rich to me as anything Uncle Henderson could desire for me, if I can only tell which of the ten plans I have thought of is the best.

Aunt Henderson gave me a little book with a very long name, which she hoped would prove, at all events, more profitable reading than Bishop Taylor. Cousin Tom had relapsed into something of the shy, half-surly manner he had when first I came, and his great eyes were flashing, and his voice was very gruff. But just as I was getting into the hackney coach, he said abruptly, "Cousin Kitty, forgive me if I spoke roughly to you; you have been very good to me; and some day perhaps I will hear Mr. Wesley." Aunt Jeanie, to whom I paid a visit early in the morning, gave me nothing—at least nothing gold and silver can buy or pay for; but, like the apostles, such as she had she gave me abundantly. There were tears in her dear kind eyes, and she called me her poor lambie, and fell very deep into Scotch, and prayed that the good Lord would keep me through all the perils of the wilderness; "for the world was a wilderness, no doubt, and temptation was strong. The Lord forgive her if it was like murmuring to say so, she had found so many pleasant places on her way; and all the way had been good to her; and every thorn needful; and the waste places as wholesome as the Elims; the water from the rock sweeter even than the fountains under the palms. And how can I dare be so ungrateful as to distrust my God for thee, my bairn," she added. "If I am old and tough, and able to bear a prick now and then without shrinking, and thou art young and tender, and quick to feel, does not He who gathered the lambs in His bosom know that better than I?"

So we cried together a little while, and then she knelt down with me for the first time by her bed-side, and poured out her heart for me in tender, pleading words, that melted all my heart as ice melts in the spring sunshine and rain.

What she said I cannot remember. It was not like words. It was like a heart poured out into a heart—a child-like, dependent human heart into the great, infinite, tender heart of God. But when she rose and kissed me, and bade me farewell, all my heart, which had been so touched and melted, seemed to have grown strong and buoyant. It seemed as if every burden became light, and every task easy, and every grief illuminated in the light and heat of that prayer.

When I reached Great Ormond Street, the butler said my lady was still in her chamber, but had directed that I should be shown up to her at once. I thought this very affectionate of Aunt Beauchamp, and stepped very softly, as when Mother has a headache, expecting to enter a sick-chamber.

But, to my surprise, Aunt Beauchamp was sitting at her

toilette, in a wrapper more magnificent than Aunt Henderson's Sunday silk. And the chamber was much more magnificent than the best parlour at Hackney, with a carpet soft as velvet, and all kinds of china monsters, on gilded brackets, and rich damask chairs and cushions; not stiffly set up, like Aunt Henderson's, as if it were the business of life to keep them in order, but thrown lavishly about, as if by accident, like the mere overflow of some fairy horn of plenty. Two very elaborately dressed gentlemen were sitting opposite her; what seemed to me a beautifully dressed lady was arranging her hair in countless small curls; while a shapeless white poodle was curled up in her lap; and a black page was standing in the background, feeding a chattering parrot.

It startled me very much; but Aunt Beauchamp, after surveying me rather critically as I made a profound courtesy, held out two fingers for me to kiss, and patting me on the cheek, said, " As rosy as ever, Kitty; the roses in your cheeks must make up for the russet in your gown.—A little country cousin of mine," she said, introducing me in a kind of parenthetical way to the gentlemen in laced coats.

One of the gentlemen looked at me through an eye-glass, as if I had been a long way off, which made me indignant, and took away my shyness. The other, in a sky-blue coat, who seemed to me rather old, rose, and with an elaborate bow offered me a chair, and hoped it would be long before I withdrew the light of my presence again from the town. "The planets," he observed, looking at Aunt Beauchamp, "naturally gathered around the sun."

Aunt Beauchamp gave a little girlish laugh, tapped him lightly with her fan, called him a "mad fellow," and bade me go and seek my Cousin Evelyn.

It seemed to me very strange to see these elderly people amusing themselves in this way, like old-fashioned children. Aunt Beauchamp is much older than Mother. I should think she must be five-and-forty. And the old gentleman's face looked so sharp and wrinkled under his flaxen wig. And I could not help noticing how close he kept his lips together when he smiled, as if he did not wish to show his teeth. He must be more than fifty.

I felt so sorry Aunt Beauchamp let her maid put those cherry-coloured ribbons in her hair. They made her face look so much older and more lined. And it is a dear, kind old face, too. She looked almost like Father when she patted my cheek. Father says she was very beautiful when she was young. I suppose it must be sad to give up being beautiful. Yet it seems to me every age has its own beauty. White hairs are as beautiful at seventy as golden locks at twenty. It is only by trying to prolong the beauty of one stage into another that the beauty of both is lost.

I hope I shall know when I am five-and-forty, and not go on forgetting I am growing old, while every one else sees it.

I am resolved that on all my birthdays I will say to myself, "Now, Kitty, remember you are eighteen, nineteen, twenty." And in that way I think old age cannot take me by surprise.

I found Cousin Evelyn in dishabille, not elaborate, but real, in her room, one hand holding a novel which she was reading, the other stroking the head of a great stag-hound which stood with his paws on her knee, while a maid was smoothing out her beautiful long hair.

Her greeting was not very cordial; it was kind, but her large penetrating eyes kept investigating me as they had on our journey from Bath. Having finished her toilette and dismissed her maid, she said, "What made you stay so long at Hackney? Did you not find it very dull?"

It had never occurred to me whether it was dull or not, and I had to question myself before I could answer.

"You need not be afraid to tell me what you think," she said.

" Mamma thinks Aunt Henderson a self-satisfied Pharisee ; and Aunt Henderson thinks us all publicans and sinners ; so there is not much communication between the families. Besides, I suppose you know that the distance between America and England is nothing to that between the East and the West of London ; so that, if we wished it ever so much, it would be impossible for us to meet often."

" I am not afraid to tell you anything, Cousin Evelyn," I said ; " but I never thought very much if it was dull. It was of no use. I had to be there ; and although, of course, it could not be like home, they were all very kind to me, especially Cousin Tom and Aunt Jeanie.".

" And now you *have to be here,*" she replied ; " and I suppose you will not think whether it is dull or not, but still go on enduring your fate like a martyr."

"I am not a martyr," I said ; "but you know it is impossible to feel anywhere quite as one does at home." And I had some difficulty in keeping back the tears, her manner seemed to me so abrupt and unjust.

Then suddenly her tone changed. She rose, and seating herself on a footstool at my feet, took one of my hands in both of hers, and said, " You must not mind me. I think I shall like you. And I always say what I like. I am only a child, you see," she added, with a little curl of her lip. " Mamma will never be more than thirty, therefore, of course, I can never be more than ten."

I could not help colouring, to hear her speak so of her mother; and yet I could not tell how to contradict her.

She always saw in a moment what one does not like, and she turned the subject, saying very gently, "Tell me about your home. I should like to hear about it. You seem so fond of it."

At first it seemed as if there was nothing to tell. Every one and everything at home are naturally so bound up with my very heart, that to talk of it seemed like taking up a bit of myself and looking at it.

But Evelyn drew me on, from one thing to another, until it seemed as if, having once begun, I could never finish. She listened like a child to a new fairy tale, leaning her face on her hands, and gazing on me with her questioning eyes quite eagerly, only saying when I paused, "Go on—and what then?"

When I spoke of Mother, a tender, wistful look came over her face, and for the first time I saw how beautiful and soft her eyes were. That expression, however, quickly passed, and when at length I came to a long pause, she said, smiling, "I am glad your Trusty is a genuine, uncompromising old sheep-dog. I hate poodles;" and then she added in her old dry tone, "It is as good as a pastoral, and as amusing as a novel. When we go back to Beauchamp Manor, I will ask papa to build me a model dairy, and will commence an Arcadian life. It would be charming."

"But," I said, bewildered at her seeming to think of me and Mother and Betty as if we were people in a poem, "your dairy would be mere play; and I cannot see any amusement in that, except for children. It is the thought that I *ought* to do the things—that the comfort of those about me depends on my doing them—that makes me so happy in them."

"The thought that you *ought!*" she said;—"that is a word no one understands here. We do what we *like*, and what we *must*. If I thought I ought to go to the opera or to Vauxhall, I should dislike it as much as going to church."

"As going to church!" I said.

"Yes," she replied. "I mean at Beauchamp Manor, where Dr. Humden reads long sermons some dead bishop wrote centuries ago, in a voice which sounds as dead and stony as if it came from the effigies of all the Beauchamps which presided over the Church. In town it is different. The archdeacon never preaches half an hour, and that in the softest voice and

5

in the most elegant language—very little duller than the dullest
papers of the *Spectator* or the *Tatler*.   And then, one sees every
one ; and the performances of the congregation are as good as a
play."

Evelyn next gave herself, with real interest, to the inspection
of my wardrobe.

It seemed almost like sacrilege to see the things which had
cost Mother so much thought and pains treated with the imperfectly concealed contempt which curled my cousin's lips as she
unfolded one carefully packed article after another.   My best
Sunday hat brought a very comical twist into her face ; but
the worst of all was when I unpinned my very best new dress,
which had been constructed with infinite contrivance out of
Mother's wedding-dress.   Evelyn's polite self-restraint gave way,
and she laughed.   It was very seldom she gave any token of
being amused beyond a dry, comical smile ; and now her rare,
ringing laugh seemed to discompose Dragon, the stag-hound,
as much as it did me.   He seemed to feel he was being laughed
at—a disrespect no dog can ever endure—and came forward
and rubbed his nose reproachfully under my cousin's hand, with
a little deprecatory moan, as she held up the dress.

She gave him a parenthetical pat, and then looking up in my
face, I suppose saw the foolish tears that would gather in my
eyes.

"You and Dragon seemed aggrieved," she said.   "I am
afraid I have touched on sacred ground, Cousin Kitty.   You
seem very fond of your things."

"It is not the things," I said ; "but Mother and all of
us thought they were so nice ; and Miss Pawsey from Truro
does go to London once in every three or four years ; and,
besides, she has a Book of Fashions, with coloured illustrations."

I could not tell her it was Mother's wedding-dress.   Rich
people, who can buy everything they want immediately they
want it, at any shop, and throw it aside when they are tired,

can have no idea of the little loving sacrifices, the tender plannings, the self-denials, the willing toils, the tearful pleasures, that are interwoven into the household possessions of the poor. To Evelyn my wardrobe was a bad copy of the fashions ;—to me every bit of it was a bit of *home*, sacred with Mother's thoughts, contriving for me night and day, with the touch of her busy fingers working for me, with the quiet delight in her eyes as she surveyed me at last arrayed in them, and smoothed down the folds with her delicate neat hands, and then contemplated me from a distance with a combination of the satisfaction of a mother in her child and an artist in his finished work. I could not say all this with a steady voice, so I fell back on the defence of Miss Pawsey ; but she only laughed, and said,—

" Do you not know, Cousin Kitty, that three years old is worse than three centuries ? It is all the difference between antiquated and antique. You would look a great deal more modern in a ruff and farthingale of one of our great-great-grandmothers in Queen Elizabeth's days. Indeed, I have no doubt, if I could see Aunt Trevylyan at this moment, I should think her quite in fashion compared with those exactly out-of-date productions of your Truro oracle. We must send for my milliner."

" But Mother thought it so nice, Cousin Evelyn," I said at length ; " I could not bear to have what she took such pains with pulled to pieces."

She looked up at me again with the soft, wistful look in her eyes, folded the precious dress together as reverently as I could have done, and, laying it in the trunk, said very gently,—

" Do not think any more about it, Cousin Kitty. I will manage it all."

I have been to the opera and to church, and I cannot wonder so much at Cousin Evelyn comparing the two.

The gloom of the Hackney Sundays seems cheerfulness itself compared to the dreary week-day glare of these. At the opera the music was as beautiful as songs in the woods on a spring morning: it was composed by a young Saxon gentleman—Mr. Handel. It was very strange to me that the people attended so little. Aunt Beauchamp had quite a little court of middle-aged and elderly gentlemen, to whom she dispensed gracious smiles, or frowns which seemed in their way as welcome, pretty severities with her fan, and laughing rebukes; and whenever I looked about between the acts, the same small entertainments seemed going on in the boxes around me. While the music went on I could see and hear nothing else.

Evelyn laughed at me when we returned. I actually was so unsophisticated, she said, as to go to the opera to enjoy the music.

"What can any one go for else?" I asked. "It is not a duty."

"For the same reason we go to church, or anywhere else," she replied,—"to meet our fellow-creatures, to play over our play, or see them act theirs. I could have told you of three separate dramas going on in the boxes nearest us, one at least of which is likely to rise into tragedy.—You liked the music then?"

"It was as beautiful as a dream," I said; "only I wished sometimes it was a dream."

"Why?"

"I felt sorry for that modest, gentle-looking young woman having to talk so much nonsense in public. I think she could hardly have felt it right."

"You strange little creature," said Evelyn, "you bring right and wrong into everything. You must not think of the actors as men and women, but merely as machines."

At church it seemed to me very much the same. Aunt Beauchamp encountered many of her little court, and distributed her nods and smiles and her deprecatory glances, as at the play.

During the Psalms people made profound courtesies to their neighbours in the next pews; and during the Litany there was a general fluttering of fans and application of smelling-bottles, as if the confessing ourselves miserable sinners were too much for the nerves of the congregation. But then it occurred to me that I was as careless as any one, or I should have known nothing of what the rest of the congregation were about; and it was a comfort to confess it in the words of the Litany. Afterwards I stood up, and was beginning to join with all my heart in the psalm, when Evelyn tapped me lightly, and said, " No one sings but the professional choir." Then I saw that several people were looking at me with considerable amusement, and I felt ashamed of my own voice, and then felt ashamed of being ashamed.

The sermon was on the impropriety of being righteous over much; and every one said, as they met and exchanged greetings in the porch that it was a most elegant and able discourse; it was a pity some of those Methodist fanatics could not hear it. Afterwards many important arrangements were made as to card-parties and balls for the ensuing week, or for Sunday evening itself.

On our way home Aunt Beauchamp said to me, " My dear child, you really must not say the responses so emphatically, especially those about our being miserable sinners. People will think you have done something really very wrong, instead of being a sinner in a general way, as, of course, we all must expect to be."

One thing that made me feel strange in Aunt Beauchamp's church is its looking so different from the church at home. I cannot help liking the great stone pillars and the arched roof, and the fretwork of the high windows, with bits of stained glass still left in them, better than this new church, with its carpeted passages, and cushioned galleries, and painted wooden pillars, and flat ceiling. The music, and even the common speech in response and prayers, seem in some way mellowed and made sacred as they echo and wind among the old arches and up the roof, which seems more like the sky.

But Cousin Evelyn says my taste would be deemed perfectly monstrous—that these old country churches are remnants of the dark ages, quite Gothic and barbarous, and that in time, it is hoped, they will be replaced throughout England by buildings in the Greek and Roman style, or by that classic adaptation of both which is so elaborately developed in the ornamental pulpit and sounding-board of the church we attended.

And then Aunt Beauchamp says some of the wood-work is of that costly, new, fashionable wood called mahogany, so that it admits of no comparison with the rough attempts of less civilized ages.

I wonder if there are fashions in architecture as well as in dress—only counting their dates by centuries instead of by years. It would be strange if these old churches should ever be admired again, like the costumes of Queen Elizabeth's time, and these new buildings be ridiculed as antiquated, like Miss Pawsey's fashions!

I should be glad if this happened! The poor old Gothic builders seem to have delighted in their work, and taken such pains about it, as if they were guided by thoughts about right and wrong in what they did, by love and duty, instead of just by fashion and taste.

There seems such a heavy weight of emptiness about the life here. The rigidity of Aunt Henderson's laws seems to me liberty compared with the endless drifting of this life without laws. In the morning the toilette, with the levee of visitors, the eager discussions about the colour of head-dresses and the shape of hoops. In the evening a number of beautifully dressed people, paying elaborate compliments to their present acquaintances, or elaborately dissecting the characters of their absent

acquaintances—the only groups really in earnest being apparently those around the card-tables, who not unfrequently fall
into something very like quarrelling.

This kind of living by the day surely cannot be the right
kind—this filling up of every day with trifles, from brim to brim,
as if every day were a separate life and every trifle a moment-
ous question.

When our Saviour told us to live by the day, He meant, I
think, a day encompassed by Eternity—a day whose yesterday
had gone up to God, to add its little record to the long unfor-
gotten history of the past, whose to-morrow may take us up
to God ourselves. We are to live by the day, not as butter-
flies, which are creatures of a day, but as mortal yet immortal
beings belonging to eternity, whose mortal life may end to-
night, whose longest life is but an ephemeral fragment of our
immortality.

Evelyn seems very much aloof from the world about her.
In society sometimes she becomes animated, and flashes brilliant sayings on all sides. But her wit is mostly satirical; the
point is too often in the sting. She is evidently felt as a power
in her circle; and her power arises in a great measure from her
absence of ordinary vanity. She does not care for the opinion
of those around her; and whilst those around her are in
bondage to one another for a morsel of praise or admiration,
she sits apart on a tribunal of her own making, and dispenses
her judgments.

At present, I believe, she has passed sentence on me as
pharisaical, because of something I said of the new oratorio
of the Messiah. At first it seemed to me more heavenly than
anything I had ever heard; but when they came to those
words about our Lord's sorrows, "He was despised and re-
jected, a man of sorrows and acquainted with grief," and around
us there was, not a hush of shame and penitence, but a little
buzz of applause, suppressed whispers, such as "Charming!"—

"What tone !"—"No one else can sustain that note in such a way !"—and at the close the audience loudly clapped the singer, and she responded with a deep theatrical courtesy—I thought of "*When I survey the wondrous Cross,*" wished myself in Dr. Watts' chapel, and felt I would rather have listened to any poor nasal droning which was worship, than to such mockery. I could not help crying.

When we were in the house again, Evelyn said,—

"You enjoyed that music, Kitty."

"No, Cousin Evelyn," I said; "I would rather have been at the opera, a hundred times, and far rather in Aunt Henderson's chapel at Hackney."

"Your taste is original, at all events," she replied dryly.

"To think," I said, "of their setting the great shame and agony of our Saviour to music for an evening's entertainment, and applauding it like a play ! One might as well make a play about the death-bed of a mother. For it is true, it is true ! He did suffer all that for us."

She looked at me earnestly for a few moments, and then she said coldly,—

"How do you know, Cousin Kitty, that other people were not feeling it as much as you ? What right have we to set down every one as profane and heartless just because the tears do not come at every moment to the surface ? The Bible says, 'Judge not, and ye shall not be judged;' and tells us not to be in such a hurry to take the motes out of other people's eyes."

I was quite silenced. It is so difficult to think of the right thing to say at the moment. Afterwards I thought of a hundred answers, for I did not mean to judge any one unkindly. I only spoke of my own feelings. But Evelyn has retired into her shell, and evades all attempts to resume the subject.

This morning at breakfast Cousin Harry (of whom we see

very little) spoke, quite as an ordinary occurrence, of a duel, in which some one had been killed, in consequence of a quarrel about a lady ; and of another little affair of the same kind ending in the flight of a lady of rank to the Continent.

I asked Evelyn afterwards what it meant.

" Only that some one ran away with some one else's wife, and the person to whom the wife belonged did not like it, and so there was a duel, and the husband was killed."

" But," I said, " that is a dreadful sin. Those are things spoken of in the Ten Commandments."

" Sin," she replied, " my scriptural cousin, is a word not in use in polite circles, except on Sundays, as a quotation from the Prayer Book. We never introduce that kind of phraseology on week days."

" Do these terrible things happen often, then ? " I asked.

" Not every day," she replied dryly. " The next thing you will be thinking is, that you have lighted on a den of thieves. A great many people only play with imitations of hearts in ice. For instance, mamma's little amusements are as harmless to herself and all concerned as the innocent gambols of a kitten. The only danger in that kind of diversion," she added bitterly, " is, that it sometimes ends in the real heart and the imitation being scarcely distinguishable from each other."

The easy and polished world around me no longer seems to me empty and trifling, but terrible. These icicles of pleasure are, then, only the sparkling crust over an abyss of passion, and wrong, and sin.

There is excitement and interest enough, certainly, in watching this drama, if one knows anything of what is underneath,— the same kind of excitement as in watching that dreadful rope-dancing Cousin Harry took us to see at Vauxhall.· The people are dancing at the risk of life, and more than life. The least loss of head or heart, the least glancing aside of one of these graceful steps, and the performers fall into depths one shudders to think of.

I tremble when I think of it. Dull and hard as the religion seemed to me at Aunt Henderson's, it is safety and purity compared with this wretched cruel levity, this dancing on the ice, beneath which your neighbours are sinking and struggling in agony.

Religion is worth something as a safeguard, even when it has ceased to be life and joy.

The sweet hawthorn which makes the air fragrant in spring is still something in winter, although it be only as a prickly prohibitory hedge.

The trees, which were a home of happy singing birds, and a treasure of shade and refreshment in summer, are still a shelter even when their leafless branches toss and crackle in the fierce winds of December. That is, as long as there is any life in the thorns, or the trees, or the religion.

If it were death instead of only winter that made the trees leafless, they would soon cease to be a shelter as they have before ceased to be a delight.

Yesterday I had a letter brought me by Evelyn's maid, written on perfumed coloured paper.

In it the writer ventured to call me in poetry a goddess, and a star, and a peerless rose. If there had been only that, I should have felt nothing but indignation; for I do believe I have done nothing to deserve such nonsense being said to me.

But at the end there is some prose, in which the writer says he has really formed a devoted attachment to me; and he seems to want me to marry him at once, for he talks of lawyers and settlements. Cousin Evelyn came in as I was sitting perplexing myself what I ought to do. She laughed at my distress, and told me she could show me a drawer full of such compositions.

"It is so trying to have to make any one really unhappy," I said; "and you see he says in the prose that life will be a blank to him if I cannot give him the answer he wishes."

"Indeed you need not mind," she said. "I myself have broken a score of hearts in the same way, and I assure you no one would know it; they do as well without their hearts. They are like the poor gentleman, whom Dante discovered, to his surprise, in the Inferno while he.was supposed to be still alive. A devil was walking about in his body while his soul was in torments; and the devil and the soul were so much alike that no one had suspected the change."

"I had never anything of the kind to do before," I said, "and I am sorry. The prose really looks as if he would care, and I want to write gently but very firmly. I wish I could see Mother." But then I thought how Mother had always told me of the one refuge in every difficulty, and I said softly, hardly knowing I said it aloud, "But if I pray, God will help me to do what is right."

"Pray about a love-letter!" exclaimed my cousin, looking nearly as much shocked as I had felt at her calling the church as good as the play. "Pray about a love-letter, Cousin Kitty! You surely would not do anything so profane."

"Surely I may pray God to help me to do right," I said, "about everything. Nothing in which there seems a question of right and wrong can be out of His care."

Evelyn looked at me once more with her wistful, soft look, and said very gravely,—

"Kitty, I believe you really do believe in God."

"You do not think that any wonder?" I said.

"I *do*," she said solemnly. "I have been watching you all this time, and I am sure you really do believe in God; and I think you love Him. I have never met with any one who did since my old nurse died."

"Never met with any religious person!" I said.

"I did not say that," she replied. "I have met with plenty of religious persons. Uncle and Aunt Henderson, and several ladies who almost shed tears over their cards, while talking of Mr. Whitefield's 'heavenly sermons,' at Lady Huntingdon's— numbers of people who would no more give balls in Lent than Aunt Henderson would go to church. I have met all kinds of people who have religious seasons, and religious places, and religious dislikes, who would religiously pull their neighbours to pieces, and thank God they are not as other men. At the oratorio I thought you were going to turn out just a Pharisee like the rest; but I was wrong. Except you and my old nurse, I never met with any one who believed, not in religion, but in God; not now and then, but always. And I wish I were like either of you."

"Oh, Cousin Evelyn," I said, "you must not judge people so severely. How can we know what is really in other people's hearts? How can we know what humility and love there are in the hearts of those you call Pharisees; how they weep in secret over the infirmities you despise; how much they have to overcome; how, perhaps, the severity you dislike is only the irritation of a heart struggling with its own temptations and not quite succeeding? How do you know that they may not be praying for you even while you are laughing at them?"

"I do not want them to pray for me," she replied fiercely. "I know exactly how they would pray. They would tell God I was in the gall of bitterness and in the bond of iniquity; they would thank Him for having, by His distinguishing mercy, made them to differ; and then they would express a hope that I might be made to see the error of my ways. I know they would, for I heard two religious ladies once talking together about me. One asked if I was a believer; and the other, who had expressed great interest in me and sought my confidence, said she 'was not without hope of me, for I had expressed great disgust at the world. She had even told Lady Huntingdon she thought

I might be won to the truth.' The woman had actually worked herself into my confidence by pretended sympathy, just to gossip about me at the religious tea-parties."

I endeavoured to say a word in defence, but she exclaimed, —"Cousin Kitty, if I thought your religion would make you commit a treachery like that, I would not say a word to you. But you have never tried to penetrate into my confidence, nor have you betrayed any one else's. I feel I can trust you. I feel if you say you care for me you mean it; and you love me as *me myself,*—not like a doctor, as a kind of interesting religious case. Now," she continued, in a gentler tone, "I am not at all happy, and I believe if I loved God as you do I should be. That may seem to you a very poor reason for wishing to be good, but it does seem as if God meant us to be happy; and I have been trying, but I don't get on. Indeed I feel as if I got worse. I have tried to confess my faults to God. I used to think that must be easy, but the more I try the harder it is. It seems as if one never could get to the bottom of what one has to confess. At the bottom of the *faults,* censoriousness, idleness, hastiness, I come to *sins,* pride, selfishness. It is not the things only that are wrong, it is *I* that am wrong,— I myself,—and what can alter me? I may change my words or my actions, but who is to change *me?* Sometimes I feel a longing to fall into a long sleep and wake up somebody else, quite new."

It occurred to me that the thought of conversion, which to Cousin Tom had, in the wrong place, become like a barrier between him and God, would to Evelyn be the very thing she longed for. And I said, "Except ye be converted, and become as little children, ye cannot enter the kingdom of heaven." It is *we* that must be converted, changed, and not merely, as you say, our actions,—turned quite round from sin and darkness to God and light."

She caught at the words "*as little children.*" She said,

"Cousin Kitty, that is just the thing I should like,—that would be like waking up quite new. But how can that be?"

"It seems to me," I said, "that it must be like the blind man, who, believing our Lord's words, and looking up to Him sightless, saw. Looking to Him must be turning to Him, and turning to Him must be conversion."

Then we agreed that we both had much to learn, and that we would read the Bible together.

Since then we have read the Bible very often together, Evelyn and I. But her anxiety and uneasiness seem to increase. She says the Bible is so full of God, not only as a King whose audience must be attended on Sundays, or a Judge at a distance recording our sins to weigh them at the last day, but as a Father near us always, having a right to our tenderest love as well as our deepest reverence.

"And I," she says, "am far from loving Him best—have scarcely all my life done anything, or given up anything, to please Him."

I comforted her as well as I could. I told her she must not think so much of her loving God as of His loving her,—loving us on through all our ingratitude and foolishness. We read together of the Cross—of Him who bore our sins there in His own body, and bore them away.

I cannot but think this is the true balm for my cousin's distress; it always restores and cheers me—and yet she is not comforted.

It seems to me sometimes as if while I were trying to pour in consolation, a mightier hand than mine gently put aside the balm, and made the very gracious words I repeated a knife to probe deeper and deeper into the wound.

And then I can only wait, and wonder, and pray. It does seem as if God were working in her heart. She is so much gentler, and more subdued. And the Bible says not only joy and peace, but gentleness, is a fruit of the Holy Spirit.

I often wish Evelyn were only as free as the old woman who
sells oranges at Aunt Beauchamp's door, or the little boy who
sweeps the crossings ; for they may go where they like and hear
the Methodist preachers in Moorfields or in the Foundry Chapel.
And I feel as if Mr. Wesley or Mr. Whitefield could help my
cousin as I cannot. If she could only hear those mighty, melt-
ing words of conviction and consolation I saw bringing tears
down the colliers' faces, or holding the crowd at Moorfields in
awe-stricken, breathless attention.

My wish is accomplished. We are to go and hear Mr. Whitefield speak at Lady Huntingdon's house in Park Street. It
came about in this way :—

A lady who is reported to have lately become very religious
called one morning, and after some general conversation began
to speak of Mr. Whitefield's addresses in Lady Huntingdon's
house. She strongly urged my aunt and cousin to go, saying,
by way of inducement, that it was quite a select assembly—no
people one would not like to meet were invited, or, at all events,
if such people came, one was in no way mixed up with them.
" And he is such a wonderful orator," she said ; " no common-
place fanatic, I assure you, Miss Beauchamp. His discourses
are quite such as you would admire, quite suited to people of
the highest intellectual powers. My Lord Bolingbroke was
quite fascinated, and my Lord Chesterfield himself said to Mr.
Whitefield (in his elegant way), ' He would not say to him what
he would say to every one else, how much he approved him.' "

" I did not know that Lord Chesterfield and Lord Bolingbroke were considered good judges of a sermon," said Evelyn
dryly.

" Of the doctrine—well, that is another thing," said the religious lady ; " but of the oratory and the taste. Garrick, the
great actor, says that his tones have such power that he can
make his hearers weep and tremble merely by varying his pro-

nunciation of the word Mesopotamia; and many clever men, not at all religious, say they would as soon hear him as the best play."

"I have heard many services which seemed to me like plays," said Evelyn, very mischievously; "and I do not see that it can do any one's soul any good to be made to weep at the word Mesopotamia."

"Oh, if we speak of doing real good to the soul," rejoined the visitor—"that is what I mean;" and in a tone of real earnest feeling she added, "I never heard any one speak of the soul, and of Christ, and of salvation like Mr. Whitefield. While he is preaching I can never think of anything but the great things he is speaking of. It is only afterwards one remembers his oratory and his voice."

And it was agreed that we should go to Lady Huntingdon's house the next time Mr. Whitefield was to preach.

"How strange it is," Evelyn said to me when the lady had left, "what things religious people think will influence us who are still 'in the world!' What inducement would it be to me to go and hear a preacher, if Lord Bolingbroke and Lord Chesterfield, or all the clever and sceptical and dissipated noblemen in England liked him, and were no better for it? They try to tempt us to hear what is good, by saying the congregation is fashionable, or that clever people are captivated, or that the preacher is a genius, or an orator, or a man of the world, when I do think the most worldly people care more for the religion in a sermon than for anything else, and would be more attracted if they would say, 'We want you to hear that preacher, because he speaks of sin, and of Christ, and of the forgiveness of sins in a way no one else does.' I wonder," she concluded, after a pause, with a little smile, "if I ever should become really religious, if I shall do the same; if I shall one day be saying to Harry, 'You must hear this or that preacher; for he is a better judge of a horse than any jockey you know.'"

We have heard Mr. Whitefield.

And what can I remember?

Just a man striving with his whole heart and soul to win lost souls out of a perishing, sorrowful world to Christ, and holiness, and joy.

Just the conviction poured in on the heart by an overwhelming torrent of pleading, warning, tender, fervent eloquence, that Christ Jesus the Lord cares more infinitely to win and save lost wandering souls than man himself—that where the preacher weeps and entreats, the Saviour died and saved.

Yes, it is done. The work of salvation is done. "It is finished."

I never understood that in the same way before.

It is not only that the Lord Jesus loves us, yearns over us, entreats us not to perish. He has saved us. He has actually taken our sins and blotted them out, washed them out of sight, white, whiter than snow, in His own blood.

It is not only that He pities. He *saves*. He has died. He has redeemed. The hands stretched out to save are those that paid the terrible ransom. He did not begin to pity us when we began to turn to Him. " When we were without strength, He died for us, ungodly."

"God was in Christ reconciling the world to Himself, not imputing their trespasses unto them."

"For He hath made Him to be sin for us who knew no sin, that we might be made the righteousness of God in Him."

I never understood this in this way before; and yet there it is, and always has been, as clear as daylight, in page after page of the Bible.

All the way home Evelyn said nothing. Aunt Beauchamp was the only one who spoke; and she said it was very affecting, certainly; but she did not see there was anything so very original. It was all in the Prayer-Book and in the Bible.

And then, after a pause, she added, in rather a self-contra-dictory way, "But if we are to be what Mr. Whitefield would have us, we might as well all go into convents at once. He really speaks as if people were to do nothing but be religious. He forgets that some of us have other duties."

Then she took refuge in her vinaigrette, and said in a very languid voice, "My darling Evelyn, you look quite pale. Much more excitement of this kind would make us both quite ill. The man is so terribly vehement, he makes one feel as if one were in peril of life and death. Such preaching may do for people without nerves, but it would soon kill me. I am only too glad I escaped without an attack of hysterics. And," she continued, "I was told that a few days since Lady Suffolk was there by invitation. I really wonder a person of Lady Huntingdon's character should invite such people to her house. My dear," concluded my aunt, "I do not think the thing is respectable; and I wonder Lady Mary proposed our attending such an assembly. Indeed I wonder at myself for consenting to go. It is not at all a kind of place for sound church people to be seen at. I would not have the archdeacon know it on any account; and I am sure Dr. Humden would think I had been out of my senses."

And soothed with so many restoratives, ecclesiastical, social, and medical, Aunt Beauchamp relapsed into her usual state of languor and self-contentment.

But Evelyn said nothing. Only when I ventured some hours afterwards to knock at her bed-room door, she opened and closed it in silence, and then taking both my hands, said, in a soft, trembling voice, "Cousin Kitty, I am very full of sin! I really think I am worse than any one, because, being myself so wrong, I have so despised every one around me. I have been a Pharisee and a publican all in one."

And then she burst into tears, and buried her face in her hands. But in a few minutes she looked up again with a face beaming with a soft, childlike, lowly peace, and she said, "But, Cousin Kitty, I am happier than I ever thought any one could be. For I do believe our Lord Jesus Christ died for my sins, and has really washed them away. And I do feel sure God loves me, even me; and I think He really will by degrees make me good—I mean humble, and loving, and kind. I do feel so *at home*, Cousin Kitty," she added. "I feel as I had come back to the very heart of my Father—and oh, He loves me so tenderly, so infinitely, and has been loving me so long. Yes, at home, and at rest," she sobbed; "at *home everywhere*, and for ever, and *for ever.*"

The next morning Evelyn came to me early, pale, but with a great calm on her frank expressive face. "Kitty," she said, "I have had a strange night. I could not sleep at all. It seemed as if the sins of all my past life came up before me unbidden, as they say the whole past sometimes comes vividly back to a drowning man. I saw the good I had left undone, the evil I have said and done, and the pride and selfishness at the bottom of all. And almost more than anything, I felt how unkind, and even unjust I had been to mamma; how ungenerous in not veiling any of her little infirmities; for I know she loves papa and Harry and me really better than all else in the world. I felt I must come with the first light and confess this to you. For one night came back to me, Kitty, years and years ago, when I was a little child. Harry and I had the scarlet fever, and I saw before me, as if it were yesterday, my mother's pale, tender face, as she moved from one little bed to the other. I remember thinking how beautiful and dear she was as she sat by the nursery fire, and the flickering light fell on her face and her dark hair, and how she started at any movement or moan I or Harry made, and came so softly to the bedside, and bent over me with such anxious love in her eyes, and said tender little soothing words, and smoothed the pillow, or kissed my forehead with the soft kiss which was better than any cooling draught. Since then, indeed, we have been much away from her, and left to governesses and tutors; but, Kitty, think what a blessing it is to recall all that early affection now, instead of by-and-by, when it would be too late to say a loving word, or do a thing to please her in return! *Now* I can bear to think of this, and of all my coldness and impatience, with the thought of the Cross and of God's forgiving love, and with the hope of the days to come. But only think what it would have been to have seen it all *too late.*"

It seems as if, in coming back to God, Evelyn had come back to all that is tender and true in natural human love.

I suppose this is conversion. The joy of such a waking must be very great. But it is joy enough to *be awake,* however little we know when and how we awoke,—awake in the light of our Heavenly Father's love, to do the day's work He gives us.

To-day she smiled and said to me,—

"I think I should not mind now their talking over my case at Lady Betty's tea-parties. I had rather not, but if there was kindness at the bottom of it, I need not mind much. Yet, Kitty," she continued, "I do think still it is not possible to talk truly and much of our deepest feelings of any kind. I think it is a waste of power which we want for action."

"We certainly need never sit down to talk of our own feelings," I said. "There are moments when they will come out. And there is so much in the Bible to speak of without talking about ourselves."

"Yes," she said; "I think setting ourselves to talk religion is weakening. Think of Harry and me having a meeting to discuss which of us loved our parents best, or whether we loved them better yesterday or to-day! Yet there are sacred times when we *must* speak of those we love."

Aunt Beauchamp is rather puzzled at the change in Evelyn.

Evelyn has tried to explain it to her. But she says she cannot at all understand it. "*Every one* believed in Christianity except a few sceptics, like Lord Bolingbroke. *Of course*, the work of our redemption was 'finished.' It was finished more than seventeen hundred years since. Mr. Humden preached about it, always, at least, on Good Friday. And why Evelyn should be so particularly anxious about having her sins forgiven, she could not conceive; she had always been charming, if at times a little *espiègle*. But if she was happy, no one could object."

There is nothing striking in this change in Evelyn, but it is pervading,—a gentleness in all she says and does; which, with the natural truthfulness and power of her character, is very winning. And this I notice especially with regard to her mother, a deference and tenderness, which, with no peculiar demonstrations of affection, evidently touch Aunt Beauchamp more than she knows. She begins even to venture to consult Evelyn about her wardrobe.

Evelyn does not ask to go again to hear Mr. Whitefield. But she has asked to go with me to see my poor old Methodist orange woman, who has disappeared from our door-steps, and now lies contentedly on her poor bed, coughing and suffering, waiting the Lord's time, which, she says, is sure to be exactly right. The dear old soul gets us to read to her chapters from her old Bible, and hymns from Mr. Wesley's new hymn-book, and repeats to us bits from Mr. Wesley's sermons. And perhaps, although sometimes the grammar is very confused and the theology not very clear, the strength of God made perfect in the weakness of a dying-bed may help us both as much as the mighty power of Mr. Whitefield's eloquence.

To-day Hugh Spencer called, on his way from Cornwall to Oxford.

At first he called me Mrs. Kitty, and was very ceremonious. But I could scarcely help crying, I was so glad. It was like a little bit of home. But he did not bring a very good account of Mother, and that made me cry in earnest. And when he saw that, he dropped naturally into his old manner,—always so kind and like truth itself.

When he was gone, Evelyn asked me who he was, and why I had not said more about him. "He looks," she said, "a man one could trust."

But why should I? He is only like one of ourselves.

I am so glad and thankful. Aunt Beauchamp is going again to Bath for the waters. And from Bath, Father or Jack is to fetch me home.

I am so happy, I can scarcely help singing all day. I hope it is not ungrateful. They have all been so very kind to me in London.

And even Aunt Beauchamp's very dignified maid, of whom at first I stood in such awe, seemed quite sorry when she heard I was going, and fell from the highest refinement of English into her native Devonshire dialect, when she took leave of me, to go and prepare the house at Bath, and wished me every blessing with tears in her eyes.

Yet I have done nothing for her, except being very sorry for her, and trying to comfort her one day when she was crying because her only brother had got drunk and gone and taken the king's money, and listed for the wars, and left her widowed mother alone.

To-day Evelyn went with me to wish good-bye to Aunt Henderson. Aunt Henderson was very kind in her hortatory way. She told me she had heard with thankfulness that Evelyn had become serious. But she advised her not to run into extremes. Young people brought out of the world were very apt to run into the other extreme of fanaticism. She hoped Evelyn, if she was indeed sincere, would keep the golden mean. It had always been her endeavour to do so, and she had found it the wisest plan.

Cousin Tom was more shy and awkward than ever. He said, when I asked him, that he had attended Mr. Wesley's preaching two or three times, but it was like daggers to him. For as to telling everything to his father and mother, he did not see how any human being could. To sit evening after evening at home a distrusted delinquent, the subject of indirect lectures, was more than he could bear. If he confessed, he must run away the next morning.

I told him I was sure he had no idea of the true love there was in his mother's heart—if he would only try it.

"Very little more idea, Tom," I said, "than you have of the love God has for you—if you would only try that!"

A gleam of light flashed for a moment from under the shaggy eyebrows, and he glanced up at me. But then the old desponding downcast look came back. Aunt Henderson and Evelyn joined us, and he said no more.

Aunt Jeanie seemed to me feebler than when I saw her last; but her dear old face lighted up as she talked to us.

And as we were going away, she rose and held our hands in each of hers, and said, in a tender, trembling voice,—

"The world is no easy place for bairns like you to find their way through. And there's no safe road through it that I know, from first to last, but just the foot-prints of the Lord himself. But you must not look to see even these in any long track before you. You'll mostly find nothing plain but the next step. Yet your hearts need not sink for that. A Saviour's hand to guide you is better than any map. It *upholds while it guides.* I have found that the times when I was longing for the map were just those when I was losing hold of the hand; and then more than once the thorns, piercing my feet, drove me back to the foot-prints and to the hand I should never have forsaken. But you need not be afraid even of the thorns," she added, her whole face lighting up with confidence and joy; "the feet in whose prints we tread were pierced for us with worse than thorns. And the hand that guides and upholds is a hand well able to bind up any wounds. It has bound up what none else could—the broken heart."

Then, as once or twice before, she seemed to forget the thought of our presence in the presence of God. Her whole spirit seemed to rise in prayer.

Evelyn and I said little as we went home together. But it was not because our hearts were closed to each other. They seemed not only too full, but too near to need the intervention of words.

IV

T home again! With what longing I have looked forward to the moment when I should be able to write those words. And now I can scarcely see to write them through my tears.

For Mother looks so ill, so terribly gentle; her step, always light, so noiseless; her voice, always soft, so low and sweet; her smile so tender, not like the dawn or the echo of happy laughter, but like the light struggling through tears.

Can these few months have made such a change, or have I been blind? Father does not seem to see it, nor Jack. Can it be, after all, only that, coming out of the glare of that brilliant London world, everything in our quiet world at home looks pale for the time?

Because the house, and the furniture, and all look so different. I never saw before how the bit of carpet in the parlour is worn and colourless; nor how the chintz curtains are patched; nor how Mother's Sunday dress itself is faded.

And these cannot have changed much in a few months.

Indeed, as it is, I should not have noticed the furniture half so much if we had met as usual in the hall, around our ordinary table to our ordinary fare. But Betty was determined to make it a high-day; and accordingly the meal was spread in the parlour, and the best Delft ware was brought out, as if I had been a stranger of distinction: and, after all, it seemed a positive wrong to notice the darns in the table-cloth, bleached to such a dazzling whiteness; and the crack in the best glass sugar-basin, monument of an ancient battle between Betty and Jack.

Yes, it was this holiday pitch to which Betty had insisted on winding everything up, which just brought me from the laughing point to the crying, which is so near it. It was the tender anxiety in Mother's eyes that I should find everything especially pleasant and bright, that so nearly turned the smile in mine into tears whenever I looked at her. It was Betty's ostentatious exhibition of all her grandest things that gave me the little pang when Father took off his best coat, which he had put on to welcome me, and Mother took it from him, and folded it so carefully in its white covers, and laid it on its shelf in the cupboard.

For it is no grievance to have to take care of one's clothes; I am sure none of us feel it so. And I would not, if I could, have our dear old furniture sink into the mere decorative ciphers such things are in rich men's houses, instead of being the dear familiar old letters on which so much of the history of our lives is written.

No; it was just the strain to be at high-holiday pitch which was too much for the carpet, and the table-cloth, and our precious Mother, and me.

For when at last Father gave a little shivering glance at the parlour grate, with its very fine decorations, which Betty would on no account sacrifice to such low considerations as warmth and comfort, and Trusty, with his paws on the sacred threshold which he dared not cross, whined an insinuating remonstrance against our exclusiveness, and our stateliness at last broke down, and Jack set a light to the fire in the great hall, and we five drew close to it, and the great festival was over, and we began to be really at home,—it could not have been only the glow from the blazing logs—Mother certainly *did* look less pale, and more like her old self, as Trusty and I sat together at her feet, she stroking my hair, and I stroking Trusty's ears.

Yet we did not remain long so; Father fell asleep, and waking suddenly, asked Jack if he had seen to the horses. The one I had ridden had been lent us, and had a cough, and must have a warm mash.

Jack had not seen to anything. Father dryly supposed not —how could any one expect it?

Jack yawned in a deprecatory way, and went out; and Father did not fall asleep again, but followed Jack in a few minutes, muttering that borrowed beasts at least must not be left to chance.

The troubled look came into Mother's face again. Trusty evidently felt she needed consolation, and after following Father to the door, paused a moment, then came back and put his paws on her knee, and attempted to lick her hand. And I felt just as dumb and perplexed as the dog, and could do little more than he in the way of comfort. I could only draw Mother's hand round my neck, and press a little closer to her, and cover it with silent kisses.

After all, we are all "dumb creatures" after a certain point. Only, dogs reach their dumb point a little sooner than we do.

And this has been going on all the time I have been away! While I have been living without care or anxiety; while Aunt Henderson has been pursuing her grave routine of household occupations, having the washing done on Monday, the ironing on Tuesday, the best parlour cleaned on Wednesday, the back parlour on Thursday, the hall and garden-room on Friday, and things in general on Saturday; while Aunt Beauchamp has been amusing herself with her complimentary old gentlemen in the mornings, and exciting herself over her cards every evening; care, care, care, keen pangs of fear, and slow gnawings of anxiety have been steadily, surely eating away at Mother's heart; and no one has seen it but Trusty! Poor faithful, per-

plexed old dog, he has seen it—he told me so with his wistful
eyes this evening, and by his low whine when Jack went out,
not closing the door, and Father followed him, decisively slam-
ming it. And I have not been here. But nothing on earth
shall ever move me from Mother's side again.

The Same Evening.

After writing these words my heart was too full for any
more, and I closed the Diary, and prepared to go to sleep, lest
Mother should see my candle burning too late, and be anxious
about me. But it was too late already. The soft touch was
on the latch of the door, and before I could possibly extinguish
the light and hide my tears in the darkness, Mother was beside
me.

"My darling!" she said—a rare word for her. "You are
overtired. You are not well. You should be in bed before
this. We must come back to our homely old country ways."

"Indeed I am not tired, Mother," I said, trying to speak
steadily.

"Has anything troubled you, darling," she said, "while you
were away?"

"Oh, no," I said; "every one has spoiled me with kindness."

"Spoiled you for the old home, Kitty?" she murmured.

She had given me a right to cry, and I sobbed out, "Oh,
Mother, it is nothing but you; you are so pale, and things have
been troubling you, and there has been no one to see it."

She was too truthful to comfort me with a deception. She
only smiled, and said, "Does no one see but you, Kitty?
Well, supposing I say I have missed you day and night, and
never knew what you were to me till you went away, will that
comfort you, Kitty? Shall we cry because it is all right again?"

"I will never leave you again, Mother, as long as I live," I
said passionately.

"As long as we both live, darling," she replied very quietly.

"If it is God's will, and not very selfish in me, I do trust not."

I was calmed by her words.

It was only after she had seen me safely in bed, and closed the door, and come back again to give me another kiss before she left me, that her words came back to me with another meaning.

"As long as we *both* live."

And then they echoed through and through my heart, like a passing-bell through a vault. And I tossed to and fro, and could not sleep, until I remembered I had not said my prayers.

The first night of my coming home ! the thing I had prayed for evening and morning, and often in the day, ever since I left home, and I had gone to rest without a word of thanks to God !

I was appalled at my own ingratitude. I rose and knelt by the window in the moonlight, which quivered through the branches of the old elms, and shimmered on the leaves of the old thorn, and chequered the floor through the diamond lattice panes.

It was that I wanted—only that—prayer with thanksgiving. It did me good from the moment I began.

And what wonder? Prayer is no soliloquy. The Bible says, when we call on Him, God bends down His ear to listen, as a father bends down to listen to a little child. Yes, God listens ! He heard me as I confessed my ingratitude and my distrustful fears. He heard me as I gave Him thanks ; He heard me as I committed Mother to His care.

Ungrateful ! God had been watching Mother all the time, understanding her inmost cares, and caring for her.

And He will care for us, "*as long as we both live.*" Yes, when I breathed even *those* words into His ear, the terrible death-chill seemed to pass from them. "As long as we both live" here on earth; and then, when we have no more cares to cast on Him, He will still care for us both for ever and for ever.

Marginal Note.—I was unjust, too, to say no one had seen how dear Mother was looking; for Hugh Spencer told me she was looking ill when I saw him in Great Ormond Street.

I am feeling much better to-day than yesterday.

In the first place, Mother is looking better.

In the second place, I have had my morning walk once more, and milked the cows, and taken the cup of new milk to Mother before breakfast. And the mere sight and sound of the sea made my heart buoyant again like its own waves : the great and wide sea, heaving its innumerable waves from its deep, still heart; the wind crisping them into foam, till they looked like a flight of snowy sea-birds; the old familiar thunder of the breakers against the rocks; the long roll of the ebbing wave, as it swept the pebbles back from the white beach far below. Then the turf was crisp with hoar-frost; and the wind on the cliff blew me about with a rough heartiness; and when I sat on the milking-stool in the shelter of the hollow, Daisy looked round at me with her large, motherly eyes, and in her calm, friendly way, recognized my right to be there. So all the dumb creatures welcomed me home again.

And in the third place, I have had a battle with Betty, which is *her* welcome and recognition that I have once more taken my old standing.

I had just taken the new milk to Mother, and to my grief and surprise had not found her in her own little closet over the porch ; she had not yet risen.

" I find that it strengthens me more to take the milk before I rise, Kitty," she said, making light of it. " I did not think you would have been stirring so early after your journey. It is cold sometimes in the mornings now," she added, apologizing to my rueful looks; "but when the spring comes, we will have our old morning talks in the porch-room again."

I tried to make as light of the change as Mother did, to her ;

but when I left her, I could not resist the longing to pour out my trouble on some one. Father was in the fields, Jack was in bed. Betty was the only human creature in the house; and I had no resource but to invade the sanctuary of the dairy where she was making the butter.

The windows were open; the low sunbeams slanted through the thick leaves close outside, flickering on the clean, cool, gray slabs of slate; the fresh morning air came in, rippling the surface of the milk in the pans from which the thick cream had been skimmed, while the one that was left with its unbroken crust of thick yellow cream, recalled countless childish feastings. Altogether, it was a delicious atmosphere of coolness, and greenness, and cream, and memories of childhood ; and I felt just as much a child beside Betty, as when Jack and I had stood there, humble petitioners to her bounty as the Queen of the Dairy, and Dispenser of all that was Delicious, scarcely tall enough to see over the brims of those wonderful pans of delight.

Betty was facing the window, lovingly patting her butter into shape, and humming to herself a low winding song, with as little beginning or end as the murmur of a brook. She did not hear me until I stood before her, and exclaimed—

"Oh, Betty, why did no one tell me? Has no one seen how ill Mother is?"

It was an indiscreet beginning. Betty looked on it as an assault. For a minute she said nothing, then still continuing apparently absorbed in her butter, she replied dryly,—

"Some folks think no one sees anything except they tell it to the town-crier. Some folks, specially young folks, think no one see anything but themselves."

"Oh, you know what I mean, Betty !" I said. "How long has Mother not been able to get up to have her milk? And why did no one write me?"

"Why no one wrote I can't say, Mrs. Kitty," she replied. "Why *I* didn't write, is as plain as why the dog doesn't speak.

Not that that is so very plain neither, leastways as regards Trusty, for he sees more than a sight of us that can."

And she continued dexterously and elaborately shaping her butter into the well-remembered dainty little rolls, as if the precise curve of the rolls were of supreme importance, and the question under discussion of none.

My disadvantages in the contest were great; a woman with her fingers occupied has always such a high vantage-ground in a debate, over one that is idle. The matter in debate can always be treated in a placid, parenthetical way, as quite subordinate to the matter in hand. Besides, Betty was in the very heart of her dominions, and I was an invader.

My only chance was to get her to perceive that I was no combatant at all, but only a suppliant, when, after guarding herself with an admonition, I knew her faithful womanly heart would open all its stores of affection and pity at once.

The tears which nearly choked my voice came to my aid, as I said,—

"Betty, I know you love her almost as I do, and you always see as quickly as any one. Is Mother ill? and can anything be done?"

Then Betty, having laid the last finished roll on its white dish, began to wipe her hands in the runner that hung behind the door, and said—

"I tell you what it is, Mrs. Kitty, I believe we make a heathen idol of Missis, and the Lord won't have it." And the runner was suspiciously drawn over Betty's face.

"Make Mother a heathen, Betty!" I said. "What do you mean?"

"I mean this, Mrs. Kitty," she said: "I have heard that parson that the other parsons can't abide, and who turned my brother-in-law into a lamb; and he said we are all born idolaters, no better than the heathen, unless we love God. And then he went on to say what were our idols. At first I thought he was going to let us all off easy. For he spoke of the rich man worshipping his riches, and I thought of the old miser at Falmouth, who counts out his money every night; and then he spoke of the great man worshipping his acres, and I thought there was a hit at our squire, who wouldn't let Master have that bit of a field that runs into ours, and would have made such a winter pasture for our Daisy; and then he spoke of the foolish young hussies making an idol of their ribbons, and I looked round on a many such that were there, to see how they liked that. But then he told of husbands and wives making idols of each other, and mothers of their children, and then I thought of all of you, Mrs. Kitty, and wished that Master and you and Missis had been there to hear : and so I do, sure; it would have done you all a sight of good. There's Master makes an open idol of you, my dear; and Missis is just as bad, only she does it in secret like; and you think no one fit to touch Missis or look after her but yourself."

Having thus delivered her conscience of her sermon, Betty had made an outlet for her sympathy; and sitting down on a bench, and wiping her face with her apron, she resumed in a gentle husky tone—

"Not that I think you need worrit yourself so much about Missis. In my belief, it's you, Mrs. Kitty, my dear, that she has been pining for : and now she's got you again, the life will come back again, like a fish thrown back into the water; least-ways if you don't go making an idol of her, and, with your tears and your woful looks watching every turn of her face, love her right away from us altogether into heaven, which at any time, in my belief, it would take little to do with Missis. For that she is fit for to go nobody can deny. But as to her not getting up so early," she continued, "that's something to be thankful for, my dear. It was me that brought her over to that, and I hope no one will over-persuade her out of it. Some folks seem to think it improves a weak rope to stretch it as far as it will strain. In my belief, it's more like to snap it."

Betty's view of Mother's health comforted me much. It seemed to bring the matter from the region of vague, immeasurable, helpless fears, into that of actual but remediable cares, which a little cheerful, tender nursing might soon relieve. I felt anxious to know more of Betty's experience with the Methodists, and I said,—

"Then the parson, after all, said nothing which particularly suited you, Betty?"

"Suited! no, Mrs. Kitty, he did not sure! as little as a rod suits a fool's back. And a fool I was to go, when Missis warned me not."

"You did not like what he said, then?"

"I should think not," she replied. "I should like to know who would like to be stuck up in the stocks before the whole parish, and pelted with dirt and stones, not in a promiscuous way like, but just exactly where it hurts most!"

"How was it, Betty?" I ventured to ask.

To my great amazement, Betty's voice suddenly failed, and she began to cry. Never before had I seen her show any sign of feeling, beyond a transient huskiness of voice or a suspicious brushing of her hand over her eyes. She was wont to be as much ashamed of tears as a school-boy. But now her tears became sobs, and it was some little time before she could speak.

"Mrs. Kitty," she said, "it was just as I was thinking who he'd hit next, and smiling to myself to see the poor fools sobbing and fainting around me, when down came the word like an arrow right into the core of my heart; and there I had to stand writhing, like a fish on a hook, while the parson drove it in;—and he as quiet all the time as if he'd been fixing a nail in the right spot to a hair's-breadth, in a piece of wood that mustn't be split. I could have knocked him down, Mrs. Kitty;

but there I stood, fixed and helpless as a worm with a pin through it."

"But what did he say, Betty?"

"Mrs. Kitty," she said, "he made me feel I was no better than a natural-born heathen, and that the idols I had been worshipping, instead of God, were things an Indian savage would have been ashamed of."

"What were they then, Betty?"

"Why, just my dairy, and my kitchen, and myself," she said; "the very pats of butter, which must be better than any in the country; and the stone floor I've been as angered to see a foot-mark on, as if it had been the king's foot-stool."

"The parson did not speak about pats of butter and kitchen floors?" I said.

"Not in so many words," she replied; "but I knew well enough what he meant, and so did he; the passions I've been in with Master Jack and you about your tricks, and with old Roger about his dirty shoes, and all."

"But, Betty," I interposed, "Jack and I and Roger were provoking and wrong often; and the kitchen and the dairy were the work God had given you to do, and you *ought* to care about them."

"What's the use of struggling, Mrs. Kitty?" Betty replied, hopelessly shaking her head. "I am not going to defend Roger. If I were a saint, I'd not say Roger's not often as bad as a born fool, and that things don't often happen aggravating. Haven't I gone over things times without number, and made out everything as clear as if I'd been a lawyer at the assizes—that I'd a right to be in a rage, and a right to care for the work the Almighty gave me to do? But it's of no use; the wound is there, and the word is there, working and rankling away in it like a rusty nail. I'm a poor sinful woman, Mrs. Kitty, and that's the end of it, and I see no way out of it."

"But, Betty," I said, "did you not go again, and try to get comfort?"

"I did indeed, although I had little hope of getting comfort," she said. "All the time he was speaking, he looked at me through and through like, but I never flinched: I looked at him back again; and I set my face, and said in my heart, 'You've caught me now, but I'll never let you try your hand on me again.' But when he had stopped and I got away, it seemed as if something were always drawing and drawing me back, like a moth to a candle. So at last I went again. A lot of folks from the mines and the fishings were met on the side of the moor, and a man preached to them from the top of a hedge. But this time it was not the parson, Mr. Wesley; it was a chap from Yorkshire—a stout, tall fellow, strong enough to throw any wrestler in Cornwall. At first I thought he was speaking a foreign tongue; but when I made him out, I found he was worse than the other. The parson drove that one nail home into your heart, and kept it there in one spot, struggle as you might; but the Yorkshire man knocked and pounded you about until there was no sound place left in you from top to toe. He made me feel I had been doing, and speaking, and thinking, and feeling wrong every day of my life, and was to this day. And that was all the comfort I got for not minding Missis."

"But, Betty," I said, "there *is* comfort, there *is* balm for such wounds; that was not *all* these Methodists said."

"No," she replied mournfully, "folks say they spoke wonderful gracious words about our Saviour and His death and His pity. But all I know is, it all turned to gall for me. They say sugar turns to vinegar when folks' insides are wrong; and I suppose the sweetest words man or angel ever spoke would be sour to me, as long as my heart is all wrong. Why, the very thing that makes me worse than the Indian savages, *is* the Lord's pity and what He went through for me, for they never heard of it, and I have."

"But, Betty," I said, "there is prayer! You can pray."

"I always thought I could, Mrs. Kitty," she said, "until I came to try. I've always said the Lord's Prayer every night, and the Belief and the Commandments on Sundays. But when I came to want something and ask for it, it seemed as if I could not pray at all; pray, of course, I might, but it seems as if there were no one there to mind."

"Betty," I said, "I think you really do know our Lord's pity and grace as little as the Indians. You speak as if you were all alone in your troubles, when all your troubles are only the rod and staff of God bringing you home."

"Maybe, Mrs. Kitty," she said; "but I can't see it. I only feel the smart and the bruises, and they worrit me to that degree I can barely abide Roger, or Master Jack, or you, or Missis, or anybody. I even struck at old Trusty the other day with the mop—poor, harmless, dumb brute—as if it was *his* fault. But he knew I meant no harm, and came crouching to lick my hand the next moment."

"Oh, Betty," I said, "the poor beasts understand us better than we understand God! They trust us."

"And well they may, Mrs. Kitty," said Betty, "for they never did any sin. The cat 'll steal the milk if she gets a chance, poor fool, and the dog cannot be trusted with a bone at all times, I won't say he can. But the Almighty made them so, and it's us that puts them out with our laws about mine and thine, which they don't understand. It's their nature. But the Almighty never made us to bury our souls in pats of butter and pans of milk, and forget Him, and fly into rages about a bit of dirt on a kitchen floor. And until that can be set right, I don't see that anything is right, or that I can think with any comfort of the Almighty."

"But our Saviour came to set all that right, Betty," I said. "He came to put away sin by the Sacrifice of Himself."

"Maybe, sure," said Betty, "but I know it's not at all set right for me."

She rose, and once more wiping the tears from her face, she went into the kitchen to set the rashers on the frying-pan for breakfast.

But before she drowned her voice in the hissing of the bacon, she turned and said to me with unusual gentleness :—

"You mean it very kind, Mrs. Kitty ; but I don't know why I should pour out my troubles on you. It's not to be expected a young maid like you should understand. But you meant it very kind, my dear ; only don't say a word to worrit Missis, and don't you lose heart about Missis yourself, for she'll get round in time, sure, now she's got you again ; if you don't go and make a heathen idol of her, as the parson said. And after all, my dear," she concluded, "I never found the work any the forwarder for worrying about it over night. You can't mend a thing before it's torn ; and if you get a hundred pieces, the rent'll always be sure just to go in the way that fits none of 'em. Things *be* perverse, most times, and there's no way that I know by, of being up with them beforehand."

Betty's prediction seems coming true, perhaps is making itself true, for her cheery words about Mother have lightened my heart, and the lightening of my heart seems to lighten Mother's. The anxious look is wearing away a little, although not the paleness. But I cannot say all is right between Father and Jack.

This morning they had one of the word-battles Mother and I so greatly dread.

We three had all but finished breakfast, and Father had been making very sharp comments on Jack's absence, when he himself came strolling in in his easy unconcerned way, and seating himself at the table after a general greeting, began to play with the home-brewed ale and bread and cheese in rather a languid manner, every now and then half suppressing a yawn.

"Over-wrought with last evening's work, I conclude," said

Father, beginning, as he usually does, with the politest sarcasm; "when young gentlemen toil till midnight, old men, of course, must expect to work in the morning while they rest."

"I believe I was rather late last night, sir," said Jack, with an easy attempt at apology.

"And in good company, sir!" said Father. "A pleasant serenade you and your companions gave us, as you parted. A little too much repetition, perhaps, in the strains, and a slight uncertainty in the close."

"I was not drunk, sir," said Jack.

"I did not say you were, sir. I spoke of your company, not of your entertainment. Any gentleman may be overtaken now and then, among his equals, of course, but no son of mine—no gentleman who bears the name of Trevylyan—shall have my leave to herd with degraded sots, who make brutes of themselves on small beer."

"There is a difference between claret and beer, certainly, sir," said Jack, daintily quaffing his home-brewed, while he glanced at the little bottle of French wine, always set for Father (he acquired the habit in the army in Flanders, Mother says, and cannot be expected to do without it now. If it is a little expensive, we can save in other ways).

"There is a difference between *you* and *me*, sir!" retorted Father, dropping his sarcasm and enforcing his words with some of those strong expressions, which Mother says he also acquired in the army in Flanders. "I give you notice that I pay no more bills at any low tavern where you may choose to make boon-companions of any rascally fellows in the town and neighbourhood."

"I quite agree with you in preferring better company, sir," said Jack; "but I cannot afford it. I have neither horses for the hunt, nor fine clothes to wear, nor fine company to keep that I can see, unless I seek the society of the Squire, who is carried to bed every night from the effects of the best claret."

"Leave the table, sir," said Father, "if you cannot speak except to insult me."

Jack rose without a murmur, throwing the remainder of his bread and cheese to Trusty; but before he went out of the door he turned back and took a cherry-coloured ribbon knot out of his pocket, which he said he had bought for me at the fair.

"Is it paid for, sir?" said Father in a tone of suppressed rage.

"I had no small change about me at the time," said Jack, "and I told them so. But Hugh Spencer happened to be near, and he lent me the money."

"No daughter of mine shall wear stolen goods!" said Father, and seizing the ribbon he threw it in the fire.

With that Jack grew warm and strode out of the house, and Father grew cool, and seeing the tears in my eyes, smoothed my hair tenderly, and told me not to fret, my own brown hair was better than all the cherry-coloured knots in the world.

"It is not for the ribbon, Father," I said.

"For what, then?" he said testily.

"For thee and Jack, Father," I said.

He was silent a moment, and then he said :—

"Perhaps I was rather hard on the poor fellow. Boys will be boys."

"It was not that I meant, Father," I said, for I felt as if I must speak, because Mother was crying; and dearly as Father loves her, he never will bear a word from her. "It was not that. It is that you are right and Jack is wrong, and yet you always let him make you seem wrong, because he is so cool and he puts you in a passion."

"Fine education you give your children, madam," said he turning to Mother; "your son puts me in a rage, like an old fool as I am, and your chit of a daughter reads me a sermon."

But he was not angry either with Mother or me.

And at dinner, like a generous gentleman, as he is, he held out his hand to Jack and said :—

" Perhaps I was hard on you, my boy. It was well-meant, after all, buying your sister the ribbon."

But that was not at all what I meant. Jack had come off from the conflict a self-complacent victor, satisfied that he had kept his temper under great provocation, and had done a very generous action in buying me a ribbon with Hugh Spencer's money; which, of course, especially now that the ribbon was burned, he would never think of paying.

And Jack is so pleasant, that when I lecture him it always ends in a joke; and when Betty and Father scold him, they always put themselves in the wrong, and end by virtually begging his pardon; and when Mother gently remonstrates, he ends in persuading her that he is on the eve of turning over quite a new leaf, and indeed had quite made up his kind to do so before she spoke.

But the new leaf is only a repetition of the old, and my heart aches to think how it will end. It seems to me people never drift by accident into the right haven.

July the Fifteenth.

I wonder if any one ever quite carried out all Bishop Taylor's rules every day. Perhaps he did not mean it to be done. It so often happens with me that one " action of piety " takes up the time of the whole seven. For instance, one morning I seem able to do nothing but rejoice in the thought how good God and my Saviour are, and thank Him for all His goodness to us. The next I am overwhelmed with the thought of my own weakness and sinfulness, and the wrong things I think, and say, and do. And this morning I seemed able to do nothing but pray for Jack. I am so anxious about him, and it is impossible to help loving him so dearly, if it were only for Mother's sake, who loves him as the apple of her eye.

I wonder if Mother is quite right. She seems to think women were only made to endure patiently whatever the men belonging to them inflict, consciously or unconsciously. But I think we should try to prevent them being selfish and inconsiderate for us, because it does them harm as well as us.

But am I right in seeing so much of " the mote in my brother's eye "?   Does our Lord mean that we should be blind to the faults of those we love, or that, *not being blind,* we should shut our eyes and say, " I *will* not see."   He cannot mean this, for it would be false, and all false things He abhors.

I think He must mean that we should love on, in spite of all we see.   How can we help each other unless we see where each needs help?   But we must see, not to exhibit but to veil, not to judge but to help.

Love is not blind, I am sure; for true love lives and breathes and has its being in truth.

It is the selfishness in our love which is blind, the passionate selfishness which says, " This is mine, therefore I *will* think it fair, and will give the lie to any who say it is not."

But God is Love, and He is the Truth, and He says to us, " You are *not* sinless, you are not fair, but you are mine ; I have pitied and redeemed you, because you were wretched and polluted, and I will make you fair."

And in our poor narrow measure I think we should try to be and do the same.

My last attempt to take the mote out of my brother's eye has certainly not been at all successful, except that it has answered the purpose of showing me more plainly the beam in my own.

After writing about Jack as I did last night, I felt this morning as if it were scarcely sisterly and honest not to tell him what I thought this afternoon.

Betty was " meating the pigs," Father was guiding the plough with Roger, the call to the labouring oxen came pleasantly across the valley, Mother was sewing in the hall, and I and Jack were alone in the kitchen, I sorting herbs on the table at the open window, and he polishing a new gun I had brought

him from London. The opportunity seemed favourable, and I
ventured to say,—

"Jack, you won't mind my saying so; but you will pay
Hugh Spencer for the cherry-coloured ribbon, won't you ?"

"How can you worry about such trifles, Kitty?" he said.
"Just a few pence, not worth mentioning between old friends,
and gentlemen's sons."

"But they were lent," I said; "and a debt is a debt."

"Let Father pay it then," he said, laughing; "he has the
property. Or you yourself, Kitty; since you are so particular."

"I would, indeed, Jack," I said; "but it is such a trifle, I
don't like to speak to Hugh about it."

"Nor do I," he said dryly.

"But it's *your* debt," I said.

"Kitty," he replied, "you are in the way to be one of the
most aggravating women I know. It's a symptom of insanity
when trifles take such possession of the brain. You should be
careful."

"But how much was it, Jack?" I persisted once more. "I
could give you the money, you know, and you could pay
Hugh."

"You may give me what money you please," he replied, "I
am not too proud to be thankful for trifles. But I shall not
pay Hugh. It would be a degradation to allude to such
nonsense. And besides," he continued, "Hugh Spencer is a
screw, and it is only what he deserved. I asked him to lend
me a few guineas a few days before, and he refused. I was
disgusted with his meanness."

I felt myself getting hot, and I said,—

"I think the meanness is in borrowing, not in not lending."

"You are always ready enough to turn against me," said
Jack; "but you may look in the Bible, and you'll find plenty
about the duty of lending, and not even expecting to be paid
again. It's like the publicans to lend, expecting to receive as

much again. And to refuse to lend at all is worse ; it's like the
Pharisees and hypocrites. An open heart and an open hand,
that's the kind of Christianity I like, and that's the kind of
Christian I mean to be when I am rich. Do you think I would
have shut my purse to Hugh if I had had money to lend?"

" Jack," I said, " Hugh is not a publican nor a Pharisee, and
you know it. You know he has impoverished himself again
and again to get you out of scrapes ; and if he ever refused to
help you, it was because he thought it right to refuse; and he
was right, I have no doubt. And with all your grand intentions,
when did you ever deny yourself anything for any one ?"

Jack had entangled me in his sophisms, and driven me to
indignant assertions, as he does Father. He was cool as usual,
and pushed his advantage.

" As to self-denial," he said, " if I had the means, it would
be no self-denial to me at all to help my friends, but the greatest
pleasure. And I never said Hugh was a publican or a Pharisee.
I only said the publicans and Pharisees disliked lending money.
I daresay they were right ; and Hugh was right, at all events,
as regarded the money."

"Oh, Jack !" I said, "how can you be so ungenerous to
Hugh? Have you forgotten the times without number he paid
for things you bought, when the people threatened to send the
bills in to Father, because you said it would break Mother's
heart? Have you forgotten how, again and again, some little
comfort or delicacy Mother needed has come in from him,
'just,' as he used to say, 'because he happened to meet with
it'? Ask all the poor toiling men and women in the parish
whether Hugh Spencer is generous or not. And you know he
is not rich, and that his father never allows him much.

" No; I believe a certain carefulness about money *is* hereditary
in the Spencer family," Jack replied.

I know he felt in the wrong, because he was so provoking. If I could only have been quiet, and let the conviction

work! But my heart was full, and my temper was up, and I said,—

"Jack, I don't know what you will come to, and what you will bring us all to. The Bible says, 'The *wicked* borroweth and payeth not again.' You seem to have no honesty nor gratitude, nor shame; and I do believe you will end in breaking Mother's heart."

"Whew!" said Jack, drawing a long breath, and for a moment stopping his polishing to look at me. "Whatever sins may be hereditary with the Spencers, a certain peculiarity of temper is certainly hereditary with the Trevylyans. My dear Kitty, Mother is coming into the kitchen, and as you are so apprehensive about her feelings, I recommend you to withdraw. You look quite excited. No doubt," he added demurely, "as Mother used to say, you will be sorry for this to-morrow."

And I had to withdraw, for I could not stop my tears; and what is worse, I shall have to be sorry to-morrow, and to apologize to Jack, for the language I used was certainly unnecessarily strong. Unnecessarily strong as regarded the immediate occasion, but as regards that habit of his, what language can be too strong? And what an opportunity I have thrown away of helping him!

It was only yesterday I was thinking how feeble my convictions of sin were compared with Betty's; and I had resolved next Sunday seriously to read Bishop Taylor's "Instruments, by way of consideration, to Awaken a Careless Person and a Stupid Conscience," and his "Form of Confession of Sins and Repentance, to be used on Fasting Days." But now there is no need to go through a course of voluntary humiliation. I am humbled enough in Jack's eyes as well as in my own. So unworthy, so hasty, so passionate, how could I ever think of setting myself up as a censor of other people? Perhaps this pride and secret self-satisfaction is the beam in my own eye. Perhaps, now I feel how really blind and wrong I am, I may be able to speak to

Jack to-morrow with more result. For he *is* wrong about the debts. Perhaps when I speak to him from his own level, as no better than he is, though in a different way, he will listen.

It is of no use. Jack received my apologies with the graciousness of an offended but merciful sovereign.

" Do not mention such a trifle again, my dear little Kitty. We all get a little excited at times ; it is in the family, although, perhaps, I am not so much troubled in that way as the rest of you."

And when I made one more feeble attempt to make an impression on him about the debts, he stopped me with—

" Perhaps I was even a little hot myself yesterday about poor Hugh. Hugh is a good fellow at bottom. We all have our little peculiarities, especially about money. I only meant that when I have my commission, and have won a few battles, and taken one or two towns, and have my prize-money, that won't be exactly *my* way. An open heart and an open hand, Kitty, that's my idea of a Christian, although it may make one's purse a little low at times."

And he kissed me benignantly, and went away whistling, " Begone dull care."

What can I do ? It is plain the price of the cherry-coloured bow is far too great a trifle for Jack's " open hand " to contract to pick up and return.

And it's plain that he considers himself, although probably touched with a little of the general infection of the sin of Adam, quite singularly free from the peculiar infirmities of the Spencers, and the Trevylyans, and every one else.

And it is plain that my hands are by no means steady enough (even if my eyes were clear enough) to take the mote out of my brother's eye.

Yet I cannot help feeling as if those habits of his were like the little low clouds gathering far out in the west, like the little uneasy interrupted gusts of wind which come when we are to have a storm,—like the little cloud no bigger than a man's hand, which the prophet's servant saw, when the heaven was so soon to be black with clouds.

I should make a bad historian. I have never said a word about our journey home from London.

Not that there is much to tell, because, after all, we came from Bristol by sea, Father, and Hugh Spencer and I; and I was so full of the thought of home, that I did not observe anything particularly. The chief thing I remember is a conversation I had with Hugh.

It was a calm evening. Father had rolled himself up in his old military cloak with a foraging cap half over his eyes, and Hugh and I were standing by the side of the ship watching the trail of strange light she seemed to make in the waves. There was no one else on deck but the man at the helm, and an old sailor mending some ropes by the last glimmerings of daylight, and humming in a low voice to himself what seemed like an attempt at a psalm tune.

" Do you know what he is singing? Hugh asked.

" Not from the tune. I do not see how any one could; but the quaverings seem of a religious character, like what the old people sing in church."

" It is a Methodist hymn," Hugh said. " He said it through to me this morning." Hugh always has a way of getting into the confidence of working men, especially of sea-faring people. The old man had been in the ship which took Mr. John Wesley and Mr. Charles Wesley to America. Several religious people were there also from Germany, going out as missionaries. They called themselves Moravians. At first he despised them all for a foolish psalm-singing set. But they encountered a great storm on the Atlantic, and the old sailor said he should never forget the fearless calm among those Christian people

during the danger. "It was," he said, "as if they had fair
weather of God's making around them, be the skies as foul as
they might." He could never rest until he found out their
secret. When he went ashore, he attended the Methodist
meetings everywhere; "and now," he said, "thank the Lord
and Parson Wesley, my feet are on the Rock aboard or ashore."

"These Methodists find their way everywhere, Hugh," I
said. "It does seem as if God blessed their work more than
any one's."

"And what wonder," he said; "who work as they do?"

"But so many people—even good people—appear to be
afraid of them," I said. "Are they not sometimes too violent?
Do they not sometimes make mistakes?"

"No doubt they do," he said. "All the men who have done
great and good work in the world have made mistakes, as far
as I can see. It is only the easy, cautious people, who sit still
and do nothing, who make no mistakes; unless," he added,
"their whole lives are one great mistake, which seems
probable."

And then he told me something of what he had seen in the
world and at Oxford; how utterly God seemed forgotten everywhere, how scarcely disguised infidelity spoke from the pulpits,
and vices not disguised at all paraded in high places; how in
the midst of this John and Charles Wesley had stood apart, and
resolved to live to serve God and do good to men; how they
had struggled long in the twilight of a dark but lofty mysticism,
until they had learned to know how God has loved us from
everlasting, and loves us *now*, and how Christ forgives sins
now; and then, full of the joyful tidings, had gladly abandoned
all the hopes of earthly ambition for the glorious ambition of
being ambassadors for Christ to win rebellious and wretched
men back to Him.

"Morning, noon, and evening," he said, "John Wesley goes
about proclaiming the tidings of great joy, in Ireland, America,

throughout England, among colliers, miners, and slaves; in prisons, to condemned criminals; in hospitals, to the sick; in market-places, pelted with stones; in churches, threatened with imprisonment; reviled by clergymen, assaulted by mobs, and arraigned by magistrates. They go on loving the world that casts·them out, and constantly drawing souls out of the world to God to be blessed."

"It seems like the apostles," I said. "It is wonderful."

"Kitty," he said fervently, "when I think, I can *not* wonder at it. The wonder seems to me that we should wonder at it so much. If we believe the Bible at all; if not now and then by some strange chance, but steadily, surely, incessantly, the whole world of living men and women are passing on to death, sinking into unutterable woe, or rising into infinite, inconceivable joy; and if we have it in our power to tell them the truth, which, if they believe it, really will make all the difference to them for ever, and if we find they really will listen, what is there to be compared with the joy of telling these truths? And the people do listen to Whitefield and Wesley. Think what it must be to see ten thousand people before you smitten with a deadly pestilence, and to tell them of the remedy,—the immediate remedy, which never failed. Think what it must be to stand before thousands of wretched slaves with the ransom money for all in your hand, and the title-deeds of an inheritance for each. Think what it must be to see a multitude of haggard starving men and women before you, with the power such as our Lord had of supplying them all with bread here in the wilderness, and to see them one by one pressing to you and taking the bread and eating it, and to see the dull eye brightening, colour returning to the wan cheek, life to the failing limbs. Think what it would be to go to a crowd of destitute orphans and to be able to say to each of them, 'It is a mistake, you are *not* fatherless. I have a message for every one of you from your own Father, who is waiting to take you to His heart.' Oh,

8

Kitty, if there is such a message as this to take to all the poor, sorrowing, bewildered, famished, perishing men and women in the world, and if you can get them to listen and believe it, is it any wonder that any man with a heart in him should think it the happiest lot on earth to go and do it, night and day, north and south, in the crowded market-places, and in every neglected corner, where there is a human being to listen?"

"I think not, indeed," I said; "but the difficulty seems to me to get people to believe that they are orphans, and slaves, and famishing."

"That is what Whitefield and the Wesleys do," he said. "Or rather they make them understand that the faintness every one feels at times is hunger, and that there is bread; that the cramping constraint, the uneasy pressure we so often feel, is from the fetters of a real bondage, and that they can be struck off; that the bewildered, homeless desolation so many are conscious of, is the desolation of orphanhood, and that we have a Father who has reconciled us to Himself through the blood of the Cross."

As Hugh spoke, a selfish anxiety crept over me, and I said,— "Shall *you* go then, Hugh, and forsake everything to tell the good tidings far and wide?"

"If I am called," he said, "*must* I not go?"

"But how can you know you are called?" I said.

"To have the bread of life to give is one call," he said; "to be able to go is another; to be willing to go is a third. If I had these three calls, Kitty, I must listen; the vocation in the Word of God to proclaim it, the vocation in my heart, the vocation of Providence."

"Have you these three, Hugh?" I said, feeling half afraid he had.

"I think I have, except the call of Providence, Kitty. I cannot see that it would be right to go directly counter to my father's will; otherwise I think I am ready to go."

My heart was heavy. Would he then leave us all so easily?
There was a long silence: the waves plashed around us and
closed in after us as we cut through them, with a sound which
in the morning light would have been crisp, and fresh, and
exhilarating; but now, in the dimness and stillness of night, it
seemed to me strange, and dull, and awful. And I thought not
so much of the waves we were bounding over and parting before us, like the future, like life; but of the waves which were
closing in on us, like the past, like death. It gave me a sad,
lonely feeling, as I thought how Hugh and I were standing
there together, and had been together all our lives, and how
soon all the sweet familiar past might slip away from us into
the darkness like the sea behind us, leaving at first a little
furrow and a track of foam, but very soon no track at all,—
and that Hugh seemed to care no more than the sea. It felt
very cold and desolate. I had been picturing life to myself as
a quiet river, always passing on indeed, but flowing by familiar
places, with its own fountains, its own hills, its own little
meadow banks to water and keep green, its own welcome at
last to the sea. And was life instead to be the mere crossing
of a great dreary sea, with one wave like another, and one great
round space like another, one horizon like another, except for
more or less of heat and cold, or more or less of storm or calm?

Ought all places to religious people to be alike,—mere spaces
of this great featureless ocean we have to cross? Ought all
human beings to be alike to us—just masses of undistinguishable
"immortal souls"?

For the first time in my life my heart felt at discord with
Hugh's, I scarcely knew why. A cold shadow seemed to have
come between us, and if it was religion that cast it, it was
wrong to wish it away.

But was it religion? I questioned myself; or was it right?
Certainly all people had not the same space or the same place
in St. Paul's heart. Only see the greetings at the end of the

epistles. And our blessed Lord Himself, if He loved all equally, surely loved each differently, each with his own *piece* of love, with a peculiar, recognizing, watchful, personal affection, which was for *that one*, and no one else !

Perhaps Hugh was feeling in some way as I did, for after that silence he said softly,—

"Perhaps I was deceiving myself. Perhaps it is just because there *is* that barrier in my way that I have been fancying I should be willing to go if there were not."

Then he began to be afraid I felt the night air chill, and brought me a little seat, and placed it at Father's side, and wrapped me up in all the warm wraps he could find. And we neither of us said anything more that night.

 HAVE had a great pleasure to-day. A letter from Cousin Evelyn, the first letter I ever received, except two from Mother, in London ; and the very first I ever received at home from any one. It has already, I believe, greatly increased my consequence in Betty's eyes. I was shelling peas in·the kitchen window when a gentleman on horseback rode up and asked Betty, who was scrubbing down the window-sill, if Miss Trevylyan lived there.

"What new-fangled title is that?" muttered Betty. "Miss Trevylyan, indeed! if it is our Mrs. Kitty you mean, she is there, and you can speak to herself."

(Betty's temper has not improved lately ; and she has relapsed into impenetrable silence about herself.)

Taking off his hat with a bow, the horseman handed me, through the open window, the letter which Evelyn had addressed in the new style.

It would have reached me before, he said, only it had met with many misadventures.

The king's mail had been robbed on Hounslow Heath ; and although the "gentlemen of the road" had most politely restored the letters after rifling the bags of their pecuniary contents, the postman had been wounded in the fray, and this had caused a delay of some days. Then there had been a flood over some part of the road which had swept away the bridges ; and finally, when the letter reached Falmouth, the farmer's lad to

whose care it had been committed, after carrying it about some
days in his pocket, forgot for whom it was meant, and not being
able to read, judiciously carried it back to the post-office nearest
him ; and there it might have been lying for no one knows how
much longer, had not the gentleman who gave it me politely
volunteered to take it to its destination on his way to his home
farther west.

The unusual clatter of horse's hoofs had brought Father into
the court, and nothing would satisfy him but that the stranger
should have his horse put up, and remain to dinner with us.
And then he had much to tell that interested Father and Jack.
Thus it was two or three hours longer before I could open the
precious packet.

Jack listened eagerly to all the stranger's news, and sighed
for the commission which was to open the world to him.

Father heard his narrative with very mingled emotions.   He
was cheered to think that the Duke of Cumberland had put
down "those canting Scotch ;" but his satisfaction was diminished by the military successes of those "rascally French."
"We taught them another lesson, sir," he said, "in Marlborough's days."   He broke into many strong military expressions at the thought of the troops of "beggarly Germans"
who had come over in the train of the Hanoverian king.

He sympathized with the London mob who, when the Hanoverian court-lady deprecated their wrath by exclaiming, in
apologetic tones from her carriage window, "My dear people,
we come for all your goods," retorted, "Yes, confound you, and
for our chattels too."   He was disgusted with the Pretender
parading as a hero at the Paris opera-house, on the strength of
the brave deeds of the Highland chiefs who were being hanged
for his sake at Tyburn.   But he consoled himself by thinking
it was just like those "confounded Papists," and with drinking
to the Protestant Succession.   But, again, his loyalty was sorely
tried by the tales of the quarrels between the King and the

Prince of Wales, and other court scandals I do not caro to write. "Terrible times, sir," ho said; "the country in the hands of scoundrelly foreigners, and tho county jails full of villanous poachers, who will poach again, sir, the instant their punishment is over. Sir, we are going to destruction as fast as Jacobites and Whigs can carry us." He was in some measure restored to hope by hearing of certain printers who had been compelled to apologizo on their knees on the floor of tho House of Lords for venturing to print reports of the debates in the Lords and Commons. "Low fellows like them," he said, "daring to report the words of gentlemen!"

But his spirits were again depressed by hearing of tho Methodist lay preachers, who drew crowds around them in every county, from Northumberland to the Land's End. "Sir," ho said, "in *my* time we should have made quick work with idle fellows who left the plough, or the mason's trowel, or the tailor's goose, to preach whatever canting trash they pleased. Wo should have dispersed the congregation, sir, at the point of tho bayonet, and set the preacher in the stocks to meditate on his next sermon. Sir, tho Papists manage to keep down such seditious fanatics; and shall wo be outdone by tho Papists?"

"No doubt, sir," replied the stranger; "but would you believe it, on my way here I met a fellow who is reported to be ono of tho worst among them, John Nelson, tho Yorkshireman, who told me he had met Squire Trevylyan, and that he was a most hospitable gentleman; for he had given him tho pasty ho was carrying for his own dinner, and had invited him to tako his bread-and-cheese and beer at his house whenever ho camo that way."

Father looked perplexed for a moment at the contrast between his fierce denunciations against the Methodists in general, and his tolerance of tho only Methodist he had encountered in particular, but he soon rallied.

"Sir," he said, "that fellow is a true-born Englishman, as

true to the Church and King as you or I. A fellow, too, with such a chest and such muscle as would be worth the King a troop of those beggarly Hessians you spoke of. And he had been knocked down and trampled on by a mob of cowardly ruffians, just before I saw him. Sir, they knocked him down, and beat and kicked him till the breath was well-nigh out of him, and his head bleeding; and then they dragged him along the stones by the hair of his head, and would have thrown him into a draw-well, but for a high-spirited woman who stood by the well and pushed several of the cowardly bullies down. I would take off my hat to that woman as soon as to the King. And then he got up and very soon mounted his horse again, and rode forty miles that very day as if nothing had happened. Sir, it is not in any Englishman, least of all in an old soldier of the Duke's, not to honour that brave fellow. Besides he was hungry; and would you have a Cornish gentleman turn a hungry traveller from his door? Not if he were the Pope himself, or the Pretender! Is it my fault that he preaches what the parsons don't like on the strength of my pasty? That fellow is no hypocrite, sir; I give my word of honour for it. A fellow with such a stout heart, and chest, and the voice of a lion! Besides," said Father softly, with some reserve, "I assure you what he said to me afterwards was excellent; none of your canting phrases, but plain sense about believing in our Saviour and doing our duty. Upon my honour," continued Father, with increasing earnestness, "I felt the better for it. He said very plain things to me, such as a man does not often hear; things, sir, that we shall all have to remember one day; and I feel grateful to the man for his honest, faithful words, and I trust I shall not forget them. An old soldier has not a few things he might be glad to unlearn, and would like to be sure will not be remembered against him."

The simple humility and earnestness of Father's manner put a stop to all further jesting; and before long the stranger, respectfully saluting him, went off with Jack to saddle his horse, and I was free to fly to my chamber and open

COUSIN EVELYN'S LETTER.

" My Dearly-beloved Cousin Kitty,—I suppose you have no more idea how we missed your dear, tender, soft, quiet, quaint, wise, comfortable, little self, than a fire has how cold the room is when it goes out. Mamma moaned for you more than she did for the poodle that was drowned in the soup-tureen ; she fancied you shivering on the Cornish moors, honey-combed, as she understands they are, with fearful abysses, your life endangered by grimy miners, your complexion by the sea-air ; and she wondered in the first place how you grew up at all, and in the second, how you could possibly grow to be what you are amidst the perils of that vast howling wilderness, or, indeed, to be anything beyond the level of a Red Indian.

" Aunt Henderson, whom I have seen twice, regrets you should be again involved in the darkness of a county she has heard to be little better than heathen ; but hopes that the sound teaching you received at Hackney may be of some use to her 'poor Sister Trevylyan, who has had so few privileges.'

" Harry swears if Mother will find him a girl like Kitty he will marry her to-morrow ; but how much he brings you forward as a golden back-ground to throw out the dark colours in which he paints the 'simpering heaps of gauze and brocade' recommended to his attention, I will not undertake to say.

" Papa roams about as unsettled as when anything detains him in London during the sporting season. He says you are a girl of the old style, such as he remembers when he was young ; not too clever to make a sensible man's home happy, 'although he may *not* be able to talk like a Frenchman about the fashions, or like an Italian adventurer about operas and pictures, or like a Bishop about religion.'

" But this again, Kitty, must not make you too conceited, as your excellences serve to barb a dart at me, in reference to a neighbouring potentate, whose estates march with those of the Beauchamps, but whose manners do not 'march' with your correspondent's tastes.

"From the silent homage rendered to your memory by Mamma's maid, and by Aunt Jeanie, the tongue of Detraction herself can, however, detract nothing. Mamma's maid has recourse to genuine Devonshire, and a genuine pocket-handkerchief to prevent genuine tears from spoiling the powder of Mamma's hair as she falters out the praises of 'the nicest and most affable young lady she ever set eyes on.' And Aunt Jeanie soars high into Scotch and the Bible, as she tells how the winsome lassie, the tender lammie, came day after day to listen to an old wife like herself; and how you made her feel as if the air of the Highlands was breathing fresh on her face once more, and the voices of old times were in her ears.

"Oh, Kitty darling, I would give all I have in the world to carry with me the fresh air you bring everywhere! There is something about you, you little witch, as much sweeter and more exhilarating than all the wit, and fashion, and cleverness of our London world, as the country air on a spring morning is sweeter than all the perfumes of a London drawing-room. What is it, Kitty, except that you are just your own sweet natural self? Yes, there is no perfume like freshness! and there is no moral or mental perfume like truth!

"And that is just the explanation of some of my difficulties, Cousin Kitty; for I *have* my difficulties, Kitty. Life—I mean the inner religious life—is not so smooth to me as you may think, as I thought it must be always henceforth when I heard that wonderful sermon of Mr. Whitefield's. Or rather, it is not so plain. For I did expect roughness, more perhaps than I have met with; but I did not expect perplexities such as I feel.

"My difficulties are not interesting, elevating difficulties,

Kitty, such as would draw forth sweet tears of sympathy and smiles of tender encouragement at some of the religious tea-parties. No one has taken the trouble to make me a martyr. I should rather have enjoyed a little more of that, which is, per-haps, the reason I have not had it. Mamma was a little uneasy at first; but when she found I did not wish to dress like a Quaker or to preach publicly from a tub, she was relieved, and seems rather to think me improved. Harry says all girls are sure to run into some folly or another, if they don't marry, and probably even if they do; and some new whim is sure soon to drive out this. Papa says women must have their amusements; and if I like going to see the old women at the Manor, and taking them broth and reading them the Bible, better than riding a thousand miles for a wager, as a young lady did the other day, he thinks it is the more sensible diversion of the two. His mother gave the people broth and bitters, and probably they like the Bible better than the bitters. I am a good child on the whole, he says; and if I ride to the meet with him in the country, and give myself no sanctimonious airs, he cannot object to my amusing myself as I like in town. Indeed, he said one day he thought Lady Huntingdon's preach-ings were far better things for a young woman to hear, than the scandalous nonsense those Italian fellows squalled at the opera. But, Kitty, although he talks so lightly, do you know, the other evening, as he had taken his candle and was kissing me good-night, he said, —

" ' By the way, Eve, if you don't fancy going with me all the way to-morrow, I'll drop you at the gamekeeper's lodge beyond the wood. His old woman is very ill, and she says you told her something that cheered her heart up; so you might as well go again. She is an honest old soul, and she says you reminded her of your Aunt Maud who died, and she was a good woman, if ever there was one.'

" So you see, Cousin Kitty, I have little chance of martyrdom.

"My difficulties are from the religious people themselves. There seems to me so much fashion, so much phraseology, so much cutting and shaping, as if the fruits of the Spirit were to be artificial wax fruits, instead of real, living, natural fruits.

"With you, Kitty, it is so different. You like what you like, and love those you love, and not merely try to like what you ought to like, and to work yourself up to something like love for those you ought to love.

"I find it difficult to explain myself. What I feel is, that religious people, no doubt from really high motives, are apt to become unnatural—to lose spontaneousness.

"I do not see this in Mr. Whitefield and Lady Huntingdon, nor in Aunt Jeanie, nor, my sweet cousin, in you. Lady Huntingdon is a queen, no doubt; but we must have kings and queens. But it is the *followers* of Mr. Whitefield, the ladies who form Lady Huntingdon's court, that trouble me in this way.

"There is a cutting down, a rounding off, a clipping into shape, like the cypresses in the Dutch gardens, and a suspicious uneasiness about any self-willed shoot which asserts its right to sprout beyond the prescribed curves, which provokes me beyond measure.

"I feel sometimes in those circles as if I were being put in a mortar and pestled into a sweetmeat; as if all the natural colour in me were being insensibly toned down to the uniform gray; as if all the natural tones of my voice were being in spite of me pitched to a chant, like the intoning of the Roman Catholic priests. It is very strange this tendency all religious schools seem to have towards monotone and uniform, from the Papists to the Quakers. And in the Bible, it seems to me, there is as little of it as in nature.

"I was becoming very rebellious when at Bath, before we escaped into the free, natural country life; and now that we are in London once more, it is coming over me again like a

terrible spell. But I am determined I will not be pestled into
a sweetmeat! The great fear is, that I shall ferment myself
into an acid.

"But if I could only keep close to God himself, to my
glorious Saviour, to His free Spirit, there could be no danger of
either. The following of Christ is freedom, expansion, and
growth. The following of His followers is copying, imitation,
contraction. And it is to the following of Christ, close, *always*,
with nothing and no person between, that we are called, all of
us, the youngest, the weakest, the meanest. You and I, Kitty!
as well as Lady Huntingdon, and Mr. Whitefield, and Mr.
Wesley, and St. Paul.

"And Christ our Lord, if we yield ourselves honestly, wholly
to Him, will develop our hearts and souls from within, outward
and upward from the root, which is *growing ;* instead of our
having to trim and clip them from outside inward, which is
stunting. He will give to each seed 'His own body.' Is it not
true, Kitty? I want very much to have a talk with you, for I
cannot find other people's thoughts and ways fit me, any more
than their clothes; and I want to know how much of this is
wrong, and how much is right.

"For instance, the other evening Lady Emily—

   *   *   *   *   *

"I had written so far, when an opportunity occurred of going
to hear Mr. John Wesley preach at the Foundry. The sermon
seemed made for me. It was on evil-speaking; and very pun-
gent and useful I found it, I assure you.

"Such an angelic face, Kitty!—the expression so calm and
lofty, the features so refined and defined, regular and delicate,
just the face that makes you sure his mother was a beautiful
woman (one of his aunts was painted by Sir Peter Lely as one
of the beauties of the day). Yet there is nothing feminine
about it, unless as far as an angel's face may or must be partly
feminine. Eyes not appealing but commanding; the delicate

mouth firm as a Roman general's; self-control, as the secret of all other control, stamped on every feature. If anything is wanting in the face and manner, it seemed to me just that nothing was wanting—that it was too angelic. You could not detect the weak, soft place, where he would need to lean instead of to support. He seemed to speak almost too much from heaven; not, indeed, as one that had not known the experiences of earth (there were the keenest penetration and the deepest sympathy in his words), but as one who had surmounted them all. The glow on his countenance was the steady sunlight of benevolence, rather than the tearful, trembling, intermittent sunshine of affection, with its hopes and fears. The few lines on his brow were the lines of effective thought, not of anxious solicitude. If I were on a sick-bed in the ward of an hospital, I should bask in the holy benevolent look as in the smile of an angel; but I do not know that he would (perhaps could) be tenderer if I were his sister at home.

"I should like to hear Mr. Wesley preach every Sunday; he would send me home detected in my inmost infirmities, unmasked to myself, humbled with the conviction of sin, and inspired with the assurance of victory.

"And yet if on Monday I came to ask his advice in a difficulty, I am not quite sure he would understand me. I am not sure that he would not come nearer my heart in the pulpit than in the house; that while he makes me feel singled out and found out, as if I were his only hearer in the crowd, if I were really alone with him I should not feel that he regarded me rather as a unit in 'the great multitude no man can number,' than as myself, and no one else.

"But I am running away from his sermon, as if I winced from it, as I did.

"He began with the words—

"'Speak evil of no man,' says the great apostle—'as plain a command as "Thou shalt do no murder." But who, even among Christians, regards this command? Yea, how few are there that so much as understand it. What is evil-speaking? It is not the same as lying or slandering. All a man says may be as true as the Bible, and yet the saying of it be evil-speaking. For evil-speaking is neither more nor less than speaking evil of an absent person; relating something evil which was really done or said by one that is not present when it is related. In our language this is also, by an extremely proper name, termed "back-biting." Nor is there any material difference between this and what we usually style "tale-bearing." If the tale be delivered in a soft and quiet manner (perhaps with some expressions of good-will to the person, and a hope that things may not be quite so bad), then we call it "whispering." But in whatever manner it be done, the thing is the same, if we relate to another the fault of a third person when he is not there to answer for himself.

" 'And how extremely common is this sin among all orders and degrees of men. How do high and low, rich and poor, wise and foolish, learned and unlearned, run into it continually! What conversation do you hear of any considerable length whereof evil-speaking is not one ingredient?

" ' And the very commonness of this sin makes it difficult to be avoided. If we are not deeply sensible of the danger, and continually guarding against it, we are liable to be carried away by the torrent. In this instance, almost the whole of mankind are, as it were, in a conspiracy against us. Besides, it is recommended from within as well as from without. There is scarcely a wrong temper in the mind of man that may not occasionally be gratified by it—our pride, anger, resentment.

" 'Evil-speaking is the more difficult to be avoided, because it frequently attacks us in disguise. We speak thus out of a noble, generous (it is well if we do not say) holy indignation, against those vile creatures. We commit sin from mere hatred of sin! We serve the devil out of pure zeal for God!'

"'Then having laid bare the disease, Mr. Wesley gave the remedy :—

"'First, "If thy brother sin against thee, go and tell him of his fault between thee and him alone." This,' he said, 'requires the greatest gentleness, meekness, and love. If he opposes the truth, yet he cannot be brought to the knowledge of it but by gentleness. Still speak in a spirit of tender love, which "many waters cannot quench." If *love is not conquered, it conquers all things.* Who can tell the force of love!

"'This step our Lord commands us to take *first,*' Mr. Wesley went on to say. 'No alternative is allowed.

"'Do not think to excuse yourself for taking an entirely different step by saying, "I did not speak to any one until I was so burdened I could not refrain." And what a way have you found to unburden yourself? God reproves you for a sin of omission, for not telling your brother of his fault ; and you comfort yourself by a sin of commission, by telling your brother's fault to another person. Ease bought by sin is a dear purchase !'

"Afterwards he exhorted us to 'hear evil of no man. The receiver is as bad as the thief. If there were no hearers, there would be no speakers of evil.'

"The close of the sermon was something in these words :—

"' O that all of you who bear the reproach of Christ, who are in derision called Methodists, would set an example at least in this ! If you must be distinguished, let this be the distinguishing mark of a Methodist—"He censures no man behind his back : by this fruit you may know him." What a blessed effect of this self-denial we should quickly feel in our hearts ! How would "our peace flow as a river," when we thus followed peace with all men ! How would the love of God abound in our souls, while we thus confirmed our love to the brethren ! And what an effect would it have on all that were united together in the name of our Lord Jesus Christ ! How would brotherly love continually increase. If one member suffered, all would suffer with it; if one was honoured, all would rejoice with it. Nor is this all. What an effect this might have even on the wild, unthinking world. Once more, with Julian the Apostate, they would be constrained to cry, "See how these Christians love one another!" Our Lord's last solemn prayer would be fulfilled—His kingdom would come. The Lord hasten the time, and enable us to love one another, not only in word and tongue, but in deed and in truth!'

"There, sweet cousin, thus did I sit rebuked and instructed, and after that you will of course never expect to hear what Lady Emily said the other evening. But as to the duty of taking her apart and telling her, I am not clear. This kind of assault is not pleasant, except to very pugnacious natures; so that this method of speaking evil *to* instead of *of* people, has further the great advantage of making one try to find out apologies for the faults one would have to condemn in this straightforward manner. And very often, I do believe, we should find the apology truer than the accusation.

"These wonderful Wesleys, Kitty! I do think they are like the apostles more than any people that ever lived; at least on the side on which they were apostles. I cannot yet get over the feeling that St. Paul or St. John, and certainly St. Peter, would have been easier to ask advice from about little home-difficulties.

" I have been hearing about them from your friend, Mr. Hugh Spencer. Papa likes him, and he has been to see us several times; and when Papa goes out, we have had long conversations concerning the Methodists, and also concerning another subject (or object) in which we are both greatly interested.

" I should like to have spent a week at that Epworth parson-age where the Wesleys were cradled—that home which was

9

free, and happy, and full of healthful play as any home in the holidays, and orderly, and full of healthful work as any school; where the 'odious noise' of the crying of children was not suffered, but there was no restraint on their gleeful laughter; to have listened to the singing with which the childish voices opened and closed their lessons; to have seen, at five o'clock, the oldest take apart the youngest that could speak, the second the next, and so on, and read together the Psalm for the day and a chapter from the New Testament; to have gone through the quiet bed-rooms three hours afterwards, and seen the rosy, sleeping faces, even the baby of a year old lying quiet although awake, or only venturing to 'cry softly;' or more than all to have watched invisibly the mother conversing alone, as she did, with one of her little ones every evening, listening to their childish confessions, and giving counsel in their childish perplexities.

"So deep was the hold that mother had on the hearts of her sons, that years afterwards, in his early manhood, she had tenderly to rebuke John for that 'fond wish' of his of dying before she died.

"There were nineteen children born in that home; thirteen of them were living at one time. The pressure of all the endless small cares of poverty was added to the labour of teaching and training those healthy, eager, clever children, all of them no doubt endued with a considerable portion of the will and character of their parents. And their circumstances were not improved by the father's uncompromising politics; many of the parishioners paid the tithes in the most inconvenient way they could, and the authorities, on the plea of a small debt, once threw Mr. Wesley into prison. Whilst there, his noble wife sold her rings to support him; other female superfluities no doubt had disappeared before, and his books were no superfluities in his eyes or hers: but in prison he read the prayers, and preached to the wretched inmates, and found the jail (so he wrote to the Archbishop of York) a larger and more important parish than his own.

" Yet burdened as she was, no one can picture Mrs. Wesley as creeping with stooping shoulders through life, a weary, heavy-laden woman. All her work was done with a hearty cheerfulness. At fifty, she said, in a letter to the Archbishop of York (tried as she had been with poverty) that she believed it was easier to be content without riches than with them.

" There was a secret spring which fed her inmost heart. Every morning and every evening she spent an hour alone with God. That morning hour of prayer (your friend Hugh Spencer said) made the day's yoke easy and its burdens light; that evening hour kept her heart and conscience at rest.

" And so fresh did those week-day sabbath-hours keep her strength, that on Sundays, during her husband's absence, she found it no toil to gather his poor parishioners in her kitchen and read a sermon, pray, and converse in a simple solemn way with them. Two hundred were sometimes assembled in this way. An unfavourable report of this ' conventicle ' was sent to her husband, and on his remonstrating she wrote that she was preparing hearers for his church-services. But if he continued to object, she simply requested, ' Do not *advise*, but *command* me to desist.' His command was God's authority for her, and she would submit unhesitatingly. His advice was man's advice, and she could not alter her convictions at his will or her own.

" The old home at Epworth Rectory is in other hands now ; the last time Mr. John Wesley went there, being refused his father's pulpit, he preached to the people from his father's grave-stone.

" Both father and mother are gone now. The family have the recollection of two saintly death-beds to crown the memory of those two noble lives. When dying, old Mr. Wesley laid his hand on the head of his son Charles, and said, ' Be steady ; the

Christian faith will surely revive in this kingdom : you will see it, though I shall not.'

"'The inward witness!' he said, at another time, 'the inward witness! that is the proof, the strongest proof of Christianity.'

"His last words were, 'God chastens me with strong pain, but I praise Him for it, I thank Him for it, I love Him for it.' His last act was receiving the Holy Communion with his family.

"The mother died only a few years since, in her seventy-third year ; calm, serene, painless, looking up to heaven, she passed away (as she had wished) whilst her children were singing around her bed a 'Psalm of praise to God.' As the praises of earth fell dim and distant on the ear of the dying, other songs of everlasting joy were beginning to burst upon her.

"I hear Mr. John Wesley preach, and read those deep heart-stirring hymns of his brother Charles, with far greater interest now that I know what their father's house was like ; what a pure sweet stream of home memories flows round their lofty devotion to God ! And this devotion seems quite unreserved. When Mr. John Wesley's income was thirty pounds a year, he spent twenty-eight and gave away two. Now that it is one hundred and twenty, he still spends twenty-eight and gives away ninety-two. The return he made of his plate lately to the tax collectors was, 'Two silver spoons, one in London and one at Bristol.'

"What wonders one man may do, without vanity and covetousness ; and with a sufficient motive ! Yet his dress is at any time, they say, neat enough for any society ; except when some of the mobs, who have frequently attacked him, but never injured him, may have considerably ruffled his attire. His temper they could never ruffle ; and in the end, his unaffected benevolence, his Christian serenity and gentlemanly composure are sure to overcome. The ringleaders more than once have turned round on their followers and dared them to touch the parson. His calm, commanding voice has been heard. Silence

has succeeded to hootings, and sobs to silence; and Hugh
Spencer says, there is scarcely a place where the Methodists
have been assailed by mobs where, from the very dregs of these
very mobs, men and women have not been rescued, and found,
not long after, 'sitting clothed and in their right mind,' at the
feet of the Saviour.

"Mr. Whitefield is very different. Any one can understand
why the Wesleys should do great things, especially Mr. John.
He is a man of such will and power, such strong practical sense
and determination, so nobly trained in such a home. But Mr.
Whitefield's strength seems to be obviously not in himself, but
in the truth he speaks. His early home an inn at Bristol, his
early life spent in low occupations among low companions, his
one great gift suited, one would have thought, more to a theatre
than a pulpit. But his whole heart is on fire with the love of
Christ and the love of perishing immortal men and women.
And he has the great gift of making people listen to the message
of God's infinite grace. The message does the rest. And *what*
it does, Kitty, I can hardly write of without tears.

"He tells people all over the world—morning, noon, and
night, every day of his life—duchesses, wise men, colliers, and
outcasts (as he told me), that we have a great burden on our
hearts; and we know it. He tells us that burden is *sin;* and
whether we knew it or not before, we know, when he says so,
it is true. He weeps and tell us that unless that great burden
is lifted off *now*, it will never be lifted off, but will crush us
down and down for ever; and half his audience weep with him.
He tells us it *can* be lifted off *now, here, this instant;* we may
go away from that spot unburdened, forgiven, rejoicing, reconciled to God, without a thing in time or eternity to dread any
more; the burden of terror exchanged for an infinite wealth
of joy, the debt of guilt into a debt of everlasting gratitude.
And then, just as the poor stricken hearts before him, each
hanging on his eloquent words as if he were pleading with each

alone, begin to thrill with a new hope, he shows us *how* all this can be. He shows us (or God reveals to us) Christ, the Lamb of God, the Son of God fainting under the burden of our sin, yet bearing it all away. And we forget Mr. Whitefield, the congregation, time, earth, ourselves—everything but the Cross to which he has led us, but that suffering, smitten, dying Saviour, at whose feet we stand. And from that moment we seem no longer to be listening, but only looking. We are looking on God. And that look is not death, but life—life everlasting, for God is in Christ reconciling us to Himself. We are looking on God and loving Him; God is looking on us and loving us. And then, as we gaze, slowly the truth dawns on us; that God is not *now beginning* to look on us with that look of infinite compassion and tenderness; He has been caring for us all our lives; He has loved us with an everlasting love. He has been drawing us, blind, wilful, unwilling, to Himself. It is *our* first look, but oh, it is not His! Then the barriers of time and death seem gone, for sin was their substance, and that is taken away; and we are *in eternity;* eternal life has begun, for Christ is our life, and we are for ever with Him.

"Kitty, I believe Mr. Whitefield has brought this unutterable joy to thousands and thousands, and that he lives for nothing else but to bring it to thousands more. And this whole generation must pass away before his sermons can be coolly criticised, or his name uttered in any large assembly of Christian people without bringing tears to many eyes.

"Dear Kitty, I have heard Mr. Wesley again, and his sermon was on our being stewards of God. I cannot tell you what that sermon did for me. That first sermon of Mr. Whitefield's seemed to lay me prostrate, beggared, utterly destitute, at the feet of my Saviour, thenceforth to be nothing and have nothing in myself, yet to possess all things in Him.

"Mr. Wesley's noble words, on the other hand, seemed to be

like God's gracious hands once more investing me with all my forfeited possessions, no more as earthly dross, but as priceless, heavenly treasures. Anything God has given me—health, youth, any power of pleasing or influencing others; every faculty of the body, 'that exquisitely wrought machine,' as he termed it; every power of the mind; our money, which he calls our poorest and meanest possession; every relationship of life, every moment of time—seem given back to me, new coined, stamped with the seal of God, and made current through eternity. If before, in the first glimpse of eternity, all the things I had most prized seemed dust and dross; now, themselves linked to eternity, they seem to me sacred and priceless. 'How precious, above all utterance, above all conception,' as he said, 'is every portion of our life. Not, indeed, that there are any works of supererogation; that we can ever do more than our duty, seeing *all* we have is not our own, but God's; all we can do is due to Him. We have not received this or that thing, but everything from Him; therefore everything is His due.'

"After that sermon I went back to the good people who gather around Lady Huntingdon, of whom I wrote to you in the beginning of this letter, or rather this book of chronicles; and in the light of that truth all seemed to me transformed. We are fellow-servants, fellow-workers; and I came to them humbly to ask them to put me in the way of doing some humble work, such as a beginner might attempt. Then, Kitty, I found that many of these good women, whose manners I had been criticising at my leisure, had meantime been·engaged in countless labours of love; and as I went with them to the schools, the hospitals, and the dwellings of the poor, the voices which brought gladness among little destitute children, and a rare sunshine into the dwellings of the London poor—which were longed for on lonely sick-beds, and welcomed with grateful smiles by wan faces drawn with pain—have passed for me into a region far beyond the icy touch of criticism; they are dear to me, Kitty. We are bound together as fellow-servants as well as brethren. It seems to me nothing unites us like a common object to work for; partly, I suppose, because working shows us our own deficiencies, and humility and forbearance spring up from one root. I think it would be a good rule if every critic were compelled by law to write a book himself. He would see then what the difficulties of those he criticises are; and the world would see what his powers are, which, in many cases, would, I have no doubt, tend to produce in the critic a wholesome humility.

"I have come to the conclusion, Kitty, that we obtain a grander and truer view of lofty things from below than from above; looking up to them from our own level instead of looking down on them, fore-shortened by their own elevation, from the height to which but for them we never could have climbed.

"And now, Cousin Kitty, I must seal up my budget, and send it this very day, or it will grow so long, you will forget the beginning before you reach the end. I had thought of sending it by the hand of your friend Mr. Hugh Spencer, when he passes through London from the University; but it is of no use to wait for him; and as there is nothing Jacobite or fanatically Whig in my lucubrations, I must trust them to the ordinary chances of the mail, and not wait till next week, when we leave London again, and they would have to be committed to the extraordinary perils of the cross posts from Beauchamp Manor. I suppose the mails, like Miss Pawsey's fashions, do reach you at least 'once in every two or three years.'

"Before finishing, however, I must tell you of a conversation which took place to-day.

"This morning two gentlemen who were calling on Papa were lamenting the degeneracy of the times.

"One was an old general, and he said—

" ' We have no heroes now—not a great soldier left. Since Marlborough died, not an Englishman has appeared who is fit to be more than a general of division. There is neither the brain to conceive great plans nor the will to execute them, nor the dash which so often changes reverses into victories.'

" My great-uncle, a Fellow of Brazennose, took up the wail. ' No, indeed,' he said ; ' the ages of gold and iron and brass are over ; the golden days of Elizabeth and Shakespeare, and the scattered Armada ; the iron of the Revolution (for rough as they were, those men were iron); the brass of the Restoration ; and now we have nothing to do but to beat out the dust and shavings into tinsel and wire.'

" ' We have plenty of wood at least for gallows,' interposed my brother Harry. ' Cart-loads of men are taken every week to Tyburn. I saw one myself yesterday.'

" ' For what crimes ? ' asked the general.

" ' One for stealing a few yards of ribbon ; another for forging a draft for £50,' said Harry.

" ' Ah,' sighed the general, ' we have not even energy left to commit great crimes ! '

" ' Then,' resumed my great-uncle, ' what authors or artists have we worth the name ? Pope, Swift, and Addison, Wren and Kneller,—all are gone. We have not amongst us a man who can make an epic march, or a satire bite, or a cathedral stand, or a picture or a statue live. Imitators of imitations, we live at the fag-end of time, without great thinkers, or great thoughts, or great deeds to inspire either.'

" ' There is a little bookseller called Richardson, who, the ladies say, writes like an angel,' observed by brother Harry ; ' and Fielding, at all events, is a gentleman, and knows something of men and manners.'

" ' And pretty men and manners they are, from what I hear,' was my great-uncle's dolorous response. ' But what are these at best ? Not worth the name of literature ; frippery for a lady's drawing-room,—no more to be called literature than these man-darins or monsters are to be called sculpture.'

" ' Mr. Handel's music has some life in it,' replied Harry ; roused to opposition (although Harry does not know 'God save the Queen' from 'Rule Britannia!').

" ' Yes, that is all we are fit for,' was the cynical reply,—' to put the great songs of our fathers to jingling tunes. We sit stitching tinsel fringes for the grand draperies of the past, and do not see that all the time we are no better than tailors work-ing at our own palls.

" ' Besides,' resumed the old general, ' Handel is no English-man. The old British stock is dying out, sir. We have not even wit to put our forefathers' songs to music, nor sense to sing them when that is done. We have nothing left but money to pay Germans to fight for us, and Italians to scream for us.'

" ' And that is going as fast as it can,' interposed papa. ' What public man have we, Whig or Tory, who would not sell his country for a pension, or his soul for a place?'

" ' Soul, nephew!' said my great-uncle. ' You are using words grown quite obsolete. Who believes in such a thing as the salvation or perdition of the soul in these enlightened times?'

" ' The Methodists do, at any rate, sir,' replied Harry, maliciously; 'and Lady Huntingdon, and my sister Evelyn, and my cousin Kitty.'

" Harry had drawn all the forces of the enemy on him at once by this assault.

" ' Sir,' said papa, ' I beg henceforth you never couple your sister's or your cousin's name with those low fanatics. If Evelyn occasionally likes longer sermons than I can stand, she is a dutiful child, and costs me not a moment's anxiety, which is more than can be said for every one; and if she visits the old women at the Manor, so did her grandmother, who lived before a Methodist had been heard of.'

" ' Methodists!' exclaimed the general, indignantly; 'it was only the other day I was told of one of them, John Nelson, who was enlisted by force, and who would have made as fine a soldier as the king has but for his confounded Methodism. They actually had to let him off, lest he should bite the other fellows, and make them all as mad as himself. Why, sir, he actually reproved the officers for swearing, and in such a respectful way, the cunning fellow, they could do nothing to him ; and when an ensign had him put in prison, and threatened to have him whipped, he seemed as happy there as St. Paul himself. The people came to him night and day, to hear him speak and preach. The infection of his fanatical religion spread in every town through which they took him. They could find nothing by which they might keep hold of him ; for he was no dissenter : he professed to delight to go to church more than anything, and to receive the sacrament. And the end of it was, the major had to set him free ; and actually was foolish enough to say, if he preached again without making a mob, if he was able he would go and hear him himself ; and he wished all the men were like him. A most dangerous rascal,—a fellow with the strength of a lion and the courage of a veteran ; and yet he would rather preach than fight. I would make short work with such fellows, if I had Tyburn for a few days in my own hands, with a troop of Marlborough's old soldiers.'

" 'It would be of no use, sir,' replied Harry ; 'they would beat you even at Tyburn. I saw a man hung there yesterday as peacefully as if he had been ascending the block for his country or his king. He said Mr. John Wesley had visited him in the prison, and taught him how to repent of his sins and seek his God, and made him content to die. The people were quite moved, sir.'

" 'No doubt ! the people are always ready enough to be moved,' said the general, 'especially by any rogue who is on the point of being hanged. These things should be met silently, sharply, decisively.'

"'The Pope has tried that before now, sir,' I ventured to suggest, 'and not found it altogether answer,—at least not in England.'

"'True, Evelyn,' said my great-uncle, meditatively. 'These outbursts of fanaticism are like epidemics; they will have their time, and then die out. In the Middle Ages, whole troops of men and women used to march through the country, wailing and scourging themselves, and in the wildest state of excitement; but it was let alone, and it passed off; and so it will be with Methodism, no doubt.'

"'But, uncle,' I said, 'those Methodists do not scourge themselves, nor any one else. They only preach to the people about sin, and the judgment-day, and our Saviour.'

"'And the people sob, and scream, and faint, and fall into convulsions,' said Harry, turning on me.

"'Of course,' said my great-uncle, 'we are not Papists. Fanaticism will take another form in Protestant countries; and as to ignorant men preaching about sin and the judgment-day, what have they to do with it? I preached them a sermon on that subject myself last Lent, in St. Mary's, and no one sobbed, or fainted, or was at all excited.'

"'But, uncle,' I said, 'the people who are to be hanged at Tyburn, and the Yorkshire colliers, cannot come to hear you at St. Mary's.'

"'However little it might excite them!' interposed Harry.

"'Is it not a good thing, uncle,' I continued, 'that some one, however imperfectly, should preach to the people who can't come to hear you at St. Mary's, or who won't?'

"'Preach in the fields to those who won't come to church to be taught?' said my great-uncle; 'the next thing will be to take food to the people at home who won't come to the fields to work, and beg them to be so kind as to eat it!'

"'But, dear uncle,' I said, 'the worst of it is, the people who are dying for want of this kind of food don't know it is hunger

they are fainting from. You must take them the food before
they know it is that they want.'

"'Nonsense, Evelyn,' he said; 'if they don't know they
ought. I have no notion of pampering and coaxing criminals
and beggars in that way. Everything in its place. The pulpit
for sermons, and Tyburn for those who won't listen. But how
should young women understand these things? There is poor
John Wesley, as orderly and practical a man as ever was seen
before he was seized with this insanity or imbecility. The
times are very evil; the world is turned upside down; and this
fanatical outburst of Methodism is one of the worst symptoms
of the times. It is the growth on the stagnant pond,—the
deadly growth of a corrupt and decaying age.'

"But, oh! Cousin Kitty, when the world was turned upside
down seventeen hundred years ago, in that ' corrupt and decaying age of ancient times,' people found at last it was only as a,
plough turns up the ground for a new harvest.

"And sometimes when I hear what Mr. Hugh Spencer tells
me of the multitudes thronging to listen to Mr. Whitefield and
Mr. Wesley, and the other preachers in America and Wales, and
among the Cornish miners, and the colliers of the north, and
the slaves in the West Indies, and of hearts being awakened to
repentance and faith and joy even in condemned cells, it seems
to me as if instead of *death* a new tide of *life* was rising and
rising through the world everywhere, bursting out at every
cranny and crevice; as in spring the power of the green earth
bursts up even through the crevices of the London paving-
stones, through the black branches of the trees in deserted old
squares, through the flower in the broken pot in the sick child's
window, making every wretched corner of the city glad with
some poor tree or blossom, or plot of grass of its own. But the
dead tree, alas! crackles in the wind,—the life-bringing spring
wind,—and wonders what all this stir and twittering is about,

and moans dryly that it is the longest winter the world ever saw, and that it will never be spring again.

"As I did once, and for so long!—

"But we have come, have we not, to the Fountain of Life; and this tide of life is not around us only, it is within us, and sometimes the joy is so great it seems quite too great to bear alone!

"And then especially I long for you, Kitty, and my thoughts buzz about you like bees around flowers in the sunshine. If you feel a pleasant little stir about your heart at any time, that is what it is!

"And where will you read this? In your sunny chamber alone, with the rooks cawing in your old elms, and the light flickering through their branches on your floor? Or in Aunt Trevylyan's closet, sitting at her feet, while 'Bishop Taylor' lies open on the little table beside her? Or by the hall fire, while uncle Trevylyan is reading for the hundredth time that book on fortifications, soothed to occasional dozes by the drone of your mother's spinning-wheel, and Jack is mending his fishing-tackle, and Trusty now and then heaves a long sigh in his sleep, and stretches himself into a posture of more absolute repose?

"I should like to see it all one day, Kitty, and I *must*, if only to tell Aunt Trevylyan all you have been to your loving cousin   EVELYN BEAUCHAMP."

"*P.S.*—Mamma and I are so much together now, Kitty. I read to her hours together, sometimes French romances and sometimes the 'Ladies' Magazine of Fashion.' They are a little dull, but they have one great merit, they imprison my thoughts as little as embroidery. But every morning, before she gets up, I read the Bible to her; and the other day, when I was a little later than usual, she pointed to her watch, and said in a disappointed tone,—

"'You are late, Evelyn, we shall scarcely have any time;' and this very morning she said,—

"'I shall be glad when Lent comes. I am tired of seeing so many people, and you and I, child, shall have more time for each other then.'

"And then she looked just as she did on that night in the old nursery at Beauchamp Manor, when she was watching by Harry's sick-bed and mine.

"*Second P.S.*—Cousin Tom is as savage as he can be to me. But he always contrives to ask for you, although he snatches at any news of you like a chained bear at a biscuit, and then shuffles off growling."

Cousin Evelyn and Hugh Spencer seem to be very intimate. That is quite natural. They must like each other. They are so suited. Nothing petty about either of them. Evelyn is just the kind of woman I used to think would understand him, so frank, and fearless, and truthful, and generous, and full of thoughts of her own; so self-possessed and ready-witted; so different from me. And she is sure to like Hugh. Every one must who knows him. And she said the first time she saw him, she felt he was just a man she could trust.

But they do seem to have become such great friends very quickly !

Already they appear to have secrets she does not tell me.

I wonder what the "subject" (or "object") was which she does not mention, in which they are both so equally interested.

When I read Evelyn's letter to Mother, she said,—

"She seems much delighted with the Methodists, Kitty. It seems to me a little dangerous for so young a woman to have such strong opinions. And I do not quite like her comparing her great-uncle to a dead tree in a London square. It does not seem respectful or kind. I am afraid she has learned that from the Methodists. I do not like young people to judge their elders in that way. But, poor child, she seems to have had her own way too much; and she is affectionate, and so fond of you, Kitty. I am glad you love each other. Kitty, I am afraid you must have tried her patience sorely with your long stories of your home. She seems to know all about us. But I am very much afraid of those Methodists. I cannot think what we want of a new religion. St. Paul says, though an angel from heaven were to preach another gospel to us, we must not listen to him. What has Mr. Wesley to say that the Bible and the Prayer Book do not say,—and Thomas à Kempis and Bishop Taylor? Betty went to hear the Methodists, and since then, for the first time in her life, she has twice spoilt the Sunday's dinner in cooking it. Evelyn perhaps has learned some good things from these people, but my Kitty will not want any other religion than that she has learned from her childhood,—in her Bible, and from the Church, and in this little closet from her mother's lips. Only *more* of it, Kitty!—more faith, and hope, and charity, more than I have ever had, or perhaps can hope to have,—*more*, but not *something else.*"

I could only assure Mother what I feel so deeply, that I could never wish for anything but to grow year by year more like what she is.

Yet when I think of it here alone, it does seem to me as if things needed to be said over again in a new way to each new generation, just as every spring has new songs and new blossoms. And even more than that, because birds do sing the same songs, and yet they are always fresh. But men's works and words seem to grow old-fashioned unless they are varied; until, as Evelyn says, they grow again into a kind of fresh youth when they pass from being antiquated to being antique.

The Bible is indeed always fresh, always new, as the songs of the birds, as the spring flowers, as the breaking of the waves, as the hearts of children, as the young man in a shining garment at the sepulchre, who must have "sung for joy" thousands of years before, at the birthday of the world.

But it does seem as if God meant His Gospel to be borne on from age to age by voices, not by books, not in faint echoes from the tombs, but in fresh, living words from heart to heart.

Certainly Betty understands Mr. Wesley and John Nelson, as she never could understand Thomas à Kempis and Bishop Taylor. I must ask Mother next Sunday about this. Mother will be sure to know better than I can.

VI

HE song-birds, for the most part, have out-lived their days of song, and are quietly chirping advice to their nestlings in a sober and practical way. Only the rooks, who seem to carry on their attachments in a very business-like style, as if they were always discussing the "settlements" and "pin-money" Evelyn used to laugh about, make as much noise as ever. The old rooks are cawing instructions to the young ones, and the young ones seem to discuss these instructions in rather a seditious spirit among themselves.

No doubt the young rooks think they are encountering quite newly-discovered difficulties with the most original arguments, although precisely the same discussions have been carried on every season in precisely the same tones for centuries, ever since rooks were.

I wonder if the cavillings and controversies of our times, which seem so modern and new to us, would sound just as monotonous to any one who had lived through seventeen generations of men, as I have of rooks!

The grave autumn winds are sweeping in slow and solemn cadences, like the throb of a dead-march, through the fading leaves of the elms; as a musician might draw a low, lingering farewell from his harp, before he laid it aside for a season of mourning. For the winds often seem to me to mourn over the wild work they have to do, sighing and sobbing through the woods they are laying bare, and passionately wailing above the waves they are lashing into fury. "We were not made for this," they seem to moan. "Of old we bore not death, but life on our wings. When will it be so again? When shall we rest? When will the earth rest and be quiet? When will all the mournful work be done, and only the good be left to do?

Hugh Spencer used to say, how thankful we should be that the part of God's work given us to do on earth is not the avenging and destroying, but the healing and the helping.

How many things I have learned from him. I suppose he will never be here much again. The work to be done in the world seems to press on him so much, and there are so few to do it; and his heart is so warm and large, he is able to do so much more than most other people. Cousin Evelyn feels what he is!

And yet this parish is like a world in itself, he used to say; and his is just the character that grows dearer to people the longer they know him, and it seems almost a pity to throw away the love old and young have for him in his father's parish. There are other people who could preach to the multitudes throughout the world. But it does seem as if no one could do what he might for the people here.

I wonder what the "subject or object" is Evelyn and he are "equally interested in," that she does not tell me!

Hugh used to tell me all his wishes and purposes. But Evelyn is so much more capable of entering into them than I ever was, and of helping him to carry them out, with her rapid ready wit; so different from me, who so often think of the right thing to say just when it is too late. And perhaps I disappointed him when he spoke to me that evening on the sea, of his feeling called to proclaim the gospel through the world, when that selfish sadness came over me, at the thought of his no more belonging to *us* all at home, but to the wide world. Perhaps he feels I cannot enter into his great, benevolent plans. And, of course, I never can, as Evelyn could. She knows so much more, and thinks so much more. Beside Evelyn's, my thoughts and feelings seem so faint and weak; like a little flute beside a clear, ringing clarion. Yes, Evelyn seems just made to understand and help Hugh Spencer. One day, perhaps, they will tell me what this great "subject" (or object) is. And I must not be selfish again, then, but must try to enter into it with all my heart; for it is sure to be something generous and good.

Jack has got his commission at last. He is wild with delight, and patronizes us all, and bestows imaginary fortunes on every one in the parish, on the strength of the cities he means to take and the prize-money he means to win.

Father seems to live over his youth again, as he talks to Jack of the perils and adventures before him; and although he warns him that the days of victory are few, and the nights of watching many, and the days of marching long, yet the old martial enthusiasm that comes over him as he fights Marlborough's battles over again, certainly has more power to enkindle Jack's ardour, than the sober commentaries at the end have to cool it.

It is pleasant, however, to see how cordial Father and Jack become over the old book of fortifications, and in their endless discussions concerning arms and accoutrements.

Meanwhile Mother and I rise early and sit up late to complete Jack's outfit. And many tears Mother lets fall on the long seams and hems—although I am sure it is easier for us both, than if we were rich, and could pay some one else to do the work, while we sat brooding over the parting. It is a comfort to put our whole heart into every stitch we do for him; to feel that no money could ever purchase the delicate stitching and the elaborate button-holes, and the close, strong sewing we delight to make as perfect as possible. Mother sews her tender anxieties into every needleful, and certainly relieves her anxieties as she does so. And I sew all sorts of mingled feelings in, besides ; repentance for every sharp word I ever spoke to Jack, and every hard thought I ever had of his little mistakes, and plans of my own for his comfort. For the bees, and the three Spanish hens, whose honey and eggs constitute my "pin-money," have been very successful lately ; and I can very well, with a little contrivance, make my woolsey dress last one more winter ; so that I shall have quite a nice little sum for Jack.

Father seems to feel as if he were going forth again to the wars and adventures of his youth in Jack's person. But to Mother it is not a going *forth*, but a going *away*. She shudders as Father goes over his battles on the table after supper, with the bread and cheese for fortresses, and the plates and salt-cellars for the armies, and talks of "massing forces," and "cutting up detachments in detail."

"My dear," she said one day, "you talk so coolly of masses and forces, and of 'cutting them up!' You seem to forget it is *men* you are talking of, and that our Jack is to be one of them."

Father smiled compassionately, and went on detaching his salt-cellars. Jack laughed, and kissed Mother affectionately, and said, "But I am *not* to be one of them, Mother. I have no intention of letting any one cut me up."

But Mother could not hear any more military discussions just then ; and we took a candle to a little table near the fire, and comforted ourselves once more with Jack's outfit.

I suppose it is meant that men must leave us one day, and go forth into the world to do their work.

But it does seem a little hard they should be so glad to go.

Yet, when I said this one day to Mother, she said, "I would not have Jack one bit less eager and pleased, on any account, Kitty ! What are women for, unless they can help men in the rough things they have to do and bear? They work and fight hard for us, and if we have our own share of the burden to bear at home, the least we can do is to bear it cheerfully, and not hinder them with repining looks or words."

"Only, Mother," I said, "it seems wronging the old happy days to part from them so easily."

"The old happy childish days are *gone*, Kitty!" she said. "Men cannot sit down on the march of life, gazing with lingering looks on the way behind them. And women should not; Christian women ought not, Kitty," she added softly. "You know *we* also have something to press forward to. Our eyes should chiefly there be fixed whither our feet are going."

"Dear Mother," I said, "if one were only sure that this step forward would be a step really onward for Jack! There are so many dangers in the army, are there not?"

"What makes you so desponding, Kitty?" she said. "It is not like you; and it seems as if you had too little confidence in Jack. We must not sit and wail together over possible evils. When such anxieties come, we must separate and pray. I know no other remedy, my child."

And I could not find it in my heart to tell her my peculiar anxieties about Jack. Besides, it would have seemed ungenerous to him.

Jack is gone. Now he is really off, and silence has settled down on the house after all the bustle. Father's apprehensions seem to over-balance his hopes. He roams restlessly in and out of the house, and then sits down to his "Fortifications," and after reading a few words, shuts the book and pushes it impatiently aside, and walks carelessly up and down, or stands whistling at the window, or goes to the door and looks at the weather, and wonders how that poor boy is getting on at sea.

And Trusty, feeling there is something wrong, goes to the door also, and also looks out at the weather, and also wonders, and wags his tail in an indecisive, meditative way, and returning to the fire, sits bolt upright before it in a cramped attitude, staring vacantly at the flames, and saying, as plainly as a dog can, that he can make nothing of it.

Mother, on the other hand, makes frequent visits to the little chamber over the porch, and comes down pale and serene, and with some little cheery observation changes the current of Father's thoughts, or reminds him of some work about the farm.

Then Trusty feels it is all right again, and stretches himself out in his easiest attitude on the hearth at her feet, and sighs, and composes himself to sleep.

I wish *I* could feel as if it were all right. But there are things about Jack which do make me uneasy.

The day before he left, I went up to him as he was packing in his own room, and slipped the little packet containing two guineas into his hand. I felt anxious he should not think it was any sacrifice to me, so I said, " The bees and those Spanish hens you reared for me, Jack, have brought me quite a fortune this year ; and besides, I had something left from Uncle Henderson's present, and there is no way of spending money here if one wished it ;—and you will want so many things."

I was going hastily down again, to avoid burdening him with thanks, when he came after me, and replacing the money in my hand, said, laughing, " Indeed, my good little sister, I cannot rob you of your frugal earnings. Hugh Spencer is a good fellow, after all, at bottom. I wrote to ask him for the loan of a few pounds, and he has sent me ten. I mean to pay him with my first prize-money. The pay is barely enough for a gentleman to live on. And besides," he added, " that good, cantankerous old Betty has actually insisted on presenting me with five guineas. I quite hesitated to take it from her. But she said it had all been earned in our service ; and ' Master's son must look like a Trevylyan ; and what use had she for money ? She was a fool ever to have hoarded it !' So that at last I actually had to take it from the dear old soul, to spare her feelings, and to show her that I bore no malice for the quarrels of my boyhood. So that you see, Kitty, with such a purse it would be mean to accept anything more from you."

Then seeing me, I suppose, look perplexed and grave, he took the packet again from my hand, and opening it, withdrew one guinea, and gave me back the other with the air of a benefactor, saying, "There, my poor little Kitty, I will not disappoint you. I will keep one for kindness' sake, and to buy you a fairing with. And you can keep the other to pay Hugh Spencer for your cherry-coloured bow, if you like ; or any other little bill," he added, "which may have escaped my memory, and which might vex father."

And Jack returned to his packing, persuaded he had done at once a very liberal and a very conscientious thing. But I could have sunk into the earth with vexation and shame. To have written to borrow money from Hugh ; to have accepted Betty's hard-earned savings ; what would he do next ? And then those terrible words, "*any other little bill,*" burnt into my heart like a drop of burning acid.

I stood irresolute.

He turned to me with his good-humoured, easy smile, and said, "What is it, Kitty ? Can I do anything else to oblige you ?"

"Oh, Jack," I said, summoning all my courage, for I dreaded very much to grieve him on that last day, "would you mind telling me if you have any idea to whom you owe those other little bills ?"

"My dear child," he said, "how can I remember in all this bustle ? Nothing but trifles, of course. Let me see : there were a pair of shoe-buckles I saw the last time I was in Falmouth, at Moses the Jew's, the newest fashion, in excellent taste, I assure you, just such as I know Father would like to see me in. Yet just the kind of trifle I would not trouble him with. But that would not matter much ; Moses is a rich man, and may wait—only Jews don't like to wait. I care more about Miss Pawsey ; she lent me half-a-guinea a few weeks since, when I had to treat some fellows to a glass in honour of my obtaining my commission. Yes ; I should like you to pay Miss Pawsey, Kitty. And if there is anything else, no doubt the people will let you know in time. I told them never to apply to Father ; so that if any one should come at any time asking particularly for me, you will know what it means, and can settle it at once, without mentioning it to Father or Mother. It might vex them. But I am glad I thought of telling you, because, of course, I could not write about these things ; and now my mind is quite easy."

And the next morning, as Jack was riding with Father, he reined in his horse, and turning back, took off his military hat to me with a low bow, and beckoned me to him, and said softly as I stood close to him :—

" Don't cry your roses away, Kitty, till I come back from Flanders, and you all have to come to Court to see me knighted. With the first good fortune I have I will send Hugh Spencer his money, unless he is a bishop first, in which case, of course, he would not need it ; and with the next I will buy an annuity for Betty, on which she will be able to live like a duchess. You see I shall make all your fortunes, and you will all of you have reason to rejoice in having befriended the hero in his adversity ; and it will be as good as a fairy tale."

So he rode away and rejoined Father, and I went back to Mother.

" What did he say to you, Kitty ?" she asked. " Is anything forgotten ?"

" He said we should all have to come to Court to see him knighted, and that he would make all our fortunes," I said ; " and that it would be as good as a fairy tale."

" Poor fellow !" she said, the tears, so long repressed, flowing

freely, as her heart was touched with this proof of Jack's generous intentions. "Poor fellow! He was always so sanguine,
and so full of generous plans."

But I could not shed a tear. I stood and felt like a stone.
The weight of Jack's secrets seemed to press my heart into
marble. And I felt like a traitor, to be making Mother glad,
when, if I had told her all, I was sure she would feel as I did.

But what am I to do? The guinea will pay Miss Pawsey, of
course, and, perhaps, the Jew, if I could see him. But I am
so grieved about Betty and Hugh Spencer. How in all my life
shall I ever be able to repay them? And they must be paid.
I would work day and night, if I could tell how to earn anything to pay them with. But fifteen guineas! It is a fortune!
How could I earn a guinea without Mother's knowing? And
would it even be true to Father and Mother to do this if I could?

Evelyn could help me. But I could not ask her without
betraying Jack.

And how shall I ever feel safe from some one coming and
"particularly wanting to see" Jack?

Ought not Father and Mother to know?

And yet would it not almost break Mother's heart?

I cannot tell her yet, at least, until the sorrow of this parting
is a little healed. For *this* is a sorrow which seems to me as if
it could never be healed. It is not the money, or the debts, or
the difficulty of meeting them. It is Jack himself that is the
sorrow. What will he do next?

I cannot bear this alone. Whatever the trouble may be, it
is clear God cannot mean it to make me untruthful. He cannot
mean it to make me to do wrong. Therefore, there must be
some way out of it, some one right way.

And God knows it. I will ask Him, and He will surely help
me also to find it, and to take it when I find it, however rough
and dark it may be.

Aunt Jeanie said we must not look to see more than the next

step. But that we *must* look to see, as sure as God is true, and has promised to lead us.

Yesterday evening, to my great surprise, Betty came into my room after I was in bed, looking wild and haggard, and she said,—

"Mrs. Kitty, my dear, I can bear it no longer. Whatever comes of it, I must go and hear that Yorkshireman again. He is to preach at six o'clock to-morrow morning on the Down above the house. I shall be back again before Missis wants me, for it won't last more than an hour. And if she is angered, she must be angered. I can get no rest night nor day. The words that man spoke are like a fire in my bones; and hear him again I must. I can but perish either way. And if I must perish, I had rather know it."

She went back to her room. But I could not sleep for thinking of her wan wild face. It haunted me like the vision of some one murdered. And I felt as if it would be hardly safe to let her go alone.

Accordingly, when Betty crept through my room the next morning very softly, that she might not wake me, I was already dressed, and, in spite of her remonstrances, insisted on accompanying her.

The appointed place of meeting was in a slight hollow on the top of the Down. We were early, and as we sat down on a tuft of withered grass, closely wrapped in our hoods and cloaks, waiting for the preaching to begin, I thought I had never been in a place more like a temple. The solemn dawn was coming up in the east; and I always think nothing is so solemn as the coming up of the morning. There is a pomp about the sunset blending with its tender lingering tints; and night is majestic with its crown of countless stars; but nothing ever seems to me so grand and solemn as the slow, silent spreading of the dawn over the sleeping world. There was

little colour yet, only that steady welling up of the light from
its deep hidden fountain, overflowing all the sky; the great tide
of sunlight rising without effort, without conflict, without recoil,
scarcely seeming to advance, yet ceaselessly advancing, and
never losing one point won; till the clouds, from mysterious,
indefinite billows of mist, became defined purple bars, through
which we gazed into the depths of golden radiance behind;
and the moon paled from a pearly lamp, illuminating the dark,
to a silver crescent floating on a silvery sea, and at length sank
with her stars into the flood of sunlight; and the sky had
become full of light, and the earth full of colour and life. Then
there were the soft twitterings of the waking birds in the wood
below us, and the murmurs of the waves far off and far below,
and the sweeping of the winds over the long ranges of the
dewy moors.

It seemed to me I wanted no other preaching, or music.
But the silent solemnity of the dawn, and the murmurs of the
great sea, and the songs of birds, have no power to lift the
burden from the troubled conscience.

That work is committed not to angels, nor to nature (as
Hugh Spencer used to say), but to poor blundering sinful human
beings, who have felt what the burden is.

John Nelson was there already. He stood earnestly conversing with a little group of men; and I watched the frank,
trustworthy face, and the tall, stalwart form, with no little
interest, remembering how he had been thrown down, and
trampled on, and bruised, and beaten by the mobs for Christ's
sake, and had dared the same rough usage again and again to
tell them the same message of mercy.

At length the congregation began to assemble. Solitary
figures creeping up from the farms and lone cottages around,
miners in their working clothes on their way to the mines,
labourers on their way to the fields, and from the nearer villages
little bands of poorly clad women and children.

In a few minutes about two hundred had ranged themselves around the preacher, who stood on a hillock, his tall figure and strong clear voice commanding the little congregation, so that he spoke more easily, more as if conversing privately than preaching. He said he would give us some of his experience, as it might be of use in comforting any who were in trouble.

" I was brought up," he said, "a mason, as was my father before me."*

" When I was between nine and ten years old, I was horribly terrified with the thoughts of death and judgment whenever I was alone. One Sunday night, as I sat on the ground by the side of my father's chair, while he was reading the twentieth chapter of Revelation, the Word came with such light and power to my soul that it made me tremble, as if a dart was shot at my heart. I fell with my face on the floor, and wept till the place was as wet where I lay as if water had been poured thereon. As my father proceeded, I thought I saw everything he read about, though my eyes were shut. And the sight was so terrible I was about to stop my ears that I might not hear, but I durst not. When he came to the eleventh verse my flesh seemed to creep on my bones while he said, '*And I saw a great white throne, and him that sat thereon, from whose face the heavens and the earth fled away; and there was found no place for them. And I saw the dead, small and great, stand before God: and the books were opened; and another book was opened, which is the book of life: and the dead were judged out of those things that were written in the books, according to their works.*' Oh, what a scene was opened to my mind! It was as if I had seen the Lord Jesus Christ sitting on His throne with the twelve apostles below Him ; and a large book open at His left hand ; and, as it were, a bar fixed about ten paces from the throne, to which the children of Adam came up ; and every one, as he approached, opened his breast as quick as a man could open the bosom of

* John Nelson's Autobiography.

his shirt. On one leaf of the book was written the character of the children of God; and on the other, the character of those that should not enter into the kingdom of heaven. I thought *neither the Lord nor the apostles said anything;* but every soul as he came up to the bar *compared his conscience with the book,* and went away to his own place, either singing, or else crying and howling. Those that went to the right hand were but like the stream of a small brook; but the others were like the flowing of a mighty river.

"God had followed me with convictions ever since I was ten years old; and whenever I committed any known sin against God or man, I used to be so terrified afterwards that I shed many tears in private; yet, when I came to my companions, I wiped my face, and went on again in sin and folly. But oh the hell I found in my mind when I came to be alone again! and what resolutions I made. Nevertheless, when temptations came, my resolutions were as a thread of tow that had touched the fire.

"When I was turned sixteen my father was taken ill, which I thought was for my wickedness; yet at that time, vile as I was, I prayed earnestly that God would spare him for the sake of my mother and the young children, and let me die in his stead; but the Lord would not regard my prayer. Three days before he died, he said to my mother, 'Trouble not thyself for me; for I know that my peace is made with God, and He will provide for thee and the children.' I was greatly surprised at this, wondering how he could know his peace was made with God.

"In one of my times of trouble I was in a stable, and falling into a slumber, I dreamt I prayed that God would make me happy. But I thought, *what will make me happy?* I also dreamt that I beheld Jeremiah the prophet standing on a large rock at the west gate of Jerusalem. His countenance was grave, and with great authority he reproved the elders and magistrates of the city ; for which they were enraged, and, pulling him down, cast him on a dunghill, where the butchers poured the blood of their slain beasts. And I imagined I saw them tread him under their feet ; but his countenance never changed, nor did he cease to cry out, ' Thus saith the Lord, If ye will not repent, and give glory to my name, I will bring destruction on you and your city.' He seemed so composed and happy while they were treading him under their feet, that I said in my dream, ' O God, make me like Jeremiah.' And since then, thou, Lord, in a small measure, hast given me a taste of his cup."

Then (he said) he prayed God to give him a good wife ; but although God gave him the most suitable wife he believed he could have had, after his marriage he loved pleasures more than God. Yet his pleasures were not happiness ; and after a day of successful hunting or shooting, he felt so unhappy that he was ready to break his gun in pieces. His conscience had found no rest. He went from home to seek work, and prayed for guidance, and the Lord blessed him in all his journey. He got into business the day he arrived in London. But the burden of sin still weighed on his heart. Forty times a day he would cry for mercy. After his day's work he sat alone, and read and prayed. He would not drink with his mates. They cursed and abused him, and he bore many insults from them without opening his mouth to answer. But when they took his tools from him, and said, if he would not drink he should not work while they were drinking, that provoked him, so that he fought with several. Then they let him alone ; but that stifled for the time his concern for his salvation, and he left off reading and prayer, in a great measure.

Then sickness came, and with it a horrible dread, not of death, but of the judgment that should follow. He recovered, and was restored to perfect health. But again his conscience was awake : he could not rest night nor day. All things prospered that he pursued, yet he felt he had something to learn that he had not learned. "*He knew not*," he said, "*that it was the great lesson of love to God and man.*"

He began to consider what he wanted to make him happy; for as yet he was as a man in a barren wilderness that could find no way out. Health as good as any man's; as good a wife as he could wish for; more gold and silver than he needed, yet no rest. He cried out to himself, "Oh, that I had been a cow or a sheep!" He thought he would choose strangling, rather than thirty years more of such a life. But then came again the terrible thought of the judgment, and he cried, "Oh, that I had never been born!" for he thought his day of grace was over, because he had made so many resolutions and broken them all.

"Yet," he continued, "I thought I would set out once more; for I said, *Surely God never made man to be such a riddle to himself, and to leave him so;* there must be something in religion, that I am unacquainted with, to satisfy the empty mind of man, or he is in a worse state than the beasts that perish."

(As John Nelson spoke these words, Betty's downcast head was raised, her hood fell back, and from that moment she never took her eyes from off his face.)

"In all these troubles," he continued, "I had no one to open my mind to; I wandered up and down in the fields thinking; I went from church to church, but found no ease. One minister at St. Paul's preached about a man doing his duty to God and his neighbour, and on his death-bed finding joy in his heart from looking back to his well-spent life. Oh, what a stab that sermon was to my wounded soul! for I looked back and could not see one day in my life in which I had not left undone something I ought to have done, or done something I ought not to have done.

"Afterwards I heard another sermon, wherein the preacher said, that man, since the fall, could not perfectly fulfil the will of his Maker; but God required him to do all he could, and Christ would make up the rest: but if man did not do all he could he must unavoidably perish; for he had no right to expect any interest in the merits of Christ, if he had not fulfilled his part, and done all that lay in his power. Then, thought I, every soul must be damned : for I did not believe that any who had lived to years of maturity had done all they could, and avoided all the evil they might. Oh, what deadly physic was that doctrine to my poor sin-sick soul ! "

Then he tried Dissenters of various denominations, Roman Catholics, Quakers, all but the Jews. To the Quakers he listened three months, because among them he heard one who seemed to describe the disease of his soul ; but, alas ! he showed no remedy.

" In the spring," he said, " Mr. Whitefield came to Moorfields, and I went to hear him : he was to me as a man that could play well on an instrument, for his preaching was pleasant to me ; and I loved the man, so that if any one offered to disturb him I was ready to fight him."

But the deliverance did not come through Mr. Whitefield, although (he said), " I got some hope of mercy, so that I was encouraged to pray and to read the Scriptures. But I was like a wandering bird cast out of the nest, until Mr. John Wesley came to preach his first sermon in Moorfields. Oh, that was a blessed morning to my soul ! As soon as he got upon the stand, he stroked back his hair, and turned his face towards where I stood, and I thought fixed his eyes on me. His countenance struck such an awful dread upon me before I heard him speak, it made my heart beat like a pendulum, and when he did speak I thought his whole discourse was aimed at me."

(Betty bowed her head with a little assenting moan, and murmured, " And so, sure, it was ! Just like him.")

When he had done, I said : " This man can tell the secrets of my heart. He hath not left me there, for he hath showed the remedy, even the blood of Jesus. Then was my soul filled

11

with consolation, through hope that God for Christ's sake would save me."

Still the conflict was not over; his besetting sin, a hasty temper, got the better of him, and his heart again felt as hard as a rock. He felt unworthy to eat and drink. " Should such a wretch as he devour the good creatures of God?" He resolved neither to eat nor drink, till he found the kingdom of God. He wept tears like great drops of rain, he kneeled before the Lord, yet he felt dumb as a beast, and could not put up one petition; he saw himself a criminal before the Judge, and said in his overwhelming sense of guilt, surrendering himself as a condemned malefactor body and soul to God, " Lord, Thy will be done; damn or save."

"That moment," he said, " Jesus Christ was evidently set before the eye of my mind, as crucified for my sins, as if I had seen Him with my bodily eyes; and in that instant I was set at liberty from every tormenting fear, and filled with a calm and serene peace. I could then say without dread or fear, 'Thou art my Lord and my God.' Now did I begin to say, ' O Lord, I will praise Thee: though Thou wast angry with me, Thine anger is turned away, and Thou comfortest me. Behold, God is my salvation: I will trust and not be afraid: for the Lord Jehovah is my strength and my song. He also is become my salvation.' My heart was filled with love to God, and every soul of man; next to my wife and children, my mother, brothers, sisters, my greatest enemies had an interest in my prayers, and I cried, ' O Lord, give me to see my desire on them; let them experience Thy redeeming love.'

"In the afternoon, I opened the Book where it is said, ' Unto Him that loved us, and washed us from our sins in His own blood;' with which I was so affected that I could not read for weeping. That evening, under Mr. Wesley's sermon, I could do nothing but weep, and love, and praise God for sending His servant into the fields to show me the way of salvation.

All that day I neither ate nor drank anything; for before I found peace the hand of God was so heavy on me that I refused to eat; and after I had found peace, I was so filled with the manna of redeeming love, that I had no need of the bread that perisheth, for that season."

The preacher went on, but I heard no more, for Betty was sitting with hands clasped, the tears raining over her rugged face, yet with such an expression of hope on it, that I felt I could safely leave her; so I told her to stay, I would see to her work, and put everything right by the time she came back.

As I went down the hill, the sound of a hymn followed me, at first faint and broken, but soon rising strong and clear through the morning air. I thought I had never heard pleasanter music; and as I lighted the fire and got the breakfast ready, my heart sang, and I prayed that there might be melody also in poor Betty's heart.

She came back before any one had missed her.

All day she went about her work as usual; her face looked more peaceful, but she said nothing, and Betty's silences are barriers no one but herself could safely attempt to break down.

In the evening, while Mother and I were sitting by the fire alone, and I preparing to confess to her my having accompanied Betty to the morning preaching, Betty appeared with the supper, and after lingering about the things until I thought she would not go till Father came back, and I should be left for the night with the burden of my morning expedition unconfessed, suddenly she stood still and said,—

"Missis, I may as well out with it at once. I am going to hear that Yorkshireman again to-morrow. It's no good fighting against it. I have tried, but I shall have to go."

I had to fill up the vacancies in Betty's narrative, as clearly as I could, hastily confessing my share in it.

Mother looked seriously grieved.

"Kitty," she said, "I did not expect this of you."

"Mrs. Kitty went to take care of me," interposed Betty. "She thought I was going mazed—and so I was, sure—and Mrs. Kitty went to keep me from mischief."

"Betty," said Mother, very gravely, "I cannot sanction your going to any such places. You know I never hinder your going to church as often as you like, and I am sure Parson Spencer is a very good man; and there are the lessons and the prayers. What can you want more?"

"I am not saying anything against our parson, Missis," said Betty; "I'd as lief say anything against the King and the Parliament. I've no doubt that what he says is all right in its way. But ever since I heard Parson Wesley, I've had a great thorn fretting and rankling in my heart, and our parson's sermons can no more take that out, than they could take a rotten tooth out of my head. It isn't to be expected they should; they're not made for such rough doctor's work. But that Yorkshireman's can. He made me feel better this morning; and I must hear him again. And then, Missis, when I've got rid of the burden on my heart, I can sit easy and hearken to Parson Spencer. For no doubt his discourses are uncommon fine. I'd as lief listen to him as to the finest music I ever heard. Only it's not to be expected that the finest music 'll stop a sore heart from aching."

"But the Bible *is* made for that," said Mother; "and you hear that every Sunday in church."

"Yes, sure, and so I do from the Yorkshireman; but he has a way of picking out the bits that suit you, picking them out and laying them on, as you did the herb-lotion, Missis, last week when I bruised my side. The herbs were in the garden before, sure enough, but I might have walked among them till doomsday, and my side been no better."

Mother sighed.

"Take care, Betty," she said, "that you do not pick out the

texts you *like*, instead of those that really suit you. Bitters," sighed Mother, "are better than sweets, often."

"And bitter enough they were to me," said Betty : "it's my belief it is the smart that did me the good."

"Well, Betty," said Mother, "I cannot sanction it."

"Bless your heart, Missis," said Betty, "of course you can't. I never thought you could. But I thought it my duty to tell you before I went."

Mother shook her head, and Betty went; for beyond this right of mutual protest our domestic government with regard to her does not extend.

Betty went, and returned, and said nothing. Nor did she give occasion to Mother to say anything. The cooking was blameless, the floors spotless, Father's meals punctual to a minute. Only there was an unusual quiet in the kitchen, and on Saturday old Roger said to me privately,—

"I can't think what's come over Betty, Mrs. Kitty. She's so cruel kind ! and as quiet as a lamb. She hasn't given me a sharp word for nigh a week, and I can't say what'll come of it. It makes me quite wisht. They say folks with Betty's tempers· fall into that way when they're like to die. And in the evening she sits and spells over the great Bible you brought her from London. It's quite unnatural, Mrs. Kitty. I didn't like to tell Missis, for fear she should take on about it, she's so tender-hearted ; but I couldn't help telling you. They Methodists be terrible folk ; they say in my country up to Dartmoor, that they know more than they ought to know, and I shouldn't like them to ill-wish Betty. I used to think her tongue was a trifle sharp by times, but the place is cruel wisht without it and mortal lonesome ; and I'd give somewhat to hear her fling out with a will once more, poor soul."

Every other Sunday afternoon has always been one of my

most delightful times. There is no service then in our parish church. The Vicar rides to a daughter-church some miles off, too far for us to reach, and we have the whole afternoon for quiet. Father and Jack used commonly to walk round the farm with Trusty, Mother sits alone in the porch-closet, and I spend the time alone in my own chamber, or in the old apple-tree in the garden.

Last Sunday afternoon I was sitting, as usual, at my chamber window. The casement was open, and it was so still that the hum of the few stray bees buzzing in the sunshine around the marigolds in the garden below, came up to me quite clearly. But the bees were evidently only doing a little holiday work quite at their leisure.

I almost fancied I could hear the waving of the grass on the hillside, as it bent before the quiet breeze ; and I could hear distinctly the crunching of the grass which Daisy was cropping at the Home-park. And below all these intermittent sounds went on the quiet, unintermittent flow of the little runnel through the stone channel into the trough where the cattle were watered.

The spring was over with its songs and nest-buildings, the summer with its power of ripening sunshine, the harvest with its anxieties and its merry-makings. The sun had nothing more to do but to smile from his depths of golden light on his finished sheaves and ripened fruit.

The earth, too, had done her work for the year, and was couching at rest, and quiet, in the sunshine, like the labouring oxen in the warm streak of gold at the top of the field opposite my window.

There was a ripe calm, and a sacred stillness over everything, which made me feel as if I knew what the Bible meant by the "shadow of the wings" of God. For where "shadow" and "God" are spoken of together, shadow cannot mean shade and darkness, but only shelter, and safety, and repose. It seemed as if the whole earth were nestling under great, warm, motherly wings.

My Bible lay open on my knee, but I had not been reading for some time. I had not consciously been thinking or even praying, my whole heart was resting silently in the presence of God, as the earth around me lay silent in the sunshine; conscious of His presence as the dumb creatures are conscious of the sunshine, as a babe is conscious of its mother's smile; neither listening, nor adoring, nor entreating, nor remembering, nor hoping, but simply at rest in God's love.

It seemed like waking, when a low murmur below my window recalled me again to thought.

It was the broken murmur of a woman's voice. The room immediately under mine was the kitchen, and as I leant out of the window and listened, I perceived that the voice was Betty's.

I went downstairs into the court, and as I passed the kitchen window, I saw Betty sitting there with her large new Bible open before her on the white deal table.

It was a long window with several stone mullions, and casements broken into diamonded panes. The casement at which Betty sat was open. The cat was perched on the sunny sill, and Trusty was coiled up on the grass-grown pavement beneath.

Betty was bending eagerly over the Book; the plump fingers she was accustomed to rely on in so many useful works, could, by no means, be dismissed from service in a work so laborious to her as reading a book; and her lips followed their slow tracing of the lines, as if she would assure herself by various senses of the reality of the impressions conveyed to her by the letters. As she bent thus absorbed in her subject, I noticed how much power was expressed in the firm, well-defined lips, and in the broad, square brow, from which the dark gray hair was brushed back; and, indeed, in every rugged line of the strongly marked face. As I approached, she looked up, startled by a little movement of the cat, and by a musical yawn from Trusty as he stretched himself, and rose to welcome me.

Our eyes met. Betty seemed to think it necessary to apologize for her unusual occupation, and she said,—

"I was only looking, Mrs. Kitty, to see if what that Yorkshireman said is true."

. I could not help thinking of the noble women of Berea; and leaning on the window-sill, I listened.

"For you know, my dear," she continued, "if his words made my heart as happy as a king's, what good is it if they were only his own words? But if it's *here*, it's not his but the Lord's, and then it'll stand."

"Then his words did make your heart light, Betty?" I said.

"My dear," she said, "'twas not his words at all. It's all *here*, and has been here, of course, ages before he or I was born, only I never saw it before."

And turning the Bible so that I might see, she traced with her finger the words,—

"*All we, like sheep, have gone astray; we have turned every one to his own way; and the Lord hath laid on Him the iniquity of us all.*"

"There's a deal more, as good as that, my dear," she said; "but I keep coming back to that, because it was that that healed up my heart."

Her eyes were moist, and her voice was soft and quiet as she went on,—

"Mrs. Kitty, the cure was as quick as the hurt. Just as Mr. Wesley's words went right to the core of my heart in a moment, and made it like one great wound, feeling I was a lost, ungrateful, sinful woman,—*these* words went right to the heart of the wound, and flowed like sweet healing balm all through it, so that just where the anguish had been the worst, the joy was greatest. Not a drop of the sorrow but seemed swallowed up in a larger drop of the joy. For it was not thinking, Mrs.

Kitty, it was seeing. I saw in my heart the blessed Lord Himself, with all my sins laid upon Him; and He, while He was stretched, bleeding, there on the cross, all alone, and pale, and broken-hearted with the anguish of the burden, the burden of my sins, seeming to say with His kind looks all the time, ' I *am not unwilling, I am quite content to bear it all for thee.*' And oh, my dear, my heart felt all right that very moment. I can't say it felt light, for it seemed as if there lay upon me a load of love and gratitude heavier than the old load of sin, but it was all sweet, my dear, it is all sweet, and I would not have it weigh an atom lighter for the world."

I could not speak, I could only bow down and rest my face on Betty's hand, as I held it in mine. We were silent a long time, and then I said,—

" Did you tell Mr. Nelson ?"

" He came and asked. I had set myself as firm as a rock, that there should be no crying, and praying, and singing over me, Mrs. Kitty, but I was so broken down with the joy, that I didn't mind what any one did or thought about me, but sat crying like a poor fool as I am, until Mr. Nelson came up to me quite quiet and gentle, and asked if anything ailed me ; and then I said, ' You may thank the Lord for me, Mr. Nelson, for to my dying day I shall thank the Lord for you, and that you ever came to these parts.' Then he asked what it was, and I told him all, Mrs. Kitty, as I have told you ; and he looked mighty pleased, and said it was being converted; and said something about the 'inward witness,' 'the witness of the Spirit.' But what that meant I knew no more than a newborn babe, and I told him so. I knew my heart had been as heavy as a condemned murderer's, and now I was as happy as a forgiven child, and all through seeing the blessed Lord in my heart. And they all smiled very pleasant, and said that was enough, and that what more there was to learn, if I kept on reading the Bible, and went to church, the Lord would teach

me all in time. But I felt I could bear no more just then, so I
wished them all good day and went home alone. For I was
afraid of losing the great joy, Mrs. Kitty, if I talked too much
about it. I felt as if I had got a new treasure, and I wanted
to come home and turn it over, and look at it, and make sure
it was all true, and all really mine."

"You spoke of *seeing*, Betty," I said, "but you had no visions
or dreams?"

"No," she said, "and I don't want any. I don't see how it
could be plainer than it is. And I found it quite true," she
went on, "about the Lord teaching me at church. It is strange
I never noticed before how the parson says every Sunday, in the
prayers, so much that John Nelson told me. 'All we like
sheep have gone astray;' and about the forgiveness of sins and
all. The prayers seemed wonderful and plain to me to-day,
Mrs. Kitty; but I can't say I've got to the length as yet of
understanding our parson. But oh, my dear," she concluded,
"it is a mercy for us ignorant folks that the Bible does seem
the plainest of all."

Then I left Betty again to her meditations, and went up for
the precious half-hour with Mother, before Father came back
from the fields. And I thought it right to tell her as well as I
could what Betty had told me. She was interested and touched,
and looked very grave as she said,—

"I don't see what we can say against it, Kitty. Your Father
thinks that John Nelson is a very remarkable man. Anything
which makes a person keep their temper, and love to read the
Bible, and go to church, does seem in itself good. But I think
Betty is quite wise to wish to be alone, and not to talk too
much about it. It seems to me we want all the strength
religion can give us for the doing and the enduring, so that
there is little to spare for the talking, or to waste in mere
emotion."

"Yet, Mother," I said, "it is love, is it not, which strengthens us both to do and to endure, and love has its joys and sorrows as well as its duties."

"Yes," she said thoughtfully, "many sorrows, and also joys. Yet, Kitty, love is *proved*, not by its joys and sorrows, which are so much mixed up with self, but by duty. God said, ' I will have obedience, and not sacrifice ;' and I think that means that God will have, not the offering of this or that in the luxury of devotion, but the sacrifice of *self;* for obedience is nothing else than the sacrifice of self."

" Yet, Mother," said I, "if the love is so deep that it makes the obedience a delight, can that be a mistake ?"

"That would be heaven, child !" she said. "But I think none but great saints have experienced that on earth, at least not constantly."

."Yet, Mother," I said, "it seems to me, the more one is like a little child, with God, the more one does delight to obey."

"Perhaps it is the little children that *are* the great saints, Kitty," she replied smiling.

" But you think we need not trouble Betty about what she feels, Mother," said I, " she seems so gentle and happy ?"

" I think we must wait and see," said Mother.

And so our conversation ended.

Can it have been only yesterday morning I was sitting mending Mother's mittens in the hall window, when Hugh Spencer came in, and, after just wishing me good day, asked where Mother was, and left me to go and find her ?

It seems so much longer.

I felt surprised that he should have no more to say to me, when we had not met for months, and he had been ordained in the meantime. I thought his mind must be full of the "subject (or object) in which he and Evelyn are equally interested."

And I supposed he wanted to consult Mother about it, thinking me too inexperienced or too much of a child to be able to give any advice worth having.

I did feel rather hurt, and then I began to be afraid I might have shown him that I felt vexed, and received him stiffly and coldly. And I resolved when he came in again (if he came) to speak quite as usual to him. What right, indeed, had I to feel hurt? Of course Mother was a better counsellor for any one than I could be; and every one could see how much better Evelyn's opinion was worth having than mine. But then my thoughts went off into quite another channel.

For some days it had been becoming clearer and clearer to me that the way out of the difficulty about Jack's debts was simply to consult Hugh. He already knew the worst of it, since Jack had written to beg of him himself. I had paid Miss Pawsey already, and I thought I would ask him to settle with the Jew, and to take the rest of what I had for his own loan (of course not saying the money was mine). So I sat thinking how best to begin, and making a number of imaginary speeches, in reply to an equal number of possible observations of Hugh's, when he returned.

He was alone, and I resolved not to lose a minute. So, without looking up from Mother's mittens (for Jack's reputation was concerned, and it was a delicate matter to negotiate, and I felt nervous), I began at once (forgetting all my speeches), at what was certainly the wrong end. I said, speaking very fast, and feeling myself colouring crimson as I spoke,—

"Hugh, some time since Jack bought a cherry-coloured ribbon for me, and he said you paid for it, and he left me some money—at least he told me about it."

"And will you not accept even a cherry-coloured ribbon from me, Mrs. Kitty?" said Hugh.

Still I did not look up; but I said,—

"It was not exactly that which Jack told me; it was about the *other* money you lent him, and I am to pay it you by degrees."

And there I stopped, having become inextricably perplexed between the difficulty of not telling a story, and of not betraying the fact that I was to pay Jack's debts with my own money.

Then Hugh spoke, and his voice was very gentle and low, for he was standing quite near me ; and he said,—

"Kitty, I came to speak to you about quite a different subject."

And then I looked up, for I thought of Evelyn's letter.

But we did not say anything more that evening about Jack's debts.

Indeed, I do not know what we said.

Nor, when Hugh went home and Mother came in, did she say much.

She only took me to her heart, and murmured, " My darling child !"

But I do not feel any more anxiety about the "subject (or object) in which Evelyn and Hugh are equally interested."

To think that Hugh had been wishing this so many years !

Only I am not half worthy of Hugh and his love.

Yet God can make me even that, in time.

VII.

I THINK no one ever had so many kinds of happiness mixed together in their cup as I have.

I can hardly ever get beyond "adoration" and "thanksgiving" in my "acts of piety" now, except when I have to make confession of not having been half thankful enough.

For Hugh is to be his father's curate, and Parson Spencer told Mother it has always been understood that, after him, the living will be given to Hugh; so that we are to have the great joy, Hugh and I, of having it for our business in life, to do all the good we can all our lives long to those who have known us from our childhood. All the good we can in every kind of way. Other people have it for their calling, the thing given them to do, to fight in the King's armies, or to make laws, or to make other people keep them, or to buy and sell, or, like Betty, to make butter and scrub floors, doing what good they can, by the way, or after their work is done; but doing good is to be our business, profession, study, always, every day, Hugh's and mine. In the morning we are to think who there are around us to be helped or comforted, turned out of the wrong way, cheered on in the right. With others, maintenance, traffic, are necessary objects. We need not have one selfish object in life. The poorest must feel there is always one door in the parish from which they will not be turned away. Those who have sunk the lowest must feel that there is always one hand that will not fear to be polluted by touching them to lift them up.

And all this will not be a romantic enterprise for us, but simple, plain duty, which is so much sweeter.

For Hugh says it is a desecration of the endowments which were given of old for sacred purposes, when the clergy treat their incomes as if they were like any common produce of traffic, or estate of inheritance, or wages of secular work. It is consecrated wealth still, he says; and when we have used what we need for a simple and unpretentious household, we owe our superfluous stores to the Church and the poor. All Christians, he says, are indeed stewards of consecrated wealth, but the clergy, he thinks, more especially. It would be a disgrace, he thinks, if the distinction between the Popish clergy and ours were that ours are *secularized* into mere thrifty farmers or little squires. It is not in *devotedness* we should differ from the ancient priesthood.

I am afraid it is the parsonesses that put things wrong sometimes. I hope I shall not be a hindrance to Hugh. I must not grudge his going out in the evening on any summons of duty, on stormy nights, even though he may seem wearied already with the day's work. I must not let any womanish fears prevent his visiting the sick, even though the sickness be deadly contagious pestilence. Should I be less brave than a soldier's wife, or a poor fisherman's? Men are meant to peril their lives and to wear out their strength in work, Hugh says; and if the Parson's calling were to be without its perils and toils, it would be less manly than the sailor's, or the shepherd's, or the miner's, or any other working man's, and therefore less Christian.

Easy things for me to intend; but not so easy to do, when the peril or the trial comes! Yet if we are to have the true blessing of our calling, we must go forth to it, Hugh says, not as a paradise, but as a campaign. And then it will be *we*, always we! and that makes all the difference.

Yet how could I bear to take this happiness if it were to

bring loss to Mother, if I caught her tender eyes every now and then watching me wistfully, and filling with tears,—and she still so feeble. But this will scarcely take me from her,—not at all at first, for we are to have our home under this dear old roof,—so that it will be all gain to Mother, and to Father too. And then I have some one to consult about everything. Because (and that is another special blessing) Hugh knows already all about us all. He has watched Mother as anxiously as I have ; and we can plan together about the best way of helping Jack, without my telling him anything more of the things I scarcely could have told even Hugh, if he had not known them before.

Hugh is not at all hopeless about Jack, although he knows all ; but he says he seems like some one in a dream, and he does think it must be a rough call that will wake him.

Father and Betty are so busy clearing out and repairing the rooms in the older part of the house, which are to be ours,—delightful old rooms with great stone chimneys, and one in a tower with a long arched window, which is to be Hugh's own den. It is high up, and from the casement, through an opening of the hills, you catch one glimpse of the sea,—a bright line of light on sunny days, at evening a dim heaving cloud of purple against the gold of the sunset; and always, Hugh says, a path for thought to sail on, out into the wide world.

Hugh and I have dived into forgotten stores in the lumber-room, and fished up wonderful pearls in the shape of old oaken chairs, which only want their backs mended, and tables which only want a leg or two to be quite stately

Betty thinks little of these discoveries, saying concisely that ten shillings' worth of furniture from the shop in Falmouth is worth them all. But then, carving and associations have no value in Betty's inventory.

She thinks much more of Mother's purchases and manufactures, although she says clothes in these days are mere cobwebs compared to the stuffs of our forefathers, when Master's great-grandmother's wedding dress survived to become a christening robe for Master, and after that a covering for the best great chair, and looked as good as new to the last.

But Mother and Betty have become quite confidential once more over the matter, Betty's sober and conservative views about woolseys and linseys having in some measure restored the confidence in her judgment, so much impaired in Mother's mind by her views about the Methodists.

Hugh said the other day there is no doubt Mr. John Wesley would recognize Mother to be a most saintly woman, if he knew her; and that he feels sure, if Mother knew Mr. John Wesley, his life of labour, his entire devotion to God, his unlimited benevolence and beneficence to man, his attachment to the Church services, she would revere him as next to the apostles. It is the greatest trial of Reformers, he thinks, that they have often to be blamed and misunderstood by the *good* men and women of their times.

He says if Mother had lived in Martin Luther's time she might probably have prayed for him in her convent as a prodigal, whilst living by the very faith he spent his life to proclaim.

" But if Mother had lived in a convent, Hugh," I said, " she would never have been married, and she would have been a Papist; which would have been impossible."

He smiled, and said,—

" But, Kitty, Mr. Wesley thinks some of the holiest people who ever lived were Roman Catholics."

" That must have been when there was nothing else for people to be," I said.

" Nay," he replied; " Mr. Wesley says now, 'I dare not exclude from the Church catholic all those congregations in which unscriptural doctrines, which cannot be affirmed to be the pure word of God, are sometimes, nay frequently preached; neither

12

all those congregations in which the sacraments are not duly administered (as the Church of Rome), whoever they are that have one Spirit, one hope, one Lord, one faith, one God and Father of all.'"

"That is a great comfort," I said. "'But I think we had better not conjecture what Mother would have been if she had lived in Martin Luther's days. Nothing bewilders my brain like thinking what might have been if something else had been. Thank God, Hugh, she did not live in those old dark days, nor any of us."

"I am very thankful *you* did not at any rate, Kitty," he said, with his quiet smile, which is as joyous as laughter, "at least unless we had all been transplanted together."

But I was intending to write about Betty, and I have wandered quite away.

One evening, about a fortnight since, Father was sitting after supper in one corner of the hall, smoking some Virginian tobacco a ship's captain had brought him lately as a present, with the Book on Fortification open before him, and Mother and I were busy cutting out garments at the deal table at the other side of the fire, when Betty, after removing the supper, announced her intention of joining the Methodist Society which met in the village.

Mother said gravely,—

"You can do as you like, Betty; indeed I suppose you *will* do as you like. This new kind of religion seems to make that a necessity for every one."

Very severe words for Mother; yet Mother being the gentlest of beings, is nevertheless in her gentle way absolutely impenetrable when once her mind is made up.

"Once for all, however, Betty," she continued, laying down her scissors, and speaking in the low quiet tone neither Jack nor I ever thought of resisting, "I think it my duty faithfully to warn you. I do not understand this religion of violent excitement and determined self-will. The religion I believe in, is one which enables us to control our feelings and yield up our self-will."

"Missis," said Betty, in a low, faltering voice, unusual with her, " I may as well speak my mind out at once too. If you mean that I couldn't keep back my tears at the Sacrament yesterday, no more I couldn't, nor I scarce can now when I think of it. For the blessed Lord Himself was *there*, and I felt as sure of it as that poor woman who washed His feet with her tears. I felt it was the Lord Himself giving Himself to me, and showing me He loved me, and had died for me, and that my sins were forgiven. Didn't old Widow Jennifer rouse up all the town with her crying and sobbing when her poor lost boy came back, that was thought to be wrecked; and didn't he sob too, bearded man as he was? And is it any wonder I should cry at finding my God? Sure enough, Missis, I was shipwrecked worse than Jennifer's son, and sure enough my God is more to me than any mother and son to each other. If you only knew how lost I had been, you wouldn't wonder. You'd wonder I kept as quiet as I did."

Mother was silent some little time. Her kind thoughtful eyes moistened and then were cast down, and she only said very gently,—

" I know such assured peace and such joys have been given to some, Betty; but they were great saints, and I think it was generally just before their death."

" Well, Missis," said Betty, simply, "I am sure I am no great saint, and I don't know that I am like to die, but I know that none but the Lord could give me joy like that; and if it's for me, surely it's for all. And John Nelson says our parsons say so every Sunday."

" The parsons say every Sunday, every one may know their sins are forgiven !" exclaimed Mother.

"Every one who repents and believes," said Betty. "Mr. John Nelson made me see how it says in the Prayer-book, ' He pardoneth and absolveth all those who truly repent and unfeignedly believe His Holy Gospel.' And if I ever felt anything truly in my life, Missis, I've felt sorry for my sins, and hated them, and they say that is repentance. And if I believe anything in the world, it is that the blessed Lord died on the Cross for sinners, and John Nelson says that is the Holy Gospel. So that, now, whenever our parson comes to that, my heart leaps for joy. For it isn't ' *will* pardon,' but '*pardoneth;*' and that must mean forgives *now.* So it's all the same to me as if the parson said, ' Betty Roskelly, God Almighty has commanded me to tell you He forgives you all your sins for the sake of Christ Jesus our Lord.' And Missis," concluded Betty, " I don't mind how little I can understand the sermon, when that's so plain. So when the parson gets into the pulpit, I listen to the text (which is most times plain too), and then I think, ' Now he's going to preach to the learned folks, like himself, but I've got my sermon already, and it's enough for me ;' so I sit and think, quite content."

" But," resumed Mother after a pause, " you have heard those words every Sunday of your life. What makes the absolution such a new and strange thing to you ?"

" I can't well say, Missis," said Betty, "unless it is the '*now*' and '*me.*' I always listened to it all as if the parson were reading good words made a long time ago about good things a long way off, to be given after a long while to I didn't exactly know who. But when I came to see that it is God *now* forgiving *me,* that makes all the difference."

" But, if the Prayer-book makes you so content, Betty," said Mother, shifting her attack, " what do you want with those new-fangled meetings ?"

" It's the meetings that make me understand the prayers, Missis," said Betty, persisting.

"I hope you *do* understand them, Betty, and are not deluding yourself," said Mother; and having thus reserved her rights to the last word, she abandoned the contest, and Betty retired.

In the course of the evening, as we were all gathered round the fire, Father said,—

" My dear, I advise you to have no more theological discussions with Betty. She turned your position neatly with her quotations from the Prayer-book."

Mother coloured a little.

" You know, my dear," she said, " we pray every Sunday against schism as well as against heresy, and I am very much afraid of people deluding themselves into a kind of religious insanity with this new religion."

" My dear," said Father, " I have seen a good many religions, and not too much religion in the world with all of them together. I am not much afraid of a schism which sends people to church, nor of an insanity which makes them good servants. These are strange times. The squire told me to-day they have sent poor John Greenfield to prison; and when I asked him why (for though the poor fellow was a sad drunkard and ill-liver in years past, since he has taken up with the Methodists he has been as steady as old Time), he said, ' Why, the man is well enough in other things ; but his impudence is not to be borne. Why, sir, he says he knows his sins are forgiven.'*   But," concluded Father, gravely, " there are some old soldiers who might think poor John Greenfield's penalty worth bearing, if they could share his crime."

Mother is always easily melted out of the rigidity of controversy by any symptom of yielding on the other side.   It is so foreign to her nature, that (as I have noticed with other gentle people) the very effort required to enter on it makes her for the time all the more stiff and unyielding when once she begins ; just as I have noticed that a captain of militia will wear his untried sword with twice as fierce and military an air as Father, who fought through the great Duke's campaigns. But now, seeing Father's pensive face, she gladly doffed her armour and laid her hand on his arm and said,—

" My love, the Bible says, 'there is forgiveness with God for all.'" And lowering her voice she added, " When I look at the Cross of our Saviour, and see Him suffer and hear Him plead, it seems impossible that God *cannot* forgive; and then again when I look at my sins, I think it is almost impossible He *can.* And so, my love," she said, " I find no comfort but in looking at the Cross of my Lord again. And perhaps it may be the same for you."

He laid his hand on hers, and said with a grave smile, looking into her dear, pure, tender face,—

" Thy sins, Polly, must be a great weight indeed ! Faith I would like to hear thy confessions. ' To-day I was too worldly and too glad to see Kitty so happy. Yesterday I was too sorry to see my husband in a passion. Every day I love every one more than I ought, and do ten times more than they deserve.' Are these thy confessions ?"

She looked a little grieved at his turning the conversation lightly, and soon after she went to rest. But this morning she told me I must not think anything of it ; it was only a way, she said, dear Father had caught in the army, and she had no doubt he thought far more religiously than he talked. Nor must I think anything of what he said about the sins of his former life ; a truer and gentler heart, she said, never beat. The bravest were always the kindest. " And then, Kitty," she concluded, " what are the perils and temptations of women to those of men ? Perhaps more women than men may creep quietly and safely into heaven ; but every man who gets there must be a hero, and a king fit to reign over ten cities."

But when Father and I were left alone, he said,—

" Kitty, it is a strange world. Here are men who set the

whole ten commandments at defiance—imprisoning a good man for confessing his sins and believing they are forgiven. And this morning, when I was out before dawn looking for a stray sheep, I heard a sound of grave sweet singing; and I found it was a company of poor tinners, waiting around John Wesley's lodging to get a sermon before they went to their work, and singing hymns till he came out. And here's Betty, with a temper like the Furies, turned saint; and your Mother, with a life like an angel's, bemoaning her sins. It's a very strange world, Kitty; but if John Nelson came this way again, I would go and hear him. I'm not clear the stout Yorkshireman mightn't preach as good a sermon as some other people we know. And there's a good deal in that idea of Betty's about the '*now*' and the '*me.*'"

"Hugh says John Nelson is a wonderful preacher, Father," I said; "and some people think Hugh's own sermons are beautiful."

"So, ho! Hugh a Methodist too!" said Father, patting my check. "But who said that Hugh's sermons were *not* beautiful?"

The Hall Farm is honoured at present by a most distinguished guest.

A few days since, Cousin Evelyn announced that it was her royal pleasure to pay us a visit.

"I shall come without a maid," she wrote; "for Stubbs is persuaded that the Cornish people are heathens, who never offer a prayer except that ships may be wrecked on their coasts; that they tie lanterns to mares' tails, to bring about the same result, the poor sailors mistaking them for guiding lights; that when ships are thus wrecked, they murder the crew, and probably eat them afterwards, but of this she is not sure; of the perils of the journey, however, she is sure. And ready as she declares herself to be for any sacrifice on my account, I feel it

would be an ungenerous return for such unlimited devotion to
strain it so far.   I have therefore dispensed with her services,
promising to secure her a slice of the pie of me, as a relic, in
case of the worst.   And, indeed, mamma says it cannot matter
much my having a maid to decorate me ; for she calls Cornwall
' Western Barbary,' and thinks that whatever fashion I introduce
may pass for the newest Court mode.   But, Cousin Kitty, you
and I know better.   Mamma knows nothing of Miss Pawsey ;
but I who do, intend to bring my most elaborate brocades, and
my largest hoops, and my choicest lace-lappets for that renowned
artist to arrange.   For spectators, what can any woman desire
better than that most courtly old courtier my uncle, and that
most perfect gentlewoman, my aunt ? to say nothing of my
sweet demure cousin, and a neighbouring gentleman who has
told me far more about her than she, fickle goddess, ever deigned
to tell me about him.   Happily for my heart, Cousin Jack is at
the wars ; but then there are Betty and Trusty.   I am wild with
pleasure, Cousin Kitty, at the thought of seeing you all.   And I
expect you will have Mr. John Wesley down on purpose to edify
me.—Your most loving cousin,   EVELYN BEAUCHAMP."

Father shook his head and said there was too much truth in
what the maid said about the Cornish wreckers, to make it a
matter for a jest.

Mother, however softened by the compliment to Father's
manners, was only half pleased with the letter, and not at all
pleased at the prospect of the visit.

"Such an extraordinary mixture, Kitty !" she said—" Mr.
Wesley and Miss Pawsey, Methodists and hoop-petticoats !
What are we to do with such a fine lady,—a young woman,
too, with such a very dangerous levity as regards the Church ?
I wish you had not drawn her such a picture of me, my poor
fond Kitty !   What will she think ?   However, she was very
kind to you, and we must do our best."

Nor was Betty more pleased than Mother.

"It was a blessing indeed," she said, "she was not to bring her maid, for she had heard that London maids were far finer ladies than their mistresses. Not that she was afraid of any fine lady, mistress or maid; for who was better blood than the Trevylyans? And she should certainly have given the maid a bit of her mind, which might have done her good."

But knowing the angular character of these "bits of Betty's mind," I cannot but be glad at Stubbs' escape.

And now, Cousin Evelyn has been here only a week, and has conquered every heart in the house, from Betty's, bristling all over with controversial assertions of the glory of the Trevylyans, to Mother's trembling all over with the sense of her own deficiencies, and the terror of Cousin Evelyn's grandeur, and wit, and heterodoxy.

The afternoon she arrived, in spite of Betty's remonstrances, the table was set as usual in the hall, instead of in the parlour. It was just growing dusk. The blaze of the great fire of logs, on the hearth, was fast overpowering with its ruddy glow and quivering shadows the pale, fading daylight. Father kept pacing the hall and gazing out of the window, declaring Evelyn ought to have been here an hour since. Mother hovered about the supper-table, arranging the plates with a nervous precision, when the clatter of hoofs was heard in the court, and the sound of a ringing voice, and in another moment I was leading Cousin Evelyn in.

She looked so radiant, it seemed to me she brought the day back again into the house as she entered it, her face glowing with air and exercise, the feather waving in her hat, her rich brown hair knotted behind with scarlet, and falling in curls over her blue habit faced with silver. She did not overpower Mother with any great vivacity, or with any violent demonstrations of affection. The ordinary tones of her voice were deep and low, with a kind of muffled power, and her manner was composed and quiet. And this evening there was a reverent tenderness in her tones whenever she addressed Father, and especially Mother, that was most winning. Because there is that kind of power about Cousin Evelyn that makes one feel her affection something *giving*, not *asking*—a strong, kind arm thrown round you to cherish you, rather than a feeble, clinging tendril, twining round you to support itself. And her reverence or admiration always seems like the condescension of a queen stooping to kiss your hand.

Trusty, having investigated her rights with that peculiar sense (whatever it is) residing in his nose, sanctioned her at once by that peculiar power of language residing in his tail.

This quiet operation was his ordinary way of receiving any new-comer; but Cousin Evelyn's case he evidently felt to be exceptional. Like every one else with Evelyn, but quite in contradiction with his own usual sentiments, Trusty evidently felt her approval was even more necessary than his in the acquaintance, and kept sitting beside her, wistfully gazing into her face, until she honoured him with a friendly pat from her little soft hand, saying, "So, you are Trusty!" when he was satisfied, and retired to his place before the fire.

The household have all expressed to me their appreciation of Cousin Evelyn in their various ways.

Mother said the next morning, as I took her the new milk—

"Kitty, I should never have thought Evelyn so clever as you say she is. She seems to me a dear good child, not at all wild, nor in the least conceited. I am sure there is nothing in her conversation to lead any one to think she knows any language but her own, nor anything in her behaviour to indicate the least dangerous tendency towards separatists and agitators; and not a particle of the fine lady about her; rather shy, I should have thought her. I am sure we must all do our utmost to make the dear child feel at home. And there is a strange, wistful look in her

eyes, Kitty," continued Mother, "that goes to my heart—a
kind of orphaned look. Perhaps her home is not so happy as
ours, with all its splendour. I feel strangely drawn to the
child. I have a kind of motherly feeling for her, Kitty. We
must do everything to make her happy."

As if it was anything strange for Mother's heart to have a
kind of motherly feeling to any creature she had to do with!

But it is strange she should notice that wistful look in Cousin
Evelyn's eyes, for I never said much to her about Aunt Beauchamp. I thought it would be a breach of hospitality. Mother
always taught us it would be such a treachery to gossip about
the secrets of any home where we are welcomed.

Father on the contrary said—

"That child is monstrously clever. I believe, Kitty, with a
very little teaching she would know as much of the science of
war as I do. She entered into my description of the great
battle of Malplaquet as intelligently as if she had been an old
soldier."

Betty has said little. She is not the person to strike her
colours at the first summons. But yesterday morning when I
came back from the milking I found Cousin Evelyn established
with Betty in the dairy on terms of intimacy it took Jack and
me many years to win, actually rolling up a pat of butter with
her dainty little hands, her round white arms bare to the ruffles
at her elbows.

And afterwards Betty said to me—

" I am not going to say Mrs. Evelyn is what she might have
been if she had been brought up in the country in a sensible
way ; but a fine lady she is not. A more free and affable young
lady I never did see. *Her* fingers are not all thumbs ; she's
sense enough for anything if she'd only been taught, poor young
thing. And," continued Betty candidly, " that's more than I
thought when I saw her first, with her feathers and her ribbons,
and her coat like a general's, with all that tinsel stuff about it.

But to hear her talk about Parson Wesley and his sermons, with that fly-away lace on her head, and her long curls, and those little high-heeled red slippers, and a petticoat like a hen coop, was more than I could quite take in."

"But, Betty," said I, "these things are no more to Cousin Evelyn than my woolsey petticoat and laced bodice to mé; or Mother's cushion and cap and muslin kerchief pinned over her dress to her; or your Sunday cloak and hood to you."

"May be, Mrs. Kitty," said Betty; "but I've spoke my mind to Mrs. Evelyn, and she's spoke her mind to me. And I hope she'll be the better for it, for I think I shall."

By this I knew that Betty and Cousin Evelyn had had a passage at arms, the usual title to such rights of citizenship as Betty can confer.

In the evening we had a long talk, Evelyn and I, in my chamber, before we went to bed. Mother had furbished up an old state bed with faded tapestry hangings representing Herodias with John Baptist's head in a charger, and had placed it in one of the rooms which have been cleared out and whitewashed for us. But Cousin Evelyn entreated not to be put into such ghostly company again.

The first night she slept there alone, and she declared that as the wood fire flickered on the livid antique forms, they glowed and stirred in the strangest way, and that she should never be able to tell whether an unnatural glare that came over the countenance of Herodias, just as she was going to sleep, was merely the dying flicker of the embers, or that princess herself revivified and scowling on her with murderous eyes. Accordingly she has taken refuge with me.

Our conversation began about Betty. Evelyn said—

"I like you all very much, Kitty, but I am not sure that Betty is not the best and wisest among you, and the greatest friend to me. Aunt Trevylyan spoils me by her tenderness, and Uncle

Trevylyan by his courteous deference, and you by your humility. But Betty knows better, and she has given me a bit of her mind, and I have given her a bit of mine. This morning I asked her to teach me to make butter, and she said, 'Mrs. Evelyn, my dear, I'll teach you what I can, although I half think you are after nothing but a bit of play. But before we begin, I must tell you what's been on my mind for some time. You may play, my dear, with Master about his battles, and with Missis at learning to sew, and with me at making butter, if you like, but I can't abide play about religion, and I can't think it's anything else when you talk about Parson Wesley and his wonderful words, with those lappets and feathers flying about your face, and tripping on your little red shoes. The Bible's plain; and I've marked a text which you'll be pleased to read.'

"She gave me her great Bible, and I read: 'In that day the Lord will take away the bravery of their tinkling ornaments,' etc. 'But, Betty,' I said, 'I don't wear any tinkling ornaments, nor nose jewels, nor round tires like the moon, nor bells on my toes.'

"'You may smile, Mrs. Evelyn,' said Betty very gravely, 'but I think it's no laughing matter. If that had been written in our days, my dear, your lappets, and furbelows, and hoop petticoats would have come in, sure enough. And it *was* written for you and me as sure as if it had been written yesterday; so we've got to understand it. But Parson Wesley's sermons are no child's play, my dear,' she concluded; 'and if you'd felt them tearing at your heart as I have, you'd know it; and till you do, I'd rather not talk about them.'"

"And what did you say, Cousin Evelyn?" I asked.

"I was angry," said Evelyn, "for I thought Betty harsh and uncharitable, and I said,—

"I *have* felt Parson Wesley's words, Betty, and I have learned from him that pride and vanity can hide in other places besides lappets and furbelows. It's a great warfare we're in, and the

Enemy has wiles as well as fiery darts ; and it is not always so sure when we have driven the enemy out of sight that we have defeated him. We may have driven him *further in ;* into the citadel of our hearts, Betty," I said ; " and one foe in the citadel is worse than an enemy in the field."

" And what did Betty answer ? " I asked.

" She answered nothing," said Evelyn. " She said, ' Young folks were very wise in these days;' and then she began to give me my lesson in making butter. But as I was leaving the dairy afterwards, she said, ' Mrs. Evelyn, my dear, I am not going to say I've no pride or conceit of my own. Maybe we'd better each look to ourselves.' I gave her hand a hearty shake, and I know we shall be good friends."

(*Marginal Note.*—I noticed after this that throughout her visit Cousin Evelyn wore the soberest and plainest dresses she had.)

Then after a pause Cousin Evelyn continued, in a soft and deep tone,—

" Cousin Kitty, I no longer wonder at your being the dear little creature you are. I do not see how you could help growing up good and sweet here, in such a home. I love you all so much ! Aunt Trevylyan has just such a sweet, choice aromatic ' odour of sanctity ' about her, as old George Herbert would have delighted to enshrine in one of his quaint vases of perfume —those dear old hymns of his ; a kind of fragrance of fresh rose leaves and Oriental spices, all blended into a sacred incense. And dear Uncle Trevylyan and I, Kitty, have talks I am afraid your mother would think rather dangerous, during those long walks of ours over the cliffs and through the fields. He likes to hear about John Nelson and the Wesleys, and their strong homely sayings, and their brave daring of mobs, and their patient endurance of toil and weariness. He said one day he had been used to think of religion as a fair robe to make women such as your Mother (how he loves her, Kitty !) even lovelier than they were by nature, to be reverently put on on Sundays and holy days, and, it was to be hoped, hereafter in heaven. But of a religion for every day and all day, *here* and *now*, to be worn by all and woven into the coarse stuff of everyday life— a religion to be girt about a man on the battle-field, and at the mine, and in the fishing-boat—he had scarcely thought till he met John Nelson."

It is a great pleasure to take Cousin Evelyn to all our old familiar haunts. She is more delighted with our wild seas and rocky shores than even I had expected. She makes me see beautiful pictures in things to which I had grown so accustomed as scarcely to observe them. The view from the shady recesses of our " Robinson Crusoe's Cave " across the white sands, and across the line of breakers to the broad sea twinkling in countless waves on and on to the horizon where it shone a line of emerald light touching the opal sky, enchanted her. She said she had no idea what a wealth of radiance floods our everyday footsteps in the open world, until she looked out on it from that cavern.

" Think, Cousin Kitty," she said, " we are walking every hour of the day in that fairy world of glory and beauty without knowing it! and people call it 'this every-day life,' and this 'work-a-day world.' Can we not understand a little," she added, " how it is that God finds it for our profit to lead us sometimes into the shadows ? "

Often she longs for some of the great old painters to be here and transfer some of these scenes to canvas ;—the sea with its amethyst and emerald tints, the strange peaks, and pinnacles, and arched bridges in the dark rocks against which the snow-white waves leap ; the little openings in our green wooded valley, through which we catch sunny glimpses of the sea. She and Father delight to compare these things with the landscapes of the great masters which he has seen in Flanders, and she in various great houses in England.

Yet, in some way, there is a difference between Evelyn's enjoyment of these things and mine. When she would pause in delight and amazement and exclaim, "What a picture! what a flood of golden light for Cuyp! what a contrast that sky and those rocks would make for Claude!"—at first I used to wonder at my own dulness in taking it all so quietly; until one day, when I said so to Hugh, he replied,—

"It is not dulness, Kitty, that makes you never think of exclaiming, every now and then, as you look at your Mother, 'What a picture that face is!' And yet I am sure Raphael never painted a countenance of more sacred purity and tenderness than hers. It is your Mother's face! You do not wonder at it; you know it too well. Its sweet beauty has been shining on your heart since you were a baby, and has grown part of you. It is so with nature. Your Cousin Evelyn has been used to see the world from the windows of magnificent mansions, and she has taste to see it is grander than any picture-gallery they contain. But still it is a picture-gallery—a collection of masterpieces to her. I think you have been better off. You have not gone to see the beauties of nature as an exhibition; you have grown up among them, and done your everyday work among them; they have been the flowers by your daily path, the familiar walls and roof of your home. You have lived, as it were, at home with Nature, close to her heart. Her glorious face has been beaming on you like your Mother's from your infancy. She is no mere picture to you, she is your friend. You do not gaze and exclaim, 'How beautiful!'. You love and enjoy. Her beauty has entered into your very heart. It does us good to admire what is good and beautiful; but it does us infinitely more good to love it. We grow like what we admire; but we become one with what we love."

I suppose there may be some truth in what Hugh says, although it is certainly coloured by his affection.

But I do feel thankful it has been my lot to live in our

humble, quiet way, seeing the sunrise as I go to milk Daisy,
not as a great sight to rise for once in a life-time; and the sunset as I come back from all kinds of homely errands; hearing
the birds, not as a concert now and then, but singing close to
my chamber-window morning and evening; the same rooks
cawing in the same dear old elms; the same thrushes building
year after year in the same nest in the old thorn.

Evelyn told me to-day she had had a conversation with Betty
on ecclesiastical history, in reference to the great multitude of
Cornish saints—St. Just, St. Neot, St. Perran, St. Ives. Betty,
it seems, has a theory that they were the John Wesleys and the
John Nelsons of those days, sent by the Almighty to wake the
folks up; and she wonders if the Methodists will ever fall asleep
again, as the converts of the old saints must have done, so that
it will be needful for fresh saints to be sent again to awake
them.

Most of all, however, I admire Cousin Evelyn when she is
talking to Hugh. She enters into his high purposes, and wide
hopes for the world, with such enthusiasm. I used to feel like
a dwarf beside her. But now I only feel like a creature of a
smaller kind, not dwarfed, I trust, thank God, but naturally of
a less size and meant to occupy a smaller space than Cousin
Evelyn, but with that little space and that humble growth so
content, so fully content!

My only fear is sometimes lest I should make Hugh's world
narrow and his purpose dwindle to my degree. When he and
Evelyn converse, they seem to ennoble each other; and I have
no power to originate anything. I can only sympathize with
their purposes, and work out their thoughts in some little homely
way. I am afraid Evelyn would have helped Hugh much better.
But I cannot help that. I could not choose for him. And he
chose me—not some ideal woman who might be ten times

better for him—but me myself, little Kitty Trevylyan, just as I am. And as it was no choice of mine, but his, and there is no doubt about its being right, it is such a sure, deep, unutterable joy. I must just accept it all, and be happy, and love God and every one ten times as much as ever.

We have had a charming little excursion round part of the coast, Father, and Evelyn, and I, and on our way home we were present at one of Mr. Wesley's great field-preachings at Gwennap Pit; and as it came in our way, so that Mother could not be grieved, I am so glad we were there. Because I would not go for the world anywhere to grieve Mother, for a *religious* pleasure, more than for any other pleasure. And although Mr. Wesley's field-preachings are infinitely more than a religious pleasure to Betty and thousands of others, I do not see that they would be so to Cousin Evelyn and me.

We started on two horses, I on a pillion behind Father; Evelyn dressed in as sober attire as she could find in her wardrobe, not to attract too much attention. This, as it happened, was a great comfort (for I must confess Cousin Evelyn's first appearance at our church, in her large straw hat trimmed with flowers, her rich violet silk dress, festooned over her green brocade petticoat, her Paduasoy mantle, scarlet stockings, and leopard skin muff, did considerably distract the congregation); and I should not at all have enjoyed her appearing in any such dainty attire under Mr. Wesley's penetrating eyes at Gwennap.

How little the ancient miners thought, as they cut deep and wide into the lonely hill side of Carn Math, how they were excavating a church for tens of thousands! When we arrived at the place thousands of people were there already, standing about in groups conversing eagerly, or sitting on the rocks and turf in silence, waiting the arrival of the preacher. Still more and more continued to stream in—whole families from lonely cottages on the moors, the mother carrying the baby, and the father leading the little ones, leaving the home empty; companies of miners, with grimy faces and clothes, from the mines; fishermen, with rough weather-beaten faces from the shores. Few of the countenances were dull; many of them were wild, with dark dishevelled hair, eager dark eyes, and rugged, expressive features. Evelyn whispered,—

"If I were Mr. Wesley, I would infinitely rather preach to this wild-looking congregation, than to a collection of the stony, stolid faces of the midland counties, or to a smooth-faced London audience. There is some fire to be struck out of these eyes. How historical the rugged faces are, Cousin Kitty! Dark stories, I think, written on some of them, but some story written on all. I should have thought John Nelson would have done better than Mr. John Wesley here."

He appeared in his blameless clerical black, with the large silver buckles on his shoes—the little compact man with the placid benevolent face. As he stood, the object of the eager gaze of those untaught thousands, so self-possessed, and clerical, and calm, I almost agreed with Evelyn, and longed for the sturdy Yorkshireman, with his stalwart frame, his ready wit, his plain, pointed sense, his rugged eloquence.

But when he began to speak, that wish immediately ceased. The calm, gentlemanly voice, the self-possessed demeanour, made every word come with the force of a word of command. In a few moments every stir was hushed throughout that great assembly.

Before the prayer and preaching began I had been thinking how small a space even these thousands of human beings occupied in the great sweep of the hilly moorland. But when the sermon began, and I looked round on the amphitheatre of earnest intent faces, not the great hills only but the sky and earth seemed to grow insignificant in comparison with any one of the listening, deathless spirits gathered there.

Before Mr. Wesley had uttered many sentences I ceased to look at the audience. My eyes also were riveted on his benevolent face.

And before I had thus looked and listened long I forgot Mr. Wesley himself altogether in the overwhelming love and grace of the pardon he proclaimed.

It was the old inexhaustible good news, that all men being lost and wandering sheep, (and probably not one present needed to have this proved to them,) the Good Shepherd had come to seek and to save that which was lost; that all men being under sentence of death, He that might have claimed the forfeit hath paid the ransom; that the way to eternal joy, once closed by sin and the flaming sword of justice, was now for ever open to all, the sword having been buried in the heart of Him who willingly offered up Himself for us, the flames quenched in His precious blood. The way was open to all; and most earnestly Mr. Wesley invited all to return to God by this "new and living way" then and there.

Soon the sound of subdued weeping directed my attention once more to the multitude around me. The most part were "listening with a close, silent attention, with gravity and quietness, discovered by fixed looks, weeping eyes, and sorrowful or joyful countenances;"* others began to lift up their voices aloud, some softly, some in piercing cries; at one time the whole multitude seemed to break into a flood of tears, when the preacher's voice could scarce be heard for the weeping around him. Many hid their faces and sobbed, others lifted up their voices in an ecstasy and praised God. At moments a deep spontaneous amen rose from all those thousands as from one voice. One or two, not women only, but strong men, sank down as if smitten to the earth by lightning; and these were borne away, sometimes insensible, sometimes convulsed as if with inward agony.

There was a hymn after the sermon. I shall never forget its power. It seemed as if the sluice gate had suddenly been opened, and the whole pent-up emotion throughout that great,

* *Vide* Letter by Ralph Erskine in Wesley's Journal.

silent, listening assembly burst forth at once in a flood of fervent singing.

" Yield to me now, for I am weak,
  But confident in self-despair :
Speak to my heart, in blessings speak,
  Be conquered by my instant prayer:
Speak, or Thou never hence shalt move,
  And tell me if Thy name is love.

" 'Tis love ! 'tis love ! Thou diedst for me,
  I hear Thy whisper in my heart :
The morning breaks, the shadows flee,
  Pure universal love Thou art :
To me, to all, Thy bowels move ;
  Thy nature and Thy name is love."

To hear that hymn so sung by thousands who but for Mr. Wesley might never have known a joy higher than those of brutes that perish, was a joy such as I would have walked, barefoot, a hundred miles to share. And then afterwards to see those whose feelings overcame their natural reserve, going up to Parson Wesley for one shake of his hand, one word of encouragement or welcome, to which they could only respond by a sobbing, "The Lord bless you," or by tears without any words at all ; and others lingering to pour out the grief of consciences awakened to see their sins, but not yet seeing the remedy ; and to observe Mr. Wesley's kindly, patient, discriminating words for each! As Father said (when in the gathering dusk we were riding away among the slowly dispersing multitudes, who seemed scarcely able to tear themselves away),—

"Men who do not know him may talk lightly of these preachings, as a bragging boy at home may talk lightly of a battle. But, right or wrong, it is no light matter. There is power in those words, as there is in a battery, or a thunderstorm ; and, Kitty," he continued softly to me, as I sat on my pillion behind him, "I believe, in my soul, it is power from heaven.   So help me God, I will never say a word against those men again."

And the next evening when we sat around the fire, and Mother said gently, in answer to our description of the scene,—

"I am only afraid that all this excitement will pass away, and leave the poor people colder and harder than it found them,"—

Father replied,—

"Mother, you are as good a woman as there is in the world, and a very gentle touch would set you in the way to heaven; but I tell you some people want a wrench enough to part soul from body to drag them out of the way to hell.   Why, but for such preaching as this nine-tenths of those people would never have prayed except for a 'godsend' in the shape of a wreck, and would scarcely have thought of a church except as a place to be married in or buried near."

"Well, my dear," replied Mother, "we shall see.   By their fruits ye shall know them."

"My dear," exclaimed Father, becoming rather irritated, "I *have* seen.   I do call it good fruit, for ten thousand people to be weeping for their sins, as people commonly weep only for their sorrows; and to feel if it were only for that one hour that sin is the worst sorrow, and the pardon of God and His love the greatest joy."

"And if only *ten* of the ten thousand believe that truth and live by it for ever, Aunt Trevylyan," said Evelyn, "is not that fruit?"

"Yes," said Mother gently, but not very hopefully.   "I am very old-fashioned.   But I confess I am afraid of conventicles."

But afterwards when she was expressing the same dread of religious excitement, and these good feelings passing away, to Betty, Betty replied,—

"Bless you, Missis, *of course* it'll pass away, ninety-nine hundredths of it.   And so does the rain from heaven, goes back to the sea and down into the rocks, and no one knows where. But the few drops that *don't* pass away make the fields green, and bring the harvest."

Every other Sunday evening through the winter a few of our poor neighbours have long been used to gather round the fire in the hall, while Mother reads parts of the evening service, especially the psalms and lessons, with such bits as she thinks they can understand out of the homilies or some of our few Sunday books. We are too far from the church to attend it always twice, and too far for the aged and sickly of our neighbours to attend it at all; besides, the fact of the walk to church being one of the stormiest we have. Father says he thinks the legends are right enough in attributing to the devil the choice of the sites of many of our Cornish churches, for they seem placed exactly where it is hardest to get at them.

Last Sunday was the first day this winter our little congregation had assembled. Father had generally found it necessary at such times to be busy about the farm, but this evening he kept hovering in an unsettled way about the room, while Mother, also in an unsettled and nervous state, turned over the leaves of the Prayer-book. At last she called him to her, they spoke for a moment or two softly together, and when the poor old men and women came straggling in I saw a look of surprise on many faces as they whispered to one another,—

"The Captain's going to be parson to-night!"

There was a little tremor in his clear, deep, manly voice as he began,—

"Dearly beloved brethren;" but when he knelt down with us and said,—

"Almighty and most merciful Father, we have erred and strayed from Thy ways like lost sheep," the tremulousness had passed, and deep and firm came out the words of confession and prayer.

When the evening hymn was sung (and I never enjoy the evening hymn as on those Sundays when those poor old quavering voices join us in it), and the neighbours had gone, no one made any remark on the change. Mother sat very quiet all the evening. But now and then her eyes were glistening, and when, as she went to bed, Cousin Evelyn said, mischievously,—

"Dear Aunt Trevylyan, I like *your* little conventicle very much,"—

Mother did not defend herself; she only said,—

"I am not too old to learn, Evelyn, and, certainly, not too old to have much to learn. But God forbid I should be setting my feeble hand against any good work of His."

And from Mother such words as these mean much.

Much as Cousin Evelyn admires our wild coast scenery, her favourite excursions are to the cottages of the fishermen and miners in the hamlets around us.

To-day we went to see old Widow Treffry, Toby's mother. Her cottage lies alone near the entrance of a little sheltered cove guarded by very high cliffs, the points of which the sea has worn into fantastic pinnacles divided by whirlpools of seething waters from the shores. In the calmest weather the steady pressure of the tide through those narrow twisted channels, makes them a perpetual battle-field; the contending waves, writhing in a deadly embrace, dash each other high into the air in jets and flashes of foam, or charge the black rocks with their thundering volleys, to recoil from their jagged edges in cascades into the black caldron below, and be sucked back in a gurgling death-struggle by the retreating wave. But in storms, when winds enter into the strife, the conflict is fearful indeed, as many a brave ship has proved, her strong timbers shivered into a thousand fragments in the mere by-play of the fierce strife of the elements with each other.

Strange relics are washed up on the white sands at the head

of the little creek near Widow Treffry's cottage, and no one wonders much to see a quaint patchwork of the produce and manufactures of various nations, in the rude little dwelling. Rare Indian woods, and mahogany from Honduras, which would be the pride of Aunt Beauchamp's saloons, are mingled with the old deal tables and chairs.

During the last year or two the old woman has recovered strength sufficiently to creep once more about her cottage. This morning we found her in a very rare attitude for her, thrifty, stirring old creature that she is. She was crouching close to the fire with her elbows on her knees, while from the chamber within came every now and then the sound of a low moan.

"Is it the rheumatism again, granny?" I said.

"Worse than that, worse than that, Mrs. Kitty," she moaned, scarcely moving or noticing either of us. "Toby's gone mazed, clean mazed, all through the Methodists. He came home from one of their preachings last week like one out of his mind, and so he's been ever since; bellowing like a bull one hour, and moaning like a sick baby the next. He says it's all along of his sins. And what they be worse than other folk's I can't see at all! The Lord is merciful, and if He sends us a 'godsend' now and then, He surely means us to be the better of it. It wasn't us who rose the storm. And Toby never set a false light on the rocks, nor gave any man a push back into the sea, like some other folks. And if, as he keeps crying out, he didn't take the pains he might, always, to bring the drowned to life, it can't be expected we should do the same for Indians and Popish foreigners as for our own flesh and blood. Would they do more for us? And if he *has* picked up a stray bit of good luck now and then, were we to save things for the dead, or for the folks from London who come prowling about where they've no business, with their pens and paper, to rob them who've got the natural right to what the Almighty sends on the shore?

Yesterday I got Master Hugh to him, and he prayed like an
angel, and did him a sight of good for the time; but to-day he's
worse than ever, he's gone clean mazed, and swears he'll go and
give up everything he ever got from a wreck to the Justices.
And that," continued the old woman, breaking into a wail,
"that's what I call throwing the Almighty's gifts back in His
face."

At this moment Toby's face appeared at the door of the inner
chamber, pale, and haggard, and wild. But his voice was quite
calm and steady as he said,—

"Mrs. Kitty, I told Master Hugh, and he said it was the
right thing to do; and Parson Wesley said the same, when I
heard him on the moors. He said the Bible speaks of ' *the*
fire,' and of ' *their* worm,' and that that means that every sinner
who is lost in hell will have *his own* torment made out of his
own sins. And he said that worm begins to gnaw at our souls
now when we are wakened up to feel our sins. And the words
had hardly left his mouth, Mrs. Kitty, when there was the gnawing begun in my heart! And it has never stopped since. And
if it has made me faint away like a sick woman with the anguish,
and has most driven me mazed in a week, what would it be for
ever? For Parson Wesley said there's no fainting away and
no going mazed in hell. We shall always be wide awake to feel
the torment. But, Mrs. Kitty, he said there is a way of escape
now for all, and for me. He said there is a way to have our
sins forgiven. He said the Almighty gives His pardon as free
as air, and the blood of the Lord can wash all the sins of the
world whiter than snow. But he and Master Hugh both say,
the Lord sees us through and through, and there's no way of
making Him believe we are sorry for our sins but by giving
them up, and making up for them as far as we can. They say
sin and hell go together, and can't be parted, nohow. So I've
nothing to do but to go to the Justices."

Evelyn was deeply moved, and when we reached home and

told Mother, she wept many tears, and said at length as she wiped her eyes,—

" Kitty, my dear, I cannot make out about the rubrics and the canons. They were made by very holy men; and Mr. Wesley does not seem to mind them as one would wish, and I cannot think it wise to set ignorant men up to preach and teach. But his words are those of the Prayer-book and Bible. And his works are those of an angel sent from God. And what can we do but give God thanks?"

" I used to be afraid," she continued, after a pause, "that Mr. Wesley's was blind fanatical zeal, well meant but misguided; but the zeal cannot surely be fanatical which spends itself in labours of love; nor blind, since it leads so many into the light."

" Mr. Wesley says," responded Evelyn, " that *true zeal is but the flame of love,* and that all zeal is false which is full of bitterness, or has not love for its inspiration."

And Mother said, thoughtfully,—

" *His* zeal will certainly stand that test. God forbid that *ours* should not."

VIII

T *is* a trouble, certainly, about Hugh and the parish, and I don't think it helps me at all to try and think it is not. Because I *have* tried to persuade myself that we could be quite as happy and as useful elsewhere, and have succeeded again and again; yet it always comes back how dear the old home is, and how the people love "Master Hugh," and how impossible it is for any one to be to them what he could, or for him to be to others what he is to them.

So that I have come to the conclusion that it is best to confess to Hugh and to myself that it is a trouble, and rather a great trouble, and to confess this also to God, and then, with all my heart, to trust myself and mine to Him and to submit.

I have also felt much perplexed as to what submission really is, whether we ought really to *like* all that happens to us, as well as to take it without complaining.

But Hugh says submission does not mean that we are to call bitter things sweet, or to try to feel them so; but that we are to take them, however we dislike them, without a murmur, being sure that the bitterest are really good because God sends them.

We are to yield up our hearts a *living* sacrifice to God, he says, with all their joys and sorrows, and fears and hopes, just as they are, not dried into insensibility, or frozen from a fountain of life and feeling to an icy conglomeration of principles.

He says it is a good test to ask ourselves in any trial, "If we could, would we take the choice out of God's hands into our own?"

And I do find this test comforting, for if God were to say to us this very day, " Choose which you think best," I do feel sure both Hugh and I would say from our inmost hearts, " Lord, we cannot see what is best. Do Thou choose for us." And He *has* chosen for us without offering us the choice ; and that, after all, is just the same.

It was a very bright future that seemed to spread out before us, when poor Dr. Spencer died. We had so many plans, Hugh and I, for getting at every cottage in the parish, and ministering to the sick and aged, and collecting the children to teach them, and inducing the men and women to come to church. I pictured the old church full of earnest attentive faces, such as we had seen at Gwennap Pit, drinking in the " words of this life " from Hugh's lips, and " in their eagerness and affection ready to eat the preacher," as Mr. Wesley said.

And Mother there too, and Father, and by-and-by Jack,— all in the old pew Sunday after Sunday, receiving help and comfort from Hugh's words !

But I must not think of it now. It is a great blessing Mother does not think so badly of the Methodists as she used, or it would have been a terrible sorrow to her to know that Hugh had lost the living because the patron had heard he had "a dangerous leaning to the Methodists."

Cousin Evelyn is especially indignant because the clergyman appointed instead of Hugh is her great-uncle, the Fellow of Brazennose, who has exchanged a living in the East of London for this. She says he is a mere dry scholar, and only looks on human beings in general as a necessary but very objectionable interruption to books.

Men and women, she says, begin to be interesting to him when they have been dead about a thousand years, and his sermons will probably be either elementary treatises on the impropriety and danger of stealing, and resisting magistrates, or acute dissections of the controversies of the ante-Nicene centuries, which Betty will have to apply as best she can.

Hugh told me first of this appointment when we were alone. We had walked to our own dear old cave. The tide was very low, and we had wandered on over the sparkling sand almost to the very entrance of the little bay. The ebbing waves broke feebly on the shore, as if they felt the struggle hopeless, and only continued it with a kind of sullen courage, as a warfare they had to wage whether it succeeded or not.

And as we paced up and down there Hugh told me of the change which makes all our future uncertain. But he told it me in such a way as made me feel, I scarcely know how, a kind of sad pleasure. I felt it was the first trial we had had to bear *together*. And it is certainly a wonderful help in trouble to have some one else for whom we must try to lighten it.

Besides, Hugh's presence is such an unutterable help and comfort, that it is only since he has left me that I have felt really what the trouble is.

After a little while he said,—

"Kitty, do you remember that evening in the ship on our way from Bristol, when I spoke of God's calling us to preach His gospel to those who had never heard it?"

I remembered it but too well, and the recollection seemed to benumb me; the three calls he had spoken of; the call in God's Word to proclaim it, of His voice in the heart, and the call of His providence. The last only had been wanting then. It flashed on me, only too clearly, that nothing was wanting now.

"So many can do the work at home, Kitty," he said, "and so few have health, or leisure, or means for the work abroad; and since the one place in the world which was home to us, to which we had ties it seemed wrong voluntarily to break, is closed—what ought I to do?"

"Oh, do not ask *me* to decide, Hugh!" I said; "only decide and I shall be sure it is right."

"It is a sacrifice we can only make *together*, Kitty," he said.

"I cannot leave Mother and Father alone, Hugh," I said, "now that Mother is so feeble, that we may wander about the world together." '

"It would be little sacrifice to me, Kitty," he said in a very low voice, "if you could."

We did not speak for some minutes. I felt how truly the sacrifice was for us both, and how very great it was. At last I commanded my voice to say,—

"Hugh, I *cannot* judge what is right for you, because I cannot know what you feel; but if you do indeed feel that God is telling you to do this, then it is simply duty and obedience to do it, and it must, of course, be done. And my duty is to help you as much as I can. And I will, Hugh," I said; "and may God help us both."

Then Hugh said a great deal in my praise; I do not mean many words, but a great deal in a few words, about my being fit to be a great hero's wife, and about no man having ever been given such a brave tender heart to sustain and inspire him as mine.

And I am afraid I was fool enough to believe what he said, not remembering how much I have always to put down to his love, and not to my excellence. For I did actually begin to feel myself quite a heroine, until Hugh went away, and I came into the kitchen and saw Betty polishing up one of the old oaken chairs Hugh and I had foraged out from the lumber-room for our home that was to be. And that broke down all my high courage at once, and sent me to my chamber to cry bitterly, all by myself, and to learn what kind of a heroine or hero's wife I should make.

And that is a week since, yet I have never found courage to

tell Mother of Hugh's purpose, or scarcely to look at the rooms which were to have been Hugh's and mine.

I have told Evelyn, however, and she enters into it with all the noble enthusiasm of her character. Cousin Evelyn, indeed, would have made a wife for a hero, or a heroine in her own person. She talks beautifully of the wonderful joy of teaching the truth that makes the heart free to the poor slaves in the West Indies, and of preaching the life-giving gospel to the · American colonists who have never perhaps heard of it except as a faint echo of what their forefathers were taught. There are scarcely twenty clergymen, she says, in all the southern colonies, and many of those are men who have taken refuge there, because their characters were too bad for them to remain in England any longer. And then, she says, there are the convicts, our outcast countrymen, working out their sentences beside the negroes in the plantations.

"How they must *want* the consolations of the truth," she said, "and what a glorious destiny to carry it to them."

Cousin Evelyn seems to feel for these people and their wants as if she had seen them. But it is always so difficult for me to feel anything like real love and interest for masses of unknown people. If I had *seen one* of those poor slaves, had *known* the temptations and sins of *one* of those poor convicts, it would be so different. And here at home I know every man, woman, and child ; and it was such a delight to think of Hugh teaching and helping them all !

When the Bible says, "God loved the world," it means that He knows and loves every individual man, woman, and child in it—loves and pities each one according to the needs, and character, and sorrows of each. But we? When we talk of loving a whole mass of people in America, of not one of whom we know anything, what does it mean? If half of them were to be swallowed up by an earthquake, I might be sorry for the rest ; but I should not shed as many real tears as if anything melancholy were to happen to Betty or Roger. And our hearts do not beat quicker for hearing of their prosperity and joys.

To hear that thousands of them really repented and had found forgiveness and peace through believing in our Lord Jesus Christ, would certainly give me great pleasure; but it would scarcely make my whole heart glad as it would to know that poor Toby Treffry was able to rejoice in his Saviour, and was proving the sincerity of his repentance by doing all the good he could.

I ventured to speak of this, a few days since, to Hugh. I am afraid it is such a great defect in me not to be able really to love a multitude of people I have never seen, as other Christians seem to do. But Hugh did not seem much troubled: he only said,—

"Kitty, our Father in heaven really loves those multitudes, each one of them. Our Saviour shed real tears over such, and really died for them all. And you love Him. Is not that enough to make you care to help them?"

And that did help me; for I feel that is enough. It would have been reward for any toil or any sacrifice to cause one look of joy to beam on the face of our Saviour when it was buffeted and crowned with thorns for us. And He is the same, and the joy of pleasing Him the same, now.

I have told Mother Hugh's purpose of going as an evangelist to America. And she is not displeased. She says she has often wondered how it was that the kingdom of Christ has not seemed to spread for so many years; that it should be limited to one quarter of the world when all the rest are still lying in darkness. She even said that she would have thought it her greatest glory that a son of hers should have gone on such an errand to the outcast, and wretched, and lost.

Cousin Evelyn has been urging much that we should all

14

return with her to London. She says dear Mother has a very delicate and suffering look, and she feels sure some of the learned physicians Aunt Beauchamp knows could restore her to health, since there seems nothing dangerous the matter. Moreover, change of air, she says, works wonders, especially with a little troublesome unconquerable cough such as Mother has.

Betty, on the other hand, is very much opposed to the move. She says it is a plain flying in the face of Providence. The Almighty, she says, knows what is the matter with Missis, and He can cure her, if she is to be cured; and if not, all the journeys from one end of the world to the other will do nothing but wear out her strength the sooner. Least of all should she expect any good thing to come out of London, which she considers a very wicked place, where people dress in purple and scarlet, and fare sumptuously every day.

She knows indeed, "sure enough," (this in answer to my humble remonstrance) that we are to "use the means;" but she will never believe that it is using the means to fly all over the country, like anything mazed, after doctors. There is peppermint and horehound, and a sight more wholesome herbs which the Almighty has set at our doors. And there's a doctor at Falmouth who has blooded, leeched, and blistered all the folks for fifty years; and if the folks haven't all got better, there's some folks that never *will* get better if you blooded and blistered them for ever. She says also that there is plenty against doctors in the Bible, and nothing for them that ever she saw. King Asa got no good by seeking after them, and the poor foolish woman in the Gospels spent all her living on them and was nothing better but rather worse. She hopes it may not be the same with Missis, although if it were, she adds significantly, it is not Missis she should blame, poor, dear, easy soul!

Nevertheless Evelyn has carried her point, and in a week we are to start.

To-day Hugh and I went to bid Widow Treffry good-bye. She was out, but we found Toby cowering over the fire in much the same hopeless attitude as Evelyn and I had found his mother. He had been to the Justices, he said, and given up the purse, but he was no better.

"Master Hugh," he said, in a hollow, dry voice, (which made me think of the words, "All my moisture is turned into the drought of summer,") "Master Hugh! I do believe that poor hand that clutched the purse was dead! They say dead hands do clench fast like that. But yet, I'd give the world to have that poor lad's body on the sands again, just to bring it up to the fire and chafe it as Mother did Father's when he was brought home drowned. All her chafing and wailing never brought Father's eyes to open again. And it *mightn't* that poor lad's. Oh, Master Hugh, the devils may say what they will, but I do think it *wouldn't*. But oh, I'd give the world to try!"

"Toby," said Hugh, very gently, stooping down, and taking both his hands, so that his face was uncovered, and he looked up. "Toby, you will never see that poor lad's face on the sands again."

"Don't I know that, Master Hugh?" said Toby, with almost a sob of agony.

"Suppose that poor lad *was not* quite dead," Hugh continued, "and you *might* have brought him to life, what would your crime be?"

"Oh, don't make me say the word, Master Hugh," said the poor fellow. "I can't, I can't, though the devils seem yelling it in my ears all night."

"It would have been *murder!*" said Hugh, very distinctly and slowly, in a low solemn tone.

Toby trembled in every limb, his eyes were fixed, and he opened his lips but could not bring out a word. Convulsively he sought to pull his hands from Hugh's grasp as if to hide his face from our gaze. But Hugh held him fast, and looked at him with steadfast kind eyes.

"It would have been murder!" he repeated. "But there is pardon even for murder. The thief on the cross had committed murder, I have no doubt, for he felt crucifixion no more than he deserved. King David had committed murder, and had meant to do it. Listen how David prayed when he felt as you do."

And Hugh repeated the fifty-first Psalm. As he spoke the fixed look passed from Toby's face. He was listening; the words were penetrating. When Hugh came to the verse, "Purge me with hyssop, and I shall be clean; wash me, and I shall be whiter than snow," he said, "The hyssop was an herb with which the blood of the slain sacrifices was sprinkled on the guilty. That prayer is clearer to us, Toby, than it was to King David, for since then the Lord Jesus has really offered himself up for us, and His blood cleanseth us from *all* sin, and cleanses us whiter than snow, so that we may start afresh once more." And then he repeated on to the end of the Psalm.

"There *is* forgiveness, you see, even for murder. Suppose it possible that the tempter is right, Toby, in whispering that terrible word to your conscience. Yet he is *not* right when he says 'there is no forgiveness for you.' That is the lie with which he is seeking to murder your soul. You must meet whatever terrible truth he says, by laying your heart open to God, and confessing all to Him; and you must meet the devil's lie with the truth, 'The blood of Jesus Christ cleanseth from all sin.' There is nothing else that can; and I am sure if you do this the devil will flee, and you will overcome and be saved."

We knelt down and prayed together, and as we rose Toby gasped out, "God bless you, Master Hugh! You do think that there is hope!"

Before we went, Hugh found Widow Treffry's Prayer-book and set Toby to learn the fifty-first Psalm. When we left, he was sitting toiling at it, spelling it over as if it had been a letter written fresh from heaven for him.

"I hope I was not abrupt and harsh," Hugh said as we walked home, "but I felt the poor fellow's anguish was too real to be lightly cured, that the *only chance* was to probe it to the bottom. It is a blessing for Toby that reading is such hard work for him. Every verse he reads costs him more labour than carrying a heavy load up from the shore. The work will bring calm to his poor bewildered mind, so that he will be better able to estimate what his sin really is. And the words I do trust will bring peace to his poor tossed heart."

And Hugh and I were to have spent our lives in bringing such help and comfort to our neighbours in their sorrows and bewilderments! But I will not murmur. If I could see all the way instead of only a step, I should wish things to be exactly as God orders them, so I will trust Him who does see all the way.

A letter has come at last from Jack. It is short and full of the most exuberant spirits. He has been in one or two skirmishes, which he describes at some length. He is longing for a battle. Hitherto his adventures have only brought him a scratch or two, a little glory, and some friends. He mentions one or two young noblemen as his intimate companions, at whose names Evelyn looked doubtful. She says they had the reputation in London of being very wild, and one of them is a notorious gambler. He finds his pay, he says, very nearly sufficient, so far, with prudence, and the kind *parting gifts* he received at home. A young officer, he says, and the son of an old Cornish house, must not be outdone by upstart fellows, the sons of Cockney tradesmen; and if he is now and then a little behindhand, some good luck is sure soon to fall in his way, and set all right.

He has not yet made his fortune. But there are yet cities

to be won, and after all, he remarks, there are nobler aims in life than to make fortunes.   In a postscript he adds,—

"Tell Kitty that some of her friends the Methodists have found their way to Flanders.   Some of these fellows have actually hired a room, where they preach and sing psalms, and make loud, if not 'long' prayers to their hearts' content.   They are, of course, laughed at unmercifully and get pretty rough usage from their comrades, which they receive as their portion of martyrdom, due to them by apostolical succession, and seem rather to glory in.   But we must give even the devil his due, and I must say that one or two of the best officers we have, and our colonel among them, will not have them reviled.   Our colonel made quite a sermon the other day to some young ensigns who were jeering at a Methodist sergeant.   'Keep your jests till you have smelt as much powder and shot as he has,' said the colonel; and as we were turning away, he continued, 'At Maestricht I saw one of them (poor Stamforth) shot fatally through the leg; he had been a ringleader in vice before he became a Methodist, and as his friend was carrying him away, (for they stick to each other like brothers) the poor dying fellow uttered not a groan, but said only, "Stand fast in the Lord." And I have heard them, when wounded, cry out, "I am going to my Saviour!" or, "Come, Lord Jesus, come quickly!" When Clements, one of their preachers, had his arm shot off, he would not leave the battle; he said, "No, I have another arm to hold my sword; I will not go yet."   When a second shot broke his other arm, he said, "I am as happy as I can be out of Paradise."   I saw the preacher, John Evans, laid across a cannon to die, both his legs having been shot off, and I heard him praising God and calling on all to love Him, till he could speak no more.   I call that a brave death for any man.   Indeed,' said the colonel, 'it might be better for all of us if we were more like them.   Drinking and dicing may be very gentlemanly amusements, but they don't make quite so good a

preparation for a battle or a hospital-bed as the psalm-singing
and preaching you despise. At least,' he added, rather sar-
castically, 'not for privates and non-commissioned officers. It
is easier at all events to collect the men from the meeting-house
than from the tavern, and on the whole their hands are steadier.
But however that may be, in my regiment I choose to have
religious liberty.' And," concluded Jack, "some of the young
officers went away looking rather foolish, for there had been a
little difficulty in our last affair, in collecting officers who were
sober enough to lead the men. And we all know our colonel
is not a man to be trifled with."

" I am glad Jack has such a commanding officer," said Father.
" But as to those Methodists, Kitty, they seem to overrun the
world, like the locusts."

To-morrow we are to start for London, Mother, and Father,
and Hugh and I.

It is getting late, but I must write down a few words Cousin
Evelyn has just said, before I pack up my Diary, because they
have made me so thankful and happy.

We had been speaking about dear Mother's illness, and about
the journey.

Cousin Evelyn said,—

" Do you remember, Cousin Kitty, my being so shocked at
your idea of praying about a love-letter? I have learned since
then, we may pray about *everything*. And when I do, Kitty,
nothing seems too great to do or to bear, or too little for God
to care for. Often I have been lost in wonder at seeing such
majesty as His stoop to such requests as mine. But since I
have been with you," she continued, " I wonder at it less."

" Wonder less at the condescension of God?" I said.

" Yes, Kitty," she said, " I wonder less, and adore more.
For in your home I have learned more of what love is than I

ever knew before. And I see that love explains everything. It is no wonder that love should stoop to any care or rise to any sacrifice. The only wonder is *the love;* that GOD should love *us.* But *He does;* and that explains all." Then she took my hands in hers, and fixed her large dark eyes on me with that soft wistful look which always goes so far into my heart, and she said, " O Kitty, how much you have taught me!"

" Taught you, Cousin Evelyn!" I said; " why, you have more thoughts in a day than I have in a year."

" You dear, foolish, wise, little Kitty!" she said, " as if *thoughts* made people wise! Do you not know that there are more power and more wisdom in one true loving heart than in all the wise heads in the world? Yes, more power," she added, " for compared with love *things* are mere *shadows;* we really possess nothing except as love inspires us to use it; and compared with love *thoughts* themselves are only the mere inanimate *things* that are moved; whilst love is the wind, the fire, the sun that moves and quickens all; the motive force, the life-giving power of the world."

Our journey to London was like a holiday-trip all the way, after Aunt Beauchamp's coach met us at Plymouth. It was stored by the especial care of Aunt Beauchamp's housekeeper, with a travelling larder of plum-cake, Dutch gingerbread, Cheshire cheese, Naples biscuit, neats' tongues, cold boiled beef, bottles of usquebaugh, black cherry brandy, cinnamon water, and strong beer, to which were added sundry homely manufactures of Betty's in the shape of pasties and pies, and a private store of Mother's containing various wholesome and medicinal herbs. Two old servants had been sent on horse-back to guard us from the dangers of the way; and two Flemish cart-horses were added to the four sleek carriage-horses to pull our massive machine up the Devonshire hills, or out of the deep ruts in the miry roads through the marshy grounds of Somersetshire. In addition to our escort, Hugh rode beside us armed with two pistols, and Father, inside the coach with us, carried a loaded cavalry pistol; so that we could have opposed a formidable front even to a combined attack of mounted highwaymen. We met, however, with no adventure beyond being once or twice nearly "stugged," as Roger would say, in the mud, and once or twice being, as he would believe, "pisky-led," and missing our way, and being belated on the moors.

Mother's conscience was rather disturbed by the pomp in which we travelled, especially when the landlords and landladies came bowing and courtesying to receive "her ladyship's orders."

" Kitty, my dear," she said, "I really think I ought to tell them this is not our coach. I feel like an impostor."

She was consoled, however, by the reflection that but for a few accidents as to priority of birth, Father might have been riding, by his own right, in a coach quite as magnificent; wherefore for his sake she abstained from such confessions. And during our brief stay at the various inns she generally penetrated deep into the medical confidences of chambermaids and landladies, so that by the time that we reached London her store of bitters and lotions had sensibly diminished.

We did not enter the city till midnight, by which time the street-lamps are all extinguished; so that we plunged into the deep puddles and ruts, in spite of our huge coach lanterns and two volunteer link-boys, who terrified Mother by flaring their torches at the windows. Once or twice her terrors were increased by encountering some noisy parties of gentlemen returning drunk from various entertainments, and showing their valour by knocking down the poor old watchmen, or wrenching off the street-knockers. One of these parties actually surrounded our coach, armed with pistols, bludgeons, and cutlasses, with hideous yells and demoniacal laughter; when Father (Hugh having left us), taking them for highwaymen, presented his cavalry pistol with some very strong military denunciations, at the head of one, demanding to know their names, whereupon the whole company decamped, leaving Father in great wrath at the constables, the king's ministers, and the whole "sluggish Hanoverian dynasty."

At length we arrived at Great Ormond Street, to Mother's unspeakable relief. She recommended me to add to my devotions selections from the Form of Thanksgiving after a Storm with that after Victory or Deliverance from an Enemy ; "for certainly, Kitty, my dear," she said, "at one time I thought we were in the jaws of death, and gave up all for lost—our goods, and even our lives. And now being in safety, we must give all praise to Him who has delivered us."

Hugh and I had more than one quiet talk by the way. The last was one evening when we had arrived at an inn early in the day, and were taking a walk in a wood near at hand, when the first primroses were beginning to dart up little golden flames through the earth. We were speaking of Jack's letter, and I was saying how his principles about money troubled me, and especially his delusion of imagining it is generosity to spend more than you have, and then beg of other people.

Hugh said, "It is very difficult for people to be convinced of faults which go with the grain of their character. If a man of tender feelings says an unkind word, it rankles in his conscience for days ; while a hard man inflicts a score of wounds in a day on his family and dependants, and never has a reproachful pang. A truthful person will not be easy until he has repaired an accidental inaccuracy; whereas a man who habitually boasts and exaggerates, tells a hundred lies or conveys a thousand false impressions in a day, and never feels a weight on his conscience. I suppose a miser who has been grinding as much out of every one as he can all his days, living for nothing but to make his hoards more and more, and safer and safer, lies down at night pitying his foolish extravagant brother, and thanking God that he has not the love of money which led his poor tempted neighbour to forge a bank-note. It is easy to repent of the sins which some temptation has led us into *against* the current of our character; but it does seem as if nothing but Almighty power could make us feel the sins which go *with* the current of our characters. And yet this is exactly what constitutes *our sin.*"

"I am so afraid, Hugh," I said, "that Jack actually prides himself on being an open-handed, generous fellow, just on the strength of what seem to me his most selfish acts. And what is to awaken him?"

"Only One Voice can," he replied, gravely, "and no one can say how. Sometimes people are aroused to the sense of their habitual sins by falling into some sin which is against their habits; sometimes by a revelation of the true excellence of which their fault is the parody."

"But," I said, "what you say about our ignorance of ourselves is really fearful. How can we ever know ourselves really?"

"I do not know that we ever can," he said, "any more than we could heal ourselves if we did. There is one prayer which seems to me the only fathoming-line for our hearts,—'Search me and try me, and see if there be any wicked way in me, and lead me in the way everlasting.' God hears us; and with His dews and His storms He does search our hearts, and sweeps and cleanses every corner. Our poor brooms," he added, "only transfer the dust from one corner to another, and often blunderingly remove the soil with the refuse. But God's rains and winds make the ground fruitful as well as pure. That very primrose, Kitty," he said (pointing to one which was springing out of the cleft of an old tree), "a trim gardener would have broomed away the soil on which it has found board and lodging, and impoverished the world of a little world of beauty. Ah! no eye but God's is true enough to search the heart, and no hand but His is tender enough to probe it. Therefore, the strongest weapon which we have with which to help each other is prayer."

It always gives me so much hope to talk these troubles over with Hugh. The mere bringing one's fears into the light is a help; and how much more his faithful counsel! It will be very hard to separate; but he has obtained Father and Mother's consent to our marriage when he has made one or two of his missionary voyages to America. And after all, it will not be more difficult for me than for the betrothed of a sailor or a soldier. So why should we venture to call it a sacrifice?

Aunt Beauchamp was at first full of the most sanguine hopes of curing Mother. She had herself (she declared) experienced unspeakable good from a concoction called "angelic snuff," which cured (at least for a time) the most agonizing headaches, the most distressing attacks of vapours; indeed, all and each of the various contradictory and inexplicable maladies to which her sensitive nerves are liable. She knew, moreover, an incomparable doctor who had effected cures that could only be called miraculous; although the ordinary physicians and surgeons, in their bigotry, were narrow-minded and envious enough to ridicule him. This benefactor of his species, after driving about the provinces in a coach-and-six, attended by four footmen in blue and four in yellow liveries, and followed everywhere by the tears and blessings of the grateful multitudes, had settled in London on his fortune; but still, at the entreaties of those who knew his worth, consented to practise in private for the benefit of a few friends of distinction. "He one day showed me," continued Aunt Beauchamp, "a patent from the Sultan of Egypt, a medal from the Emperor of Persia, and a certificate from the King of Bantam; but this was only as an especial favour. The excellent creature has not a particle of vanity in his composition, and sedulously avoids all display."

This gentleman, after many entreaties, at length consented to undertake dear Mother's case.

Feeling her pulse, as Aunt Beauchamp said, " in that inimitable manner of his, at once tender and scientific," and asking a few questions (evidently, Aunt Beauchamp declared, only for form's sake, since he had already anticipated all the answers), he drew from the silken pocket of his laced azure coat a pillbox, which he said he had placed there that very morning, and which contained precisely the one only sovereign remedy for Mother's ailments.

Such penetration and prescience combined Aunt Beauchamp declared to be nothing short of inspiration.

But these laudations he modestly disclaimed as extravagant. " The medical faculty," he admitted, " like the poetical, like beauty (and he bowed profoundly to Aunt Beauchamp), could not be made or called up at will. The gift was congenital; it was incommunicable." Beyond this he humbly disclaimed any merit.

Then, after minutely describing the nature of Mother's symptoms in English which sounded like Latin, and which delighted Aunt Beauchamp as much as it bewildered me, he took his leave, assuring Mother that, with time, the pills, and reliance on himself, her cure was as good as accomplished.

But whether because Mother's reliance is not perfect, or because she is not a lady of sufficient distinction for such sublime and sovereign remedies, or whether Betty's medical views are right after all, I cannot say ; she is worse rather than better, the noise of the street distracts her, and Aunt Beauchamp is becoming every day more annoyed with her for not recovering, and so doing justice to those marvellous pills ; and accordingly it is decided that we are to move to Aunt Henderson's tomorrow.

I do not find the household in Great Ormond Street the same as when I left. Evelyn has more to suffer at home than she ever hinted to me; not, indeed, exactly persecution, but little daily annoyances which are harder to bear—those little nameless irritations which seem to settle like flies on any creature that is patient and quiet, as Evelyn certainly is.

Poor Aunt Beauchamp has become fretful and irritable, and keeps up a continual gentle wail against Evelyn and her eccentricities. Cousin Harry, from his masculine heights of the racecourse and the gaming-table, treats her "Methodism" with a lofty superiority as a feminine peculiarity.

Uncle Beauchamp alternately storms and laments. He was very seriously annoyed at her refusing the neighbouring Squire, whom she mentioned in her letter to me, and since then has absolutely forbidden her attending any of those "canting conventicles," as he calls the preachings at Lady Huntingdon's, the Tabernacle, or the Foundry. Moreover he actually made an *auto-da-fe* of all her religious books. But this Evelyn considers to have been rather a help than a hindrance, as at the particular time when her further acquaintance with this literature was arrested, it was falling deep into fiery controversy concerning the Calvinistic and Arminian doctrines; and she says she finds it more profitable to draw the water of life from the source, before the parting of the streams. By the time the streams are open to her again, she hopes they will have met once more, and each have left its own deposit of mud behind.

But although I have seen her face flush and her lip quiver often at many an unjust and bitter word, she will by no means be pitied.

" I am so sorry for you all," I ventured to say to her one day; " I wish you understood each other. You have many things to suffer, dear Evelyn."

" I am no martyr, Cousin Kitty," she replied, with something of her old scornfulness, though it was turned on herself; "and please do not try to persuade me I am. Half my troubles are no doubt brought on by my own wilfulness, or want of tact;

and the other half are not worth calling troubles at all. I think we sometimes miss the meaning and the good of little trials, by giving them too long names. We bring a fire-engine to extinguish a candle, and the candle probably burns on, while we are drenched in our own shower. We take a sword to extract a thorn, and drive it further in. It is a great thing to know at what page to look for our lessons, because if we look for the multiplication-table among the logarithms, we shall probably persuade ourselves we are advanced scholars, yet not be clear about two and two making four."

"But, Cousin Evelyn," I said, "we must not, I think, on the other hand, call God's chastening rod a trifle, because I suppose He means it to hurt us, if it is to do us good. And all the time, while we are setting our faces not to show the pain, He knows it *is* hurting us, and perhaps He is only waiting for us to be humbled and to sob out our sorrow at His feet, to lay it aside and take us to His heart. At least, Cousin Evelyn," I said, "I think I have found it so sometimes."

She coloured, her lip quivered, and, after a little struggle with herself, she looked up with her eyes full of tears, and said, in a broken voice,—

"It does hurt me, Kitty, oh, so much, so terribly! Perhaps after all it was pride and not humility that made me try to think it did not. But I was so afraid of flattering myself that I was a martyr, and that I was suffering for my virtues and not for my faults. If *you* had been in my place, Kitty," she said, "I have thought so often you would have made them all love you and religion together."

"Dear Evelyn," I said, "perhaps I might have made them content with me, it is so natural to me (as to all creatures without horns, and hoofs, and stings) to creep out of difficulties. And perhaps I might have persuaded myself that, in escaping reproach, I was recommending religion. But our blessed Lord did not make every one pleased either with religion or with

Him. And when we have really painful things to take up and bear, unless we glide out of the way to avoid them, I think it ought to help us to remember what He said about taking up our cross."

"But, Kitty," she said, "the cross! think what it was to Him—shame, agony, death, worse than death. Shall I call my little discomforts crosses?"

"Jesus said, Every one who followed Him was to take up His cross," I said.

"He did," she replied thoughtfully. Then looking up with one of her bright looks, she said,—

·· "Well, Kitty, nothing on earth shall persuade me I should not get on better with every one, if I *were* better! But perhaps some little portion of my troubles could *not* be avoided; and if this is my cross, it certainly makes it feel lighter to call it so; remembering that if it hurts me so much, it is not so much because it is so heavy, as because I am such a child, and so little used to bearing anything. So, Kitty," she continued, "by no means draw my portrait as a meek-eyed maiden bowed down under a picturesque burden beautifully fashioned into the shape of a cross; but as a foolish and awkward little child, stumbling along under a load which other people could lift with their fingers. But, O Kitty," she said, her whole countenance suddenly changing into an expression almost of anguish, "what miserable selfishness to talk of *my* burdens! Think of the void, the pangs of those who are dying from the hunger of their hearts for God, and will not call it hunger, but 'sensibility,' or 'repressed gout,' or 'the restlessness of youth,' or 'the irritability of old age,' or 'the inevitable worries of life,' or anything but that great hunger of the souls God created for Himself, which proves their immortality, and proves their ruin, and might lead them to Him to be satisfied. How am I to help them to find it out?"

"You can *pray*, Cousin Evelyn, and show them your whole

soul has found that rest in God ; and the time will surely come when you may tell them how.   Who knows how many of the bitterest words come from the sorest hearts? No doubt the writhing of his poor hands on the nails, and the very sight of the patience of Jesus on the cross beside him, made the reviling of the thief all the bitterer.   But in another moment that divine patience had overcome : the railing was changed to— 'We indeed justly ;' the reviling to—'This man hath done nothing amiss ;' the curses into—'Lord, remember me ;' and the agonizing beginning of an eternity of anguish into the— 'Paradise to-day.'   Ah, Evelyn," I said, "who knows how near the joyful answer to your prayers may be? who knows how soon your cross may blossom into a tree of life?"

She made no reply for some minutes; she had buried her face in her hands.   But when she looked up again, it was with a look clear and solemn and awed and bright as a child's in prayer, and she said,—

"Kitty, I think I understand better.   Henceforth I will not try to trip on under my burden as if it were nothing.   I will confess to myself and to God when it wounds, and humbly ask Him to lighten or to heal.   But hope shall make my tread lighter than ever pride could.   For who knows indeed how soon my cross may blossom into a tree of life?   It is in the nature of all crosses made from the fragments of His, is it not?   Not *nothing*, Kitty.   Our trials are not even trifles; they are the precious withering grains of a harvest of eternal joys ; they are the fiery furnace of incorruptible graces for us, and, perhaps, for others too."

We are at Hackney, Father, and Mother, and I.   This grave orderly household, too, is changed.

Cousin Tom is gone.   I knew he had made a voyage to America, but until I came here I thought it was only on some business of his father's.

But when I asked Uncle Henderson for him, he scarcely made any answer, so that I felt something was wrong. And the first time I was left alone with Aunt Henderson, to my great amazement she sat down, and covering her face, burst into a flood of tears. I think I should scarcely have been more surprised if it had been the stone effigy of the lady in a ruff in our church at home, or more entirely at a loss what to do to help her.

"Ah, Kitty," she sobbed out at length, "Kitty, child, you loved the poor lad, you were always kind to him; and he loved you like a sister. And I must speak. Your uncle won't have his name mentioned. He calls him an ungrateful wretch, an Absalom, and says he is not going to behave like king David in his dotage, that he will never have him under his roof again. My poor Tom, my boy, my only son !"

"But what has he done?" I asked; "it cannot be so very bad."

"No !" she exclaimed, passionately, "it is not indeed; it's your uncle's hard, cold, miserable religion that makes him judge the poor lad as he does. Poor Tom," she wailed again, "poor misguided lad, if I'd known better before, he'd never have run away !"

And then she told me how he had come and openly confessed to his father one evening about his going to the theatre and other amusements, and having contracted some debts; and Uncle Henderson had called him a liar and a coward, and had wondered how many more sins he would confess now he had begun; and how Tom had grown crimson, and had said that if it had not been for his Cousin Kitty and John Wesley he would never have confessed what he had, for he believed they had true religion, and they showed him the sin of deception, and the little religion he had got from them was what had given him courage to speak the truth now. And then Uncle Henderson was more angry than ever, and said John Wesley was an

Arminian and a Jacobite, and Tom was a thief and a hypocrite;
and Tom grew very white, and said if he had been a hypocrite
he would be one no more, that he would never set foot in those
Pharisaical meeting-houses again, nor have any more to do with
a religion which had no kind word for the returning prodigal;
and then Uncle had turned purple with anger, and had ordered
him from his presence, and dared him to enter his house again
until he could come on his knees and say he was ashamed and
sorry, as such an ungrateful wretch should be.

"I could say nothing, Kitty," Aunt Henderson continued,
"and I was humbled and bewildered so that I did not know
what to think; but I resolved to go the next morning to the
poor lad's chamber and try to soothe him. But when I went,
O Kitty!" and she broke out sobbing again, "he was gone—
he was gone! The bed was cold; he had been gone for hours.
His chest was there, but not a thing was taken from it except
one change of linen in his little valise. On the table was a
note to me. I have kept it in my bosom ever since."

She gave it to me to read.

"Dear Mother," it said, "we shall be best apart. I trust my
clothes and books will pay my debts, if Father will sell them.
(Here follows a list of the amounts owed—not large.) You
will not grieve much, I hope, at my going, for I have been a
poor comfort to you. I shall write when I have anything good
to tell you. I am going to the American colonies. Perhaps I
may yet live to show Father I am not such a wretch as he
thinks me, and to be more of a son to you than I have been.—
Your poor son,   TOM."

"Ah, Kitty," she said, "he hoped I should not grieve! Poor
dear lad, if he had only known how I loved him! If I could
only see him for a moment to tell him! I am afraid I made
the house too dull for him, Kitty; but I did it for the best. I
thought I had kept him so safe from temptation, and oh, I used
to glory in my foolish heart over poor Sister Beauchamp. I

have little enough to glory in now, and little to comfort me except John Wesley's sermons, which I attended first for his sake, poor fellow; and now and then a talk with Aunt Jeanie and our old gardener. They tell me the good things he said and did, and we cry together over him. They loved the lad; he was a kind lad, Kitty; all the servants loved him. Oh, I might have won him! It might have been so different! But it is too late now. Your uncle has taken a nephew of his from Glasgow into partnership, a hateful, smooth, demure man, who never laughs, or looks you in the face. And this stranger sits at our table and fares sumptuously every day, while our Tom is working for aught I know for a crust of bread."

Poor Aunt Henderson! I had little comfort to offer, but she said it was a comfort to speak of him to one who loves him, as I do.

Aunt Henderson is indeed much changed in many ways. She is softened and humbled; and, even more than that, her heart seems to have opened and grown. She has become a devoted disciple of Mr. Wesley. Yet I cannot say her example is altogether calculated to recommend Methodism to dear gentle Mother, who, not knowing how far trouble and a more humbling religion have altered her, sees only the rather controversial spirit and the self-assertion which yet remain. For the conviction that whatever she did, and believed, and said was the one standard of right, having been rooted out as regarded her domestic life and plans, has taken refuge in her religion. She is vehemently persuaded that Methodism is not only a good thing, but *the one* good thing; that Mr. Wesley's arrangements about his societies and bands, class-meetings, prayer-meetings, and dress and demeanour, are the sole model left upon earth of Scriptural piety; that his Arminian doctrine is the truth, the one truth, which all Christians would receive in every detail if sin did not unhappily darken their eyes. And since no conviction remains passive in her mind, not only does she lay aside every ornament as a vestige of the corrupt world, but she deems it her duty to bear plain testimony on the subject to all around her. Gold and pearls and costly array are, she declares, plainly prohibited to women professing godliness, and she glances significantly at the little gold brooch encircling a lock of Father's hair, with which Mother clasps her neckerchief. The one Scriptural decoration for females, she vehemently and authoritatively asserts, is a meek and quiet spirit. And dear Mother's own meek and quiet spirit has certainly been sorely tried by these attacks against the cherished keepsake which was her one bridal gift, and is her one ornament.

Aunt Henderson's chief controversies, however, are with the cool and demure Scotch nephew. She declares him to be at once a red-hot Calvinist, a lukewarm Laodicean, and a frozen Antinomian. She attacks his doctrines with bitter and fiery assertions of the universal love of God ; and he meets her with cool and irresistible logic about the eternal predestination and final perseverance of the saints, until between them the texts of the Scriptures fly about more like bullets than the sweet dews of life. The Bible seems to become no more than a book of arithmetic—men and women the figures, heaven or hell a kind of sum total, God himself a mere term, and eternity a cipher to give value to the figures.

Aunt Henderson's favourite doctrine, however, is the perfection of the saints in this life. She is very indignant with the Moravians for denying this, and declaring that to the end of life we remain "poor sinners," in daily need of pardon, and only safe in distrust of self. She has several lamentable stories and very severe sayings against this "poor sinnerism" of theirs and its consequences ; although, from what Hugh told me once about the Moravian settlement at Herrnhut, and their self-denying labours among the slaves and outcasts abroad, if by creed they are "poor sinners," in life they seem to be great saints.

But this favourite doctrine of perfection is unhappily precisely the one against which dear Mother thinks herself bound in conscience to do battle. How the love of God to every human being is combined with the election of grace and the perpetuity of faith in the elect, is, she says, a great mystery which she cannot fathom, and will not discuss. But it is no mystery at all to assert that any poor sinful man or woman can ever in this life get beyond the need of confession and daily absolution. Aunt Henderson admits that she herself has never lived under the same roof with one of the "perfect," although she has had many pointed out to her as such in the pews at the preaching-house.

The effect of all this controversy on Mother is to make her cling more than ever, "like a bewildered child" (she says), to the arms of her dear mother the Church. As it is Lent, she and I attend morning and evening prayers every day in a church close at hand, to which Aunt Henderson, as a disciple of Mr. Wesley, cannot openly object, although she drops many strong hints about depending on external ceremonies.

Both Mother and I find the quiet of the old church and the calm lowly devotion of the old prayers very great refreshments. It does seem to me a blessing to have a set of beautiful fixed prayers, which cannot be turned by the party-spirit of the moment against some other section of Christians. Because, when the makers of the Prayer-book itself had to make prayers *against* people (as against the Papists, in the service for the Gunpowder Plot, and against the rebels, in the Restoration service), they did make them so very bitter, they sound very much like curses.

But the controversies recorded in the Prayer-book were finished so very long ago that the bitterness has faded out of most of them for us, and in general there is very little controversy in it except with the world, the flesh, and the devil.

Yet I cannot help seeing that rougher and less melodious

words seem needed to startle people out of their slumber, so
that they may awake and learn to pray at all.

It is rather a relief sometimes when Aunt Henderson's warfare is turned from all the misbelieving Christians against "poor
sister Beauchamp's quack doctor," as she irreverently calls that
benevolent gentleman who failed to cure Mother.

Aunt Henderson has on this subject a theory of her own.
She says it is evident folly to imagine that medicine can be anything but nasty, and the process of being cured anything but
difficult. And this theory she has carried out by inflicting on
the patience of Mother such a series of unpalatable nostrums
and irritating applications, that yesterday Father rebelled on
Mother's behalf; and Aunt Henderson, after expressing her
mind very plainly on the consequences that ensue when people
presumptuously refuse to use the means and expect, ("like the
Calvinists,") to get well, by an irresistible decree, or, (" like the
Moravians,") by "sitting still and doing nothing," has subsided
from a very severe physician into a very tender nurse, overwhelming Mother with beef-teas and jellies, and sick-room deli-
cacies of every description, sparing no trouble or expense in
behalf of her infatuated patient.

It is in this matter of expense that I see the greatest change
wrought on Aunt Henderson by Cousin Tom's flight and Mr.
Wesley's preaching.

With Tom, she seems to have lost the object of saving.
"Why," she says, " should I hoard up for that Antinomian
Scotchman, who is a Jacobite into the bargain, I have little
doubt, if he had the manliness to confess it." And Mr. Wesley's
teaching is no mere mysticism, contemplating the heavens from
a height only to be climbed on Sundays ; and no mere bristling
fence of prohibitory rules. If it is anything, it is "*spirit* and
life," inspiring labours of love, opening the heart, and the hand,
and the purse; it does not sell the trinket to change it into

bank-notes as a better investment; it does teach and inspire to give abundantly and cheerfully, it creates a link between rich and poor, the golden link of common faith working by love.

The most pleasing change in Aunt Henderson's house is in the kitchen, where the servants are now recognized, not as a kind of animated brooms and cooking machines, but as "sisters in the society," and where the sick and aged are bountifully provided for, and hospitably welcomed and fed.

I have watched Uncle Henderson very closely, and I am not sure he does not feel Cousin Tom's departure almost more than Aunt. He is so very silent, and he goes so much less to business; and when his nephew brings him home tidings of the money-market, and the state of trade, and the prospects of his ships, he listens with a kind of forced and languid attention, so different from his old keen though repressed eagerness about loss and gain.

And then what makes him so peculiarly tender to me? He was always kind. But now, when I bring him his pipe or a footstool for his gouty foot, his voice almost trembles as he thanks me. And he said once to Mother that a *daughter* was a good gift from God.

And his hair has grown so white!

Oh! Cousin Tom has done so wrong, has made such a terrible mistake! I am sure he will never find any real peace or good, nor really learn what the love of God is, until he humbles himself and comes back, however hard it may be, and submits.

Unless, indeed, (for I must not presume to make predictions as to the way in which God in His wonderful love may lead any one,) he should learn *first* the love and forgiveness of our Father in heaven, and then come home to confess and amend, and learn the love of his father on earth. For if he only did learn that, he would learn the rest, I have no doubt.

And then we have a little secret hope of our own, Hugh and

I, (for Hugh is gone; he went a week since; but I am not yet able to sit down and write about our parting, it was so very sad!) We hope Hugh and Tom will meet, for he knows all about Tom; and although America is a very large place, it is not so full of people, Hugh says, as Cornwall. And there is more chance of people finding each other on our Cornish moors, I think, than in this crowded London.

But it is not to chance Hugh and I trust. It made it a little easier for me to part with Hugh, to think of this plan of rescuing poor Cousin Tom. It makes me feel as if he were safer—as if that loving plan were a kind of shield thrown around him.

Yet I know Hugh has a better shield than that. And I do not really believe God will take care of him because he has this one good work to do, but because God loves us both—oh, so tenderly!—and because we trust and love Him.

Of all the people Mother has seen in London, she likes Aunt Jeanie best of all. Whenever I miss her, I always know where she is; and when I go across the garden to dear Aunt Jeanie's bed-side (she does not leave her bed now), there I find Mother sitting beside her, singing a hymn of her beloved George Herbert's or perhaps reading one of Aunt Jeanie's beloved Scotch psalms, or, oftener still, the Bible.

Those two have taken a wonderful love for each other, which it is very sweet to me to see.

One day dear Mother was expressing to Aunt Jeanie her great perplexities at all those controversies and divisions of which we have been hearing so much.

"My dear Mistress Trevylyan," said Aunt Jeanie, "I think if we could see back through all the years, we should find it had always been just the same. The apostle Paul was sore tormented with the good people of his time, and their bit notions and fancies. One thought the resurrection was past already;

and a stranger fancy than that has, I consider, never yet possessed any crazy brain among poor sinful mortal men. It is less difficult, surely, even to fancy ourselves or others perfect, than to fancy ourselves raised from the dead ; though I'll not say it's less dangerous. But, my bairns," continued Aunt Jeanie, who, from the height of her threescore and ten, sometimes seems to confound Mother and me in one generation—"my bairns, I think it would be a wonderful help in quarrels among Christians, if, instead of trying to find out how bad each other's mistakes may be, they would try each to find out what the other really means. Now, as to this 'perfection,' Mistress Henderson bewildered me not a little when she began about it. But then I thought, Mr. John Wesley is a good man, and no doubt has his meaning ; not so very far out of the way, perhaps, if we could find it out. But he's a man of a strong will, or he'd not have done and foregone what he has ; and perhaps his will has got mixed up with his faith, and made him say more than he would, if people had tried to understand him right at first. And so, after pondering it over, I came to think that maybe Mr. Wesley had seen too much of people talking of forgiveness, as if it were to make sin easy, instead of making holiness possible, which is, no doubt, its true end—as if their faults could as little be helped as the rain or sunshine. And if Mr. Wesley saw this, I can conceive his honest heart rising against it, and his saying, ' You are not called to keep sinning and repenting ; you are called *to be holy,* to be *perfect.* And what God calls you to be, he means you to be, and will enable you to be.' And that is what I think Mr. Wesley must mean by ' perfection.' The rest followed when he began to cut and shape his desires into a doctrine, and to send it out bristling at all points, to fight its way through the world. It alters a house awfully when it is turned from a home into a fortress, as I've seen done in my time ; when the nurseries are turned into ammunition-rooms, and the fireside into a guard-room ; and great guns bristle out at the windows, where the children's faces used to smile, and the garden fences are spiked into palisades. And it fares sometimes just as ill with doctrines when they have to take to the wars. You would scarcely know them again."

This was a very long speech for Aunt Jeanie; but it comforted Mother greatly, as also what she said one day about the great Calvinistic and Arminian controversy.

"God forbid," said Aunt Jeanie, "that I should think His truth so low or so small as that I could see to the bottom or to the top of it. But I have sometimes thought a great part of the difficulty springs simply from people getting out of God's presence. In the Gospels it is mostly '*I*' and '*ye*' and '*now.*' But when men write theology, they make it '*he*' and '*they*' and '*then,*' which makes all the difference. The Lord says to us, 'Come now,' 'Come ye;' and our now is *to-day,* but His is eternity. I would like to hear John Wesley," she added, "and George Whitefield, and my early friends of the Covenant, and yours (good Mr. Herbert, and the others), on their knees—not *together,* Mistress Trevylyan, in a public prayer-meeting, for the prayers in public are apt to freeze into sermons; but *alone* before God. I think we should find the prayers wonderfully simple, and wonderfully alike."

"Perhaps," said Mother, "before long it may be given you to hear such prayers and to join them, where prayer in the company of the great multitude will be as simple as that in solitude; and where we shall learn all we are to know by looking, not at the past or the future, but into the face of God!"

But when Aunt Jeanie and dearest Mother begin to talk about heaven, it is almost more than I can bear; their faces light up, and their voices grow deep with such an intimate and reverent joy, that it seems as if they must be very near it, and it always makes me tremble.

For Mother does look very wan and thin, and does not improve as we hoped, in spite of all the doctors, and all the care and change.

But Aunt Jeanie says I am one of those who always want to be living on " a land like the land of Egypt, which is watered by the foot." " And very wisely you would water it all, my poor bairn, no doubt, as far as you could," she said. " But the Lord will not have it so," she added, taking my hand in her dear thin old hand, and smiling on me with her old tender smile. " The Lord will not have it so for any of us. He will have us live in ' a land that drinketh of the rain and the dew of heaven.' And although you may have to prove hunger and drought thereby, my poor lambie," she added, solemnly looking upward with a far-seeing look, as if she saw into things invisible, " you'll be sure to find it best in the end; and one day—one day, my sweet bairn—I shall hear you say so. And we shall turn it into a hymn together, you and yours, and I and mine; and it will be a hymn to which all the holy angels will delight to listen. And as far as they can they will join in it; *as far as they can*," she added, rising as she did now and then when very deeply moved it seemed almost unconsciously into prayer, " For, O Lord, Thou tookest not on Thee the nature of angels; and it is we, it is *we* only who can say, ' Thou hast led us all that long way through the wilderness, Thou hast humbled us and suffered us to hunger, and fed us with manna. Thou hast redeemed us to God by Thy blood.'"

IX.

THANK God we are at home again, which a month since I scarcely expected to be.

At Hackney on Friday morning, March the 8th, I was startled out of my sleep in the early dusk before dawn by a heaving and a jarring, which made me think in the confusion of waking that I was at sea again with Father and Hugh, and that the ship had struck against a rock, and was grating over it.

I sprang up instantly, with a vague fear of drowning; but I shall never forget the horror of utter helplessness which followed, when I perceived that it was Aunt Henderson's great crimson-damask four-post bed which was thus tottering—that it was the gigantic polished oak wardrobe whose doors were flying open, and the familiar white jug and basin which were rattling in that unaccountable way against each other.

It flashed on me at once that it was the *earth* that was moving—the solid earth itself heaving like the sea!

My first impulse was to throw myself on my knees by the bed-side. Then I committed myself to God, and felt there was something yet that "could *not* be moved."

Then followed another shock and jarring motion. The fire-irons rattled, the water jug fell and was broken, the wardrobe tottered and strained. And there seemed something more awful in the unwonted noises among those familiar things than there would have been in the roar of a cannonade or any other strange sound.

But besides these noises, and through, and behind, and underneath them, came a low distant rumble like thunder, which yet was not thunder; not above, but beneath, for it seemed quivering through the earth.

I sprang to my feet, and wrapping myself in my great-cloak, rushed out to Mother's room.

The frightened servants were already gathered on the landing, crying that the end of the world was come, and wringing their hands and wondering what would become of mistress, who was gone to the early prayers at the Foundry. Uncle Henderson appeared in a night-cap and blanket, and then Father in a military great-coat.

All had rushed together with the instinct of frightened cattle. No one had thought of striking a light.

I crept to Mother's bed-side, and kneeling down, pressed her hand in both mine.

"My darling," she said, "I am so thankful we are together. If only Jack were here, Kitty! If only I could feel he was safe, whatever happened! Kitty, let us be still, and pray for Jack."

For Mother thought, like most of us, that the end of the world was come.

Another shock, and jar, and rumble of that awful underground thunder; and then a fearful crash above us; and a piercing shriek from all outside, with sobs, and cries of "Lord, have mercy on me!" Another crash, and another burst of shrieks and sobs.

And Mother said nothing, but solemnly clasped her hands in prayer.

Then there came a stillness and a hush in the voices outside, and through the stillness we heard the wind rustling in the tall elm-tree close to the window, and saw that the dusk was slowly creeping into dawn.

And Mother said solemnly,—

"It was to be in the morning, Kitty! At least I always thought so. And O child, it must be less terrible than death! If only I were sure about Jack! What are lightnings and thunders, and the rolling together of heaven and earth as a scroll, compared with the severing of soul and body, of husband and wife, of mother and child? And then," she said, as if that hope absorbed all terror, and all other hopes, "*His appearing!* His glorious appearing! It is to come one day, and suddenly, we are told. Who can say when it may not come?"

It was very strange, the awful apprehension which terrified so many that night out of all their dreams of security, seemed to give Mother a calm and an assurance I never heard her express before.

If at other times the question had been asked her, "Lovest thou me?" she would have answered, "I hope so. I fear it is very little; but I only trust it may be called love."

But now that she thought He might indeed be at hand, all thought of her short-comings seemed absorbed in the thought of Him. She never thought of her love. She loved, and looked for Him.

I remember it all so distinctly, because, after that little prayer by my own bed-side, I cannot think why, but my terror seemed to vanish, and almost my awe. I felt almost ashamed of myself, as if it were an irreverence that I could not feel the apprehension others did. But after all, though the house trembled, it did seem to stand quite firm. And when that great crash came, I could not help thinking it was like a chimney falling; for afterwards I heard the stones and mortar rolling down; and when no harm followed, I thought, "Now all that is likely to fall has come down, and the danger is over."

I felt quite angry with myself for being so insensible; but I could not help it. I suppose it was because I had so little imagination.

In a few minutes I heard Father's voice rising in a tone of quiet command above the sobs of the maids, desiring one of them to bring him a tinder-box. Then the house-door was unbarred, and very soon Father re-entered the room with a light, and said,—

"It is an earthquake, but not very violent. I have felt far severer shocks when I was on service in the West Indies. The crash was the chimney falling through the roof of the old part of the house. The danger is over for the present, but it may recur; and we should be prepared."

Not long after, Aunt Henderson came back in her sedan-chair from the Foundry.

She told us that they were all assembled in the large preaching-house, when the walls were shaken so violently that they all expected the building to fall on their heads. A great cry followed, and shrieks of agonized terror. But Mr. Charles Wesley's voice immediately rose calmly above the tumult, saying, "*Therefore will we not fear though the earth be moved, and the hills be carried into the midst of the sea: for the Lord of hosts is with us; the God of Jacob is our refuge.*" * Evelyn was there, Aunt Henderson said, and observed to her that "it would be worth while to have an earthquake a week, to see the hearts of the people shaken as they were then." "Evelyn is a strange girl, but there is more in her than I thought," she concluded.

And I thought, "How strangely we shall all be revealed to each other, when the Day really comes which will strip off all disguises and take the blinding 'beams' out of all eyes!"

The danger was not over. One messenger after another continued to arrive with accounts of the tottering walls and falling chimneys they had seen, and with wild incoherent rumours of the ruin and destruction of which they had heard.

At eight o'clock Aunt Beauchamp's coach drove up to the

* *Vide* Wesley's Journal.

door, and she herself crept out of it with Evelyn, her gray hair streaming in dishevelled locks under her hood, her face wan and haggard with terror and the absence of rouge.

" My dearest sister," she exclaimed, throwing herself hysterically into Aunt Henderson's arms, " the chimney-stacks were crashing through the roofs in Great Ormond Street, the tiles raining like hail on the pavements, the people shrieking and crying, the streets full of flying coaches and men on horseback. I wanted to have escaped from the city at once, but Sir John said it was impossible for a day or two; so I have taken refuge with you for the night."

Poor Aunt Beauchamp was very tender and subdued. She was ready to listen to any amount of sermons, (provided she were in a safe place,) from Aunt Henderson, even when they descended to such details as hair-powder and rouge-pots; although she decidedly objected to accompanying her to Mr. Wesley's five o'clock early morning service at the Foundry.

" My dear sister Henderson," she sobbed, " you and Kitty, and Evelyn, and every one, have become so good ! and I am a poor, foolish, worldly, old woman. I am sure I do feel I want some kind of religion that would make me not afraid to meet whatever might happen. If you really think it would make me safe, I would attend that Chapel at the Foundry, or Mr. Whitefield's Tabernacle, or anything. But I cannot go back among the tottering houses now. It is too much to expect. If you could only find any one to preach in the open air, we might go in our chairs, and there would be no danger."

" My dear sister Beauchamp," replied Aunt Henderson,. grimly, " we cannot go in our chairs to heaven."

" What do you mean, sister ?" was the reply ; " the Methodists do not recommend pilgrimages, do they ? I am sure I have often wished we Protestants had something of that kind. Lady Fanny Talbot comes back from her retreat in Lent looking so relieved and comfortable, feeling she has arranged everything

16

for the year. But the worst of the Methodists is, they seem never to have done."

Aunt Henderson's horror at this suggestion was so great, she seemed to have lost the power of reply.

And then Mother said very quietly,—

" Dear sister Beauchamp, the Bible and good men say religion is not only a shield against destruction, it is a staff in all the troubles of life, and a cordial which we *never want to have done with.* For, if religion does anything for us, I think it leads us to God; and that is our joy and our rest."

Tears gathered in Aunt Beauchamp's eyes, not hysterical tears; and she looked at Mother with something like one of Cousin Evelyn's wistful, earnest looks, and said very softly,—

" I am afraid I do not know much of that, sister; I wish I did."

On the following night Aunt Beauchamp insisted on whirling Father, and Mother, and me away to Bath in her coach.

She would not wait an hour after Sir John was ready; and we started at midnight. Link boys ran beside us through the dark and silent streets. The city seemed deserted. We met no noisy rollicking parties. Only in two places did we encounter a crowd. One of these places was Moorfields, where a crowd of men, women, and children had collected, weeping and lamenting with no one to comfort them; and the other was Hyde Park, where Mr. Whitefield was preaching to a multitude who had gathered around him in their terror, as little children round a mother's knee.

It was a strange scene, as we drove slowly on the outskirts of the crowd. Here and there the uncertain flare of torches revealed a group of awe-stricken faces, many of them wet with silent weeping; while the dense throngs beyond were only manifest from that peculiar audible hush which broods over a listening multitude, broken here and there by an irrepressible sob or wail, or by agonized cries, such as, "Lord, have mercy on me a sinner," or "What shall I do to be saved?" ·

We scarcely spoke to each other all that night, and it was very strange when the dawn crept up the sky to see the highways thronged with coaches, and horsemen, and pedestrians flying as from a doomed or sacked city, and to feel of how little avail it was to fly if, after all, it was the earth itself, the solid, immovable earth that was being shaken.

It was very pleasant to me to see what a kind of tender reverence crept over the manner of both Father's sisters towards Mother, before we left London.

Aunt Henderson, as she packed up for us a hamper full of jellies and cordials, on the night of our departure (inserting one large phial of her favourite compound of snails and mashed slugs), said to me authoritatively, as if she were completing an act of canonization,—

"Kitty, my dear, your Mother and Aunt Jeanie are the best women I know. They are as good examples of perfection as I ever wish to see. They may argue against the doctrine as much as they like, but they prove it every day of their lives. You understand, my dear, Mr. Wesley only argues for *Christian*, not for *Adamic* or *angelic* perfection. He admits that even the perfect are liable to errors of judgment; which your poor Mother also proves, no doubt, by her little bigotry about the Church, and Aunt Jeanie by two or three little Presbyterian crotchets. But your Mother's patience, and her gentleness, and her humility, Kitty, and her calmness in danger I shall never forget. I should be very happy, Kitty," she concluded, decisively tightening the last knot of one of her packages, "with all my privileges, to be what she is. And how she attained such a height in that benighted region is more than I can comprehend."

"But, dear Aunt Henderson," I ventured to say, "the grace of God *can* reach even to Cornwall!"

The parting between Mother and dear Aunt Jeanie was like a leave-taking of sisters; and for keepsakes Mother gave a beloved old volume of Mr. George Herbert's hymns, and Aunt Jeanie an old worn copy of the letters of Mr. Samuel Rutherford.

We stayed three or four days at Bath, during which Aunt Beauchamp's spirits revived, and also her colour, and her interest in cards; "For, after all," she observed to Mother, "we have our duties to our children, and to society, and there is no religion, at least for us Protestants, in making ourselves scarecrows."

But on the morning we went away, when we went to her bed-side to wish her good-bye, she said to Mother,—

"My dear sister Trevylyan, if ever I should be ill, for we are all mortal, and my nerves have been terribly shaken, promise me that you will come and see me. For I am sure you would do me more good than any one."

And nothing would satisfy her but to send us all the way to Plymouth in her coach; although the coachman vehemently remonstrated, and declared he would not answer for the consequences to the horses on those break-neck Devonshire hills, and Evelyn said such an instance of rebellion against that potentate's decrees had never been known in the family before. And so we reached home again; and dear Mother thinks (as Evelyn says no doubt the sun does) that this is a very warm and genial world.

There was a strange tenderness in Aunt Henderson's manner as she took leave of Mother and me; and as we sat in the coach at Hackney waiting for the horses to start, she came forward again and took Mother's hand with a lingering eagerness, as if she had some especial last words to say. Yet after all she said nothing, she only murmured, "God bless you both."

And when I glanced back at Cousin Evelyn when we left

Bath, expecting one more of her bright looks, she was gazing at Mother with a strange wistfulness, and then suddenly she burst into a flood of tears and turned away.

Can Mother, and Father, and I, have been deceiving ourselves? She says she feels better and stronger, and so often on the journey, she used to plan how we would resume all our old habits, and she would rise early again. "There is such life," she said, "in the morning air at home," and I should bring her the cup of new milk as of old to the porch-closet; and "then, Kitty," she said, "we will read the lessons for the day always together. Perhaps I have not sought the especial blessing promised to the '*two or three gathered together*,' as I ought. And you shall read me sometimes one of those. hymns of Dr. Watts or of Mr. Charles Wesley. I am an old-fashioned old woman, and I shall never be able to understand why people cannot be satisfied with the Bible and the Prayer-book, nor how they can speak of their inmost feelings in those Bands and Classes your Aunt Henderson speaks of, without danger. But I do like the hymns, and I am sure we ought all to feel grateful to the Methodists for helping the people no one else ever thought there was any hope of helping, or of teaching anything good."

And although dear Mother has not been able to begin all the old ways just yet, that is no more than is natural. She is fatigued with the journey. In a few days it will be all right.

And as to Betty, it is of no use asking what she thinks, or minding what she says, because it is her way always to take the dark side, especially if other people look on ·the bright. And Betty's reputation as a prophetess, moreover, is bound up with the ill success of this London expedition.

It was rather a sad greeting the night we came near home. It was growing dusk, and everything was very still, when a low chant broke on us from the opposite hill. Solemnly the mea-

surcd music rose and fell, like the rise and fall of waves on a
calm day, with silent measured pauses between, until, as we
drew nearer, the hill side sent the sound back to us so clearly
we could distinguish it to be the deep voices of men singing as
they moved along the moorland. From the slow, steady movement, we knew too well what the sad, dark procession must be.
We did not say anything to each other. But when we were
sitting at supper in the hall, Mother asked Betty which of the
neighbours was dead.

"It was old Widow Treffry," said Betty; "and Toby has
joined the Methodists lately, and the members of his class carried her to the church-yard to-day, singing one of Parson
Wesley's hymns as they went."

"It was very solemn and sweet," said Mother. "It made
me think of the stories my Father used to tell me when I was
a child, of the ancient Church, and the funerals of the martyrs."

"Poor old Widow Treffry was no martyr, and not much of a
saint," said Betty candidly; "though they do say, poor soul, she
changed latterly. Nothing would save her. It was spotted
fever. Poor Toby takes on dreadful. He did all that could
be done for her, and spared no expense; and they gave her
sack, cold milk, apples, and preserved plums, as much as she
could swallow.* But it was all of no use, as of course nothing
is, when the Almighty's time is come for any of us."

"I wish we had returned a little sooner," said Mother. "I
have a wonderful prescription for fever."

"So had the doctor from Falmouth," said Betty grimly.

Trusty's welcome was far more manifest. Having exhausted
all his ordinary modes of expressing satisfaction with his tail,
and gone through all his limited vocabulary, from a rapturous
bark to a whine, he let off the remainder of his exuberant
spirits in an eccentric excursion into the poultry-yard, causing
great quackings and cacklings and flutterings there, by his

* *Vide* Wesley's Journal.

rough extempore jokes; and finally spent the evening in a sober and intelligent way, snuffing about each of us, until he evidently felt satisfied that he had smelt out the whole history of our absence.

The contrast between Betty's deeds and words was even more apparent than usual on our return home.

Every little detail of Father's and Mother's comfort, and even of my fancies, was remembered, on the supper-table, in our chambers, everywhere; the chairs set in the very corner we liked, the preserves and biscuits we preferred, a little fresh packet of Virginian tobacco for Father, and in Mother's chamber her favourite books placed on a little table by her bed-side, every corner of every room sweet and fresh with laborious sweeping and rubbing. Welcomes glistened from every white table-cloth and sheet, and gleamed from every bit of metal or polished wood in the house.

It was evident indeed that for weeks Betty had been revelling in a paradise of washing-tubs, scrubbing-brushes, wax and oil, and soap, uninterrupted by any of the hindrances interposed by the disturbing processes of ordinary life. But in words and manner she received us like a band of delinquents who, after vainly flying from home and duty, had at length perceived their folly, and were now returning in penitence and humiliation.

I knew there was much bottling up in Betty's mind to be uncorked on the first convenient occasion; and to-night the occasion arrived, as I was going to bed, when I took her out of my chest a beautiful copy of Mr. Wesley's collection of hymns bound in red morocco, as a present from Cousin Evelyn, with her affectionate remembrances.

"Good reason indeed, Mrs. Kitty, we have to remember Mrs. Evelyn," she said, "and are likely to have. However it's a mercy Missis has come back at all."

"The doctors all say she is better, and she feels so, Betty," I said.

"Poor, dear Missis," said Betty, "yes, sure, she's ready enough to feel what the doctors or any one else like to impose on her. However, after all the signs and tokens I have had, it's a mercy we're all together again, and I'll say no more."

"What signs and tokens?" I asked.

"I am not superstitious, Mrs. Kitty, my dear," said Betty. "Some folks be always looking out for wonders, and of course such folks see plenty; but I'm not one of *them*. I never see'd a ghost in my life, man, woman, or beast, though my mother did; and of course I've heard of many. But the house has been mortal wisht, I can't deny, these last days. The dog don't howl all night in that way for nothing. He was glad enough to see you all come back, poor fool; and no doubt he had his reasons. They do say beasts see more than we see at times. Nor do the birds come pecking at the window after dark without being sent; nor will the old white owl hoot himself hoarse only to please himself; nor the dishes tumble down from the dressers, where I set them as firm as a rock, nor the bells ring, without ever a hand going near them."

"There are mice, Betty," I suggested.

"There *be* mice, Mrs. Kitty," said Betty solemnly; "but it's my belief no mouse or rat pulled Missis' bell that way three times at midnight, leastways no *mortal* mice or rats; for what beasts there may be in the other world is not for me to say."

A strange chill came over my heart at Betty's words, and still more at her tones; and at length I said,—

"But, Betty, whatever strange things or creatures there may be about us, the other world is God's world as much as this, and nothing can go beyond His will. There is no dark, terrible corner of the world left out of His presence, Betty; and where He is there is light."

"That's been my only comfort, my dear," said Betty. "No doubt there's no darkness with the Almighty; but there be a good deal that's not quite light and plain to me. Do you think,

Mrs. Kitty," she concluded in an awe-stricken whisper, "that I'd have bided here alone all this time, with all these noises going on, and no one but Roger to speak to, and he with not as much sense as the dog, if I hadn't had the Almighty to look to, and if He hadn't taught me to *pray?* I'm not timorsome nor fancical, but the sweat has stood on my face like dew many a time; and I be cruel glad to see you all home again!" she concluded. And these were Betty's first words of welcome; and she left me, to go to bed in her own room inside mine, but in a minute she came out again and said,—

"Don't you take on about anything I said, my dear. You know it may have been only poor Widow Treffry after all; and anyway we must trust the Lord, Mrs. Kitty, my dear, we must trust the Lord."

But somehow poor Betty's attempts at consolation have made my heart fail more than all her signs and tokens.

I have always prayed so much that I might not blind my eyes, but look in the face whatever God sends, and try to bear it as it is. It always seems to me that we should meet troubles as Mr. Wesley says he likes to meet mobs. "I always like to look a mob in the face," said he. Yet we ought not to go *out of our way* to meet the mob, or the troubles. That would not be true courage. It would be a nervous apprehension and fear, able to bear anything better than the suspense of *waiting to see what is to come.* It seems to me to require far less courage to rush at the enemy than to wait for him; and yet this *waiting courage*, this patience is just what we, at least we women, seem most to need in this life.

Not a year since, as regarded those dearest to me, I could walk by sight rather than by faith; Mother, and Father, and Jack, and Hugh, all here together. And now Jack is in the army in Flanders, and Hugh on the Atlantic Ocean. At any hour I know not what may be happening to them. Mother, indeed, our precious Mother, I can be with every moment; I can watch her every look, I can anticipate her every want; and yet sometimes it seems as if Mother were even less within my grasp, less to be kept by any clinging touch of mine, than either Jack or Hugh !

I watch her night and day, and yet I cannot tell whether my fears delude me, or my hopes.

She has not, indeed, gained much since last year, but to-day she looks a little brighter than yesterday, and to-morrow she may be a little stronger than to-day ; and so by degrees all may be well.

Yet it is just when I have reasoned myself into most hope that the old fears come back most powerfully.

And then, as now, I have but one resource—but one.

Thinking may drive away many cares and lighten many sorrows ; but for suspense, for uncertainty, for anxieties whose issues we *cannot* know, it seems to me there is no remedy at all but prayer.

But, oh, how could we bear the overwhelming thought, " *Thou knowest,*"—the thought that there is a certainty somewhere,— unless we had also the conviction warm at our hearts, " *Thou lovest,*"—the certainty that the deepest certainty of all is the love of Him who orders all ?

Yesterday afternoon, when Mother and I returned from a little walk to the entrance of our cave, where she had rested a little while on a rock to drink in the air from the sea, which was as soft as milk, and made the heart glad, like wine when one is weary, we found the parlour occupied by our new Vicar, Cousin Evelyn's great-uncle. Betty was talking to him at the door ; and when he had greeted us, the Vicar observed in rather a nervous way to Mother (Evelyn had not told us how shy and nervous he was),—

" Your servant, madam, seems a woman of shrewd sense and much observation ; and I grieve to say she confirms the worst reports I have heard of the parish, as to wrecking and other lawless proceedings."

"Indeed, sir," said Mother, smiling, "we have lived here very peacefully for many years; and Betty does not always see the world on its brightest side."

"Madam, you relieve me considerably," he replied; "the accounts that good person gave were really appalling—I may say, without exaggeration, in many respects really appalling. A clergyman, madam," he resumed, after taking a pinch of snuff from his gold snuff-box, "has many things to discover on his first arrival in a new locality; especially, I may say, I trust without offence, in a locality which has, at all events, not as yet attained the point of civilization on which we stand at Oxford, —that is," he continued, qualifying his assertion in a nervous way, as if he were correcting something written, "not in all particulars—not precisely in all particulars."

As the assertion was, at least in that modified form, rather undeniable, Mother could only say,—

"You must indeed, sir, find the contrast great."

"Madam," he replied, "I do; yes, I think I must admit I do." And then, fortifying himself with another pinch of snuff, he rushed at once (as I have noticed nervous people frequently do) at the point he had to reach.

"Madam," he resumed, "I have been informed that there is a *conventicle* held on Sunday evenings in this house."

Mother coloured, and rose; but it had evidently cost the Vicar too much to make the assertion not to pursue it; he could not rely on his own courage for a second charge, and accordingly pressed it. "Yes, madam, a conventicle, in which is also perpetrated the further enormity of female preaching. I was also informed that in this conventicle the most pointed allusions are made to the clergy; that it is spoken of as a 'great marvel' that any good gift or grace should be given to bishops or curates; and that last Sunday evening it was actually stated, in the most offensive manner, that it would be a good thing indeed if the priests showed forth God's glory, either by their preaching or by their living. Madam," concluded the Vicar, having, I suppose, exhausted his ammunition, and relapsing into his usual nervous and courteous manner,—"madam, a clergyman, a stranger, does not know what to believe. I would have preferred seeing Captain Trevylyan; but since your servant told me he was out, I did not like to wait."

"Sir," said Mother, who by this time had resumed her seat and her composure, "you have acted with true courtesy and frankness. On the winter Sunday evenings we have been in the habit of collecting our two servants with a few of our ailing and aged neighbours to read the Church service to them and some passages from the homilies."

"The Church service and the homilies? A very primitive and praiseworthy custom, madam," said the Vicar, evidently greatly relieved. "And only a few aged people? Within the legal number, no doubt; not more than thirty-nine?"

"I never counted, sir," said Mother.

"No doubt, my dear madam, no doubt; but you should in future be particular on that score. The times are perilous, madam, and these Methodists seem to have penetrated even here. No doubt my informant was mistaken."

"Perhaps, Mother," I ventured to suggest, "the Vicar's informant was a dissenter. You always read the prayer, 'O God, who alone workest great marvels, send down on all bishops and curates'—and last Sunday Father read the litany— and you remember 'both by their preaching and living.'"

"Exactly," said the Vicar, seizing at the escape; "the young lady's suggestion shows great acuteness. And my informant may himself be a dangerous person, a nonconformist,—perhaps even himself a Methodist!"

At this point Father entered; and over a bottle of claret, the unequalled greatness of Marlborough, and the degeneracy of the times, the misunderstanding was finally adjusted; the only combustible element again introduced being Cousin Evelyn, on the mention of whose name and our relationship the Vicar observed that she was a young person of much ability, but with a tendency to dangerous opinions, a decided tendency to very dangerous opinions.

At last he left with many profound bows, saying,—

" Madam, such society and such hospitality as I have found under your roof have gone far to remove the unfavourable impressions previously produced by that good person, your housekeeper's statements. Her accounts of the moral state of the district were alarming, I may say appalling, to the highest degree."

" It is very strange, however," said Mother when the Vicar had left, and she related the interview to Father, " that any one should confound me with the Methodists, and suspect me of holding conventicles. It is very strange!" repeated Mother, in a tone of no little annoyance.

" Very strange, my dear," said Father with a mischievous twinkle in his eye; " but I have always observed it is the cautious people who get into the worst scrapes."

" But, Betty," I said this morning, " what did you tell the Vicar, to frighten him so about the parish ?"

" Well, Mrs. Kitty," said Betty, " I told him pretty nigh everything I could think of; about the wreckers tying lanterns to horses' tails to entice the ships on the rocks, and murdering the crews, and firing on the king's men, and about the poach- ing, and the fights among the miners, and all the worst things that have happened these last thirty years. I was set on it he should know. What right had he or any stranger to come here a prying and spying into our country, and specially into our own town-place, and to turn away Master Hugh, who has got the hearts of every man, woman, and child in the parish? I only wish I could terrify the old gentleman out of the country."

Finding Betty in an approachable mood, I took the opportunity of asking what her opinion was on Mr. Wesley's doctrine of "perfection."

"Well, Mrs. Kitty," she said, "I've got my thoughts on that matter;" and she began to elaborate the ornaments on the pie-crust in a way that betokened a long discourse. "In the first place, my dear, it's my belief that when a man's not a fool in general, when you do understand him, it's a wise thing to think he's not a fool when you don't understand him, but to try to make out what he does mean. That's my way; some folks, Mrs. Kitty, go just the other way; however that's no concern of mine. Now, my dear, when I heard the folks say that Parson Wesley said there are some poor mortals on earth who've got beyond sinning, I said to myself, Parson Wesley's no fool, that's plain if nothing else is, and he must have *some* meaning. And so I said to some of the folks, 'Did he say *you* were perfect, and had got beyond sinning?' And when they said 'No,' I said, 'Well, least-ways he's right enough there.' And that quieted *them* for a bit. So I was left to think it out for myself.

"And, Mrs. Kitty, it's my belief Parson Wesley means this: He has seen, maybe, some folks sit down moaning and groaning over their sins as if their sins were a kind of rheumatism in their bones and they had nothing to do but to bear it. For *I've* seen such folks, Mrs. Kitty, I can't deny, folks calling themselves Christians, who'd speak of their tempers, or their laziness, or their *flesh* as they call it, as if their *flesh* were not *themselves*, but a kind of ill-natured beast they'd got to keep, that *would* bark and snap at times, and no fault of theirs. Some folks, if you speak to them of their faults, will shake their heads and say, 'Yes, we're poor sinners, and the flesh is weak, but when we get to heaven it'll be all right. We can't expect, you know, to be perfect here.' And if Parson Wesley ever came across such I can fancy his being aggravated terrible, for they *be* aggravating, and have many a time angered me. And I can fancy his going up to them in his brisk way and saying, 'You poor foolish souls, you'll never get to heaven at all in that way, and if you don't get sin out of your hearts *now* you'll find it'll be *death* by-and-by. Get up and fight with your sins like men. The Almighty never meant you to go on sinning and groaning, and groaning and sinning. He says you are to be *holy,* you're to be *perfect;* and what the Almighty says He means. Get up and try, and you'll find He'll help you.' And if they do try, the Almighty does help them; and instead of keeping on sinning and moaning, they'll be singing and doing right. They'll be loving the Lord and loving each other. And," concluded Betty, " that's what I think Parson Wesley means by perfection."

" Some folks," she resumed after a pause, "seem to think going to heaven is a kind of change of air, that'll make their souls well all in a moment, just as other folks think going to London'll make their bodies well all in a moment. But I don't see that changes of place make the body any better, and I don't see why it should the soul. Parson Wesley says eternity and eternal life, and forgiveness of sins, and holiness, and heaven itself, must begin in the soul here and now, or they'll never begin there and then. And," she concluded, " Mrs. Kitty, my dear, it's my belief that's what Parson Wesley means by 'perfection;' and if he means anything else, or anything wrong, it's no concern of mine, my dear, for Parson Wesley's not the Bible, and it isn't at *his* judgment seat we've got to stand."

And so saying, Betty laid her pie-crust on the dish, put the dish in the oven, and finished the interview.

She seems to have arrived at much the same conclusion as Aunt Jeanie.

Mother said this morning she thought all danger of infection from the spotted fever from which poor Widow Treffry died must be over, and that we might go and see how poor Toby was getting on.

"I cannot bear the idea of his being alone in that dreary place," she said, "with all those melancholy thoughts he had when Hugh and you went to see him; and he must want many little comforts."

So Mother and I went off together, she on the old gray pony, a basket full of "little comforts" hanging from the pommel of the saddle. We found the cottage door open, but no one within. The widow's donkey, now in a good old age, was standing with closed eyes and an expression of the most stupid repose near the door. As I went a few steps from the cottage towards the sea, I heard the sound of low singing broken by occasional hammering, and mingling with the plash of the ebbing waves which were creeping lazily up the sands in the calm of the summer noon.

In a few minutes we found Toby mending his boat on the shingle, the gray pony was turned loose to graze on the short sweet turf near the cottage, the contents of the basket were disposed of within, and Mother and I seated ourselves on a rock beside Toby.

There was a look of order about the cottage and about Toby's dress, rather new to both, and Mother commended it.

"Well, Missis," said Toby, after a shy pause, "there *is* a. difference. There's something more like order and comfort inside, I trust, than there was, thank the Lord."

"You think Mr. Wesley and the Methodists helped you, Toby," said Mother.

"Bless your heart, Missis, I *know* they did. But it was not them only," he resumed with some hesitation, pulling his hair and making a shy nod at me, "it was partly Mrs. Kitty and Master Hugh. The first thing I believe that did me any good was seeing Mrs. Kitty in a rage all along of the old donkey."

And then he went on to tell us how on that morning many years ago, when I met him on the cliff, beating his donkey, (he said,) and had spoken so sharply to him about it, and then looked so kind and given him a drink of new milk, he had ridden on laughing in himself at the "tantrums" of young ladies, and wondering equally why I should care about the beast being beaten or about his being hungry.

But he said it was curious how my words and looks stuck to him. It seemed somehow to waken him to the thought that there was such a thing as right and wrong, and that the right thing was kindness and goodness; and he said that from that time he never lifted his hand against the donkey without some-how feeling a soft kind hand pulling him back; and in time, (it was very odd,) but he found the donkey went as well for good words as for bad.

Then Master Hugh used to go out with him in the boat, and in return for what Toby taught him of fishing and boating, offered to teach Toby to read. And Toby used to say in a surly way that "he didn't mind trying;" not that he or his mother saw much good in it, but he didn't like to vex Master Hugh. And Master Hugh made him learn many good words out of the Bible, and although he heeded the words little then, they came back afterwards, and often were just the end of the rope which kept his soul above water. But the great lesson that got into his heart from Hugh, Toby thought, was that goodness and mercy are not the mere softness and ornament of women, but the glory of men.

But all this time, his own life was rough and dark enough; their cottage had always been a refuge and plotting-place for wreckers and wild characters of various kinds. Often when Toby as a boy lay in bed in the inner chamber, on stormy nights, he has heard eager voices discussing the harvest likely to be reaped from the tempest, the chances of wrecks on various

17

points of the coast, and the hope of prizes, as eagerly as if the poor tossing ship had been freighted with no human lives, and worked by no trembling human hands,·but charged with a mere inanimate cargo of merchandise for their especial benefit. Toby said some of their words haunted him to this day : " She's making straight for the rocks "—" Couldn't you help her, Granny, by a little friendly light in the window ? "—" She has gone down like a shot ! " or " She makes a good fight ! "—" Fire your guns, there's no hand to help, the wind 'll beat you ! "—" Never mind ; the waves 'll do the rest "—" There 'll be a godsend for some lucky folks in the morning."

And then in the early dusk, he has heard mysterious rollings of casks into the outhouse by his bed.

In time he grew up to take his share in the watching, the work, and the spoils, to look on the storms as his natural harvest-field, and to think with scarcely more tenderness of a wreck than of a haul of mackerel.

The crews struggled, he reasoned with himself, and so did the fish. Of course they neither of them liked it; but ships he supposed were made most of them to be wrecked one day on some coast or other, just as fish were made to be caught in some net or other ; and if some folks must be better for it, why not he ? There was, indeed, a dull sense of the work not being quite as harmless as fishing, which prevented his ever speaking of it to Hugh. He knew there was *something* " up to London," which objected to such proceedings, and occasionally came down fiercely, in a blundering way, on some unlucky poor soul or other, although very commonly not on the worst man, or when he was doing the worst work.

And he knew there was also *something* somewhere up in heaven which shared these objections, and also in a blind blundering way (like a great water-wheel if you get entangled in it) came down every now and then on some chance offender and hurt or crushed him.

And he had also a dim notion that there was some mysterious connection between this great destructive and avenging something and the Ten Commandments.

There were moments, also, when the dull sense of all not being right with him, which made him afraid in passing lonely burial-grounds, or in the dark in strange places, or at any strange noises in familiar places, would be quickened into a sharp pain, when on the bodies of the drowned was found some linen marked by careful hands, or some little fond relic or locket containing a child's or a woman's hair, showing that the dead belonged to some who had loved them at home,—a pain which became intolerable after the death of that poor drowned sailor-lad, whose face he never could forget.

And then, he said, came Parson Wesley, preaching on the downs not far away, and made him feel that the *something* which was against him in heaven was no blind machine, but the living God, whose eyes are in every place beholding the evil and the good, and searching to the bottom of every heart and every work ; that the thing God is against is *sin ;* that sin is in great part doing wrong to others, or *not doing them the good we could ;* that there is nothing in the least uncertain in His ways, but the most absolute certainty that sooner or later, but in exact proportion to the sin, will come the punishment ; that the most terrible things that can happen to wicked men on earth are nothing but the prick of a momentary gnat-bite to the gnawing of the worm that dieth not ; but as the tingling of a hand placed for an instant too near the fire, to being plunged in the heart of the flames which never will be quenched ; "*the* fire " for all sinners, "*their* worm " for each ; and yet that the most terrible agonies of hell are the agonies that begin *now ;* the gnawing of hopeless remorse at the conscience, the sense of the presence of God, from whom we cannot escape, and whom we dare not approach, who holds us full in His searching gaze, and through His eyes, *which we cannot avoid,* looks through our eyes, *which we cannot veil*, into the black spot in our hearts, which He knows, and *we know*, which we cannot cover or wash out, and which He abhors.

"And that was how I felt, Mrs. Kitty," said Toby, "when you came to see Mother, and heard me moaning in the chamber inside."

"But that is changed now," Mother said.

"Yes, Missis," said Toby solemnly, "my sin is the same. I think I hate it more; it's seldom out of my sight. King David says, 'My sin is ever before me,' and I find him pretty right. And the eyes of the living Lord are on me searching me through and through, it seems to me deeper and deeper 'most every day; and I can't avoid them any more than I could—but thank the Lord, *I don't want to.* There's the difference,—I don't want to. I wouldn't be out of the sight of His eyes for the world."

"And what helped you thus at last?" said Mother.

"It was mostly the hymns," said Toby; "first the Bible, and then mostly the hymns, for they are the Bible for the most part, only set to music, like, so that it rings in your heart like a tune. It was the hymns, and what they said at the class-meeting. Before I went to the class, and heard what they had to say there, I thought I was all alone, like a castaway on a sandy shore under a great sheer wall of cliffs,—a narrow strip of sand which no mortal man had ever trod before, and which the tide was fast sweeping over bit by bit. To spell out the hymns in the book by myself was like finding footprints on the sands, and that was something. It made me feel my trouble was no madness, as poor Mother called it, no mad dream, but *waking up* from the maddest dream that could be. It made me see that others had felt as I felt, and struggled as I was struggling, and had *got through*. But when I went to the class and heard them sing the hymns, it was like hearing voices on the top of the cliffs cheering me up, and pointing out the way. Our class-leader is no great speaker, but he's got a wonderful feeling heart, and a fine voice for the hymns, and it's they that has finished Parson Wesley's work, and healed the wound he made :—

> 'Depths of mercy! can there be
> Mercy still reserved for me?'

That was the first that settled down in my heart. I couldn't listen any further, and I couldn't get that out of my head for days, until another took its place :—

> 'Jesu! let Thy pitying eye
> Call back a wandering sheep;
> False to Thee, like Peter, I
> Would fain like Peter weep.
> Let me be by grace restored,
> On me be all long-suffering shown;
> *Turn and look upon me, Lord,*
> *And break my heart of stone.*
>
> 'For thine own compassion's sake,
> The gracious wonder show;
> Cast my sins behind Thy back,
> And wash me white as snow.
> If Thy bowels now are stirred,
> If now I would myself bemoan,
> *Turn and look upon me, Lord,*
> *And break my heart of stone.*
>
> 'Look as when Thy languid eye
> Was closed that we might live;
> "Father," (at the point to die
> My Saviour gasped,) "forgive!"
> Surely with that dying word,
> He turns, and looks, and cries, "'Tis done!"
> *Oh, my bleeding, loving Lord,*
> *Thou break'st my heart of stone!*'"

That hymn, Toby said, seemed to put a new picture in his heart. Instead of the pale face of the poor lad lying lifeless on the sands, which had lately haunted him night and day, another

Countenance rose before him, pale and all but lifeless, but with the hollow eyes, large with pain, fixed in the tenderest pity on him. He understood that *"God was in Christ reconciling the world unto Himself."* He felt that it was the face of the Judge that looked so tenderly on him from the Cross: that suffering beyond any he had ever dreaded had been borne for him by the Lord Himself, made sin for him. And he felt he was forgiven.

Then all day his heart seemed bursting with the joy of reconciliation, and he was singing,—

> " Thee will I love, my joy, my crown,
> Thee will I love, my Lord, my God;
> Thee will I love, beneath Thy frown
> Or smile, Thy sceptre or Thy rod:
> What though my flesh and heart decay,
> Thee shall I love in endless day."

Everywhere that dying face of his Saviour seemed beaming on him in the fulness of pity and love; and those words, *"'Tis done! Father, forgive!"* filled all the world with music. He could see or hear nothing else.

" And now ?" said Mother.

" Now, Missis," said Toby, " I see all things once more, as they are ; but it seems as if everything were changed inwardly, though the outside is the same. The curse is taken out of everything. Even that poor dead lad's face, I see it now, and I am not afeared. For it seems to say, ' Not to me, Toby, it's too late, I want nothing ; *not to me*, but to all the rest, for my sake.' And the two Faces seem to get mixed up in my mind, Missis, the poor drowned lad's and His ; and still the words the dumb lips speak are the same,—*' Not to Me*, all is well with Me ; *but to all the rest for My sake.'* And that," concluded Toby, " is what I live in hopes it'll be given me to do, before I die."

" How, Toby ?"

" Why, Missis," he said, " I watch for the wrecks more than ever I did in old times. I watch for the crews as I never watched for the cargoes. And one of these days it's my belief the Lord 'll give me to save some of them, and to see some poor lifeless souls wake up to life again up there by mother's fire. And then I shall feel those two Faces smiling on me up in heaven, the poor drowned lad's, Missis, and the blessed Lord's Himself. And that'll be reward enough for an angel, let alone that an angel could never know the shame, and the sin, and the bitter reproaches in my heart, that makes it like heaven to me to dare to look up in His face at all."

"And meantime?" said Mother.

"Meantime, Missis," said Toby, "Parson Wesley says that the end of all the commandments of God is love; and since I once saw that,—that what pleases the Lord is for us to be good and kind to each other, it's wonderful how many chances I've got of pleasing Him. There's hardly a day without them."

And as she rode home on the gray pony Mother said, "Kitty, our Saviour said, 'The last shall be first,' and I think I never understood so well what He meant as to-day. As I left that poor fellow's cottage, with the open Bible on the window ledge, it seemed to me as sacred as a church."

X

HE post-mistress at Falmouth will begin to think me quite an important personage. This morning two letters arrived for me—one from London from Jack, and another from New York from Hugh.

Hugh's letter contains a kind of brief narrative or journal of his travels, which I read to Father and Mother.

It also contains a little especial piece for me, which I do not read to any one.

I am quite surprised to find what large towns and what a number of people there are in the American colonies.

I always thought America was a kind of place of exile, where every one always looked unsettled, as if they were only staying there for a short time, and where things were always at the beginning. I never thought of people being really *at home* there. Of course it was a foolish thought. Hugh says some of the towns are a hundred years old, and some of the houses look quite venerable.

Hugh went through a great deal of Ireland on foot on his way, and took ship at Cork. During his wanderings he lodged in the little, dirty, smoky Irish cabins, or wherever he could find shelter; and preached in all kinds of wild places, or in crowded streets, wherever he could find people ready to listen.

"Sometimes," he writes, "the poor peasants at first took me for a new kind of mendicant friar, and seemed rather disappointed when, at the end of my sermon, I did not proceed to beg. Their warm Irish hearts are easily touched—tears and blessings pour forth readily (as also on other occasions curses).

The spontaneous responses are strange enough at times. As I read the 'Prodigal Son,' a voice cried out, 'By all the saints, that's me!' or, on some home-thrust, in an angry tone, 'What traitor then told you that of Pat Blake?' perhaps accompanied with a handful of mud;—or oftener, 'Holy Mary, Mother of God, pray for us, miserable sinners;' or, 'Sweet Jesus, have mercy on us;' or, 'By the Mass, that's true!' I try to speak of the love of God to men, and of the sacrifice of the Cross, and of the joy of God in welcoming the returning sinner, and of the joy of the forgiven child; and those truths which we hold in common with the Church of Rome, (although, unhappily, too much as the green meadow where Daisy feeds has a common soil with the bare patch beyond it, which the tinners have covered with destructive rubbish). It is more and more amazing to me, the more I see of the world, to find to what an extent, and by what an infinite variety of means, the Enemy has contrived to bury out of sight the great life-giving truth that God is love and loves the world—that He has redeemed us at infinite cost—that His one command to us is to return to Him, and be welcomed and blessed, and find the joy we were made for in serving Him.

"Sometimes, however, my reception is very different. The reputation of the new heresy of 'Methodism' has gone before me. 'Swaddlers' is the term of reproach here taken up by the ignorant mob, from a sermon preached by Job Cennick on the text, 'She took the babe and wrapped it in swaddling clothes, and laid it in a manger.' In such cases the whole population rise together, especially the women, and vociferate and curse, as I think only Irish voices can, until they are tired, and have to give me a hearing from sheer exhaustion; or until they excite themselves to a fury ready for any violence, and pelt me out of the place.

"In Cork the excited mob attacked the 'Swaddlers' in the streets with clubs and swords, wounded many dangerously, and began to pull down one of their houses. In spite or in consequence of this persecution, nowhere, Mr. Wesley says, have there been more living and dying witnesses of the power of religion than at Cork. Already Methodism has had more than one martyr in Ireland. Persecution draws the persecuted together with a wonderful strength of affection. It is not the mobs we have to dread as the worst hindrance to religion in Ireland ; it is the excitable, variable spirit of the people themselves, so easily touched and so easily turned aside. And Mr. Wesley says the lifeless Protestants, who hate Christianity more than they do Popery or Paganism, are the worst enemies of the gospel in Ireland. But the excitement of speaking to an Irish audience is great. The quick comprehension of any allusion, the ready response in the expressive faces to every change in your own emotions, are very exhilarating, after the slower and heavier masses of our Saxon countrymen. Yet to see an English multitude once really stirred to the heart, is a sight which moves me more deeply than anything. It is like the heaving of the great sea on our own coasts. Those great massive waves do not easily subside, and rocks crumble before their steady power like sand-banks.

"Charles Wesley's hymns have immense power in Ireland. There is a strange story of a bitter persecutor at Wexford hiding himself in a sack in a barn where the persecuted Methodists assembled, with the doors shut for fear of the people. He intended to open the door to the mob outside. But in his hiding-place the singing laid such hold on his heart, that he resolved to hear it through before he disturbed the meeting. After the singing, the prayer laid hold on his conscience, and he lay trembling and moaning in the sack, to the great alarm of the congregation, who thought it was the devil. At length some one took courage to open the sack, and there lay the persecutor a weeping penitent ! His heart had really been reached, and his conversion proved permanent.

"Thus again and again the hymns lull the jealous sentinels of Prejudice to sleep, and leave the fortress of Conscience open to the assaults of the Truth.

"I have only once myself encountered a really furious mob. I had been speaking to an attentive crowd in an open place in the middle of a town. Some had been moved to tears, and the general attention had been profound. While I spoke, I had observed the keen eyes of one old woman intently fixed on me with an ominous, searching gaze. When I finished with prayer and a hymn, her eyes suddenly flashed into rage, and she exclaimed in a shrill, piercing voice, ' *Where's your Hail Mary ?* '

"The change in the audience was as if a spell of witchcraft had been cast on them. Loud cries and deep curses suddenly poured forth against the heretic, the deceiver ; stones and sticks began to fly from all sides around me.

"It is a terrible experience to find yourself thus suddenly face to face with an angry mob, every member of which is a human being with a heart like your own, capable of pity and kindness, and physically no stronger than yourself ; but which all together is a fierce, inhuman monster, capable of tearing you in pieces, with no more difficulty and no more pity than a hungry lion. It is a trial to courage to feel yourself, with all your strength of manhood, helpless as an infant in the grasp of hundreds of men, no one of whom, perhaps, could make you yield an inch. But it is a far sorer trial to faith and love to find hundreds of your fellow-men, and even of women, no one of whom, perhaps, alone would refuse you help and shelter, transformed into a dreadful, merciless monster, with the brain of a man, the heart of a wild beast, and the strength of the sea in a storm.

"To me the danger seemed lost in the sorrow. It was like having a glimpse into hell, thus to have unveiled before me the terrible capacities for evil in the heart of man, which make it possible for *men* to be transformed into a *mob.*

"The danger was soon over, for (I know not how) a division arose among my assailants; they began fighting among themselves, and I escaped with a graze or two on my forehead.

"But, Kitty, it was not until I had spent more than one

night in prayer; it was not until I recollected *another* mob, which *accomplished its purpose;* until once more above such a sea of cruel, mocking, inhuman, human faces, I had seen by faith, One sublime, suffering, human Face uplifted, divine in unruffled love and pity ; until once more by faith I had heard those tones faint with pain, but unfaltering in compassionate love, ' Father, forgive them; for they know not what they do;'—it was not till then that I could take heart, and hope to go forth once more with the message of pardon and grace.   But *then*, I think I never gave the message, I am sure I never felt it, with half the power before.

" And then I recollected yet another mob which also accomplished its purpose, mercilessly pelting its victim with stones until he ' fell asleep,' and what *one* of that merciless mob became. Such possibilities of *good* are there even in hearts out of which fanaticism may seem to have scorched all humanity.

" Here in America I have found no mobs, but, instead, throngs of eager listeners ; men, women, and children, riding scores of miles through forest and wilderness, and encamping in the open country for nights to hear the preacher.

" The honoured name here is not so much Wesley's as Whitefield's, and the love for him is immeasurable.   I think the accents of this apostle from our country have to the colonists the double charm of novelty and of home.   There is still much affectionate reverence here for the ' old country;' although I think, with many, partaking more than we should think flattering of the reverence for old age.   Perhaps they have as little idea here in the colonies of the freshness and youth left in the heart of the old country, as we have in England of the manhood and strength which the new country has attained.

" The field labour in the warm Southern States is mostly carried on by black slaves imported from Africa.   Some of the simplest and most fervent converts are among these negroes. Susceptible and impressible even more than the Irish, easily moved to tears and laughter, their circumstances of bondage, (and in many cases) of exile, making the tidings of *free grace*, of a Saviour loving black and white alike, and paying the ransom for all, peculiarly welcome.

" The first missions to the slaves were those of the Moravians in the West Indies. And there have been persecutions there for Christ's sake, in some respects like those of early times, bonds and imprisonments, ' cruel mockings and scourgings,' inflicted, not by mobs, but by masters.

"These diabolical possibilities of cruelty which unlimited power (whether in masters or mobs, kings or priests,) develops in the hearts of men, are things I dare not dwell on, except on my knees.

" But God is stronger than Satan ; and love is mightier and more enduring than malice.

" The Cross, not the Sanhedrim, has triumphed."

*   *   *   *   *

" *P.S.*—I have seen Tom Henderson.

" He has been successful in his schemes, and is on his way in time to be a rich man. He was full of magnificent projects of returning to his father's house like a prince, and entreating forgiveness with a fortune in his hands, that should make it plain he sought forgiveness for its own sake and not for the sake of any advantages it might bring. I have endeavoured to persuade him that his duty is to write if not to go home at once, not as a prince, but as a repentant runaway—to throw himself on his father's forgiveness, bear his reproaches, and help him in any way he can.

" He fought against this very much at first, but I told him, Kitty, what you told me you had seen of his mother's grief, and had suspected of his father's ; and I can perceive it is working, if by nothing else, by the vehemence and testiness with which he meets my arguments."

Jack's letter is very brief, and very different from Hugh's. It begins a little bitterly, alluding disparagingly to some former friends, especially to one young gambling nobleman Cousin Evelyn warned us against. He has found them out, he says, and although his reliance on human nature has sustained a shock, and although, (as he writes emphatically,) he will *never* be able to understand the *pretensions* to *gentlemanly character* of people who live on the friendliest terms with you as long as your purse is full, and *cannot see* you *across* the *street* when you happen to be in want of a *little assistance ;*—still he has no doubt the wheel of fortune has yet its good turn for him. But in the postscript his tone changes from these rather cynical reflections to the most sanguine anticipations. He has found, he says, a mine of gold, in the shape of a company for farming the mines in Peru, where, as he observes, the Spaniards found the half-civilized natives, centuries ago, eating off silver and drinking out of gold. And if these simple natives with their poor implements contrived to extract such *untold wealth* from merely *scratching*, as it were, the *surface* of the earth, what may not Englishmen in the eighteenth century discover by penetrating into its *heart ?* The secretary, he says, who has suggested these *very obvious* conclusions to a hitherto *marvellously blinded* public, is a *wonderfully clever* fellow, and his *particular friend.* He is appointed under-secretary, *good names* being of great value, he says, in the commencement of such enterprises, and already he has received a hundred pounds as the first instalment of his salary.

In a second postscript he adds, that the *sale* of his *commission,* now, of course, with such *brilliant prospects,* useless to him, especially since the war is over, and there is no *honour* to be *won,* and no *service* to be rendered the *country,* has brought him in a trifle to meet his more pressing debts. So that, (he adds, considerately,) we need not have an anxious thought about his *trifling liabilities,* which are, indeed, already all but discharged.

"Poor, dear fellow," said Mother, with a sigh, as she laid down the letter; "he is always full of kind intentions."

Father was out when the letters arrived, and he did not read them till to-day. I never saw him in such a passion as Jack's letter put him in.

" '*Brilliant prospects*,' indeed," he said, " to be the servant of a beggarly trading company ! ' *Good names !* ' too good, at least, to be dragged through the mire by a set of scoundrelly swindlers, just like the old South Sea Bubble."

Irritated more and more by his own indignant words, he first attacked Jack, next himself, and finally Mother and me. He said we had all been a set of doting idiots, and that the only way to have saved Jack would have been to let him have his own way from the first, and go to sea. It had been an instinct of self-preservation in the lad, and we were all more to blame than he. Now he had been crossed, everything had gone wrong. But it was too late now. He would go to Falmouth the next morning, have the old place put up to auction, take the first ship that sailed for the colonies, and so be out of hearing when Jack came to the gallows: for there it would end ; nothing short of that, there could be no doubt.

At first Mother's tears fell fast, while I was too frightened to cry ; but afterwards I saw Mother growing whiter and whiter, until at last her tears quite dried, and she sat quite still with steady eyes and compressed lips, and her hand pressed firmly on her heart. Then I burst into tears, and knelt beside her, and took her hands in mine and sobbed out, " Oh, Father, look, look, see what you are doing ! " He stopped in the full current of his wrath, looked at Mother, stooped and kissed her forehead, and said in a husky voice,—

" Polly, I am a brute. I always have been ; and you are an angel. Don't take it so to heart. You know I don't mean half I say. There, the boy's a kind fellow after all. It'll all come right ; be sure it will. I'm ten times as good-for-nothing as he is, Polly. Cheer up, sweetheart. The wild oats must be sown. Jack'll be an honour to the old name yet."

But words cannot heal the wounds words can make. Mother did not say a bitter word or shed a tear; but I do not like her look.

All day she has been moving gently about, saying cheering words to us all, especially to Father, who is as subdued and gentle as she is. But her face has had an unnatural fixedness, and when I kissed her good-night in the porch-closet, she folded me in her arms and said,—

" Kitty, darling, indeed I would not have kept him from sea, if I had been sure his heart was set on it. I am afraid I have been very selfish; but oh, Kitty, God knows, I would have given up seeing him again all my life to do him good. Poor Jack! God forgive me! Yet, Kitty, it cannot be too late? Say you do not think it can?"

There was something in that childlike appeal to me which pierced my heart more than if I had seen her sobbing in anguish.

But she did not shed a tear. Her eyes were dry and bright, and I tried to keep my voice quite firm and cheerful, as I said,—

" Of course, it is not too late, Mother. We will have him back to us. He shall take up the farm again with Father; and they will get on so much better than they ever did before. You will see."

She shook her head; but she smiled, as if a faint hope began to dawn in her heart; and I said,—

" Mother, it is *never* too late. We can pray for him night and day. And that must help him."

But as I sit down here alone, my own heart sinks and sinks below the worst fears Father expressed in his anger.

What ever will make Jack understand about *right* and *wrong*? Oh, if Hugh were only here!

Yet, alas! if Hugh had been here, could he ward off all evils? Could he have warded off one of these evils from those he loves?

The echo of my own words brings the words of another sister to my heart,—"If *Thou* hadst been here, my brother had not died."

He could have been there! He knew all. But he *kept away.* The sisters drank the bitter cup to the dregs. The brother died.

Then through the anguish came the deliverance and the unutterable joy.

. I *will trust.* I will *never give up* trusting. There is reason. "The same yesterday, and to-day, and for ever."

We have passed through a storm of trouble since I wrote last. For weeks I have not had heart to write a word, if I had had time.

Have we got *through* the storm? Are we on dry land once more? This trembling and anxiety, and restless expectation of something worse, is it only like the uncertainty and giddiness one feels when one steps on dry land after a rough voyage? or are we still on the waves, and is this only a temporary lull?

The day after Father's reading that unhappy letter of poor Jack's, Mother tried to rise as usual, and come downstairs; but she fainted whilst dressing; and Betty and I found it difficult to lift her into the bed again, so heavily did her slight frame lie in our arms in its helpless unconsciousness.

Father was distracted with alarm when he came to breakfast and heard Mother was ill. He would not touch a morsel of food, but saddling a horse at once galloped off to Falmouth for the doctor.

When the doctor came, Mother was better, and made so light of her ailments, that he, himself a stout, florid little man, who looked as if he had never been ill in his life, persuaded us we had all been unnecessarily alarmed. "A momentary suspension of the action of the heart, a slight disturbance of the circulation, would frequently bring on consequences," he said, "of the most alarming kind. Of the most alarming kind, Mr. Trevylyan, to the uninitiated! There is a slight flushing and trembling. Sometimes, in ordinary cases, I would have recommended bleeding or a blister; but your good lady seems not quite in a state to bear much additional loss of strength. This evening I will send an especial messenger with an electuary, of which I had the prescription lately from the surgeon of a Spanish ship. I have no doubt we shall be well enough to do anything—to ride after the

18

hounds if we please, Captain Trevylyan, in a week or two. A generous diet, and, above all, cheerful conversation, such as, I am sure (he concluded, making a bow to me), cannot fail, my dear young lady, with you for the nurse. Above all, cheerfulness. The first and last ingredient in all my prescriptions is cheerfulness. Life is not long enough, with all our science, Mr. Trevylyan; with all our science, life is not long enough for care."

And the rosy doctor mounted his horse, and rode cheerily away, leaving Father, Betty, and me in very different states of mind.

"A very sensible man," said Father; "a very skilful and penetrating man. Kitty, you see, we must cheer up."

And going up to Mother's bedside, he said,—

"My dear, the doctor gives us the most cheering accounts. In a few days you will be as usual ; indeed, perhaps, better than ever.—It really seems quite a blessing, Kitty," he said to me, as he took his long-delayed breakfast, "that your Mother had this little attack. It may be her restoration, quite her restoration. That doctor has such a quantity of life in him he seems to put it into his patients."

But Betty took a very different view, and a very gloomy one. She would do nothing but shake her head ominously, except when she launched out into an attack on the medicine recommended by the Spanish doctor, who, she had little doubt, was sent expressly by the Pope or the King of Spain to murder as many English folks as he could in a quiet way. "Not," she concluded, "that I think medicine has much to do with poor dear Missis, one way or the other."

So I went back to Mother's chamber, to look as cheerful as I could, with my heart full of a terrible dread, of which Betty's "tokens" were but the echoes.

All day the flush in Mother's face deepened, and no effort of mine could keep her from talking with an eager rapidity quite unlike herself, of having Jack back to us, and how bright we would make the old home for him, and how this was the turning-point, and all would soon be well. " For you know it is not too late, Kitty," she kept saying. " It is never too late." Father kept restlessly hovering about the house all day, occasionally coming in with a gentle step, and saying some pleasant word to her. And at meals, those desolate meals, he repeatedly said to me,—

"You must not be so anxious, child. You have seen so little of illness. You take on too much. The doctor said there is nothing to alarm any one who understands the matter, nothing in the least alarming; and whenever I go in, Kitty, she is quite cheery, Kitty, quite cheery. There is nothing to be anxious about."

And then he would rise with his food scarcely tasted, and go to the door and whistle for Trusty, and come back in a minute to assure me, with more vehemence than ever, there was nothing to be anxious about, nothing at all; and to beg me to keep up my heart, and look very cheery in Mother's chamber.

But when, as night came on, Mother's eyes seemed to grow brighter and larger than ever, and her utterance more rapid, and at last, instead of those sanguine eager plans about Jack, she began to talk as eagerly about all kinds of trifles, and at length I crept out to tell Father I was sure she was *not* better, and he came in, and she asked him eager rapid questions about things she did not care about in the least, I shall never forget the look of anguish which came over his face.

" Oh, Kitty," he said when I came down afterwards and found him sitting by his untasted supper with his face in his hands, " oh, Kitty, I have killed her ! "

After that we were obliged to keep him away from her room, his presence seemed to excite her so painfully. Again and again, when I left the room for anything during that night, I found him standing listening at the door with hushed breath, and a face haggard and sunken as if he had been watching for nights.

It was a dreadful time, listening to Mother's dear gentle voice raised to that unnatural eager tone, saying things that were no thoughts of hers, demanding replies to all kinds of wild questions,—with the knowledge that that other dear despairing face was watching at the door outside, and that every one of those quick unnatural tones was piercing his heart.

In the morning when I came out of the room, he was standing at the head of the stairs with Trusty sitting bolt upright beside him. Father laid his hand on my shoulder with questioning looks, which he did not dare to put in words, while the poor faithful old dog licked my hand with a little perplexed whine. There was something in his old kind familiar ways which broke the spell of unnatural calm to which the excitement had kept me strained, and I laid my head on Father's shoulder and wept.

"Poor little Kitty!" he said, "my poor little maid!" and we went down to the hall together, while Betty stayed in Mother's room.

After that, Betty took us all in hand, and reigned as I suppose the most capable people always will for a time when there is a storm, and every one feels in danger.

I made a faint proposition that we should send again for the doctor, chiefly because I thought the ride to fetch him would be the best thing for Father.

But Father's confidence in the cheery man's skill was broken, and Betty decidedly prohibited any such expedition.

"There be strange tales," she said, "of folks that live on the lives of other folks. I don't say I believe them altogether, but I can't abide his double chin and his round fat face; nor I believe can Missis."

"But the ride might do Father good," I said.

"I don't see folks have any right to go imposing on grown-up people as if they were babies," said Betty. "Poor dear Missis was too much that way herself always, and if Master mustn't go into the room, and can't be kept from hovering about the door like a ghost, the best thing is to make him of some use."

So Father was appointed carrier; and now, many a time, it was as difficult to bear as Mother's wandering words to see him creeping up and down stairs without his shoes, carrying little cups and trays as laboriously as if they had been tons weight, with his efforts not to let a drop be spilt or a spoon jingle.

Betty's treatment was very simple. She let dear Mother have what she liked, and do whatever she thought would make her most comfortable.

"It's my belief *they* know oft-times, Mrs. Kitty," she said to me mysteriously, "what's good for them. And if not, God Almighty only can keep the life in any of us, and in my opinion we've no right to make them more wretched than they need be."

Therefore, contrary to all rules I ever heard of, when dear Mother seemed oppressed for breath, Betty opened the window and let the sweet fresh air in; and when she complained of thirst, Betty brought her cool fresh water.

On the third night she insisted on sending me and Father to bed.

"You can't work miracles, my dear," she said, "and the Almighty doesn't see fit to work them now-a-days. And if you sit up gazing at Missis another night, you'll be as bad as she is, and that'll be more of a handful than I can manage."

So at last, on the condition that I should have Mother all to myself on the following night, while Betty rested, and with the solemn promise that I should be called instantly if Mother asked for me, I went to my chamber.

How hard it was to turn from those dear wandering unconscious eyes! To close the door between us seemed like rolling the stone before a sepulchre. I should have turned back by as irresistible an attraction as that which draws a poor bird with clipped wings down to the earth from which it struggles, but for the knowledge how the opening of the door made that fragile frame start and tremble, and how eagerly she looked for that unknown something any sound seemed always to rouse her to expect. I did not expect to sleep for a moment.

Yet after I had lain down and had begun a prayer for Mother, comforting myself with the thought I could help her in that way, the next thing I was conscious of was the quiet dawn stealing up through my casement, and a sound, not in my ears, but in my heart, of these words, "*I shall not die, but live, and declare the works of the Lord.*"

I rose up and looked around towards the window. Everything was so still in that sacred calm of early morning, that I think it would not have surprised me to catch the glistening of the white garment of an angel going up through the still, pure air, beyond the old thorn, beyond the old elms, beyond the green hill, beyond that soft gray cloud into the pure light of the dawn, pure as if it streamed through the gates of pearl.

But there was nothing to be seen, nothing to tell *whose* whisper that was which was echoing softly through my heart when I woke.

For it *was* a Voice, I am sure, a heart and spirit speaking to mine; so distinct, so outside me were the words, and yet so mysteriously within.

They lingered in my heart with a power beyond that of any music, and filled it with an unspeakable rapture of calm and peace.

So I rose and dressed, and said my morning prayers, looking out of my open window.

Those words seemed to have taken all fluttering and hurrying haste and terror from me.

I said to myself,—

"I will not be superstitious; I will not build my hopes on signs, or omens, or even on these words. Oh, my Saviour, my Father, I will build on *nothing* but Thy love. But yet I will not put away the comfort of those words from me. They are Thy words, and whatever else they mean, they mean love. And I will lean—I will rest—I do lean and rest my whole heart and soul on that—on Thee.

It seemed to me as if my whole being had been bathed in a

well of living water, when I went back to Mother's chamber,
so fresh it felt, and strong. At the door stood Father listening
as if he had been there long. I stood and whispered him some
words of comfort. And when I opened the door so noiselessly
that Betty did not turn to look, and crept to Mother's bedside,—
she *looked at me!* She looked into my eyes, with quiet conscious
love, she stretched out her thin hand and laid it in mine ; and
then as I sat down and held it in both mine—afraid to show
too much of what I felt—the feeble grasp relaxed, her breathing
came and went, evenly, softly, as a child's. It was the soft even
breathing of sleep.

She slept on until dawn had deepened into day, and all the
many-coloured changes by which the hours are illuminated and
distinguished from each other when the day is new, had passed
into the changeless radiance of mid-day, and there was nothing
left by which to mark the time, but my own hopes, counting every minute of such repose as a priceless treasure; and
my fears for Father, watching, ignorant of all, at that closed door.

At length she opened her eyes, and Betty, who had been
watching her, as still and silent as I had been, rose and brought
her some jelly.

And then she asked for Father.

There was no need for me to call him. As soon as the words
had left her lips the door opened without a sound, and his poor
haggard face appeared, inquiring with mute touching looks what
he ought to do.

I rose and led him to the bedside.

Mother held out her hand to him, and said,—

" Dear, I shall get well."

As he had been so often enjoined by Betty, he tried hard
not to betray his feelings, but just to look quietly pleased, as if
it was just what he had hoped, and to say some easy, cheering,
natural words. But the quiet look was quite a failure from his
poor sunken eyes, and with the attempt at the cheering word his

quivering lips failed altogether, and with one passionate sob he sought to withdraw his hand from her and leave the room.

But she laid her other hand on his, and he had no resource but to fall on his knees and bow his face over her hands, and weep like a child.

Betty lifted up her hands in horror, but when she tried to speak, her voice failed too ; so she turned away, and I knelt down by Father, and in a few minutes led him gently away.

It was not till Mother was sleeping again, and we were in the hall together, and Betty brought in the supper, or whatever that nondescript meal might be called which was our first and last that day, that she recovered her self-command enough to say, in answer to an apologetic remark of Father's concerning his disturbing Mother,—

" Well, Master, I don't see that there's much to choose between us all as to that matter : it is no doing of ours, and *we've* nothing to boast of, if the Almighty has seen fit to work a miracle ; for that it is a miracle I have no manner of doubt. There have been signs and tokens enough to prepare anybody for another drowning of the world, and we've all done our best to kill her ; and there's Missis sleeping as innocent and as quiet as a lamb ! "

Sweet hallowed nights of hopeful watching, when I lay awake till I heard her breathing fall into the even cadences of sleep, and woke to hand some little nourishing draught or refreshing drink to her, and to hear her dear voice murmur thanks, or perhaps some sweet old verses from her beloved George Herbert !

Then those delicious days of her gradually returning strength ! To watch day by day the precious little steps of recovery ! It was like watching the leaves open, and the flowers in spring, each day bringing a new delight ; only the life whose precious tide was slowly rising thus from point to point, was no unconscious flood of natural growth—it was Mother's life !

Then that first Sunday when she was lifted into her own little porch-closet, and laid on the couch by the window! She had insisted on being lifted there in the morning, and that all but Betty should go to church;—she had wanted Betty also to accompany us, but no authority in the house reached to that.

As I left her, she broke out again into Herbert (which is her music), murmuring,—

> "Christ hath took in this piece of ground,
> And made a garden there for those
> Who want herbs for their wound.

> "Thou art a day of mirth:
> And where the week-days trail aground,
> Thy flight is higher, as thy birth:
> Oh, let me take thee at one bound,
> Leaping with thee from seven to seven;
> Till that we both, being tossed from earth,
> Fly hand in hand to heaven."

With such holy strains echoing in our ears, and such gratitude in our hearts, a very happy walk was Father's and mine to church that sunny Sunday, across the corn-fields, with the little quiet waves plashing against the rocks far below.

And very real and living were the prayers, and thanksgivings, and responses of the service. They seemed just as if they were a new song, made expressly for Father and me that morning.

As we returned, Father said to me confidentially,—

"Kitty, do you understand that poetry of Mr. Herbert's?"

I said, "I thought I did, and that I liked it."

"You do!" replied Father despondingly; "well, I suppose all really religious people do. But I never could."

When I sat by Mother in the quiet afternoon, I told her something of what Father had said; and she told me how it had gladdened her as she lay there to hear Betty singing hymns in her dear old cracked voice, as she went about her work.

"I am afraid, Kitty," she said, "I have been too dainty about words and forms. The holy angels no doubt do not need the delicate spices of quaint fancies, to make the true prayers and praises of the poorest sweet as incense to them.   I felt it to-day as I lay here, and found the smell of the dewy grass and the new-mown hay sweeter than any perfume, and the sound of Betty's Wesleyan hymns sweet as the singing of a cathedral choir.   Yet still," she added smiling, " my own thoughts flowed back into the channel of old Herbert's poetry, and I sang in my heart,—

> "My joy, my life, my crown!
>   My heart was meaning all the day ;
>   Somewhat it fain would say :
> And still it runneth muttering up and down,
> With only this, 'My joy, my life, my crown.'"

And when Father joined us, she made me read to him the hymn,—

> "O dreadful Justice! what a fright and terror
>   Wast thou of old,
>   When sin and error
> Did show and shape thy looks to me,
> And through their glass discolour thee!
> He that did but look up was proud and bold.

> "But now that Christ's pure vail presents the sight,
>   I see no fears :
>   Thy hand is white,
> Thy scales like buckets which attend,
> And interchangeably descend,
> Lifting to heaven from this well of tears.

> "For where before thou still didst call on me,
>   Now I still touch
>   And harp on thee.
> God's promises have made thee mine,
> Why should I justice now decline?
> Against me there is none, but for me much."

Father endeavoured to look pleased, but I could see that he was much perplexed.   Nor was his cheerfulness restored until I repeated to him, at Mother's request, Mr. Charles Wesley's hymn,—

"Hark ! a voice divides the sky :
Happy are the faithful dead,
In the Lord who sweetly die ;
They from all their toils are freed.
Them the Spirit hath declared
Blest, unutterably blest ;
Jesus is their great Reward,
Jesus is their endless Rest.

" Followed by their works they go
Where their Head hath gone before :
Reconciled by grace below,
Grace hath opened Mercy's door :
Justified through faith alone,
Here they knew their sins forgiven ;
Here they laid their burden down,
Hallowed, and made meet for heaven.

"Who can now lament the lot
Of a saint in Christ deceased?
Let the world, who know us not,
Call us hopeless and unblest :
When from flesh the spirit free,
Hastens homeward to return,
Mortals cry, 'A man is dead '—
Angels sing, ' A child is born.' "

In the evening, when Father and I were alone, he asked me what I thought Mr. Herbert meant by that poetry.

. . I repeated to him the text, " Whom God hath set forth to be a propitiation, through faith in his blood, that HE might be just, and the justifier of him that believeth in Jesus." " I suppose that is what Mr. Herbert meant, Father," I said.

" Then if he meant that," replied Father, rather testily, " why couldn't he say it ? Religion is good, and riddles are good in their way, but I don't see the good of mixing them up together. I shall never be able to understand the pleasure of twisting the Bible-texts into a puzzle for the sake of untwisting them again. It's rather hard on me, Kitty, for I've taken more pains than I can tell to like that stuff, for your Mother's sake. However, Mr. Charles Wesley's been a great friend to me, with his hymns.

It's a great mercy for me that I've fallen on times when a man may hear sermons as easy to make out as commanding orders, and religious poetry as plain as prose."

I little thought that hymn of Herbert's would so soon come into use as an apology for Mother.

The Monday after that Sunday which was such a great high day to us, Betty, coming down in the dusk, and going to the dairy, fell over the stable-bucket, which Roger had left in the way, and broke her leg. The Falmouth doctor came at once and set it, and says it is not at all a difficult or serious case.

But Betty, never having had an illness which prevented her moving about in her life, grimly sets the cheery doctor at defiance, and takes it for granted that she is dying.

"And it's a comfort to me, Mrs. Kitty," she said to me this evening, "to think I am. Leastways a comfort in some ways. It'll be a warning to Roger as long as he lives, that's one thing; for if I've told him once about leaving that bucket in the way, and said it would be the death of some one, I've told him so scores of times; and now he'll see that I told him the truth. That is one thing, Mrs. Kitty; and another is the signs and tokens. They'll all be made plain,—the pulling of bells, the howling of the dog, poor fool, and all. And I'm mortal glad, Mrs. Kitty," she continued, "that it's me after all, and not Missis." Here her voice faltered, and she hesitated a minute before she went on, and said, "I may as well speak out, Mrs. Kitty. It's my way, and maybe you won't be troubled with me or my ways much longer. I'm mortal glad it's me and not Missis, Mrs. Kitty, because of the assurance, the inward witness in the heart. I got it, my dear, last year. And one day when Missis was ill, poor lamb, and I asked her, she said she hadn't. So it's better I should be taken first."

At first I felt a flush of indignant surprise that Betty could possibly think herself more ready to go to heaven than Mother; but gentler thoughts came as soon as I looked at the poor, kind, rugged face, down which a few tears were trickling slowly, not I knew from pain; and I said as steadily as I could, "Betty, you surely don't mean that you are more fit to meet God than Mother is!"

"My dear," she said, "it's the inward witness. Poor dear Missis, when I spoke to her about it, I'm not even sure if she knew what I meant. It's God's gift, my dear, and He gives freely to the poorest sinners. Better than Missis!—I might as well think I'm better than an angel. But I've got to feel that my sins are forgiven, my dear, and I'm afraid Missis has not. And there's the tokens; so, if the Almighty would take me instead of her,—I'm a cross, cantankerous old woman, my dear, at best, and can never look for anything but quite an under place in heaven, if the Lord spares me ever so long. So I'd as lief go at once."

Then as I looked at her as she turned her face away to hide the tears, like an old Spartan as she is, my whole heart bowed down before her, and I would have knelt to her.

She would have died for any of us with joy, to gain us time to be made more ready for heaven, or to win us a higher place there!

For some time I could scarcely speak. And then I remembered that hymn of Herbert's on God's justice, and said part of it to Betty (explaining as I went), where he says to Justice,—

> "For where before thou still didst call on me,
> Now I still touch
> And harp on thee.
> *God's promises have made thee mine.*
> Why should I justice now decline?
> *Against me there is none, but for me much.*"

And I told her how dear Mother's eyes had glistened as she listened to those words.

"Is not that assurance of being accepted by God?" I said.

"Well, Mrs. Kitty," said Betty, "it do sound cruel like it. And I suppose the Almighty must allow folks to say things in their own way; and if it isn't as plain as might be,—it isn't given to every one to speak plain,—and the Lord can understand,—Mrs. Kitty, my dear, the Almighty can understand, no doubt. I do think sometimes we are all like lisping babes before Him; and if we don't always make out other folk's lispings, He is the Father of us all, and no doubt He can. No doubt He stoops down and listens till He does make it all out; and by-and-by, no doubt, He'll teach us all to speak plainer, so that we may understand each other. Mrs. Kitty, my dear," she concluded, wiping her eyes in a candid way with a corner of the sheet, "you've given me wonderful comfort, wonderful comfort, and the Almighty bless you for it, my dear."

"And so, Betty, you mustn't die yet," I said, smoothing back a wandering lock of her gray hair which was falling over her eyes; "you must do your best to get well. We can't spare you, any of us, for a long time."

"That's as the Almighty pleases, my dear," she said; "we can all be spared a deal easier than we like to think when His time comes. But there *be* the cows, and the pigs, and the poultry, and the butter; and it would be a trial to leave the beasts and fowls, poor fools, to nobody but Roger. I don't deny that it would; not but that he means well, and didn't set that bucket on purpose to break my leg, poor soul, I've no doubt, and all folks can't be blessed with brains. But if I do get over it, Mrs. Kitty," she concluded, "don't you ever say it was the doctor, for I couldn't abide it; and if anything could have killed me it would have been his grinning face, clucking and chuckling away like an old hen when he was nigh driving me mazed with the pain. If I do get well, it will be the Almighty, my dear,—the Almighty, and you, Mrs. Kitty. I only hope, my dear," she said, shaking her head ominously, "you're not born to trouble; for surely the Lord gives you a wonderful gift of cheering and nursing folk, and the Almighty don't most times give His gifts in vain."

XI

HREE months since I wrote a line in these pages! The last words seem faint and distant, like a voice across a chasm, as if the earth had opened beneath my feet and made a great gulf between me and the day when they were written.

Mother had recovered wonderfully. It was as if some lingering malady had been lowering over her life, which spent itself in the tempest of that fever, and left her relieved and almost refreshed, like the air after a thunderstorm. The enforced rest, the duty of saving and considering herself, and letting herself be taken care of, had no doubt much to do with it.

Also, no doubt, there was a merciful Hand at work, and a most tender Providence.

One day Mother and I were sitting sewing at the great window of the Hall. Betty, although limping a little, was once more in office in dairy and kitchen. Father had just whistled for Trusty, and was off for the farthest part of the farm. It was the stillest part of the day, early in a hot afternoon. There was not a sound but the trickling of the water into the cattle trough in the court, the occasional buzzing of a fly against the window, or the hum of a stray bee settling on the marigolds and thyme outside, and Betty's voice humming at her work in the kitchen with scarcely more variety of intonation than the bee.

Mother and I had been talking of Jack. We had written to him some time since, begging him to come back to us, at least for a time, saying we thought the farm was becoming too much for Father, that the old place was large enough for us all, and that we were all longing to have him with us again, and then at all events we could talk over his future plans together.

We had not had any answer. We had explained to each other again and again how natural it was there should be some delay. The posts were so irregular at all times; and although Father had repeatedly ridden to Falmouth to inquire if there were any letters, and had found none, there were endless ways in which accidents might have occurred before letters reached Falmouth. Besides, Jack would no doubt have many things to arrange, especially if he decided on coming back to us; and perhaps, being no very ready writer, he might not send a letter at all, but bring us the answer in person. We were planning how the country might be made less dull for him, and entering into all kinds of arrangements by which we would make home bright for him, (partly, I believe, to persuade ourselves of the reality of our pleasant picture by multiplying its details,) when suddenly a horseman galloped on a foaming horse into the court-yard, making the old walls echo and the windows vibrate with the noise.

Mother and I looked at each other. I suppose I was as pale as she was, for she said,—

"Sit still, Kitty. Let Betty see what it is."

Betty, never easily hurried, was always especially deliberate when she thought other people were in an unnecessary bustle. It seemed an age, while she stood lecturing the horseman, and then before she limped to the open window and gave me the letter, muttering that some folks always liked to make a dash at the end of anything and finish in a fume, putting themselves and other folks in as much fuss as they could; but that it was

her belief such hurry-scurry was most times only a cover for
their own dawdling.

"Bless your heart, Mrs. Kitty, my dear," she concluded,
catching the alarm in my face, "don't look so scared. It's
only a servant of Sir John Beauchamp's; nothing but some
fancy of Mrs. Evelyn's, startling folks out of their wits."

"Betty, give the man refreshment, and ask him to stay and
rest as long as he can," said Mother quietly.

And Betty retired.

It was indeed a letter from Evelyn to me.

It began with tender, soothing, lingering words, quite unlike
her usual way of dashing into the midst of things. It was
meant to "break the news." It only threw my brain into such
a bewilderment, that when I came to the news my heart beat
and my head swam so that I could scarcely read it. But when
I did take it in, I was calm again in an instant. For I could
only think of Mother.

I stood a minute afraid to look at her, and irresolute what
to do, when she said softly,—

"Kitty, don't read it, tell it me. I know quite well it is
not good news. And it's about Jack."

I looked at her. She was sitting with her hands clasped as
if in prayer. And I knelt down by her and whispered (how, I
can never remember, for the words seemed to hiss from my
lips like some one else's voice) that Jack had done something
for which he was arrested and was in prison at Newgate.

"Kitty," she said, "there is no time to be lost. Go and
fetch your Father."

Poor Father! When I found him, and told him, he never
uttered a word of reproach against Jack or any one. He said,
"Poor fellow, poor fellow, I was too hard with him!" and that
was all. We walked home across the fields in silence.

When we returned Mother beckoned to us from the window
of the porch-closet. Father joined her there. I remained in

19

the Hall below. In a few minutes Mother called me, and I went up.

"It is quite plain, darling, what we must do," said Mother; "it is a great mercy it is so plain."

"Father and I must go to him at once," said I.

"Yes," said Mother, "to-morrow." And she pointed to a postscript of Evelyn's letter, which in my excitement I had not noticed, and in which she desired us if we liked to send the servant home by sea, and take his horse to ride to London on at once.

Everything was arranged before dawn the next day.

Father was to take his own horse, and I the man's. We might thus be in London in less than a week, and have besides the great comfort of making the journey alone, not exposed to the questions or prying looks of fellow-passengers.

Betty was too thoroughly one of us not to know our trouble, at least as far as that Jack was in prison. She believed it was for debt; indeed we scarcely understood ourselves whether it was for that or worse.

All night she was up making provision for the journey, insisting that I should keep quiet in my bed. In the morning, as I was dressing, she said, in a rapid eager way, as she was packing and pressing my things into as small a bundle as possible, without pausing a moment in word or work so as to give me a chance of interrupting her :—

"Mrs. Kitty, I've put five guineas in an old stocking in a corner of the bundle. I should have given them to Master Jack when he went to the wars; but Mother told me to keep them for my burying, and I promised I would. However, I've been thinking well about it, and I don't see it would be any sin to break my word.

"For a long time I've been of two minds about it; for what's the use of a fine burying to me, any more than to the rich man in the Bible? Fine buryings won't keep sinners out of the fire, nor will the sores of the poor body, nor the licking of the dogs, poor fools, keep off the blessed angels from carrying the soul home. When I die, Mrs. Kitty, it's my wish that the class members should carry my body to the grave singing Mr. Wesley's hymns, while the angels are carrying my soul, singing *their* hymns. Not that I'm altogether sure, Mrs. Kitty, the angels even will be wanted; for heaven seems nearer a good bit now, since the Lord died, than it was before, and maybe we shall step into it all at once, quite natural, without help from any one. But that's neither here nor there. It wasn't the burying that made me of two minds, but my word to Mother. I've prayed many times about it; and last night I saw it all as clear as the sun. It's my belief that we are to do as we'd be done by, by the dead as well as by the living. And if I were dead, and had got any one to make a foolish promise like that, I should think it the greatest kindness if they broke it, and put the money to a better use. So I shall do the same by Mother, Mrs. Kitty. You needn't say anything to Master Jack about what I've told you. But it's my belief Mother'll be smiling on them guineas from heaven, if she knows about it, if it helps Master Jack; which is more than she could do in conscience, if they were spent making brutes of folks on rum and gin at my burying."

So saying Betty limped down the stairs, leaving me sobbing out the first easy natural tears I had shed since the dreadful news came.

Mother insisted on coming down to breakfast with us, and as she bid me good-bye, while Father was seeing to the bits and girths, she looked so calm and cheerful, I could not help saying,—

"Oh, Mother, don't keep up so. You will break down so much worse when we are gone."

"No, Kitty," she said, "I shall not. I am not keeping up. I believe I am *kept* up. I cannot understand myself. I cannot feel hopeless about this. I have a persuasion not like persuading myself, but like a prophecy, that good is to come out of this for Jack and all of us, and not evil, and the hope strengthens me to pray for him as I never prayed before in my life."

And so we parted.

It was certainly a comfort that the rapidity of our journey depended not on the will and convenience of indifferent coachmen or sailors, to whom we could not have explained our terrible reasons for haste (and who would have looked on our trembling eagerness to get on merely as the fussiness of a fretful old gentleman and of an impatient girl), but on our own exertions and on those of our horses.

How the noble generous creatures seemed to catch the infection of our eagerness! until, for their sakes, and for the sake of greater speed in the long run, we had rather to restrain them than to urge them on.

I only remember distinctly two incidents of that journey, so completely were we absorbed by its purpose.

One was on a fine clear morning, as we were riding down a steep, stony hill in a narrow lane, when we saw before us a gentleman, in a clerical dress, on a horse which was shambling along at its own pace, with the reins on its neck, whilst the rider was reading from an open book laid on the saddle before him.

Father was so impressed with the peril of the proceeding, especially as the clergyman's horse made a very awkward stumble just as we passed him, that he took off his hat, and said to the stranger,—

"Sir, you will excuse an old soldier; but I should think myself safer charging a battery than riding in that way on that beast of yours."

The stranger bowed most politely, and said something in a calm, pleasant voice, about himself and the horse understanding each other; but as he thanked Father for his advice, his face

quite beamed with that cloudless benevolent smile no one who
has seen it can forget; and I saw it was Mr. John Wesley.

The second incident which stands out from the dreary mist of
anxiety which hangs about that journey, happened on the next
morning.

It was not five o'clock, and still rather dusk. We were
always in the saddle as soon as we could see. But at the end
of the town we were leaving, a large crowd was already gathered.
We had to ride through it, and I never liked the look of faces
in a crowd less. Many were of the very lowest type, dull and
brutish, or fierce with a low excitement, and above them rose a
dreadful black thing with arms. At the outskirts of the crowd
we encountered some rough jests. But when we got into the
thick of it, all was quite still. Every eye was riveted on one
spot, and every ear was listening to one calm, solemn voice,
fervent and deep, but always natural and never shrill (he held
it a sin to scream); and before we came in sight of him I knew
it was Mr. John Wesley preaching.

"Come on, Kitty," said Father in a low, trembling voice,
laying hold of my rein as I paused an instant; "don't you see
what the people are waiting for?"

I looked at his quivering lips, and did not venture to ask.

But as I glanced back for a moment, it flashed on me what it
was. It was Mr. Wesley preaching to a crowd collected to see an
execution. That terrible black thing with arms was the gallows.

I shall never forget the respectful kindness with which Uncle
Beauchamp welcomed Father when we reached Great Ormond
Street, nor his tender gentleness to me.

Aunt Beauchamp was as kind in her way; but she went into
hysterics; which was perhaps a relief to every one, as they converted her into an invalid who must be kept quiet, and left
Cousin Evelyn and me free for each other.

Evelyn explained everything to me, as Uncle Beauchamp did to Father.

Jack was in Newgate; not in the debtor's side, but worse.

He had taken some money from that Company, only anticipating his salary, he said, by a few weeks, and, of course, intending to replace it. But the law does not deal with intentions, and the act was felony, and he had to stand his trial. Uncle Beauchamp and Uncle Henderson had engaged the best lawyers to defend him, and Evelyn said they assured them there was much hope.

"But if the defence fails," I said, looking into Evelyn's face, " what is the penalty ? "

"It may be anything, or it may be nothing," she said, avoiding my eyes with an evasiveness quite unusual with her, "the law is so uncertain, every one says."

"It might be *anything !* " Evelyn and I understood each other, and we said no more.

Father and I went the next day to Newgate. It was arranged that we should each see Jack alone, to spare his feelings.

Grim walls with windows placed so as to let in as little light and pleasantness as possible, clanking of chains on prison bolts, grating of clumsy keys, the careful locking behind us of reverberating iron doors, and through all a sense of being watched by curious prying eyes, and then the dreadful certainty that to so many these cells were but the ante-chamber to a dishonoured grave, made me feel like a prisoner myself, almost like one buried alive myself, as I stood alone in a gloomy little room with barred windows looking on a dull court, trying to pray, trying to think what I would say to Jack, but unable, try as I might, to do anything but mentally repeat words without meaning and count the window-bars and chimney-stacks; so that when at last Father came, and I was led into Jack's cell and left alone with him, I was entirely unprepared, and could only throw my arms around his neck and sob out entreaties that he would forgive me for all the rough and cross words I had ever spoken to him.

"Poor little Kitty," he said, with a deep voice more like Father's than his own, "my poor little sister, you and Father are both alike,—not a reproach, not a complaint;" and then placing me on a chair, while he paced up and down the cell, he said, "I did think he would have been in a passion, Kitty, and, I am sure, I wish he had! It would have been much easier." Then, after a pause, he added in a tone more like his own old easy, careless way, "It is the most unlucky thing in the world. I am the most unlucky man in the world. Only three days and then my salary would have been paid, and everything would have been right. However, one must never look on the dark side. Something may turn up yet." And then he asked eagerly all that the lawyers thought.

I said they seemed to have much hope of success.

He seized at this in his old sanguine way, as if success had been certain, and after talking some time about his unluckiness, he concluded,—

"But you know, Kitty, it's a long lane that has no turning. I always knew that there would be a change of fortune for me some day. And now I shouldn't wonder if it's on the point of beginning; for, to confess the truth, they were rather a low money-making set after all in that Company. The secretary's a screw, and a perfidious hypocrite into the bargain. Although not exactly in the way one might have chosen, I've no doubt it will turn out a good thing in the end to have done with them. And as to any little hasty words you may ever have said, Kitty," he concluded, as we heard footsteps approaching, "never mention such a thing again. We all have our little infirmities, and you were always the best little soul in the world."

But as I drove back with Father, my heart seemed absolutely

frozen. Here were we all breaking our hearts about the sin, and doing what we could to make it weigh less heavily on Jack. And his conscience seemed as light as air. He seemed to have no conception that he was anything but unlucky.

How could he ever be made to understand about right and wrong?

The next evening Uncle Beauchamp came to me from an interview with the lawyers, in the greatest perturbation. They said Jack would not enter into their line of defence, and it seemed doubtful if he could be got to plead not guilty.

"You must go and talk to him, Kitty," he said, "and persuade him. If any one can you will. For as to myself," he added, "people's ideas of morality and religion seem to me so incomprehensibly turned upside down since the Methodists came into the world, that I cannot make out anybody or anything."

So the next morning early I was admitted to Jack's cell.

"Uncle Beauchamp says you and the lawyers cannot understand each other, brother," I said, "and I have come to see if I can be of any use."

"The lawyers and I perfectly understand each other," said Jack. "They want me to swear to a lie, and I can't. I did take the money; and if my only defence is to swear I did not, why then, Kitty, there is no defence, of course, and I see no way out of it. I thought they would have found some other way, but it seems they can't."

I felt my whole heart bound with a new hope for Jack, and I went up to him, and took his hands, and said, looking up in his face,—

"You would rather suffer any penalty than tell a lie, brother?"

"Of course, I couldn't swear to a lie, Kitty. What do you mean?"

"Thank God!" I said; and I could not help bursting into tears.

Jack paced up and down the cell a minute or two, and then he paused opposite me and said very gravely, "Are you *surprised*, Kitty, that I will not tell a falsehood—that I will not perjure myself? Did you think I *would?* Did you think because I had anticipated a few days the salary due to me from a set of beggarly trades-fellows, that I could tell a deliberate lie, and take a false oath!"

"O Jack," I said, hiding my face in my hands, "how could I tell! since you took what did not belong to you? It troubled us so much!"

Jack turned from me angrily, and as I sat leaning my head on my hands, I heard him pacing hastily up and down. And then, after some minutes, not angrily, but softly, and in slow, deep accents, very unlike his usual careless manner, he said,—

"I understand, Kitty; you thought if your brother could *steal*, he could do anything else."

"But you will *not*, Jack!" I said, kneeling beside him. "*You will not*. You will suffer anything rather than do what you feel to be wrong,—to be sin. Thank God! thank God!"

He sat for some time quite silent, and then he said, a little bitterly,—

"You seem very thankful, Kitty, for what every one might not think a very great mercy, to have the way cleared to the gallows, as it is to me. I suppose you know a poor woman was hanged the other day for stealing sixpence; and I have stolen fifty pounds. Do you think Father and Mother will be as glad as you are?"

"Oh, Jack!" I said, "you *know* what I mean, you *feel* what I feel. We will move heaven and earth to get you set at liberty, and I feel such a hope that we shall succeed. I feel that God is on our side now, brother. And He is so strong to help!"

But I felt that if we succeeded beyond my brightest hopes

(and I was full of hopes, for there was prayer, and I had thought of a plan), I think I shall never know a truer thrill of joy than that morning in Jack's gloomy cell, when he chose anything rather than do what he felt wrong.

For it seemed to me my brother was then for the first time his true self, the self God meant him to be. He was in the far country still, in the country of husks, where no man gave him even husks; but might I not hope he was "coming to himself"?—that the temptation to a sin *foreign* to his character was (as Hugh once said it might) awakening him to the sin *habitual* to his character, which was indeed *his sin?*

My plan was at first regarded as exceedingly wild by every one but Evelyn. But at last one objection after another gave way; and Cousin Evelyn and I were suffered to drive in Aunt Beauchamp's coach to the residence of Elias Posthlethwaite, Esq., Secretary of the Original Peruvian Mining Company.

Mr. Posthlethwaite wore beautiful ruffles and very brilliant jewels, but his face wanted that indescribable something which makes you *trust* a man, and his manners wanted that indescribable something which makes a gentleman. He received us with most officious politeness, taking it for granted that we had come for shares (many fashionable ladies, Evelyn said, having lately acquired a taste for such gambling, as more exciting than cards). He was afraid that at present not a share was to be purchased at any price. The demand was marvellous. But he did not seem much relieved when Evelyn told him we had no intention of investing in the Company. And his manner changed very decidedly when I contrived to stammer out the object of our visit.

"It is a most painful business, young ladies, a most painful business. The young gentleman was, moreover, an intimate friend of mine. I thought it would have been an opening for the poor young fellow."

I pleaded Jack's youth, I pleaded his refusal to plead not guilty, I even pleaded for Father's sake and Mother's, though it seemed like desecration to make them and their sorrows a plea with that man. But he could not be moved. He said it was exceedingly painful, and quite against his nature, but there were duties to the public which young ladies, of course, could not understand, but which, at any cost, must be performed. At last he grew impatient, the boor's nature came out under pressure, and he remarked with a sneer that those kind of scenes were very effective on the stage, in fact always brought down the house; but that, unhappily, society had to be guided not by what was pretty, but what was necessary. In conclusion he said that, in fact, it did not rest with him; the Governors were suspicious, and had found fault with the accounts before, and it was essential an example should be made.

Meantime Evelyn had been reading (I thought absently) over the printed paper on the table, describing the objects of the Company, and giving a list of the Governors, and at this moment fixing her fingers on two or three of the principal names, she read them aloud, and said calmly,—

"These are the Governors, Mr. Posthlethwaite; and you say the decision rests with the Governors. We will drive to their houses at once. Lord Clinton is one of my father's most intimate friends."

The manner of the Secretary changed again. "Lord Clinton," he said nervously, "Lord Clinton, madam, knows very little of our affairs. In fact, he will no doubt refer you back to me."

"We will see, sir," said Evelyn coolly, fixing her calm, penetrating eyes on him.

He winced evidently.

"Lord Clinton," he said, pressing his forefinger on his forehead, as if endeavouring to recollect something; "ah, I remember, there was a little mistake there, a little mistake which, but for press of business, should have been corrected long ago. Lord Clinton's name was put down inadvertently, without his having been consulted."

"Then the Hon. Edward Bernard, or Sir James Delaware will do as well," said Evelyn. "Come, Cousin," she added, rising, "there is no time to be lost. I suppose, Mr. Posthlethwaite, those two gentlemen were consulted before their names were printed?"

"Certainly, my dear madam, certainly!" he replied. "But, excuse me, what will you say to these gentlemen that they do not know already, or that I could not explain as well, and save you the trouble?"

"Thank you, the trouble is nothing, Mr. Posthlethwaite," said Evelyn quietly. "I will recommend these gentlemen," she continued very deliberately, "who, you say, have had their suspicions roused about the accounts, to look into the accounts and to see if no other victim can be selected for the office of scape-goat except my cousin Mr. Trevylyan."

His keen fox-like eyes quailed visibly before her clear, open gaze.

"My dear madam," he said after a pause, "Mr. Trevylyan is your cousin; your cousin, and an intimate friend of mine. The Governors, I confess, are much irritated, but we must not too easily despair. Leave the matter to me, and we will see what can be done."

"Very well, sir," said Evelyn; "if *you will* see what can be done, *I will not.* You will let us know to-morrow."

And she swept out of the room, Mr. Posthlethwaite bowing her to the steps of the carriage.

"What do you think will be the end of it, Evelyn?" I said when we were alone in the carriage, for I felt very much bewildered.

"The end of what?" said Evelyn.

"Of this terrible affair of Jack's," I said.

"I cannot see quite so far as that, sweet little cousin," she said; "but I think I see the end of Mr. Posthlethwaite and the Original Peruvian Company."

"And the prosecution?" I said.

"How can there be a prosecution, dear little Kitty," she said, "when the prosecutor is hiding his head, for fear of finding himself in Jack's place, and when the Company is scattered to the winds?"

"He seemed a terribly hard man," I said; "I never saw any one like him before, Evelyn. It makes me quite shudder to think of him. And you really think the whole thing was a deception?"

"Well, children," said Uncle Beauchamp, when we returned, smiling as he caught Evelyn's triumphant glance, "safe out of the lion's den at all events! I thought Kitty was to have brought the lion himself in chains of roses, like a fairy queen as she is. But she looks as if she had suffered in the encounter," he said, patting my cheek, which was wet with tears.

"Kitty is only half pleased," said Evelyn. "She scarcely knows whether to rejoice about Jack, or to weep over the wickedness of human nature in the person of Mr. Posthlethwaite; whereas I, on the other hand, having a hard and impenetrable heart, scarcely know whether to be most pleased that Cousin Jack is safe, or that Mr. Posthlethwaite is not safe. I always have thought it one of the most delightful prospects held out to us in the Psalms, that the wicked are to be taken in their own net; but to draw the net tight with my own hands was a luxury to which I scarcely dared to aspire."

Then she narrated the interview. Uncle Beauchamp assured Father and me that all would be right; and I was permitted to go at once to Jack, and tell him all we had accomplished.

Jack was very thankful, and most gentle and affectionate to me; but he said,—

" Don't think me the most ungrateful fellow in the world, Kitty; but I am not sure really, after all, whether it wouldn't have been easier on the whole to have been sent to the colonies, or even put out of the way altogether, than to have to meet every one, and feel, as I do, that I have been the most selfish, cowardly dog in the world, all the while I thought myself a fine, open-hearted, generous fellow. And," he added in a lower voice, " I'm not sure that *that* isn't easier than to have to look at one's self as I have had to do for these last few hours. It's a terrible thing, Kitty, to be disgraced in your own eyes."

" Don't talk so, Jack," I said. " Say what you will to yourself and to God, but not to me. It will do you no good ; and I can't bear it. You don't know, Jack, how good and noble you may be yet," I said, and I put my arm within his, and looked in his face, and said, " I should feel proud to walk with you, Jack, now through London, in that very dress ; the people might say what they would, but I shouldn't mind a bit, for I should feel ' That is my brother, who would rather die than swear to a lie.' "

" It's a brave little Kitty," he said in rather a husky voice ; " but, hush, Kitty !" he added hastily, " hush, for God's sake ; don't lift me up on my fool's pedestal again !"

But as I went away he called me back, and said softly,—

" You have hope of me, Kitty ; don't give it up, for Heaven's sake, don't ! and try to make Father and Mother have hope of me. It does me good to think you have, for God knows I have little myself."

The next day Father and I went to him together ; but that interview I cannot describe, because I never can think of it without crying, much less write. How Father begged Jack's pardon, and Jack Father's, and they both fell into weeping. It is such an overwhelming thing to see men like Father and Jack hopelessly break down, and cry like children.

To women, I think tears are a natural, easy, overflowing of

sorrow. But from men they seem wrung, as if every drop were almost bled in anguish from the depths of the heart. With us tears are a comfort, to men they seem an agony.

But Evelyn was right. In a few days the Original Peruvian Mining Company's splendid offices were to be let, and Elias Posthlethwaite, Esq., was nowhere to be found.

And the prosecutor having come to nothing, of course the prosecution came to nothing too.

But that was not the chief joy; not by any means the chief joy to me, great as it was.

The day after I had told Jack the effect of our interview with the Secretary, I was permitted to sit with him some time in his cell.

At first I talked to him about home, but I thought he seemed absent, and after a little while he said abruptly,—

"Kitty, I had a very strange visitor yesterday evening after you left,—an old sailor called Silas Told,—who it seems finds his way into all the prisons and to the hearts of the prisoners in a very remarkable way. He was a sailor in his youth, and a very bad fellow from his own account; involved in all kinds of horrors in kidnapping blacks from the African coast. At last he grew tired of his wild life, and settled down in business in London, and married. Not long after this a poor workman got him and his wife to go and hear Mr. Wesley at the Foundry. They were not convinced in a moment, but before long everything was thoroughly changed with them. They found great happiness in religion; and after a time he gave up his business to teach poor outcast children at a school in connection with Mr. Wesley's meeting-house at the Foundry, at a salary of ten shillings a week. For seven years he worked from morning till night for these destitute boys. He trained three hundred of them, teaching them to read and write, and fitting them for all kinds of trades. But one morning, when he and his boys were attending Mr. Wesley's five o'clock morning preaching, the text was, 'I was sick and in prison, and ye visited me not.' The reproach pierced his heart, he said, as if our Lord had looked sorrowfully at him while he spoke the words. For some days he was wretched, and from that time he has made it his work to visit every cell in every prison to which he can find admittance. He has gone in the cart to the gallows with criminals, praying for them all the way. He has brought joy, absolute joy, with the news of God's mercy, into condemned cells. He has made the most hardened criminals weep in an agony of sorrow for their sins,—such an agony, Kitty, that afterwards, when they were able to believe God had forgiven them their sins, it seemed nothing to go to the gallows. And what seems to me more wonderful still* (this the jailer told me), sheriffs, hangmen, and turnkeys have been seen weeping as he exhorted or comforted the prisoners. The authorities, civil and ecclesiastical, have tried again and again to keep him out of the prisons, but he will not be kept out. And so yesterday evening, Kitty, he found his way to me."

I said nothing, but waited for him to go on. After a little pause he continued,—

" He found his way to me, and when I am free, if ever I am, I will find my way to him ; for he prayed with me ; and prayer like that I never thought there could be. He prayed as if he saw my heart, and saw our Saviour. I shall never forget it,—I trust I shall never forget it. What the words were I am sure I cannot tell. They did not seem like words, so fervent, so sure, so reverent, so imploring, so earnest, it seemed as if he would have stormed heaven ; and yet all the time the great power of them seemed to be, that he felt God was on our side, *willing* to give, *delighting* to give, stretching out His hands to give!"

"You had told him something of yourself," I said, when he had been silent a little while.

"I don't know what I told him, Kitty, or what he found out

* Stevens' "History of Methodism."

I only know I intended at first to tell him nothing; I thought he was going to treat me as one case among a thousand of spiritual disease. But he came to me like a friend, like a brother, so full of respect, so full of pity, there was no standing it, and before he left I was telling him what was in my inmost heart."

"And it has done you good, Jack," I said.

"It has opened a new world to me," he said. "It has made me see that what you and Father felt for me in my sin and trouble, God felt infinitely more. He has been *grieved* at my doing wrong, because sin is the worst misery, and His one desire and purpose is to lift me out of it up to Himself. And He will do it, Kitty; I do believe He will do it."

It was some days before the formalities about Jack's liberation could be arranged, and very precious days they were to him. Silas Told saw him often, patiently encountering his variable tempers, and meeting his shifting difficulties : for at first Jack had many difficulties; and occasionally, I must confess, he was in an irritable state that did not always contrast favourably with his old complacent equanimity. He often reminded me of a sick child waking up with a vague sense of hunger and discomfort which it could only express by fretting. But the great fact remained. He was no longer asleep; his whole being was awake. At one time he would defend himself captiously against his own previous self-accusations; at another he would bitterly declare that all hope of better days for him was an idle dream, —he had fallen, not perhaps beyond hope of forgiveness hereafter, but quite beyond all hope of restoration to any life worth living here. Yet although often, when I seemed to leave him on the shore, I found him again tossed back among the breakers, and buffeted by them hither and thither, nevertheless, on the whole, there was advance. There was a steadily growing conviction of his own moral weakness, and a steadily growing confidence in the forgiveness and the strengthening power of God, until on the day that he came out, when he and I were alone in the study in Great Ormond Street, he said,—

"It is the *beginning* with forgiveness, Kitty, that makes all the difference ! *Easy* forgiveness, indeed, may make us think lightly of doing wrong, but God's is no easy forgiveness. The sacrifice which makes it easy for us was *God's*. It is pardon proclaimed with the dying words of the Son of God, and sealed with His blood. It is wonderful joy to know that God does not hate *us* on account of our *sins ;* but I think it is almost greater joy to know that He hates our *sins* for *our sakes*, and will not let our sins alone, but will help and encourage us, yes, *and make us suffer anything* to conquer them, and to become just, and true, and unselfish."

Many outside difficulties remained. It seemed difficult to find any career open to Jack. He was ready to try anything, and to bear any humiliation ; but the suspicion and distrust which doing wrong necessarily brings on people are a cold atmosphere for anything good to grow in. If he smiled, for instance, Aunt Henderson was apt to think him impenitent. If he was grave, Uncle Beauchamp was disposed to consider him sullen. It is so terribly difficult for any one who has fallen openly to rise again. If he stands upright and looks up, some people call him shameless ; if he stoops and looks down, others call him base. At first we thought of home and the old farm life ; but much as I should have liked to have him with us again, I could not help seeing with some pain that although Jack made not an objection, and endeavoured to enter into it, the thought evidently depressed him.

One morning while Father and I were debating these matters, to our amazement the footman quietly ushered in "Mr. Spencer."

Hugh had that day arrived with Tom from America. Father left me to tell him all the sad yet hopeful history of the last few weeks, and when, almost before we had come to the end of it, Jack came in, I went away and left them alone together.

Jack told me afterwards that Hugh's warm welcome, and his honest and faithful counsel, were better than a fortune to him. " It is such a wonderful help," he said, " to feel you are trusted by one everybody can trust like Hugh."

I know so well what that is. At one time I used to be afraid to give myself up to the feeling lest it should be idolatry; but I have got over that fear now, after talking it over with Hugh, because he says I am just as wonderful a help to him, which makes it plain that it must be because God makes it so. Hugh says it is no more worshipping each other to feel we can work twice as well together, than it is worshipping the sun to feel we can work better in the daylight.

Hugh has set it all right for Jack,—Hugh and poor Cousin Tom, who came back with him. Hugh thinks the old life at home would not be good for Jack; he thinks Jack and Father naturally fret each other a little, and if they control themselves so as not to fret each other, they will fret themselves all the more by the effort. Besides, he thinks the life would be very depressing for Jack. It would be like a life of old age begun in youth, that monotonous routine of work pleasant and calm enough, with the busy day of life *behind,* but most depressing and trying, with nothing behind but lost opportunities, a closed career, and a wasted youth.

It was therefore arranged that Jack should go to America, and take charge of a tobacco plantation, which Tom had recently purchased in South Carolina, while Tom remained at home to assist his father. The relief to Jack was evidently very great; and I was glad it was all settled before we returned home, as the discussions might have been painful to Mother.

In order to complete these arrangements we spent some days at Hackney. Aunt Henderson informed me, with a grim satisfaction, that Uncle Henderson's demure nephew had disappeared with a considerable sum of money. The loss of property was evidently more than compensated by the fulfilment of prophecy, and by the manifest discomfiture of Calvinistic doctrine in the person of her Presbyterian foe.

Uncle Henderson abandoned that field of controversy altogether; and if any one at any time lifted up a faint protest in favour of Mr. Whitefield and Lady Huntingdon, the utmost Aunt Henderson would concede was, that "there were exceptions, merciful exceptions; that there was, in short, no limit to the divine mercy; that she believed there were even Papists that would be saved."

The disappearance of the nephew and the money was, in his way, as great a relief to Cousin Tom as to his mother.

"You see, Cousin Kitty," he said, "I was determined to submit to anything, for I felt I deserved it. But it is a comfort to feel that I can be of some use to Father, and that I am coming back to work for them, and not only to eat fatted calves."

"I have no doubt, Cousin Tom," I said, "that, after the welcome, no hired servant of his father's worked like the forgiven son did."

"And I have no doubt," he replied, "that he enjoyed toiling in the sweat of his brow as much in its way as the feast."

"I think the forgiven children our Lord meant all do," I said.

A glimmer of understanding glanced out from Cousin Tom's shaggy brows, and he said,—

"Do you remember, Cousin Kitty, once telling me that conversion was not a closed door between us and God, but an open door through which I must go? Well, I was a long while getting to understand that, but I think I am beginning now."

Those were very happy days at Hackney. Aunt Henderson was so interested to hear all about Mother. When I related to her Betty's treatment of the fever, she said Betty was quite right in considering her recovery a miracle, for that such conduct was nothing less than murder and madness.

But her heart was too softened and humbled with joy—the joy of having her boy home again—to be very severe on any one's errors,—except the demure nephew's, without whose delinquencies and misbeliefs her controversial weapons might have rusted on the shelf.

When I attempted to thank her for Tom's generous conduct to Jack about the plantation in South Carolina, she stopped me at once,—

"Kitty, my dear, every shilling we have in the world would be nothing for me and mine to repay to you and yours. What you and Mr. Spencer have done for Tom and for us is beyond thanks or payment, and compliments are not in my way. Poor dear Sister Beauchamp understands that kind of thing. But I never did. But, my dear, if at any time any of you are ill, don't hesitate to send for me to come and nurse you. I do know something about physic, which is more than can be said for any of you, poor Sister Trevylyan among you ; and I'd go from one end of the earth to the other, and wear myself to a skeleton with pleasure, to do any of you any good in my power. So only you promise, Kitty, my dear, and I should feel it quite a burden off my mind."

I could not help inwardly trembling at the thought of the snail's broth, the severe medical discipline, and the collisions that must inevitably occur in such a case between Aunt Henderson and Betty. I could only say I trusted we should all keep well for a long time, and that it would be a delight to me to render the same service to Aunt Henderson.

So we are once more at the dear old home. Our own old

party,—Father, and Mother, and Jack, and Hugh, and I; for Hugh always was one of us, although now he is one of us in a nearer way.

How nearly we have all been severed in the storms of this "troublesome world." And how sweet the past dangers make the present calm.

There is much, indeed, still to remind us that we are at sea, on the open sea, with no promise of exemption from storms in time to come. But we are not without a Pilot; and we have proved Him, which is something to gain from any storm.

Mother is much more willing to part with Jack for America than we dared to hope she would be. She says she feels it easier to part with him now than when he went to the army in Flanders. She feels he is not going alone. And by that, we know well, she does not only mean that Hugh is going with him to settle him in the new country.

For Hugh *is* going, but with a hope that makes his going easier for us both than when he left us last.

Because, a few days after our return, we had a visit from Evelyn's great-uncle, our new vicar.

He looked more aged and thinner than when we saw him last; and he was more nervous than ever.

He said he believed it was too late to transplant an old man like him from the centre of civilized and learned life at Oxford to what, he hoped he might term, without offence, a region rather on the outskirts of civilization. He said, between wrecking and poaching, aversion to paying tithes, their Cornish dialect, and what he could not help calling remnants of native barbarism, on the one hand, and Methodism on the other, he could make nothing whatever of the people, and if any one else could, he was sure they were welcome to try.

He had therefore come to propose that Hugh should take the curacy, with a liberal salary. He himself would settle in London. He had spoken to the patron, who, considering the circumstances, said perhaps it was the best thing that could be done. So all is settled.

Hugh and Jack are gone. They sailed from Falmouth.

I feel more anxious now they are actually gone than when it was first proposed. From not having much imagination, I never can measure the pain of things beforehand, which sometimes makes it worse afterwards.

The ship they sailed in is an old one. I heard some sailors talking disparagingly of her as we left the quay.

And the evening after they left was stormy. Heavy masses of thunder-cloud gathered in the west as I looked from the cliffs, just where I thought the ship must be.

And Betty shakes her head again, and says it is of no use boding ill, but she has seen and heard very dismal things of late.

And when I combated her fears, and reminded her what terrible things she had heard about Mother, she only nodded and compressed her lips, and reminded me that, if miracles were worked, and Mother was spared, nevertheless she broke her own leg, to say nothing of Master Jack; and miracles can't be expected at all times. She only wishes she had not been a poor crippled old woman, or she would have gone herself to take care of Master Jack. She has heard terrible tales of the Indians and blacks; and who was to get up his linen and darn his stockings? However, she will hope for the best. Folks *have* got out of their hands alive, she believes, and she trusts Master Hugh will, and that we shall see him back again safe and sound; but she shall be thankful when we do, that is all.

"But, Betty," I said at last, struggling between tears and anger, or rather between anger at her for her forebodings and at myself for minding them—"Betty, it is no better than the heathens to heed such fancies. We must open our hearts wide

to the Bible, and let the light of the truth and the breath of the
Spirit shine and search through every corner. What are all the
forebodings in the world to one hour of hearty prayer? Remember, prayer was stronger even than St. Paul's forebodings;
for he said he 'perceived that the voyage would be with much
hurt and damage, not only of the ship, but also of their lives.'
Yet, afterwards, when he had fasted and prayed, he stood forth
and said that *God had given him the lives of all* that were in
the ship; and though the ship was wrecked, not one life was
lost."

"There *be* some prayers," said Betty, "that can move heaven
and earth."

"And prayer was stronger than prophecy once," I said—
"not the prayer of an apostle, Betty, but of a poor sinful heathen
city. Nineveh was saved, let Jonah be disappointed as he
might at his words being set aside."

"Well, Mrs. Kitty," said Betty dryly, becoming very busy
and energetic about her work, "I hardly take it kind of you to
put me down with that poor selfish old Jew. I've thought
many a time it as wonderful the Almighty should speak by him
as by Balaam's ass,—running away from his work, nearly sinking the ship and the sailors, and then sulking and creusling
like a spoilt child, because the Lord was more pitiful than he,
and the poor sinful men and women of that great city, and the
poor harmless dumb beasts, were spared. I can't say but I do
feel hurt to be likened to him. All I know is, I pray night
and day for Master Jack and Master Hugh; and if Master
Jack and Master Hugh do come back safe and sound, cruel glad
I shall be."

"Betty," said I, "you know I never meant to compare you
to the prophet Jonah; I only said that God even turned from
His own threatenings when people prayed to Him long ago; and
who can say how much even our prayers may help those we
love now? He can send His angels, and one of His angels is

stronger than all the storms on the ocean; or He can stretch
out His hand, and then poor sinking Peter can walk on the sea.
I want you to think of God's promises, and not of signs, and
tokens, and our forebodings. I want you to hope, Betty,
because I know you love us all so dearly; and the more we
hope the better, I think, we pray; and sometimes I find it
hard to hope myself, and I want you to help and not to hinder
me."

"Well, my dear," said Betty relaxing, "young folks most
times find it easy enough to hope. If the sun shines for an hour,
they think there'll never be winter again; and if old folks don't
keep their wits about them, where'll the fire-wood be when
winter comes? And, Mrs. Kitty, my dear, I meant no disrespect
to the prophet Jonah; poor fearful soul, he had his troubles,
sure; and if I'd been in his place, I won't say I mightn't have
been worse than he, although I do hope the Almighty would
have kept me from caring for some poor bits of leaves, that
grew up like mushrooms in a night, just because they made me
cool, more than for all the people in that great town, specially
the innocent babes and the dumb beasts. I'm a cross-grained
old soul, Mrs. Kitty, my dear, and my temper's a little particular at the best of times; but I'd be content to sit a helpless
cripple all the rest of my life in the chimney-corner and watch
Roger, poor fool, or that poor clumsy hussy, blundering away
at the beasts and the butter (though I won't deny it might
worry me into my grave), if I might see you and Master Hugh
and Master and Missis all here together, and know Master
Jack was doing well,—and who knows but I may? For I
don't deny that the Lord's mercies are beyond everything; and
if *He* disappoints folks, it's most times by giving them more
than they ask and better than they hope. Leastways, Mrs.
Kitty, my dear, that's been His way with me."

XII

T is now two months since Hugh and Jack left us. We have had letters, full of hope and promise; and all the weight of forebodings which settled down on me in the long days of silence between their leaving and our hearing seems melting away. Every breath of this soft spring air, every smile of this life-giving spring sunshine, seems to blow and shine my cares away.

I think the delight of seeing new things is nothing compared to the delight of, seeing old things grow to a new beauty, in a new season, or in the light of a new joy,—that is, living things, things of God's making. I can never fancy taking half the pleasure in seeing all the wonderful forests Hugh writes about in the New World that I do in seeing those very same dear old elms, that have bent down over me from my childhood, wake up, branch by branch, and twig by twig, and spread their delicate leaves in the air till they are thick enough to hide in deep bowers of shade the soft nest those two happy thrushes have been so busy building and lining, and where the mate is now singing in low tender tones, while the mother-bird broods over her nest, and the gentle winds rock the cradle.

Those American forests, with their brilliant climbing-plants, would be only a picture to me,—a glorious picture, indeed, painted by God's hand, but wanting the sweet perfume of time and home which breathes to me from every blossom of the hawthorn under my chamber window.

And now there is another new light on all the dear familiar old places; for Hugh is coming back so soon, so soon! And we are to work together all our lives for the good and happiness of the old parish and the old friends, to bring new eternal hope and life, I trust, into many a heart and home.

It is the wonderful power of *life* in everything which seems to thrill the heart with the conscious presence of the Life, far more than the most glorious scene which we cannot look at long enough to see it grow and bloom and change until, instead of lying on the surface of our minds as a vision, it possesses our hearts, and grows into them as a part of our life.

The beauty of all beautiful places says, *God has been here.* But the life in the lowliest living thing—in the tiniest moss which puts forth a fresh green stem to-day—in the little leaf which has burst the gummy casing in which it was encased yesterday, and flutters in the air and sun to-day, with the crumples of its long winter packing not yet fluttered out of it— in the trembling snowdrop, which a touch can crush, but which all the weight of the inanimate earth could not keep from bursting up into the sunshine—*life* in its lowliest development says not, God *has been* here, but *God is here;* not only "The Master's hand has been on us; do you not see the perfection of His work?" but "The life of the Life-giver is breathing through us; do you not feel the joy of His presence?" and that seems to me to go much deeper into the heart.

I was sitting to-day by the little well-spring in our wood, from which the water wells up so gently, so peacefully, without noise or stir, that it often makes me think of the pool which the angel troubled and made its waters healing; so strong is the power of life for every creature near that seems to flow from that little spring! The first spring-flowers always come there, which is one of the reasons why I know it so well, because I gather the first nosegay there every year for Mother; and so deep and hallowed is the quiet, that, as a child, I used often to fancy it must be something more than wind and water which made the flowers quiver and the leaves flutter, as if with the touch of a hand they loved; and, as it is, I often wonder if there are not a great many more living beings busy in the world around us about God's work than we know of. Because *we* use machines to save toil and to spare hands; but where work is not toil, but delight, and where the workers are ten thousand times ten thousand and thousands of thousands, why should lifeless machinery do what living hands can always do so much better?

But however that may be, Hugh says, matters comparatively little; because nothing is done in God's world by dead laws made long ago, nor by lifeless machinery set going long ago, and generally superintended from a distance. Everywhere the agency is living, not mechanical; whether the work of happy ministering spirits, or of the one living Presence, which is better and dearer and nearer than all.

Mother and I have been having long talks as we have been sitting at our spinning or sewing; and it seems to me it is our transplanting those poor limited thoughts of ours into heaven that makes half the difficulties, if not all, in those questions of predestination, and assurance, about which some Christian people have been fighting so bitterly of late.

We want to have everything sealed and settled, and written down in unalterable decrees and irrevocable title-deeds; forgetting that deeds and decrees are of value to us simply because the people who make them may die or change.

But the grand security of the gifts of God is that it is God who gives them. The Giver lives for ever, and is always at hand. I do not think He will give us any other security, and I am sure we can have none so strong.

Unbelief, like Eve, craves a security independent of God. But independence of God is death; and faith, accepting the living God as the security of His own promises, finds in such dependence, not only security, but life. Unbelief would have some sentence, some irrevocable decision, to build on. God gives us no such poor abstractions to rest on apart from Him. His promises are all personal, all made to present faith. He says, " My sheep shall never perish, neither shall any pluck them out of my hand "—" I will never leave thee nor forsake thee "—" What shall separate us from the love of Christ ?"

If the cold heart, craving security against itself, asks, "But can *I* pluck *myself* out of Thy hand ? Can I forsake Thee ?"— though neither things present, nor things to come, nor life, nor death, can separate, may not *sin ?* still no answer comes but, " I love, I keep—*abide in Me.*" If we seek one promise to a past faith, one word of encouragement to any except those who are turning to God, we may look through the Bible in vain. Turn to God, all is light; turn from Him, all is shade. God gives no promises except to faith, and faith in exercise.

But if the trembling, clinging heart asks, weeping, the same question, " Can I ever tear myself from Thy hand ? can I ever leave Thee ?" it is still the same answer, though in a different tone, the tone of tenderest pity—" Abide in Me ; *I love, I keep.*" To strong faith this is full and absolute assurance. . To feeble faith no stronger assurance can be given. If all the ingenuity of all the divines and lawyers in the world were taxed to find a formula stating in abstract terms the security of a believer, despondency would be sure to find some flaw to exclude itself. Therefore I think God takes another way, and drives the trembling, doubting heart, through the very destitution of security, to Himself; to the security which is safety, whether it is felt to be so or not, and which, when it is felt to be safety, is life and joy besides ; to the fortress of the Father's house— to the sanctuary of the Father's heart.

And once there, what child would not smile at all the security of documents, weeping on His bosom, " I would rather trust Thee ! "

God will not suffer us to rest on things, on words, on anything

in our past, or anything even in His promises, apart from Himself. "Communion with God," Mother said, "is the end and
object of redemption. 'Thou hast redeemed us *to God* by Thy
blood.' And God loves us too much to suffer that anything
shall be a substitute for prayer, for the communion of the soul
with Himself."

*   *   *   *   *

It seems that, during our absence in London, when Betty
and Mother were left alone together, they had many discussions.
At first these were at times rather hot and controversial. But
one day Betty said it made her head so dizzy, she felt like going
mazed, to be spinning round and round always in the same
place, as it was her opinion Missis and she had been doing.
She therefore proposed that, instead of talking so much, they
should read the Bible together, with one of Mr. Wesley's hymns
by way of a prayer; and it was wonderful, Mother said, how
much better they grew to understand each other after that.

"For," said Mother, "to confess the truth, Kitty, I never
forget something Betty said to me about assurance and the
witness of the Spirit, when I was ill." So at last, one evening
after their reading, Mother had the conversation which she thus
related to me :—

They had been reading the eighth chapter of the Romans,
and had stopped at the verses, "There is therefore now no
condemnation to them that are in Christ Jesus," and "The
Spirit beareth witness with our spirit that we are the children
of God." Betty told Mother what she had told me before,—
how, after weeks of gloom and wretchedness, in which the sense
of her sins weighed on her like a darkness that could be felt,
one evening she saw the burden of her sin laid on her Saviour,
so that all her heart suddenly overflowed with gratitude, and
love, and peace. She felt that He had borne her sins, and that
they were borne away, and that she was forgiven.

Mother replied that she had more than once felt her heart

melt into thankfulness and joy when she had looked at the
Cross, but that afterwards the recollection of her sins had
weighed her down again, and she thought the utmost she could
ever hope for was that at last hope might overbalance fear,
God's mercy outweigh her sins, and that so, perhaps on her
deathbed, a trembling hope might be vouchsafed her that she
might depart in peace. She did not deny that such an assurance as Betty spoke of might be given to some, but she believed
it was to great saints or to people with very strong faith. At
all events, she had never thought it could be anything but pre-
sumption for her to expect it.

But Betty said she did not think the Almighty meant His
children to creep through the world with a rope round their
necks, as if they were never sure of not being condemned at
last. If God Almighty's service was to be such a *wisht* thing
as that, she did not think many would be drawn to it. And she
was sure no father with a heart in him would treat the worst
child who wanted to become better in such a way, much less
the Lord.

"But," said Mother, "the tenderest parent can see his child
suffer anything if it is for the child's good. The more God
loves us the more He will bear to be grieved with our griefs, if
it is to end in our joy. And since we are such wilful and rebellious children, it may be safer for us to wait for our pardon
until we are safe from sinning any more."

"That wasn't your way, nor Master's, leastways Missis'," said
Betty.

"Better perhaps if it had," replied Mother, thinking mournfully of Jack.

"Well, Missis," said Betty, "all I know is I couldn't work,
nor I wouldn't, for a master who had no way of keeping his
house right, but spying on the men and maidens like a jailer,
and never dropping them a good word or a smile for fear they
should forget their places. Even the beasts feel the difference,

poor fools. And as to Master Jack," she added in a softened, faltering voice, "I can't deny that if you and Master were to treat him like a good-for-nought, and never give him a kind look nor a word of welcome, but sit in the Hall, like judges, for him to come and bow and make fine speeches before you, and then send him to take his meat along with Roger and me in the kitchen, if I were Master Jack I'd run away again for good; and as to me, I'd take myself off in no time;" and Betty all but cried at her own picture, when a new view of the matter struck her, and she broke into a smile. " Well, Missis, what an old fool I be to think of you and Master setting up *play-acting* like that. Why, any one would see through it fast enough. Roger, himself, poor innocent, would wait, laughing in himself, to see what was to come next; and the very dog would see through it, and whine and fawn on Master Jack, and jump from him to you, as much as to say, 'Why, don't you see it's young Master!' But Master Jack would see through it first of all, and before you or Master could say one of your fine improving speeches, he'd be at your feet, Missis,—he'd be on your heart, and you'd be sobbing your heart out over him for joy."

Mother made no reply for some little time, and Betty resumed in a low voice,—

"And God Almighty is a sight better than that. The father in the Bible didn't sit in the house waiting for the son to come back, and making up faces and speeches to make him feel what a fool he had been. His only fear was that the poor foolish lad would be too ashamed to come. He was watching all the while from the door, and the moment he saw him he ran to meet him, that they might come back together, that every soul in the house might see the poor fellow was welcome. He stopped the poor speech the lad had made up in the foreign parts with kisses, so that he never got through it, and fondled him as if he had been his mother more than his father, and set all the men and maidens to work, and then set them to feasting and dancing and merry-making, as if it had been a wedding or a christening, instead of a poor wild lad creeping back home for a bit of bread, with scarce a rag on his back nor a shoe to his feet. He wasn't afraid the poor boy would make himself too much at home. He couldn't do enough like to make him feel he *was* at home; and the Lord says that's how the Almighty feels when one of us comes back to Him. And HE knows the *inside* of the Father's house," concluded Betty, "which is more than any of us do yet awhile."

Mother admitted that the parable of the prodigal son did indeed show quite plainly God's joy in receiving the penitent sinner. But how were we to know we were penitent? It was so easy to deceive ourselves, to persuade ourselves into anything we wished.

"Well, Missis," said Betty, "I didn't find it so easy; the more I wished it the less I felt I could get it."

Some people, sincere and truthful Christian people, might feel that, Mother admitted, people who were reserved and truthful with themselves; but who could answer for the delusions into which excitable sanguine people might work themselves if they were told that the beginning of religion was to feel that their sins were forgiven?

"Of course some folks will deceive themselves," said Betty. "Some folks always will. The apostles couldn't keep them from it. But the warnings of the apostles even to such always ended, not with 'go away,' but 'come back;' and it may give folks a better chance of turning right altogether at last if their faces have been turned the right way only for a few hours. It's my belief folks are more easily got to try again if they've had but a glimpse of what a terrible thing sin is, and what joy God can give, than if they'd lived all their lives without having a thought beyond the brutes, and doing everything worse than the beasts. But," concluded Betty, "I can't be sure, Missis.

that if they don't turn right in the end it won't be worse for them. And I think the apostle Paul felt the same."

Mother returned to the point,—How was any one to know the false joy from the true ?

And to that all Betty could say was,—

" Well, Missis, I can't say I think folks can know unless they try. As far as I know it's a kind of joy that makes you ready to let all the world trample on you and never mind a bit. It's a joy that makes you feel as if you could forgive even your greatest enemy, and indeed as if no one could do anything so hurtful to you as to be worth calling an enemy, because if they could only feel what you feel, they would be like your brothers at once. It's a joy that lifts you above all the joys of the world as if they were poor forgotten dreams, and makes you ready to stoop beneath any burden or trouble in the world, because of the hand that fits on the yoke. It's a joy that makes you feel lower than the lowest upon earth, because you've been forgetting and neglecting Him who died for you; and it's a joy that makes you feel higher than all the kings of the world, because He loves you ; and it's a joy the whole world cannot take away, but the least puff of pride or breath of sin can dim and soil and stain. If we lived in it always we should be as meek as lambs, and as busy as bees, and as happy as angels, and as brave as Master, and as kind, Missis, my dear, as you : and when we lose it there's nothing for us but to go back where we found it, to the Lord who won it, to the Almighty who gave it. For we're as weak as Samson with his hair shorn without it, and as strong as Samson when he took up the city gates when we've got it ; and though it's never to be found by looking for it, it's always to be found by looking for the Lord. For when the Almighty calls us to forsake the world for Him here and now, do you think He has nothing better than the world to give us here and now? And," she concluded, "if we're always to be climbing up the rock out of the waves ourselves, and never sure we're on it, how are we to turn and have our hands free to help the rest who are still clinging to the wreck or buffeting the breakers?"

"And what did you say next, Mother?" I asked.

"I said nothing to Betty," Mother replied. "I went up into the little porch-closet, Kitty, and knelt down and prayed God to teach me."

"And then, Mother?" I asked.

"Why then, Kitty, I read the Bible, and I thought a long time, and then I prayed again, and at last I began to see that it was a sin not to believe in the love God has to us, and a duty to be glad."

And is not this the good news which the Methodists are bringing to thousands and tens of thousands all over the world, —a religion which promises present life, and joy, and strength to all who receive it, and which keeps the promise; a religion which speaks not only of a past creation, finished and made, and very good, but of a living present Creator and Father, creating now and living now; not only of the past finished redemption, but of a present living Redeemer; not only of a past miraculous Pentecost, but of a present living Holy Spirit, teaching and comforting here and now?

> "Not thankful when it pleaseth me,
> As if Thy blessings had spare days,
> But such a heart whose pulse may be
> Thy praise."

This morning I awoke with these words of good Mr. Herbert's singing in my heart, and before noon I felt my need of them. There has been a letter from Hugh. Jack's affairs will take longer settling than we thought, and meantime Hugh finds plenty of missionary work among the poor blacks, so that I must try not to wish him back before the autumn, to which time his return is delayed ; and not to let the intervening days be merely a kind of waste border country between two regions of life, but to fill them with their own work, which, no doubt, if I ask God, He will give me to do.

One piece of work has come already. Toby Treffry, when Mother and I went to visit him to-day, asked me as a great favour if I would let him come to our house for an hour now and then, and help him on a little with his reading, which, with all his pains, he still finds to be a very laborious and rather uncertain method of gaining information or edification. This evening he came for the first time, and with some hesitation the chief reason for this desire of improvement came out. He has contrived to collect a few of the idle boys of the parish on Sunday afternoon, when there is no service, to teach them reading and singing, and the attempt to help others has taught him his own deficiencies.

This accounts for the sounds Father and I heard issuing from Toby's cottage as we were walking through the fields last Sunday. The singing was hearty enough, at all events. From time to time the voices seemed to grow uncertain and few, and to wander with no very clear purpose or connection with each other ; but after such intervals Toby's voice was heard again like a captain's collecting his scattered forces, and the whole body came in together at the close with a shout which Father and I concluded was the chorus.

I suggested to Betty that a little instruction in music in a humble way, such as I can give, might not be useless to Toby if he is to be choir-leader as well as schoolmaster.

"More than that, Mrs. Kitty," said Betty, "Toby Treffry is appointed local preacher through our district."

This announcement was made as Betty was taking away the supper, and the demand on Mother's faith in Methodist arrangements was more than it could stand.

"Toby a preacher, when he can scarcely read!" she said.

"It's my belief, Missis," said Betty, "folks can learn to read a deal easier than they can learn what the Almighty's learned Toby, poor soul. There be things seen in the depths Toby's been taken through, not written in any spelling-book I ever see."

"But whatever the profit may be to others," said Mother, "it must certainly be dangerous to Toby himself to set himself up to teach when he has so much to learn."

"Well, Missis," said Betty respectfully, but very determinedly, "it seems to me, if folks wait to teach till they've no more to learn, they may wait till doomsday. And more than that, the folks that do set up to teach because they've done learning are most times mortal dull teachers. Nothing comes so fresh, in my opinion, as a lesson the teacher himself learned yesterday from the Almighty. However, Toby's not set himself up to teach, at any rate; folks found they were the better for what he'd got to say up to class, and so do I, and they would make him speak to them, so that he couldn't help preaching, and that's the end of it."

"An audience that *will* listen is certainly a good beginning for a preacher," remarked Father. "I would not object to a little more of the same test; and I suppose Toby's salary is not very great."

"Well," replied Betty dryly, "Toby's pay, and most of the local preachers', is most times the wrong way, as far as this world goes. He walks often ten and twenty miles to his preaching, and when it rains he's got to preach in his wet things, and sit in them till they are dry, which is all very well when folks are young, but can't last always. As far as I can see, Toby's pay is weary bones now, and is like to be rheumatism when he's old. But he's content, sure enough, and well he may be, and the rest of them too. They've got good part of the pay they look for now, and all the rest well kept for them."

But when I afterwards questioned Toby himself about his expenses and his self-denying labours, he coloured and stammered very little like a man accustomed to public speaking; but at last he said, "They've only taken me on trial for a year, Mrs. Kitty; and as to the *pay*, the times I have alone in my walks, thinking of the Lord and his goodness and all I've got to tell them, are pay enough for a prince, let alone the joy of seeing the folks' hearts melted by the words, and the hope of meeting them and thanking the Lord all together, by-and-by."

These last weeks have been full of events. Uncle Beauchamp died rather suddenly two months since. The shock brought a slight attack of paralysis on Aunt Beauchamp, which has disabled her from entering any more into society.

Cousin Evelyn is left in possession of a large fortune, bequeathed to her sole use on her father's death, by the will of her paternal grandmother. She has announced her intention of paying us a visit, if convenient. Aunt Beauchamp, in her feeble health, keeps recurring, like a sick child, to a promise she says Mother made her of coming to nurse her if ever she should be ill. And since it is impossible for Mother to leave home, the doctors think, (Evelyn writes,) that, difficult as the journey is, the most probable chance of recovery is for her mother to come at least for a little while to us. Mother's tender, gentle nursing may restore her shattered nerves, or at least soothe them.

Betty's anticipations of this visit are not bright. A fine London man and maid, and an old lady who, she has heard, paints her face as no one ever did in the Bible except Jezebel, are very serious apprehensions to Betty. Indeed she said to-day it was quite enough in her opinion to account for all the evil signs and tokens; so that perhaps (she admits) there's some comfort even in such an upset as this, for such sights and sounds might have boded worse.

. Betty's spirits are much relieved now that our visitors have come, by discovering that the "London man" turns out to be a Methodist collier lad, promoted by Evelyn to the dignity of groom, that Mrs. Sims is entirely engrossed with her mistress, that my poor Aunt has relinquished the rouge, and that in a very short time the whole party are to emigrate to the Parsonage.

For Cousin Evelyn has bought the next presentation of the living for Hugh, for which she says no thanks are due, as she intends to rob us of the Parsonage, and to convert it (with the exception of such rooms as she and her Mother want) into an orphan house for some destitute little girls she has discovered in London, for whom she believes the great hope is to take them quite out of reach of their bad relations into such a new world as this will be to them.

We, she says, are to struggle on as we can in the old house. She insists, however, on repairing and restoring the whole fallen side of the old court, in which are situated the rooms formerly appropriated to our new home. The masons and carpenters are at work already. There is not much to be done. The old walls are as firm as when they were built; and the stone mullions only need to be repaired here and there. The chief alterations are the replacing of broken floors and ceilings, the glazing of the old windows, and the dethronement of Betty's poultry, which from time immemorial have made their roost in the deserted old chambers.

Already, under Evelyn's eager hastening, the work is advancing. And when Hugh comes back he will feel as if an enchanter's wand had been waved over the old place, so delightfully like and yet unlike is it to its old self.

Evelyn is altogether graver and gentler and more peaceable than I ever saw her. Her strong will seems to find its element in action, and no more drives her restlessly against other people's wills merely by way of exercise. At the same time she seems to me more of a queen than ever; and I delight to watch how instinctively every one yields to her control;—every one except poor Aunt Beauchamp; and in her sick-chamber I love to see Evelyn even better than anywhere else. The stroke, and the bereavement, and the change of circumstances have brought a vague feeling of irritation and helpless opposition into my poor aunt's brain, very painful to see, and this chiefly vents itself on Evelyn. She seems to feel as if something, she knows not what, were always preventing her doing what she wishes; and, when Evelyn appears, this tyrannical something seems to represent itself to her as poor Evelyn's will. At times she blames and reproves Evelyn as if she were a wilful child; at other times she weeps and wrings her hands, and entreats her, as if she herself were the child and Evelyn the harsh parent, to be allowed to do some impossible thing or other.

And Evelyn, so strong and commanding elsewhere, by that sick-bed is tender and yielding, and patient with every sick fancy. Now and then she is rewarded, after a paroxysm of anger or fretfulness, with a few tender words of love and thanks, as a gleam of clearer light breaks on the poor troubled brain. And then it is always as to a little child Aunt Beauchamp speaks to her, calling her old tender pet names, at which poor Evelyn's eyes fill with tears.

The doctors say this form of the disease will probably pass, and already Mother's presence and firm kind nursing seem to exercise a soothing influence.

The time for Hugh's arrival is come. Any day may bring us tidings of his vessel. Evelyn is hastening the preparation of the Parsonage for the reception of her mother and the orphans. Two rooms looking on the garden she has had fitted up with every luxury her mother is accustomed to—china vases, and images on gilded brackets, caskets of aromatic woods, soft carpets, leopard and tiger skins, mirrors with little china cupids peeping round at their own reflection from the garlanded frames, everything to make her poor mother feel as much at home as if her windows looked on Great Ormond Street, instead of over a patch of garden sheltered with difficulty from the storms of the Atlantic.

The rest of the house is a strange contrast. In Evelyn's own rooms the only luxuries are flowers and books, and a view, through an opening in the valley, of the sea. The furniture is nearly as simple as that of the dormitories and the schoolroom for the orphans, to whom the remaining rooms are devoted.

Every one of the little white beds for the orphans has its own little dressing-table and washing apparatus, and chest of drawers, and its tiny set of book-shelves. These are all alike. Evelyn means to add by degrees little gifts of pictures or books, as she learns the tastes of the little inmates. She wants to supply the place of a home, as far as possible, to the children, not, she says, by the assumption of names of relationships which are untrue, but by getting to know each child individually, and by giving each some little peculiar possessions, so as to make each feel not a little unit in a sum total, or a thing in a store-house, but a little person in a family. Her plan is to give each, perhaps, a hen or a fruit-tree, that they may learn early the connection between taking care and having, and between self-denial and giving. She intends also, whenever it is possible, to encourage their cherishing little memorials of the past, that they may feel they are not taken into the orphan-house to be taken out of the order of God's providence, but only to be removed from some of the world's dangers and Satan's temptations.

"That is my blank-sheet, Kitty," she said to me one day. "It will be strange in after years to watch how what is written on it corresponds with my plans. For though the scheme is in my hands, the history, you know, is not."

"Cousin Kitty," she said suddenly, as we were walking home across a reach of sandy shore, "Mr. Wesley thinks riches the

meanest of God's gifts; but I do think they are a grand gift
when one is young and free. So few have wealth until their
wants and habits have so grown up to it that it is, after all,
only just what they want; that is, not riches to them at all.
Now with me it is different. My tastes are as simple as possible. I have no pleasure in splendour, and no need for luxuries. God has given me riches in my youth and health; and,
moreover," she continued in a trembling voice, "He has given
me to see something of the great poverty and misery there are
in this world; and also He has brought me, at the threshold
of my life, face to face with Death. And there is nothing in
the world I should like so much—I mean really *like* and *enjoy*
so much "—she continued, emphatically, "as to give up *myself*
and all I am and have, to helping, and cheering, and saving
the sorrowful, and neglected, and destitute, and lost people
around me, all my life long; and leading them to feel all the
time that the love and help they found in me are only a little
trickling from the great fountain of the love and power of God."

As she spoke she was looking far out over the sea to the
west, where the sky was glowing with sunset. But the glow
and light in her eyes and on her beaming face seemed, as I
looked at it, to make the glow of the sky seem a lifeless thing
in comparison. It came, I felt, from a Sun "unseen and
eternal," and the light was not sunset, but sunrise.

*   *   *   *   *

While Evelyn and I stood together by the sea-side that evening, I noticed at one point a bank of clouds just rising slowly
above the horizon. As we walked home, the wind rose in those
strange fitful gusts which Father says are like the flying skir-
mishing parties sent to clear the way before the main forces of
a storm.

I felt terribly anxious; and I knew every one felt I was,
because all through the evening they tried to keep up the conversation, and spoke eagerly of Evelyn's work at the Parsonage,

—of the work we were doing—of Father's old military days—
of any one, except Hugh—of anything, except the wind which
had now ceased to be gusty, and kept surging up the valley in
great waves, as regular and almost as strong as the billows it
had been urging on in its course, and whose salt spray it dashed
against the rattling windows, mingled with the great plashes of
the rain.

Evelyn wished me good-night in an easy, careless voice, as if
it were quite an ordinary night, and no one we cared about
were on the sea ; and Mother made no attempt to come to my
chamber, or to invite me to hers, as she did in any common
anxiety. Only Father's voice had a faltering tenderness as he
came back from an exploration of the weather outside, and
said, as we separated for the night,—

" This storm is nothing sudden ; it cannot have taken any
good seaman by surprise. It has been brewing since yesterday
evening, and, no doubt, every one who knows this coast is
either far enough from it, or safe in port."

But, long afterwards, I heard Mother's closet door shut, and
low voices close what I felt had been an earnest parley, and
with every sense quickened as it was that night, I heard Evelyn's
soft step creep stealthily past my chamber to her own.

Only Betty ventured to speak to me.

She knocked at my door, and came into my chamber from
her own, while I was still standing at the window to undress,
listening to the storm.

" Mrs. Kitty, my dear," she said with an old tone of authority,
which carried me back to my childhood, and made me feel
submissive at once, " Mrs. Kitty, my dear lamb, you mustn't
stand hearkening and gazing like that ; " and she began to un-
fasten my dress as when I was a child. " There's nothing folks
can't see and hear if they hearken in nights like this. I have
heard the wind screech, and moan, and scream in that way, I
could have sworn it had been folks in mortal trouble ; and in

the morning, when I came to ask, nothing had happened out of the way; so take heart, my dear, take heart."

How thankful I felt to Betty, for the want of tact which made her come bluntly out with her sympathy, so that I could just lay my head on her shoulder and cry like a child, and be comforted.

"I'm not out of heart, Betty," I sobbed. "Why should I be? His ship may not have left America yet, you know, or it may be in port quite safe, close at home, close at home!"

"It may, my dear, it may," she said; "but it isn't maybe's that'll comfort you, my lamb; we must look to the Lord."

"I do," I said, "indeed I do. But He promises us no security from danger now,—none from any danger, does He?"

"Well, Mrs. Kitty," she said, "I can't say I think He does. But He promises to care; and He tells us to trust; and we must. The Lord is sure not to hurt us more than He can help. His promises are great, my dear; but the Lord Himself is better than all His promises. He always means more than He says;— more, and never less; because He is better than words can say. So, Mrs. Kitty, my dear," she concluded, "I'll leave you alone with Him. You'll find it better; for all the great fights, it's my belief, have got to be fought out alone with the Almighty. And you'll find, when you kneel down and give yourself up to Him heartily, that you don't want any more promises than He has given —not one. For all the words in the world end somewhere, and leave something they cannot reach; but the love of the Lord ends nowhere, but flows right down to the bottom of every trouble."

And when she had gone I did kneel down, and proved what Betty said to be true. I proved that all possible promises are included, comprehended, and absorbed by the one, " *I will never leave thee!* " that all hopes of deliverance are weak compared with simple trust in the Deliverer.

I would not blot out the lessons of that night for twice its pain.

For at last I was able to put out my light and lie down in the

darkness, without terror, alone with the storm, although the
rush of the wind up the valley, as gust after gust broke against
the house, made the branches of the old elms strain and groan,
and the windows rattle, and the old house tremble to its foun-
dations ; yes, without terror, for the tones of an enemy's voice
had passed from the storm. I could take refuge beneath the
arm that wielded it—take refuge with God for me and mine.

And this was something to prove. For it would certainly
have been far easier to have been myself at sea by Hugh's side,
tossed helplessly, as I thought he might be, from the crest of
one wave to the trough of another, with the ship staggering in
every timber from the blows of the winds and waves, than to
be thus listening, sheltered and alone, to the surging of the winds
as they broke in the valley after spending their force on the sea.

In the morning Betty came to me as I was dressing, with her
face white and her eyes large with fear. Toby, she said, had
just come down from the cliffs, and had said there was a dismasted ship of British build, out of her course, and quite un-
manageable, making as fast as she could for the fatal rocks at
the entrance of his bay. He was going back to his cottage, with
one or two of his class, to pray for the crew ; and then they were
to keep watch on the points from which help was most possible,
ready to throw ropes, and offer any assistance they could.

None of us could rest in the house with such a catastrophe
at hand. Father and Roger went up on the cliffs to join the
old seamen and fishermen already watching there. Evelyn and
I tried to accompany them, but the wind would not let us
stand, and it was arranged that we, with Betty and Mother,
should remain in Toby's cottage, keeping up the fire, taking
thither blankets and warm wraps, and all kinds of restoratives,
in case any of the shipwrecked crew could be rescued.

But that moment on the cliffs had been enough to imprint
the terrible sight on our hearts for ever.

Dismasted, helpless, but full (we know) of our countrymen, driven on their own shores—the shores they had been eagerly looking for so long—to perish!

Not one of us spoke a word as we busied ourselves in making every possible preparation, or in the still more terrible moments of inaction which followed when every possible preparation was made.

Then Toby came for an instant to the door, and shouted, "There is hope! there is hope! don't give over praying. She is jammed in between two rocks. If she can hold together till the ebb of the tide, there is hope."

A sob of relief broke from us all, and we knelt down together. But no one could utter a word.

Soon Toby came again.

"They are making signals," he said. "We have made signals to them to wait. But either they don't make us out, or she won't hold together. One of them is tying a rope around him, to throw himself into the sea. We can see him from the beach. We could make them hear, if it wasn't for the roar of the wind and the sea."

Then we could remain in the cottage no longer. Evelyn and I went back with Toby to the point of the beach nearest the wreck.

"He hopes to reach us, and get the rest in by the rope," said Toby. "But he'll never do it. The sea is too strong."

And then, in a low tone, "He must know the coast. He is climbing the slippery rocks by the only point where they can be climbed—where Master Hugh and I used to hunt for gulls' nests."

He stopped, and his eye met mine.

"Ah, Mrs. Kitty, take heart, take heart," he said. "Master Hugh knows what he's about; and the Lord 'll never let him be lost."

The form we were watching plunged from the rock and disappeared. There was a shout among the seamen. Again another. He had re-appeared above the waves. Once more he was hidden. There was a long low groan among the seamen; then a terrible silence. What happened in the next moments I never saw. A mist came before my eyes, blotting out sound and sight.

And the next thing of which I was conscious was waking up in Toby's cottage, with my head on Mother's bosom, and seeing some one stretched on Toby's little bed, drawn beside the fire, but not too close, while Toby and Betty on each side were chafing the hands and feet, and the face was motionless and pale as death.

But slowly, almost before I was fully conscious, slowly the eyes opened, and met mine. And in an instant I was kneeling beside Hugh !

They had been chafing, and rubbing, and trying every means of restoration, for an hour; but it was only just before I re-covered consciousness that the first gasp, the first pale flush of colour, gave signs of returning life. But as I knelt beside him his breast heaved slightly, his eyes opened again and rested (with such rest !) on mine, and he rather breathed than said, so faint was his voice, " Are the rest saved ? "

And Toby said, " They're all safe. The Lord bless you, Master Hugh. The waves which dashed you a drowned man, as we feared, on the beach, did not break the rope which bound you to the wreck. One or two of the boldest were saved at once, and all the rest when the tide went out."

Then Hugh was satisfied, and asked no more questions, but kept firm hold of my hand, and closed his eyes. His lips moved, tears pressed slowly out from under his closed eyelids, and an expression of the deepest peace settled on his face.

And before night we were all kneeling beside him, the ship-wrecked crew at the door, while in distinct though feeble words he was thanking God, whose " mercies are new every morning, whose mercy endureth for ever."

That was the way in which God answered a thousand prayers at once. Life was given back to the perishing by Toby's fireside ;

and through his hands the wrecker's house of death became the threshold of life ; the den of thieves became the house of prayer.

And Hugh was given back to me. That was the first service in which Hugh led the prayers and praises of his parishioners. A "prosperous journey had been given him, such as was given to St. Paul of old," beyond all we could have dared to ask.

He had reached his native shores with a nobler triumph than if he had been convoyed by a fleet and greeted by a royal salute ; cast on the beach a shipwrecked man, all but dying for those he had plunged into the waves to rescue. The amens of his first thanksgiving service had been sobbed from the lips of those whose lives he had risked his own to save.

We accepted it as a token.

When the storm of life is past, when we wake to our first thanksgiving service on the other shore, will there be such a company of rescued men and women around us then, rescued from wreck more hopeless, pouring out their hearts, not indeed to us, but to Him who loved us and hath redeemed us to God by His blood, not from hell to heaven only, but from sin to God?

For these storms never cease on earth. And even when Whitefield, and the Wesleys, and John Nelson, and Silas Told, have passed from earth, and all the noble men and women who work with them, rescuing wrecked souls from destruction, and chafing fainting hearts into life, Hugh says the storms will still continue, and the wrecks. For till heaven and earth shall pass away, the work of rescuing the lost will have to begin again, generation by generation, and day by day. But there is no fear, (Hugh says,) but that with the storms God will send the workmen for the work of rescue ;—the old work of rescue from the old perils, wakening the new song of redemption, fresh as at first in every heart that learns it fresh from heaven.

The End.